The Patriot

The Patriot

Evan S. Connell

COUNTERPOINT
BERKELEY

Library of Congress Cataloging-in-Publication Data is available
ISBN 978-1-61902-328-4

Cover design by Ann Weinstock

COUNTERPOINT
2560 Ninth Street, Suite 318
Berkeley, CA 94710
www.counterpointpress.com

Printed in the United States of America

For Donna, Janet, and Matthew

Our country! in her intercourse with foreign nations may she always be in the right; but our country, right or wrong!
—Stephen Decatur

God grant that not only the love of liberty but a thorough knowledge of the rights of man may pervade all the nations of the earth, so that a philosopher may set his foot anywhere on its surface and say: "This is my country."
—Benjamin Franklin

The Patriot

1
★

One August evening in 1942 a small, dapper man about fifty years old whose name was Jacob Isaacs came briskly walking into the lobby of the Union Station at Kansas City, paused, looked over his shoulder with an expression of impatience, and beckoned urgently. The door swung open again and his daughter Leah came sauntering in, gazing about the lobby with no particular interest; she was a dark, sturdy child whose glittering green eyes and suggestive manner made her seem older than twelve. She was followed by her mother, Hannah, a rather squat, graying woman in a shapeless polka-dot dress, who was carrying a bright red coffee can. And at last, after quite a bit of difficulty getting his suitcases through the door, in came a tall spindly boy with curling black hair, big feet, bony arms, and a hooked nose, which somehow contrived to give him the appearance of a long-legged, awkward bird, earnest and a little despondent; apologetically he hurried to catch up with his parents and his sister. His name was Melvin and this evening he was to leave home for the first time. He was going into training to become a naval aviator.

His father was already at the entrance to the station restaurant and, looking back once again, seemed to be astonished that Melvin was so far behind.

"My shoe came untied," the boy explained when he caught up. "I had to stop to fix it, and then somebody asked me if I knew where the train to—"

"All right, you're here. That's the main thing," his father said, motioning the family into the restaurant. "Put the suitcases to one side or the waitresses will trip over them. They never look where they walk, I don't know why. Now what are you doing?" he demanded sharply. "We could be sued."

"Nobody's going to trip over them," Melvin said, but without much conviction, and seated himself, "or even if they did, it'd be their own fault."

"Run outside and check the suitcases. Here, I'll give you the money. And don't dawdle around, for once in your life. I'll order dinner for you. I know what you like."

Melvin sighed, but obediently worked his feet out from beneath the table and got up, bumped into the waitress, and took the suitcases away. By the time he got back the soup was on the table.

"There was a big line of people—" he began.

"All right, I'm not doubting you. Sit down. The only thing that puzzles me is why you always seem to be at the end of a line. I get things accomplished, why can't you?"

"I don't know," said Melvin.

"Never mind. I'm not criticizing. I was joking. I've ordered you a nice big sirloin steak, just the way you like it. While you were away I was telling your sister some interesting facts concerning the history of our family. Someday I would like to find time to write the history of the family. It would be fascinating. Everybody would be amazed. Your grandfather, for example, if he had lived a hundred years earlier—a little more, perhaps—he would be famous, his name on the Declaration of Independence like John Hancock. Today we do not have such men. What a subject! How much do we know of our past? Practically nothing. It's true. I'm amazed. We get up, we rush to work, at night home exhausted. It's true. Then another day, precisely identical. We don't know who we are. How do men communicate when words have failed? By knowing their ancestry. We should study history." He reached across the table to pat his daughter's hand, saying, "If the war continues, you will someday be able to join this new Women's Auxiliary Army Corps. Would you like that?"

"Jacob, she is a baby!" exclaimed Hannah. "What is it you're saying? The war will end soon. Everyone says so."

But Jake Isaacs continued as though he had not heard. "Last

December what occurred? We all know too well. The Japanese attacked Pearl Harbor, a successful sneak attack, succeeding because America trusted Japan, trusting the treacherous envoys in Washington, our nation's capital. Long before then, to be frank, I was saying this was a mistake. Do not trust the Japanese, I said, but who listened? Nobody. We want peace, so does everyone else, this is what I heard on every side. Look at the result, hoping for peace, trusting. So what's happening in Europe? This very moment what atrocities are being committed, all because America and her allies wanted so much to avoid antagonizing the Axis? Hitler is running wild. Thank God for the Russians! Where would we be without them? I shudder to imagine what would happen to England and America without the brave people of the Soviet Union, a nation like our own in many respects. Now, however, the Nazis have crossed the Don River, in Africa the British garrison at Tobruk has surrendered. A little while ago Rommel was seventy miles from Alexandria and the Suez, God alone knows where he will strike next. No, this war will not soon be over." He reached across the table to grasp his wife's hand. "Hannah, we have no choice! What will happen if the Nazis are successful? Years ago," he went on, looking first at his daughter, then at his son, "although it seems to me like yesterday, I served in France. I would have preferred to remain home—who wouldn't?—but I was obliged to think not only of myself. The situation today is similar. We have no choice. We cannot consider peace. Melvin is going to fight for us. He is pleased and proud because he understands the consequence of a Nazi victory. Our lives depend on success," he added, grasping his son by the elbow. "What's the trouble? Aren't you hungry?"

"Not very," the boy replied in a low voice and picked at the rim of his plate.

"The fact is—why should I pretend it's untrue?—we are proud of you, Melvin. After graduation you will be wearing a tailor-made uniform, a commissioned officer of the United States Navy, with gold wings. Have you thought of that? It's a great honor. The course of training, however, is unusually difficult, for good reasons. I've been told all about it. You will have to study harder than you did in school. Your grades were not good. I regret to say this, but we all know it is true. You can do much better if you

5

try. It isn't that you are not bright; it is that—to be frank, I don't know. You are a puzzle."

Melvin grinned and took a sip of water without looking at anyone.

"Do exactly what you are told. I know all about the Army. Here, eat this dish of turnips. You'll be getting hungry on the train."

Melvin pushed the turnips away, hunched his shoulders, and remarked after a pause that he was not going into the Army, he was going into the Navy, and at this his father gestured impatiently.

"It amounts to the same thing. Now, Hannah, I have a surprise. For Leah, too. Are you listening? If Melvin makes it through the training program we will go to Pensacola to watch the graduation. I understand the ceremony is very beautiful and impressive. Leah will be excused from school. Would you like that?" he asked his daughter.

"All right," Leah said. "If I don't have to make up the homework."

"To judge from your report card, you don't do it anyway. When I was—what are you doing?" he asked Melvin. "Stop pulling at your collar."

"It's tight," Melvin said. "I was trying to loosen it a little bit."

"You are no longer a schoolboy, you must learn to wear a necktie without discomfort. Eat the turnips. You'll get hungry on the train."

Melvin again pushed the dish away; he groaned and looked desperately toward his mother, who had been staring at him and who had not responded to anything for the past few minutes.

"You've got to eat. Here!"

Melvin, his voice trembling, said, "Listen, I actually don't want those turnips! *Please*—can't you understand? Stop shoving them at me!"

"Whatever you wish. Don't blame me if you get hungry on the train. It's a long trip, overnight."

"Let me alone! Let me be hungry!"

"Did you lock the automobile?"

"Yes," Melvin said.

"Are you sure? It pays to be careful."

6

"Go and look, if you don't believe me!"

"I believe you. Just answer yes or no. It's only that I am not convinced the door is locked. You have always been careless about locking up. You walk out of the house and leave it open. Anybody could enter."

"I don't know," said Melvin gloomily. "Maybe I did forget." He stared through the window of the coffee shop at the people in the lobby.

"Show the Navy—demonstrate to the officers you are sincere and ambitious. This will go on your record. Nothing is more important than an excellent record. Are you listening?"

"I'll do the best I can, as long as it makes some kind of sense."

"Don't argue, do whatever you are instructed. There will be reasons you can't possibly know about." He paused, glancing at the clock on the wall while a departure was announced, and continued: "We have the finest soldiers and the best generals in the world, as well as the most modern equipment, consequently it's just a matter of time until the enemy is defeated. For example, General MacArthur is deliberately allowing the Japanese to advance. He is letting them overextend their lines, the same as at Bataan where the Japanese suffered severe losses, not only of men and materials but in prestige. They are rapidly losing face, as they say; this is very important to them. Any day now we will hear the trap has been sprung and the Japanese Army annihilated. It has been proved in a number of encounters that they are poor soldiers, lacking particularly in imagination. They are underpaid and badly equipped, with obsolete weapons, and, in contrast to the Americans, have been forced into this war by their leaders. Furthermore, I have seen comparisons between Japanese and United States warships and airplanes—how much thicker the armor plate on our ships and how much faster the airplanes. American air power is occupied elsewhere at the moment but will soon launch a major assault. One high-ranking Japanese general, whose name, unfortunately, I have forgotten, is unable even to read, and signs his orders with an X. I meant to show you, last night, a few items I have kept from the First World War. They are in the trunk in the attic—a trench knife, an Iron Cross from the breast of a German major, some photographs, I don't know what else. You can see them on your furlough. I don't understand why you're not eating. We still have a few minutes. Do you want something else? You love to eat. I've watched you eat more than your mother and sister together. Fantastic! I don't know where you put it."

"Can I have your V-five pin?" Leah asked. "You promised."

"I did not!" Melvin replied, looking at her in surprise.

"Give the pin to your sister. That would be a nice gesture."

"I sort of wanted to keep it," Melvin said.

"Give the pin to her, Melvin."

"All right, if you insist, but she'll just lose it." He removed the pin from his lapel and handed it to her. It was a blue and bronze shield with a miniature pair of wings; he had worn it wherever he went ever since he had been accepted for cadet training.

"I won't either lose it," Leah said. "You lost your overcoat last winter."

"Children," Hannah said, clasping her hands and shutting her eyes. "At such a time, children. Shame. Don't argue, please. Now what do we say, Leah, when there's a gift?"

With a look of boredom the girl answered, "Thank you for the pin, Melvin." Then she sat forward eagerly, her green eyes shining. "After the war are you going to take me for an airplane ride? You promised you would."

Melvin looked at her in astonishment; she was lying again. "I did *not* promise," he remarked irritably, and he continued to gaze at her. During the past few months she had grown much heavier, but less clumsy. There was sometimes in her eyes and on her lips an expression that fascinated him.

"We will take a ride, one after the other," Jake Isaacs said, patting his lips with a napkin. "Each of us will go up in the airplane."

"Maybe you will, maybe you won't," said Melvin. "I could get washed out. Then I couldn't take anybody up."

"Don't talk like that! Nonsense. Do your best, you'll succeed. The Navy does not expect to commission every cadet, only the best, however we have no doubt of your ability. One thing is important: keeping your nose to the grindstone. You can do it. We know you can. We'll be looking forward to watching you graduate at Pensacola."

Melvin noticed that they were all staring at him; apparently

8

they were waiting for him to assure them that he would not fail. He could not think of anything to say.

A few minutes later they accompanied him to the gate. His father insisted on carrying both suitcases and continued to give advice. Trains rumbled beneath the station; the floor was trembling with vibrations. From below came the odor of steam and coal smoke, and the distant clank of a hammer on an iron wheel. Bells were tolling with curious insistence and he was seized with an urge to leave, to tell them good-by and begin the trip.

His mother and father were both talking to him—she had given him the coffee can, which he knew was packed with chocolate candy. He could hear their voices but he was unable to concentrate. He realized that he was smiling at them, and that they assumed he had been listening to everything they said; he heard himself speak, and saw his mother step backward, as though in a dream, with her hands clasped and her eyes tightly shut. He understood, then, that his departure was painful to her. All at once Leah flung both arms around his waist and hugged him, lifting him off the floor; he was startled by her strength. His father was giving the ticket to an official in an old-fashioned blue serge uniform with brass buttons and a queer round cap which appeared to be made of cardboard; the ticket was punched. Melvin nodded gratefully, as though he were indebted to the official for this service, picked up his suitcases with a feeling of confusion, nodded blindly, and plunged into the crowd descending the ramp.

Late afternoon of the next day the train arrived in a small Iowa town called Vernon which was surrounded by cornfields. Melvin got off the train and waited a while, having no idea what to do.

The depot was crowded with men carrying suitcases; a few of them seemed to know where to go, but most of them, he noticed, were either looking around in bewilderment or walking uncertainly back and forth. Several of them asked him if he knew how to get to the naval base. He replied that he did not know and that he was going there himself. He decided he might as well inquire about a bus or a taxi, but soon found he could not get through the crowd to the information window; in fact the crowd had become so large he could not go anywhere, and men were still getting off the train. Someone's elbow knocked the candy out of his hand, someone else accidentally stepped on it and then deliberately kicked it, and he found himself being shoved along the platform toward a big gray truck where a naval officer in a wrinkled khaki uniform was standing on the hood with a megaphone in one hand and a whistle on a lanyard around his neck. The officer was looking down on the crowd without much interest. After a few minutes he blew the whistle, waited until there was silence, and then gave orders through the megaphone that all incoming cadets were to hand over their luggage to the enlisted men in the back of the truck, after which they were to form a double line on the road and stand at attention.

Having gotten his suitcases into the truck, Melvin wandered to the road, where he joined the line, hooked his thumbs in his belt, and gazed around at his companions. Presently he discovered that one of them—a stocky, muscular, red-haired farm boy in a cheap, tight suit and an engineer's cap—was staring at him with disapproval. At that moment the whistle sounded and the officer bawled through the megaphone, "*Right face! Forward—harch!*"

The head of the column started walking and after a while the movement carried down the line to Melvin, who found himself paired off with somebody wearing fancy pointed shoes and a paper carnation. It seemed to Melvin that his partner marched unevenly, taking shorter steps with one foot than with the other; in any event they could not get together and went along the brick road, up and down, following the heads that bobbed along in front of them. After a hot, tiresome walk they turned a corner and marched through the center of town where myriads of locusts sang in the elm trees.

There was no naval station, only a small college, half of which had been requisitioned by the government. In front of a dormitory that now bore the name of an aircraft carrier the column was brought to a halt and quarters were assigned for the night.

The next morning at five o'clock they were wakened by a bugle call over a loudspeaker. After a breakfast of beans, powdered eggs, coffee, and cold, greasy bacon, they left the dining hall and were mustered into platoons in front of the dormitory. A lieutenant commander, who turned out to be the executive officer of the base, addressed them from the steps.

"You have signified your desire to become naval aviators. Your presence on this station indicates your wish to wear the gold wings of the United States Navy and by so doing to perpetuate a worthy tradition. Some of you will achieve that goal. Others" —and he paused—"will not."

At that moment one of the college girls came walking by, her pleated skirt swaying from side to side, and the men stirred restlessly. Melvin, who was standing in the last rank of the fourth platoon, turned his head.

"You, there!" the executive officer cried, striding down the steps and advancing halfway to the fourth platoon. "You in the last rank! What's your name?"

"Melvin Isaacs," he responded, flushing and grinning.

"Let me hear that again," the executive officer demanded.

"Melvin Isaacs!" he called, still grinning, and heard somebody advise him in a low voice to add "sir," but the warning had come too late.

"Isaacs!" the commander echoed, "Isaacs! The first thing a cadet learns is that an officer is to be addressed with respect. Following this muster you will report to the flagship *Langley* to be assigned four hours of extra duty and ten demerits. The second thing you will learn—this applies to the entire company—is that you will have neither the time nor the energy to be looking after women."

He turned on his heel, mounted the steps, and spoke to an ensign who was standing by with a clipboard.

"Mr. Sarkus," the cadets heard him say in a positive voice, "you will take over."

"Aye, aye, sir," the ensign replied. They exchanged salutes. The commander strode away.

"Now hear this!" Ensign Sarkus began. "These will be your permanent quarters." And he started reading the list.

As soon as the company had been dismissed Melvin hurried into the dormitory and ran up to the second floor and along the corridor, hunting for his room; he had been billeted with a cadet named Horne and wanted to beat Horne to the room in order to get first choice at the beds. He planned to lie down on whichever he wanted until Horne appeared, then, having established a claim, he could go over to the *Langley* to see about the extra duty and demerits. He found his room, flung open the door, and stepped inside. There were two bunks, one above the other. On the lower bunk lay the ugly farmer, and his cap was resting firmly in the center of one of the desks.

After a pause Melvin asked, "Are you sure you're in the right room?"

The farmer's eyes were extremely cold and blue, pink-rimmed, close together, yet despite their coldness they burned wickedly, like the eyes of a savage little pig. He arched his back away from the bunk, expanded his chest until it looked as thick as a keg, flexed his arms, exhaled, and collapsed so heavily the springs creaked.

"You must be Isaacs," he said in a hoarse, rasping voice. "You're off to a great start, Isaacs. Ten and four the first day." Suddenly he doubled up his legs and kicked the underside of the top bunk. "I was afraid this was going to happen. Horne and Isaacs. Out in front there I said to myself, 'Well, Sammy boy, cross your fingers and pray that ain't him.'"

"What do you mean?"

"What do I mean? I mean that I was afraid you were going to draw the other half of this room because your name begins with an I and mine begins with an H, that's what I mean."

"I know that, but I want to know why you didn't want me for a roommate."

Horne bounced himself on the bunk and appeared to be thinking. "Go get your demerits," he said finally. "You got enough to think about for one day."

"I'm not going anywhere till we get this settled," Melvin said.

"All right, you asked for it," Horne replied, and sat up. His nose had been smashed at one time and crookedly set. There was an indented white scar on his forehead just above his right eye, as though he might have been kicked by a mule. "I didn't want nothing to do with this war, see?" he remarked. "I was working on my old man's farm and doing all right. I just wanted to be left alone, then I found out I was going to get drafted because I got a kid brother who can help out on the farm, so I signed up for this program ahead of the draft and I'm going to get through this program with no strain. I don't want anybody hanging around my neck, see?"

"I don't hang around anybody's neck."

"Good. You go your way and I'll go mine. We got snookered into this rat race, so we got to make the best of it."

"That's fair enough as far as I'm concerned, and in case you haven't realized it, we're here for a damn good reason. Hitler and Hirohito have got to be stopped and it's up to us to do it."

"My busted banana!" the farmer muttered. "Isaacs, we're cannon fodder. It's the same old story. In every war the suckers get mowed down like ducks. When are you going to wise up? One thing I can't take is a hero."

"You'll change your mind."

"Beat it! Go get your demerits before he gives you twenty."

"You said you were afraid this was going to happen, that you and me would get thrown together. I'll tell you one thing: you're no sorrier than I am." They stared at each other for a few moments, then Melvin left the room. As he walked across the campus toward the administration building he attempted to calm himself. After all, there was more than one point of view to anything. But in the end he could feel nothing except contempt and disgust. He thought about reporting Horne's attitude to the officers, but decided they would discover it soon enough.

"Just what do you suggest?" he inquired that evening. "Allow the Nazis and Japs to overrun the world?"

"Knock it off," Horne replied, "I got work to do." He had begun to study the textbooks they had been issued, although they had not yet attended their first class. He glanced across the desk, saw that Melvin was writing a letter, shook his head, and resumed studying.

In the days that followed they said very little to each other, and yet, somewhat to Melvin's surprise, Horne evidently bore no grudge and even went out of his way now and then to be friendly. Melvin first noticed this one afternoon during the boxing period. The gymnasium was crowded with cadets, all boxing at once, while officers walked back and forth on the balcony and shouted at them through megaphones to stop dancing and start fighting. From the beginning it had been apparent that Horne knew how to box; when the first gong sounded he had advanced with a menacing shuffle, his shoulders hunched professionally, feinted quickly, and then all at once Melvin came to his senses on the canvas. He got to his feet with blood dripping from both nostrils and rushed forward flailing away, and Horne carefully knocked him down again. But a few minutes later while they were in a clinch Horne glanced up at the balcony to see if any officers were watching, and whispered, "Take it easy, Isaacs. If you don't rush me I won't have to hit you." Melvin was outraged by this; he burst free and crouched, panting desperately, prepared to spring forward, but lost his balance at the last moment and fell down. He jumped up, wild with anger, and Horne, with an irritated expression, knocked him down again.

That was the way it went whenever they boxed, and after about a week Melvin's nose had become swollen and extremely sensitive; he thought it might be broken but he did not go to the dispensary to find out because he was afraid the doctor would keep him there.

In the dormitory one evening Horne had difficulty studying; several times he passed a callused hand across the reddish-blond stubble on top of his head, and at last he slapped the desk. "Honest to God, Isaacs," he said, "I don't know about you." And he continued in his hoarse, belligerent voice, "I really don't! What makes you so eager?" He began to get excited; the indignation of his own voice was arousing him. "Where do you think you are—in the South Pacific? You can't win the war in a gymnasium! And as far as that goes you ain't going to win it in any navigation class either—like today. Why didn't you simply do what the man told you instead of asking him why?"

"I wanted to know the reason," Melvin said, gazing at him in mild surprise.

"Officers don't like to be asked why," Horne replied. "Officers usually don't know why. That's why they don't like to be asked.

You don't understand officers. You should watch how I treat officers. I give them no trouble, they give me no trouble."

Melvin had already noticed this and wondered at it. "I suppose you're right, but in navigation class I just wanted to know the reason."

"That's beside the point!" Horne shouted, jumping up from the desk with his fists clenched.

"I don't feel that it is," said Melvin. They stared at each other a moment and then Horne sighed as though he were confused.

Later that evening he asked, "You figure you're going to make it through this program?"

"I don't know," Melvin answered. "I hope so, but I don't know."

Their days began about sunrise, which was nothing new to Horne, who was accustomed to dressing by the light of a kitchen stove or a lantern, and who had often been in the fields at dawn; but Melvin could not get used to being awakened while it was dark. For the first few days he had not known whether he would be able to get out of bed, partly on account of the medical injections which had almost paralyzed him. Immediately after receiving these injections the company had been sent to the athletic grounds to play football, and after the football game they went on a cross-country race—a circumstance so unbelievable that while he was running over the hills with an arm full of serum he continually and plaintively inquired of no one in particular if the order had not been a mistake; he thought they should have been sent back to the dormitory to rest. But it was no mistake. An officer drove along behind them in a station wagon and honked the horn and occasionally leaned out the window to shout at them to run faster. The cadets who fell down and were unable to get up were placed in the back of the station wagon with a medical corpsman who looked after them but also passed their names to the officer, who put them on the pap sheet for ten demerits and four hours of extra duty. After the company had been running along the road for about half an hour Melvin became sick at his stomach, but managed to keep running while he vomited and presently he felt a little better, though quite weak and dizzy, and when the company ran past the depot and through the middle of town to the campus he felt rather proud that he was no more than a hundred yards or so behind Horne, who had led the race all the way.

He understood by then that so much exercise immediately following the injections had not been the result of confusion in the battalion office; it had been deliberate, not punishment so much as an example of what they might expect in the future. The Navy was advising them that if they were not prepared to accept such treatment for the next year they should resign from the aviation training program.

Room inspections occurred several times a day. Ensign Sarkus came around, followed by an enlisted man with a clipboard. If the ensign felt displeased with a room he would hunt about until he found some reason for giving the occupants the customary number of demerits and extra duty. Melvin and Horne would stand side by side at rigid attention looking straight ahead while Sarkus prowled around and picked up the chairs to examine the bottoms of the legs for dirt and leaned out the window to see if the ledge had been scrubbed, and if he could find nothing objectionable there, or anywhere else, he would flip a coin on Melvin's bunk and no matter how high the coin bounced he would then observe that the cover had not been stretched taut and the corners had not been squared; with this he would suggest that some little triangles of cardboard be slipped into the corners beneath the cover in order to square them, and having offered this advice he would then nod to the enlisted man, who, after about three weeks, no longer needed to ask Melvin his name. Why it was that Ensign Sarkus never flipped the coin on the lower bunk and gave Horne the demerits was something Melvin could not understand.

In addition to boxing, football, and cross-country races, the athletic schedule consisted of some calisthenics which he thought were extraordinary—such as lying on one's back with one's feet held precisely six inches off the ground for a period of ten or fifteen minutes—an obstacle course built of logs, ropes, barrels, hurdles, walls, and various traps, nets, and parapets joined by trenches and pits filled with water, and a game which the Navy called basketball. This was played on a court, with a basketball, and there were goals at either end; otherwise there was no similarity to basketball. No fouls were called. In fact there was no referee. There was, however, the usual officer who ran back and forth bawling through a megaphone and threatening them with demerits unless they played harder. Horne seemed to have an instinctive grasp of the fundamentals of this game, knocking down anyone who got in his way, and the officer looked on him with approval. He also broke the battalion record for the obstacle course, and in the gymnasium he established a new mark for climbing a rope hand over hand to the ceiling. Melvin displayed a great deal of energy in these various athletics, but was frequently brushed aside or stepped on, and it seemed to him that a day never passed without at least one officer shouting at him.

Most of their time, however, was spent in classrooms where they studied military sciences: navigation, recognition, communications, and theory of flight, all of which Sam Horne assimilated with no apparent difficulty; whenever an examination was given he scored not far from the top of the battalion. Melvin's score was apt to fall somewhere near or slightly below the median. Aircraft recognition gave him the most trouble. Lantern slides were flashed on the classroom wall, or on the ceiling or in a corner, for a fraction of a second—one-tenth, one-fiftieth, sometimes one-hundredth of a second—and the cadet wrote down what he had seen. As often as not Melvin saw only a flash of light with a blur in the center. He had been issued a deck of recognition cards, and every night after the conclusion of the study period he would remain at his desk until taps, turning over these cards, squinting, rubbing his face in an effort to concentrate, attempting to recall what he had learned.

One evening, unable to stand this any longer, Sam Horne crumpled a magazine he had been reading and threw it at the wastebasket. "Now look," he began, spreading his hands in the lamplight and staring truculently across the desk. "You make everything tough for yourself. Relax! Take it easy!"

Melvin ignored him, turned up another card, and said, "SBD Dauntless. Forty-two."

"Forty-one," Horne remarked patiently. "Forty-*one* feet, stupid, not forty-two feet. Forty-two feet is the wingspan of the SNJ, not the SBD. Why can't you remember such a simple thing? You're going to need this information for gunnery at Pensacola. If you ever get to Pensacola."

"Forty-one, you're right," Melvin answered nervously, and repeated while shuffling the deck, "SBD forty-one. SBD forty-one. SBD forty-one."

Sam Horne watched, listened, and occasionally corrected him, and presently the notes of the bugle came echoing through the corridor. Horne switched out the light and rolled into his bunk with the powerful ease that distinguished him on the athletic field. "Good night, Isaacs," he said in the darkness, and Melvin was oddly touched, though he did not know quite why—Horne had never bothered to tell him good night before.

"Okay," he answered brusquely, "good night, Horne," and sprang into the upper bunk. After the security patrol had gone by the door he pulled a flashlight from beneath his pillow and resumed studying the cards.

September was over, and with October came their first free Saturdays, the first evenings of liberty in the dusky bronze Iowa autumn. There was not much to do in Vernon—it was a very small town lost among the great fields of corn—and cadets were restricted to a radius of three miles from the *Langley*; furthermore the liberty period lasted only five hours, but they looked forward to it all week. And it was in this month that Melvin became attracted to one of the civilian girls employed by the Navy to serve food in the dining hall. He did not care much for Navy food and even when he was hungry he had been in no hurry to join the line, but now, all at once, to Sam Horne's astonishment, he often asked what time it was and then observed that it would soon be time to eat. In the line he would stand on tiptoes trying to see where she was, but when he got to her he would gaze seriously in another direction while she, with phlegmatic lack of interest, dropped an ice-cream dipper of scrambled eggs or coagulated beans on his tray.

It seemed to him that she was lovely and sensitive, and between visits to the dining hall he berated himself for lacking the courage to speak to her. He decided it was because there were so many cadets around; they began to push and mutter, as he himself did, whenever it appeared that someone up ahead was delaying things.

Then, one Saturday in early November, he and Sam Horne were walking along the main street trying to find something to do when he saw her drinking a soda in a drugstore and he promptly stopped with his face pressed to the glass.

"What's the matter with you?" said Horne. "What makes you so pale?" Then he looked into the drugstore. "Well, I'll be damned," he said, rather idly, and scratched his head, "there's that broad from the chow hall."

"Let's go in and talk to her. Come on," said Melvin. But Horne did not want to. "Come on," Melvin insisted, and took hold of his roommate's sleeve. "We'll see if she's got a friend."

"Let go!" cried Horne, twisting away. "You almost tore my shirt. What the hell's got into you?" He examined his sleeve and grunted, took a hitch at his belt, and said he thought he would go to the movies. There was a Western picture in town and he was very fond of these. He peered into the drugstore again, scowled, and began walking away.

"Wait a minute!" Melvin said, hurrying after him.

"You coming or not?" Horne demanded.

"I don't know," Melvin said, and stood first on one foot and then the other. "I guess so," he said earnestly. "No, I guess not. Come on back with me."

"I got better ways to waste my time," said Horne. "I'll see you at the barracks, if you don't wind up in sick bay with the clap." He took another survey of his sleeve and marched across the street to the theater as though he had been offended.

"Go on! See a movie!" Melvin shouted after him, meanwhile hoping Horne would change his mind, but when he did not, when he had bought a ticket and disappeared into the theater without so much as a backward glance, Melvin unwillingly retraced his steps to the drugstore. He did not want to go inside and approach the girl; now that she was actually available he decided he would rather go to the movies with Horne, but he had thought about her so much that he felt obliged to make use of the opportunity.

He emerged from the drugstore a few minutes later with her on his arm and they went for a walk around the town. This developed into one of the memorable walks of his life, because near the end of it he slipped a hand into the pocket of her coat and she allowed it to remain. He spoke volubly about himself, his opinions, his plans and difficulties, and about a Navy fighter plane called the Corsair which he hoped to fly when he was commissioned at Pensacola; and when they said good night at the boarding house where she lived he kissed her with such enthusiasm that an ugly little dog came dashing up and began to snap at his heels. He tried nonchalantly to kick the dog in the ribs, but the dog was too quick for him, and too persistent, and since he was afraid that he might be washed out of cadet training if he returned to the dormitory with his trousers ripped, he was forced to let go of her.

They went walking together every Saturday after that. Her name was Becky McGee, and if she was repelled by his cheerless uniform of khaki and brogan shoes, topped by a coarsely amorphous fatigue hat which looked as though something vital had been removed from it, she did not let him know. These walks, which began taking them progressively farther along the country lanes outside the town, became more and more gratifying as far as Melvin was concerned. His hand was always in her pocket. There, of course, he could enjoy the feel of a sturdy, bulging thigh, or they could passionately and suggestively intertwine fingers, and before long it seemed to Melvin that he would go out of his mind if he could not possess her.

One frosty Sunday morning, after a particularly frustrating Saturday night during which he had come closer than ever to his eventual object—with the result that he tossed to and fro on his bunk until Horne woke up and kicked him from below—while they were both leaning out the window to fill their lungs with the morning air, Melvin confided that he had fallen in love. Sam Horne, if he heard, paid no attention; he drew his head in the window and swung his arms to snap the kinks from his spine, then stretched out on the linoleum and started doing pushups with one hand behind his back.

Melvin, who could not imagine why anyone would do calisthenics voluntarily, seated himself on the window sill and observed with indifference the tanned, sculptural arch of his roommate's torso methodically rising and descending.

"Well, as I was saying, this girl is different. She has a brilliant mind, for one thing, and then, too, a marvelous sense of humor. And, obviously, I mean, she's—well, let me put it this way. Frankly, don't you admit she's one of the most beautiful women you've ever seen in your life? Tell the truth. I'm not asking you to say so unless you believe it."

20

Sam Horne bounced to his feet and went shadow-boxing around the room.

"They're all beetles," he declared. "Listen, Isaacs," he continued, feinting, jabbing at the lamp, "before we get through this program"—he ducked, danced sideways—"even a woolly dog is going to look beautiful." All at once he stopped boxing and glared around, his fists clenched. "Where are my shoes?" he demanded excitedly. "Who took my shoes? By God, somebody's run off with my shoes!"

"They're underneath the wastebasket," said Melvin.

Horne danced nimbly out of the room, down the corridor, and back into the room, bobbing and weaving and throwing punches stiffly in every direction, shuffling his feet, snorting, and exclaiming triumphantly, *"Hah! Hah!"*

"What are they doing under the wastebasket?" he asked suddenly, with his hands dangling at his sides.

"They don't smell very good," Melvin explained, "so last night I turned the wastebasket over and put them under it."

Horne straightened up with an ominous expression, but just then another bugle call rang through the corridor, followed by a metallic announcement on the loudspeaker: "Now hear this. Now hear this. There will be inspection of quarters in five minutes. Inspection of quarters in five minutes. Quarters not shipshape will result in cancellation of liberty privileges next Saturday. That is all." There was a crackling, crashing noise as whoever had read the announcement began shuffling papers beside the microphone; then the loudspeaker fell silent. Horne and Melvin were already at work cleaning up the room.

On Thanksgiving Day he received a special-delivery letter from his father. The letter was quite long, and after finishing it he gave it to his roommate, who read it attentively and turned back to read parts of it a second time; so absorbed was Horne, in fact, that Melvin became embarrassed and fidgeted and finally said, "It's nothing really, just a lot of dry family history," but Horne went on reading. Melvin wandered around the room cracking his knuckles and pulling the tip of his nose.

"I mean, after all," he suggested once, and shrugged.

"I'd like to know your old man," said Horne, folding up the

letter. "My old man couldn't write a letter like that. Is what he says true about your ancestors immigrating to this country in seventeen twenty-eight?"

"His folks did. My mother's people came here recently. She's still got relatives in Europe, in Holland, I think. I know she's worried about them, because of the Nazis. But my father's ancestors were about as American as you can get, I suppose, probably wrestling with Betsy Ross in some cornfield," he added, thinking of his latest evening with Becky McGee.

"He says there were two brothers named Isaacs who fought at the battle of Kings Mountain during the Revolutionary War. Is that the truth?"

"Well, my father has spent a lot of time doing research in our family history, so I guess it is."

"He says one of your ancestors was decorated by General Wolfe after the battle for Quebec."

"Yes. I've seen the medal. It's in a bank vault."

"And you were in the Civil War, too, huh?" Horne asked, scratching his head.

"Oh, yes, I've heard about that war lots of times. My ancestors got all mixed up in that one. They were mostly Confederates, but there were a few who sympathized with the North."

"Well, there's one thing for damn sure—your old man is expecting big things of you in this war. Twenty-five Japs and the Congressional Medal."

"At least," Melvin said.

"Yuh, yuh," Horne remarked, tightening his belt.

Then, for just a moment, their eyes met, and Melvin wondered if he was quite as cynical as he had been three months ago.

3

★

Snow was sifting from a hushed blue-gray sky one morning early in December when Sam Horne, who had been appointed a cadet officer, brought his platoons to attention and stepped forward to salute the executive officer of the base. Moments later he once again saluted and stepped backward. In his left hand was a large manila envelope containing the company orders: the company would proceed to the War Training School at Albuquerque, New Mexico.

During the trip Melvin and Horne sat together, and the envelope rested in Horne's lap. He had received the highest rating in the battalion. Melvin, who had nearly failed, was determined to do better at Albuquerque, and reminded himself there was no reason he and Horne should not be standing together at the head of the class on graduation day at Pensacola. After Pensacola they would be sent to the Pacific, to the war. From movies and magazine stories he knew what to expect—the sea and the sky and the Navy blue planes peeling out of formation and plummeting toward the Japanese, tracers setting fire to flimsy Zeros, brilliant explosions, debris and flames on the ocean, battleships rocking through the heavy seas, submarines with brooms tied to the conning towers to signify a clean sweep, and the carriers on the horizon. He imagined himself in the war, taking off at dawn with bombs slung beneath the wings of a Corsair, and returning, spiraling down on the carrier while everyone watched, and later, standing at attention on the deck of the flagship. Perhaps Sam Horne was standing beside him—the two of them receiving a decoration of some sort from an admiral. He thought of Admirals Nimitz and Halsey, and it did not seem impossible that after the ceremony the admirals would invite them ashore somewhere for a drink, or to have supper—there was a hotel with palm trees in this dream, and there were mustachioed British major generals in pith helmets being introduced, and native entertainment, discussion of the campaign—and finally it would be time to go. He and Sam Horne would rise, take leave of their commanders; then in a few minutes the generals and admirals and congressmen at the hotel would look up as two Navy fighters in perfect formation, each with an uncompleted quadrangle of Japanese flags stenciled on the fuselage, roared over the palm trees in the direction of the fleet which swung at anchor a mile off shore, or which had weighed anchor and was steaming toward Japan.

Sam Horne had spoken to him. Melvin blinked and sat up.

"What's the matter with you?" Horne inquired.

"Nothing," Melvin answered. "I was just thinking." He pulled out his wallet, looked to see how much money was there, and said, "If you want to know the truth, I feel lucky. What about you?"

"You're not lucky," Horne replied, smiling.

"I have a dollar that says you're wrong."

"Do you really think you're lucky?" asked Horne. "All right. All right, if that's the way you feel." He took a coin from his pocket, shook it between his palms, and clapped it expertly on his knee. Melvin did the same.

"We're alike," he decided.

"We're not," said Horne, and lifted his hand from the coin. "Now do you believe me?" he asked as he was putting Melvin's dollar into his wallet. "There are people who win and there are people who don't win. That's the way things are and there's nothing you can ever do to change the situation."

"I'll match you again," said Melvin.

"It's your dough," said Horne. As he put away the second dollar he continued. "I try to explain things to you, but you never listen. I win, you lose. Is that so hard to understand?"

"It doesn't make sense," Melvin said after a moment of thought.

"That's absolutely irrelevant," Horne went on patiently. "It's the same in this program. Like on that final exam in recognition. Neither of us knew for sure what that heavy cruiser was, but I guessed right and you guessed wrong. It's fate. Stick with me, though, and I'll see if I can get you through Pensacola."

24

"I'll get through. Nobody needs to help me get anywhere."

Horne looked at him quizzically, grunted, and resumed staring out the window, tapping his blunt strong fingers on the envelope.

"The Deacon's going to get through," Melvin remarked a few minutes later.

"He might," said Horne.

"How can he miss? Already got a private pilot's license, and besides, he's a college graduate. He won't have a bit of trouble."

"He's got a license for a Cub. Flying a Cub is not the same as flying an F6F. He got a little head start on us, that's all. I'm not so sure he's going to make it."

"Why do you say that?"

"Call it a hunch. I see him stumbling around the obstacle course in those baggy sweatpants like he was half-crocked and I say to myself, What's with this clown? What's he doing here? You know how he is. He hates being in the Navy. The Nazis and Japs have overrun half the earth but he doesn't much care. The only thing he's sore about is that he couldn't stay home and make more money."

Melvin looked at him in astonishment.

"So all right," Horne added, "I know what you're thinking—couple of months ago I was sore as hell about being trapped in this rat race. Well, I still am, but it looks like we haven't got any choice. I want out as bad as anybody. Jesus, I could be cleaning up with that farm."

"I see your point. I can see his point, too," Melvin said. "If you look at the situation objectively."

"That's the whole trouble. In war you can't afford to be objective. Either the Axis is going to be destroyed or the free world is."

"You don't have to tell me. I know that as well as you do. In fact that's what I was trying to point out to you right from the beginning. At the moment, however, I'm simply attempting to look at it from somebody else's point of view."

"I hope to God if you and I end up in the South Pacific flying missions together you don't start looking at it from the Japs' point of view."

"Listen, I agree with you," Melvin said. "Don't tell me."

"Okay, but just don't forget it," said Horne.

"Where *is* the Deacon?"

"Down the corridor shooting craps, where else? Why? What do you want with him?"

"I was just wondering how come he volunteered for an outfit like this. You know what I mean—there's such a high mortality rate in naval aviation. It's strange that he'd volunteer."

"It's strange anybody would volunteer," said Horne gloomily. "I could kick myself."

Melvin suddenly got up and began walking through the coach; Horne jumped up and hurried after him.

The Deacon was on his hands and knees rolling dice against the door of the lavatory. Beside him was a paper cup nearly filled with coins, and some dollar bills, and from his lips drooped a white clay pipe which gave off a rancid, pallid smoke.

"No gambling on this train," Horne remarked, pushing his way through the crowd. "I'm in charge of this detachment and I'm giving an order. Break it up. All of you people are on report for gambling aboard a Navy conveyance."

Nobody paid any attention. The game went on.

"You people, I say, are on report, by God, and I'm not fooling, not only for gambling but for showing disrespect to the company commander—and that's me."

Then the Deacon said without looking up, "G-get lost, fruit. No-nobody cares what you say. That's a fact."

Melvin had been staring at him with great curiosity. "What are you doing in this outfit, Deacon? What made you join this program when you didn't have to?"

"I was dodging the frigging draft, what do you think?" he replied irritably. "Christ almighty, what a question! Leave it to nature's ready-mades," he added, blinking, and reached for the dice. "S-seventy-five dollars a frigging month! I agree with S-Schopenhauer."

"You say you're dodging the draft, but you volunteered for this."

"I'm a patriot," he answered. "Now get lost, because I'm a busy man, god-g-goddammit." He shook some coins out of his paper cup and began to blow on the dice.

"Come on," Horne muttered, "let's get out of here," and when they had returned to their seats he said, "I tell you, I don't get him. One night in the barracks out of a clear blue sky he opens his yap and says, 'Your p-patriot is the most d-dangerous man alive because he is b-both willful and s-s-sin-sincere.' I don't figure him at all."

The train stopped for half an hour in Kansas City. Melvin telephoned his family and they reached the station a few minutes before the train was ready to depart. Horne seemed very much surprised by Leah; after staring at her he began to talk loudly and officiously to Melvin's mother, saying that as soon as the company reached Albuquerque he was going to have Melvin appointed his adjutant.

"He thinks being an officer is important," Melvin explained. "See, he gets to wear a black tie instead of a khaki tie because he's a cadet officer and he likes that."

"I worked hard for it," Horne said, turning on him. "Don't think I didn't!"

"It's an honor, unmistakably," exclaimed Jake Isaacs, and stepped backward as though to have a better look at the black necktie. "You should be working harder, Melvin, and get to be a cadet officer like your friend. This will all be placed on the records. Being an officer is important, I agree."

"We all get commissioned at the same time."

"You mean maybe," said Horne, tapping him heavily on the chest. "Not everybody's going to get through this program."

"But you intend to get through, don't you?"

"You bet I do, and no mistake!"

"Well, I'll be right alongside, don't worry about me," Melvin retorted.

Later, several hours after the train had left Kansas City, Horne coughed, loosened his collar, and drummed his fingers on his knees. "How old did you say your sister was?"

"Twelve," Melvin said absently. Then he sat erect with an embarrassed expression. "She's thirteen. I just now remembered, she had a birthday a couple of weeks ago."

"Is that so? She's quite a bit—ah, well, larger than I expected. I mean, she—ah—" Horne paused, scratched his head, and sighed. "Jesus O'Grady, what a long miserable trip," he mumbled, and did not mention Leah again.

They traveled all that day and through the night. A wind was blowing from the mountains. The coach swayed and rattled. At midnight the lights were dimmed and after a while Horne went to sleep, but Melvin sat up wide awake. A full moon appeared from behind a plateau, was reflected in the river, moved behind a farmhouse and some trees, and gradually seemed to grow lighter in color, higher in the windy, cloudless sky, and then, far to the south, the sun was rising.

In Albuquerque they got off the train, formed into platoons without waiting for an order, and with Horne to one side hoarsely singing the cadence they marched up the hill toward the University of New Mexico. As soon as they came within sight of the football stadium Horne angled toward the fourth platoon and said, "Holy cats, what have we got here, the Alamo?" The stadium loomed over the pines, a deep adobe color. "And look!" he said, and pointed toward a gravel parade ground where several cadets wearing green garrison caps and hairy green mackinaws were practicing the manual of arms with wooden rifles.

"All right, okay," said Melvin. "I see them. Extra duty, so what?"

"Wanted to make you feel at home," Horne replied with a cheerful grin. He stepped away from the platoons and continued calling cadence until they were in front of the stadium. There he brought the company to a halt.

"Right face!" he bellowed. "Isaacs, front and center!"

Melvin stepped out of the ranks, marched up to him, clicked his heels, and saluted. "Aviation Cadet Isaacs reporting. Have you got a problem? Can't you figure out where the chow hall is?"

"Don't get smart," Horne remarked, blowing on his hands to warm them. "I'm liable to put you on report—insubordination, by God."

"That'll be the day. Let's get this show on the road, whatever you're going to do. It's cold."

"You want to go in with me to present the orders?"

"Okay. I sure don't want to stand out here in this wind."

"At ease!" Horne bawled to the company. Then, after looking around, he added just loud enough to be heard, "You people stand fast and don't goof off because some creep officer is probably watching us. Come on, baby," he said, gesturing for Melvin to follow, "let's see what this roach trap looks like."

They walked between two squat naval guns which flanked the stadium entrance and stepped inside and found themselves at the foot of a wide gray staircase with a black iron railing in the center. At the top of the staircase an enlisted man was reading a magazine with his chair tilted back and his feet on a desk. To either side of the staircase was a long, dimly lighted corridor lined with plaques, knotboards, blackboards with colored chalk diagrams, and cutaways of naval vessels, from which came a dank subterranean odor as though there were a dungeon somewhere below. The seaman had gotten to his feet, the magazine out of sight; he had felt the draft of air they let in and was peering down the staircase to see who had entered.

Next day they were issued green wool trousers, the green mackinaw, and a heavy green wool garrison cap with a blue and yellow V-5 insignia. They were notified that on liberty they would be required to wear the garrison cap; at all other times they would wear the canvas fatigue hat with the brim turned up.

"What gives?" Melvin asked as soon as the formation had been dismissed. "All the time in Iowa we had to keep the brim turned down."

Horne didn't know.

"Well, why don't you ask one of the officers?"

"I should ask *why?* Are you out of your head?"

"There's got to be a reason for it."

"Whether there's a reason, or whether there's no reason, is absolutely irrelevant," said Horne in exasperation. "How many times have I got to tell you that?"

"Maybe it's because Roosevelt wears his hat brim up."

"I don't care if it's because that little dog of his wears a hat with the brim up. All I know is, that's the regulation and I'm not about to ask why. You go ask the skipper if you want to."

"It isn't that important," said Melvin.

"I guess," said Horne dryly.

This was the only change in the regulations, and with the exception of flight lessons the daily program was almost identical to that in Iowa: they ran the obstacle course, did calisthenics and played football in the snow, and continued to attend ground school.

On a mesa west of the city was the airport. Except for a few cottonwood trees around the hangars and along the arroyos the mesa was barren, sunny, and freezing cold, covered for miles in every direction with dry, glittering snow. The winter air was stable, without currents even on windy days; the wind when it did come sweeping over came like a deep river and the small airplanes that headed into it would stand motionless or would be blown backward.

About an hour before dawn the company left the stadium and boarded an old Navy bus which rolled down the hill and came up the opposite side of the railroad underpass with a smoking exhaust and clashing gears, passed through the main street of downtown Albuquerque, and started the long grade to the mesa while the stars faded and the Sandia mountain peaks gradually became distinguishable against the sky. When the first rays of the sun struck the airport the cadets were warming themselves around the stove in the ready room and fat Rosa was at work in the kitchen. Fat Rosa had the restaurant concession and was convinced there was nothing so good for an aviation cadet as a plate of tortillas, tacos, enchiladas, and fried beans, together with a few green peppers.

Since most of the Navy pilots were overseas the instructors at the War Training School were civilians; the only naval aviator at the base was a sullen old ensign named Ilstrup who had long, greasy hair and a big belly. He did not have much to do; he was the check pilot and spent most of his time asleep at a desk with a newspaper over his face. He seemed puzzled and vaguely resentful when a cadet could not learn to fly, and after each check ride he would recommend that the cadet be dismissed from flight training.

The first cadet to have trouble was the Deacon; shortly before Christmas he was notified that after the holiday he would be scheduled for a check with Ensign Ilstrup.

Melvin was surprised by this, and said to Horne, "When we were at Iowa I used to ask him about flying. You know how he'd build a plane out of some chairs and then sit in the middle of it with a broomstick? Well, it's strange—do you know what I mean? He told me about crosswind and how to correct for drift, and about freezing to the stick during a spin. He taught me so much—all about wing loading and instrument lag and the emergency procedure."

"Knock off worrying about him and worry about yourself," Horne answered. "He's finished. He hasn't got a prayer."

To everyone who assured him he would pass the check, the Deacon replied, "They can send me to Gr-Great Lakes, who cares?" and, sucking on his pipe, he usually added, "I didn't ask for this frigging war. Everybody go to hell."

Christmas morning there was a telephone call for Melvin from Kansas City.

"The packages, did you get the packages?" his father shouted into the telephone. "We sent packages! Christmas! Merry Christmas!"

"Merry Christmas," said Melvin. "Yes, I got the packages. Thank you."

"Here is your mother! Can you hear me? Now I'm giving the telephone to your mother! Say hello! Here she is! Merry Christmas! Everybody is thinking of you!"

"Hello, Mother," Melvin said.

"You're all right, Melvin?"

"Yes, I'm all right."

"You sound unhappy. Is something wrong?"

"No. I'm fine."

"You're getting enough to eat, Melvin?"

"I suppose so," he said with indifference.

"We miss you. This is your first Christmas away from home. Leah is right here and wants to talk to you."

"Hi! When are you coming back?" Leah asked.

"I don't know. When the war's over, I guess."

"Can you fly an airplane?"

"Oh, sort of. Not very well."

There was a pause, then his father was on the telephone again.

The call was awkward; when it ended—he had promised to take good care of himself, to wear his overcoat on cold days, and to see the doctor if he felt ill—he returned to his bunk exhausted and depressed, and found that a special-delivery letter had arrived. It was from Becky McGee. He had not thought much about her since leaving Iowa; there had been too much to do, too many other things to think about, and, besides, she was a thousand miles away. The letter was militantly cheerful. He suspected she had rewritten it a number of times in order to give an impression of vivacity and sophistication. How was he getting along? she inquired. Very well, she was willing to bet. Had he lost his heart to one of those New Mexico girls? She hoped not. Would the Navy be sending him in her direction again? She certainly hoped so. If he could arrange to be in Omaha some week end she might be there, too. She knew of a marvelous little old Italian restaurant with candles and checkered tablecloths where the veal scaloppine was divine.

By the time he had finished reading this letter Melvin had begun to feel guilty, for it implied he had committed himself; he did not think he had, but evidently she did. He could not make up his mind what to do. He thought he should write to her, but he did not want to. Finally he put the letter in the bottom of his locker, hoping it might somehow disappear.

The next morning quite early, while the mesa sparkled in the winter sun and a few birds soared in the wind above the city and the river, Ensign Ilstrup put on his helmet, his sheepskin jacket, and his gloves, and with a clipboard beneath his arm he walked across the concrete apron in front of the hangar to a small red and black airplane where the Deacon stood at attention. They got into the cabin side by side and a few minutes later the plane taxied rapidly toward the downwind end of the field, the tail bouncing crookedly over the frozen ruts as though a child were pulling it along by a string.

Soon it rose a few hundred feet into the air, rising almost vertically because of the wind, buzzing like a bumblebee, circled half around the field, and flew away to the west. Melvin, Horne, and several other cadets had stepped outside and were standing in a row against the sunny side of the hangar to catch what little heat was reflected; with their hands tucked in their sleeves and mackinaw collars turned up around their ears they stamped their feet and critically watched the vanishing plane.

When the red and black Lycoming did not return by noon an instructor took off and flew toward the area where it had last been seen and he located it without much difficulty, he said, because it was the only brightly colored object on the entire mesa.

It lay in an arroyo like a brilliant red T—so incredibly red that the snow all around, by contrast, seemed faintly yellow. Inside the cabin the two men hung head down from their safety belts. Their necks were broken. The officer's left hand was speckled with blood and was frozen fast to the handle of the door, as though he had been trying to push it open as he died. His other hand, like both of the Deacon's hands, reposed on the roof of the cabin a few inches below his head in the nonchalant finality of death, and there was no expression whatsoever on either face.

When the Deacon's body was removed from the cabin a stream of silver coins poured out of his pockets and showered into the deep snow. There had been a dice game in the barracks the previous night, Christmas night, but neither the station officers nor the instructors who flew the body in from the mesa knew about it, and they thought it extremely odd that he had been so fond of coins.

Death had always seemed a trifle ludicrous to Melvin. Had not the Deacon himself given his impression of death one evening in the barracks?—clutching at his heart and sinking to the floor with a droll expression so that everyone laughed. And he smoked his pipe while he lay there with a dead look, his eyes rolled back in his head, and finally got up and dusted his trousers, for he had always been fastidious.

"We ought to write his brother, don't you think?" Melvin suggested that evening.

Horne scratched his head and thought and at last said, "Go ahead. It suits me. You write the letter and we'll both sign it. That's a good idea."

"I was thinking you should write it. You're the cadet officer."

"What is there to say?"

"How should I know?"

"You think we should write they had him rolled up in a piece of oily canvas—and he was nothing but a little bundle—and his shoes stuck out the end? What should I do? Write that in a letter to his brother? We better forget it. There's nothing we can do. We might just make matters worse. Let's go shoot some pool."

They put on their mackinaws, went down the long staircase, and began walking across the campus toward the recreation hall. The night was clear. The stars were very bright.

"This seems like any other night," Melvin said, and Horne turned on him swiftly.

"What'd you expect—a flaming sword in the sky? Forget it, from now on! Get this through your head: nobody told us this was going to be a picnic. When you signed up for this outfit you knew it was going to be dangerous. You could have waited; you could've gold-bricked around till the draft finally got you, and chances are you could've got into the Supply Corps or some damn thing. So what are you doing here now? And another thing—what makes you keep saying you want to fly night fighters after you get commissioned? Those guys have got about the same life expectancy as a rat in a laboratory. Why do you think they get double flight pay?"

"I know it's dangerous," Melvin said, feeling awkward and defensive, "so it's something I ought to do."

Horne was apparently satisfied with this answer. He continued walking toward the recreation hall.

"This program is rough and we got a long way to go. Stop complaining."

"I'm not complaining," Melvin remarked irritably. "I'm just wondering. It's different than I expected."

In brogan shoes and khaki fatigues that were now slightly faded Sam Horne led the company through the winter at Albuquerque. Once more he received the highest grades and Melvin again ranked not far from the bottom. At the beginning of February the company mustered before the stadium.

"Well done," the commandant said. "Here are the orders, Mr. Horne. You will proceed without delay to the naval pre-flight school at Athens, Georgia. Good luck."

"Thank you, sir. I hope we never need it," he replied with a grin. Confidently he saluted and turned around.

"Right face!" he bawled. "Forward—*harch!*" and with another manila envelope in his hand he sang cadence as he led the way to the depot.

"We could skip this next base," Melvin said when they were on the train. "You could alter the orders and we could just go straight to primary. It'd take the Navy months, maybe years, to figure out what happened. We could get all the way through Pensacola before anybody discovered we never went to preflight. And that's another thing: why do they refer to it as preflight when we've already learned to fly? That doesn't make sense. Well, I'll tell you," he exclaimed, rubbing his hands, "we're over the worst of the program and it ought to be no strain from here on. I'm sure looking forward to those wings!"

"You must be off your rocker," said Horne.

"Not at all! Only one thing does puzzle me: when we signed up at the recruiting office—at least when *I* did—they said that within nine months of reporting for duty I could expect to be with a combat squadron in the South Pacific, but we've already been in the program about six months and we're a long way from finished. I can't figure it out."

"It's no mystery. The Japs were running all over us when we signed up, and the Navy was throwing everybody out there trying to stop them. So now the Japs have been slowed down and the result is that we spend more time in training. It suits me. I don't want to go up against those Zeros until I know everything there is to know."

"Their planes are flimsy. We have the best equipment in the world, and the best personnel."

"Will you please knock it off!" Horne said with disgust. "When are you going to grow up? Honest to God, talk about a babe in the woods! Don't you know we've already been stuffed so full of propaganda it's leaking out our ears?"

"First you talk out of one side of your mouth and then the other. Right now you sound as cynical as you did six months ago."

"I'm realistic, which is more than anybody will ever be able to say for you. Those Japs are hot and the Zekes are better than the press lets on. I'm not afraid of them, I'm not afraid to fight, but I'm not going out there like a Boy Scout after a merit badge, and anybody who does isn't going to come back. Don't kid yourself."

"Maybe. Maybe you're right, I don't know. The whole business is so strange."

"It is, for a fact."

On a cold, rainy morning the cadet company reached Athens; but by noon the clouds had begun to lift, shafts of wintry sunlight reached down to the parade ground in front of the barracks, and suddenly the building in which they were unpacking trembled with a wild whistling roar. Windows rattled and dust sifted from cracks in the ceiling. The weird whistling roar was heard again and once more the windows rattled.

"Corsairs!" somebody shouted.

The building had again begun to vibrate; Melvin saw Horne shouting to him but was not able to hear anything and as the third plane passed overhead with a scream like a stricken animal he thought it was about to hit the barracks; he realized that he, too, was shouting but was not able to hear himself and had no idea what he had said. Then he was outside on the parade ground shading his eyes from the sun and looking up through the broken white clouds into the pale sky, seeing for the first time that winter was nearly over. The sky was mild and warm above the clouds. There was no sign of the airplanes.

"Two o'clock," someone said, and he turned half around and looked again. There were the Corsairs high above the administration building spiraling slowly out of sight.

"You never see one before?" asked the cadet who had spoken. His name, Melvin knew, was Roska. He was the oldest cadet in the battalion and had been an enlisted man for several years before he transferred to the pilot training program.

"No, but I recognized them right away—you can't miss those gull wings and that fuselage. And the way they sit in the air! They go like they were sliding on tracks!" He hooked his thumbs in his belt and shook his head in admiration.

Roska was grinning. "You're the eagerest cadoodler that ever was, I do swear."

"They came over so fast!" Melvin exclaimed. "Why, for a

36

minute I didn't know what happened. I thought it was an earth-quake, or somebody had dropped a bomb. I wonder how fast they were moving. Four hundred at least, don't you think?"

"Sounded that way."

After a pause Melvin said, "I hear you were at Pearl Harbor when the Japs attacked."

"I was," Roska said, "and I like to got my can blowed off."

"Why did you transfer to this outfit?"

"I wish I knowed. I wish I'd had sense enough to stay put."

"I have a feeling the program gets easier from now on."

"It don't figure to get no easier for me, Isaacs. I never made it through public school and all this here book crap is killing me. This aerology and aerodynamics, boy, I'm in deep."

"Well, at least there isn't much new at this base. I talked to somebody in the battalion ahead of us who said about the only thing is a course in relaxation. If that means what it sounds like, I'm all for it."

"This Navy sure is changing," said Roska.

The purpose of the course in relaxation was to teach the cadets to minimize muscular tension. At Pensacola and later with the fleet they would be in the air for long periods of time; so each afternoon at one o'clock the company returned to the barracks and got ready for the class. Each cadet removed his shoes, loosened his belt and necktie, and lay flat on his bunk with his hands at his sides and his eyes closed. The instructor then moved quietly from one bunk to another, murmuring suggestions and praising those who appeared to be the most relaxed.

Melvin grew to love this class. He would lie on his bunk exactly as he was supposed to, and with a tranquil smile on his lips he awaited the wonderfully soft and reassuring pressure of the instructor's hand on his shoulder and for the beginning of that mellifluous, kindly, and hypnotic lecture; and while he lay there digesting his lunch and listening it seemed to him that the abrasive, jarring world in which he lived from dawn till noon, and all afternoon and half the night—this wretched, fearful world of militant savages somehow disappeared in a whorl like water down the drain. So much at ease was he, so unutterably relaxed and secure, that one especially balmy afternoon he fell asleep while the instructor was talking to him.

That evening, seated on a bench outside the recreation hall with Sam Horne, he explained what had happened.

"What did he say when you woke up?" Horne asked. He was eating a pint of ice cream as he customarily did after finishing supper.

"Well, he was mad, that's the funny part of it," Melvin said. "He wrote down my name and told me to report to the administration building."

"What did they say over there?"

"Nothing much. Just another ten-and-four is all."

Horne finished the ice cream, crumpled the carton in his fist, and threw it at the trash can. "I don't think you're going to make the grade, not at this rate."

"We'll see about that," said Melvin. "By the way, what's that piece of machinery they're installing in the pool?"

Horne didn't know; he thought it had something to do with life-saving. The device consisted of a scaffold on which was mounted the fuselage of an airplane. The fuselage was fastened by chains to a length of narrow-gauge railroad track which inclined steeply into the water.

A few days later an announcement was made over the public-address system that a course in survival procedure had been instituted.

The first step in survival when forced down at sea was to escape from the sinking airplane. Each cadet, fully dressed in flight clothing, climbed a ladder to a platform on top of the scaffold and there was strapped into the cockpit, after which the airplane was turned loose and went screeching down the track, crashed into the water, submerged, and turned over on its back as it continued sinking. A few seconds later the cadet was supposed to bob to the surface, take off his shoes, and swim to the shallow end of the pool as rapidly as possible. An officer stood by with a stopwatch and a clipboard on which the time was recorded. Meanwhile a winch was in operation, dragging the fuselage to the surface and hauling it back up the track while water spouted from the seams and rivet holes.

Occasionally a cadet did not break the surface when he was expected. Then, quite suddenly, there would be absolute silence, broken only by the lapping of water at the sides of the pool. The

38

man at the winch looked expectantly at the officer while the seconds ticked away. Finally the officer would nod, and the fuselage came out of the water with the cadet struggling frantically, choking and gasping for air, tangled in the harness, or with a radio cord looped around his wrist; or, at times, unconscious.

Escaping from the plane was the first step toward survival. Reaching shore was second. Third was finding enough to eat once you had reached the shore, and fourth was getting home again. So it was that one Sunday evening approximately a month later, while the cadets were cleaning up their quarters for Monday-morning inspection, the barracks echoed from top to bottom with the familiar voice of Iron Mary, the public address system. Melvin was on his knees waxing a section of the floor for which he was responsible. Horne, whose bunk was across the aisle, was polishing a pair of shoes.

"Now hear this. Now hear this. Second Battalion. First Company. Platoons Able and Baker. Platoons Able and Baker muster on the parade ground in ten minutes in front of the *Wasp* prepared for survival trip."

"Now hear this! Now hear this!" Melvin exclaimed as soon as the loudspeaker fell silent. "I'm sick of listening to that thing! All we do is muster! Platoons Able and Baker fall out for muster in five minutes in PT gear. Platoons Able and Baker muster in five minutes for church. Muster for special instructions, muster for personal inspection, well I'm fed up! Yesterday they gave us four minutes to muster for chow and then what happened? It was thirty-six minutes until we got inside out of the rain. Oh, and then what? What did they serve us? Beans and powdered eggs again. Survive, hah! After what they feed us here I could survive anything."

"Save your breath, you're going to need it," Horne remarked briefly.

Late that night a Navy bus went bouncing along a country road a good many miles from the base and at intervals of fifteen minutes slowed down just long enough for one cadet to jump out. Melvin got out of the bus about three o'clock in the morning. He was already hungry and tired and somewhat depressed, having had nothing to eat during the long ride. Horne and Roska and several of the others had rushed over to Ship's Service to buy candy bars and malted-milk tablets which they stuffed into their pockets before mustering, and he wished he had done the same. A light rain was falling and he had forgotten to bring his overcoat. He was dressed in the daily work uniform of brogans, khaki pants and shirt, necktie, and a dark blue cotton jumper with a plastic name tag pinned to the breast. On his head, pulled well down over his ears, was a knitted cap. He was no sooner outside the bus than the cap and jumper were saturated; he could feel his head growing wet inside the cap, which was a disgusting experience, so he pulled off the cap and threw it away. He stood in the middle of the road and gazed unhappily at the diminishing tail light of the bus. He had no idea where he was. The windows of the bus had been painted black and this had annoyed him, although he did not know exactly why. He had a map and a compass, a canvas-covered canteen of water hooked to his belt, K rations, a sheath knife, and a waterproof box of matches. He could not see anything at all, it was so dark. He took out the matches with the intention of lighting one and having a look around, but the box slipped through his fingers and splashed into a puddle at his feet and he could not find it. For a while, then, he stood by the side of the road unable to think of anything to do. He was sorry he had joined the Navy; it was not at all the way he had thought it would be. He had expected everyone would look up to him because he was an aviation cadet, but nobody cared.

He began to wish for his father, who knew no more about the woods than he did himself and could not possibly be of any help; in fact, his father's presence here would only make matters worse—they would start arguing about something. All the same it would be nice to have him around.

Melvin sighed. He squinted, leaning forward a little in an effort to see something, anything, but he could not even see the branch into which he pushed his face. There was a strong odor of turpentine and of moldering vegetation. He squatted down, holding up his arms for protection, and turned around several times, breathing shallowly through his mouth because he had begun to smell a putrid odor; there was either a dead animal or a swamp nearby, but he could not tell where it was. He thought about walking up the road to meet Sam Horne, who was still on the bus, but he knew Horne would do what the Navy expected him to do; as soon as he got off the bus he would take a compass bearing and then begin to study the map. In a minute or so he would have made up his mind how to go about reaching civilization and he would plunge into the forest. Horne had grown up in the country and it did not frighten him. He would be out of sight and hearing almost immediately. Even if they did meet each other on the road, Melvin suspected Horne would ignore him because they had been ordered to find their way back to the base individually.

But then he thought of Roska, who had gotten off the bus just fifteen minutes ago. Roska was a reasonable sort. Furthermore, he had been in the Navy a long time and ought to know what to do in a situation such as this.

Melvin took a sip of water from his canteen, screwed the cap on again, tightened his belt, and started walking back in the direction from which he had come, but he had not gone more than a few yards when he stepped into a hole and fell. He landed on the box of K rations. It was as hard as a brick, and he thought at first he had fractured his leg. He clenched his fists and gritted his teeth and rolled over so that he lay on his back in the middle of the road with one foot still in the hole, which brimmed with stagnant water. The road was slimy, the rain came pattering down. Some loons were calling in the woods.

After a while the pains stopped shooting through his leg, so he sat up and pulled his foot out of the hole and then reached for his sheath knife in case an animal or an Indian should attack him, but the sheath was empty. Despondently he groped around in the mud, but the knife was gone.

For a long time he remained where he was with his head bowed, but finally got up and went limping along the road, or what he thought must be the road; he could not see it, so every once in a while he stooped and explored with his fingertips, and while doing this he touched what felt like a snake. Instantly he sprang high in the air and came down among a clump of ferns, and after that he was not able to find the road again. He went stumbling through the forest, holding his arms in front of his face, and eventually he came to the shore of a lake. He could not quite see it, but he could hear the water and he could smell it, and he knew, besides—whether from the breeze on his cheek or through some other sense—that he had come to a lake. He tripped over a log and fell down again, got up, and then, feeling exhausted, he sat on the log and crossed his legs.

After meditating for a while he decided to smoke a cigarette; he was relieved to find that he had not lost his cigarettes, and they were dry, but the matches were damp and crumbled away. He was struck by the fact that after losing the waterproof matches he had not until this moment thought of these paper ones—but the implications, whatever they might be, all at once seemed tiresome, so, after putting the cigarettes back in his pocket, he rested his chin on his hands and did not move for a long time.

It occurred to him that all his life he had been expected to *do* something, and he decided he was sick of doing things, sick of every possible kind of activity; he remembered that when he was a child he had read somewhere about a pioneer who was wounded and who crawled inside a hollow tree and whose skeleton was found there many years later, and he now considered crawling inside this log. Nobody would ever learn what had become of him; the Navy would simply inform the family that he had perished on a survival hike. Quite probably there would be such a public outcry when the newspapers got hold of the story that there would be a Congressional investigation, and the base would be closed, and then finally, many years later, some hunter would find this skeleton.

Melvin sighed, blinked, and peered around. He was not sure which side of the road he was on because he could not recall in which direction he had jumped. He took out the compass and by holding it close to his eyes, tilting and squinting, he was able to see the needle, which was slightly phosphorescent. The compass must be correct, but he was positive somehow that the needle pointed south; he tapped it with his fingernail, shook it vigorously, held it away from his belt buckle, stood up. Still it pointed south. He thought about studying his map but decided the night was too dark to read it, and then too, even if he could see it, he did not think he would be able to figure out where he was.

Finding nothing else to do at the moment, he decided that he might as well eat. He took out the package of K rations, scratched through the wax paper and tore off a flap, and got hold of an envelope full of powder. He was uncertain whether it was supposed to be taken dry or mixed with water; he thought of emptying it into the canteen, but then of course if it tasted bad he would not have anything left to drink, so he tilted his head back and tapped the powder into his mouth: it was grainy and crystalline, with a tart lemon taste, and he thought it was probably meant as a dessert. Next he tried a biscuit, which was completely tasteless and so uncompromisingly hard that it hurt the fillings in his teeth; he threw it away. Next he found a packet of tiles. He could not tell by sniffing at them, or by feeling them, just what they were, but undoubtedly they were very nourishing; quite probably a single one of these strange little objects contained as many proteins and vitamins as a turkey dinner. He tried to break one of the tiles, but found he was not strong enough, so he licked it; it had a chalky taste, like cement or plaster, and he did not want it, but, reminding himself that if he intended to survive he would need some nourishment, he slipped it between his teeth and began sucking it, meanwhile shaking the rest of the K rations out of the box. There were three cigarettes, which he added to his own supply; some gum, which he also kept; a cube of sugar that he popped into his mouth; and a flat round tin can with a key soldered to the top. He opened the can and tasted a little. In the darkness, not knowing what to expect, it was difficult to identify, but he thought it was some sort of dehydrated and compressed ham and eggs. After a few minutes he began to feel bloated, though he had not eaten much, and in a sudden fit of temper he threw the rations in the lake and relapsed into a state of aggrieved rumination.

He considered the months he had spent in the Navy, the many hours he had spent studying such things as celestial navigation; now he was lost in the woods, seated on a rotten log in the middle of a forest without the slightest idea as to where he was or what to do. Perhaps this made sense, but he was too depressed to care. He felt betrayed and vaguely sacrificial.

The rain had turned into a drizzle and finally began dissipating into a cool pre-morning mist. The foggy clouds were beginning to lift and to give a sense of motion, and here and there a bird chirped. Melvin was able to distinguish the ground and the foliage. He thought about getting up, but it was too much trouble. Dully he contemplated the misty lake. He supposed there might be fish in the lake. But even if there were he would not be able to catch them. He noticed a few V-shaped ripples near the shore and recognized them as being made by snakes swimming around on some God-forsaken business; he considered throwing rocks at them, yet even this seemed barely worth while. Apparently the sun had risen, because the clouds were discernible, and the air was growing warmer. He noticed that one of his ankles was swollen and mottled, and as he examined it he became uneasy. There were no fang marks, however, and the ankle was neither painful nor especially stiff, so he concluded it was poison ivy or poison sumac, or whatever poisonous shrubs they had in Georgia; it was either that or a spider bite, and, having smeared it with mud, which was what primitive people always did in the movies, he forgot about it.

The breeze was becoming stronger, blowing the mist from the lake; it looked as though the sun would be out before long.

Gradually, as he sat there waiting, he became conscious of a certain odor. He sniffed. It was sweet and acrid. Vapors were still rising from the lake, but above them he saw what looked very much like a plume of smoke. He sniffed again and stood up but immediately fell down because his legs had gone to sleep. He lay on the ground slapping his legs and sniffing without taking his eyes from the smoke, and after a while, with the assistance of a stick, he got up and went hobbling eagerly along the shore.

The smoke was farther away than he had estimated, but after crashing through the brush for about an hour he heard voices. It occurred to him that they might be officers. He had not done anything wrong, unless it was being attracted to human voices; even so, if they were officers, he did not want to be seen. He crept forward as cautiously as possible, placing one foot carefully ahead of the other and bending at the waist, for he had a vague recollection of someone in *The Last of the Mohicans* doing this; he climbed over a fallen tree with hardly a sound, but was then somewhat taken aback to find himself at the entrance to a privy. The wooden door was open, a swarm of flies hung about, there was nobody inside, nothing but that round, convincing hole and a cardboard box labeled PEACHES which was half-filled with corncobs. It was all so final somehow, so decisive and incontestable, that he could not move. He thought about making use of the facilities, did so, and continued on his way. A worn path led through the trees. He took this path and before long he caught sight of a clearing in the forest.

There was a gasoline station with a paved road going by. There was a barbecue stand with smoke billowing from the chimney.

He stepped off the trail and squatted down behind a giant fern. His stomach was awake now, evidently having been informed that breakfast was a possibility. He peeped through the leaves and scrutinized the clearing. In a few minutes an old man wearing a soiled apron came out of the barbecue stand and looked at the sky, spoke to a dog that lay in the road near the gas pump, and then went back inside the shack, wiping his hands on the apron.

"On your feet, cadet," said an impersonal voice, and at this Melvin uttered a pitiful little sob, so shocked was he, and pitched forward into the fern as though he had been stabbed in the back.

However, it was not an officer; it was Sam Horne. He had stumbled across the barbecue stand during the night and had camped nearby, waiting for it to open. Roska had also found it. The two of them had built a shelter against the rain and had the floor lined with newspaper, moss, and pine boughs. Roska was lying flat on his back in the shelter with his overcoat for a pillow and was licking his fingers. He had just finished eating barbecued spareribs. Beside him was a portable radio he had rented from the old man and his wife, and empty beer bottles were scattered all around.

"Well," Melvin said after being informed of the situation, "I think I'm ready for breakfast."

Horne walked with him to the edge of the clearing. "Listen, there's a couple of officers cruising around in a station wagon. They went by about half an hour ago, so if you hear anything coming, take out for the woods—and don't head this way."

"I won't get caught," Melvin said. He studied the road and

the buildings. "What about the people who operate this place? Do they know who we are? I mean, do they know we're on a survival hike?"

"Why, of course they know it," said Horne. "The old duffer told Roska he's feeding between fifty and sixty cadets every week. Why, he says some of them camp here two or three days. He says he's thinking about having a little map printed because some of the guys have got lost trying to find this place."

"What does the Navy think about it? The officers, I mean."

"Oh, Jesus," Horne muttered, clutching his head. "You think any cadet is stupid enough to let the officers know what's going on? Now look," he continued a moment later, and opened his wallet, "as long as you're going, you might as well get me another sandwich."

"What kind would you like?"

"I think maybe I'd like another barbecued pork on a bun with sesame seeds, and a couple more beers. Tell him that last beer wasn't very cold; see if he's got any that's been on ice longer. Oh, and some pickles. And we need more toothpicks and paper napkins."

Melvin returned a few minutes later with the food and the beer in a bag and said, "He gave us these old movie magazines, and says if we decide to stay overnight he can let us have a card table and some camp chairs."

"He's a nice old man," said Horne. He sat down cross-legged and began to unfold a paper napkin, but paused, pointed across the clearing, and all at once whistled shrilly through his teeth.

Melvin saw a sudden movement in the shrubbery, fronds waving to and fro as though someone had just dropped out of sight.

A few seconds passed.

Then two cadets jumped over a fallen tree and came walking boldly toward the shelter. Their names were Elmer Free and Nick McCampbell. Elmer Free was a loose-jointed, long-legged Texan with prominent upper teeth that gave him the look of a porcupine or a beaver. Tied to his belt by a string was a small owl which he had killed with a rock and which he had planned to cook and eat, but now, when it became obvious that he could get all the food he wanted at the barbecue stand, he drew his

46

sheath knife and slashed the string and tossed the owl into the brush.

"Adios, old bird, I'm tellin' you," he remarked. He balanced the knife on his palm, crouched, and with a swift underhand motion he threw it; the knife glittered across the camp and lodged in the center of a rotten log with a thump.

"We done seen them crooked officers, boys. Done parked theyselves in that station wagon down the road about a mile by that there motel."

"By the *what?*" Melvin asked.

"That there motel where Stuart got hisself picked up."

"He slept in a motel last night?"

"Sho." Seeing the expression on Melvin's face, Elmer grinned. "You slep' on the ground, boy, but Stuart's going to get washed out the program."

"Oh, they wouldn't wash him out for that. They may give him about fifty hours of extra duty, but they won't wash him out."

"That's all you know, Isaacs boy. He done sacked hisself in that there motel with a girl."

Melvin had been reclining on the pine boughs. Immediately he sat erect. "What did you say?"

"Sho! Old Stuart, he had hisself a night, from what I hear."

"I imagine he did. Who is she?"

"Don't rightly know. Less she's that there motel keeper's daughter."

Melvin slowly wiped the grease from his chin. The motel was not far away and he had not planned on doing anything for the rest of the day.

"Do you suppose she might still be there?"

McCampbell spoke for the first time. He had a dour, saturnine face almost concealed by the wool cap pulled down over his ears. "You act like you were on a fraternity picnic," he muttered.

"That's right," Horne agreed, eating a pickle. "What do you think this is? You're supposed to be learning how to survive under adverse conditions. What are you going to do when you get shot down over New Guinea?"

Melvin ignored them and lay down, belched, loosened his belt, and opened the bag to see what else he could eat. The conversation stopped. He glanced up and noticed that they were all watching the road. A Navy station wagon had come around the bend.

At the barbecue stand it stopped while an officer got out to talk to the old man; they could see the old man shake his head again and again. The officer returned to the station wagon and drove away. The back end was packed with cadets like royalists in a tumbril.

A moment after it disappeared there was a rustling in the underbrush and another cadet stood up and came strolling toward the shelter with a cigarette in his hand. He was quite tall, with broad shoulders and a handsome face. He looked bored, as though through no fault of his own he had been placed in an absurd situation. His name was Pat Cole. He was from the second platoon.

He wandered into the camp and surveyed it critically.

"I understand the Greyhound stops here."

"Sho," said Elmer Free, looking at him with respect.

"The *what?*" cried Melvin, rising up on one elbow. "Do you mean to tell me a bus comes along this road?"

"Didn't you know?" Cole remarked, glancing down at him with cynical amusement. "No, of course you wouldn't."

Elmer nodded. "Goes smack dab to Athens."

Melvin looked at Cole. "Do you mean you're going to ride it?"

"Why else would I have asked?"

"But how could you get away with it? Suppose there was an officer at the depot?"

Elmer grinned and wagged his head. "You don't hardly ride all the way to town. What you do, you ask the driver to let you down long about a mile shy and you hike her home the rest of the way. I aim to circle around the rear and come a-clompin' through the obstacle course like I'm mighty pooped. Them officers, they ain't got hardly no brains, I know for a fact."

"I'll camp here tonight and catch the bus tomorrow evening," Cole said. "That is, if no one objects to my company," he added with an unpleasant smile. He did not look at anyone as he said this, but stared into the distance and seemed to be waiting for someone to tell him either that he was welcome or that he was not.

48

After a prolonged silence Melvin asked, "Why tomorrow?"

"Oh," he said, turning around casually, "if I should arrive by midnight tonight, or early tomorrow, the officers would be too suspicious. Regardless of our friend Elmer's opinion, officers do have brains. They're quite aware of our distance from the base and they know, consequently, approximately how long it will take us to return." He walked a few steps and said over his shoulder while he stared into the forest, "You're thinking to yourself that they'll get me, aren't you? Don't worry, they won't. I'm not stupid."

"But what if they did?"

"He'd be on his way to Great Lakes in twenty-four hours," Horne said. "Why the hell do you think this area is being patrolled? If you think the only officer around here was the one in that station wagon you better think again. They mean business. This flight program is full of gold-bricks and the Navy knows it. They're going to clean out guys like Cole and it's all right with me, because I'm not about to have any deadbeat flying wing off me in the South Pacific."

"Bravo," said Cole, and clapped lightly.

Horne pointed a finger at him. "I could make things rough for you, Mister. In more ways than one."

"Mr. Horne, I'm terrified."

"You better be," Horne answered, and Melvin noticed that he had begun to shift his weight from one foot to the other and was nervously toying with his belt buckle. He was ready to fight.

"Elmer," said Melvin, "how about you? You taking the bus?"

"Most surely am. Come along."

Melvin looked at Cole. "What about you?"

"Did you think I was sounding off? Walk if you please. I'm not attempting to sell anything." He turned his back deliberately on Horne. There was a mirror nailed to a tree; he stooped and began to comb his hair.

Horne took a step toward him and half-lifted one hand, but then stopped, shaking with anger, and stepped back. Suddenly he turned to Melvin. "We've invested better than six months of hard work in this outfit. Don't throw it away just to save yourself a couple of days' walk." He paused, and seemed to be expecting Cole to say something.

"Sho, Sammy boy, except she's a mighty long row to hoe," said Elmer.

"Hell's bells!" Horne exclaimed, gesturing furiously. "I used to go on Boy Scout hikes rougher than this."

Melvin glanced from one to the other. Cole and Elmer obviously were intending to ride the bus. Horne wasn't. McCampbell probably wouldn't; he was scraping the mud from his shoes with a stick, and somehow it was apparent he meant to follow orders. Roska would probably go along with Horne, if for no other reason than that Horne was a cadet officer. It was, of course, a problem in morality, and of all the problems he could have imagined on a survival hike this was not one. To ride the bus, he knew, would be deceitful; on the other hand, everybody was doing it—not everybody, perhaps only a few, but there were sure to be others besides Cole and Elmer, lurking in the woods until the bus came along and then springing out to flag it.

Melvin began to feel uncomfortable. He could not make up his mind, and he was irritated that such an insignificant matter was giving him such difficulty. He stood up, thrust his hands into his hip pockets, and wandered around the camp, kicked at the stump, lit a cigarette, and tried to make a decision. At last, in an ill temper, he flung down the cigarette, ground it under his heel, and announced that he would hike to the base. He saw that Cole had been watching him.

"All right," Horne said loudly, "let's get started, whoever's walking. It'll take a long time—three days if we run into more swamp."

The old man packed a box lunch for each of them, except for Nick McCampbell, who had vanished into the forest while they were talking. In addition to the lunch they took along a wicker basket filled with spareribs, fried chicken, hard-boiled eggs, salami, cheese, pork, and dill pickles. In the middle of the morning they broke camp: Horne, Roska, and Melvin. Roska's canteen was full of beer.

"Look out for snakes," said Cole.

At the edge of the clearing Melvin turned around to wave good-by and to wish Cole and Elmer luck on the bus ride, but they were tossing a baseball back and forth and paid no attention.

"They think they're so smart," Horne muttered, jumping over a log. "Just wait and see. The officers'll pick them up. And won't I be glad!"

That afternoon on the mucky shore of a brackish pond they came across some footprints emerging from the water. The marks in the mud were very small, with the heel scarcely visible, and so pigeon-toed they might have been made by an Indian.

"That's McCampbell," Horne said. "What the hell was he doing in the pond?"

They followed his tracks into the brush, by some flowers and a spray of wild ginger growing at the base of a sweetgum tree, around a bog, and then on dry ground they lost his trail.

Several hours later, just before dark, after picking their way through a cypress swamp, they found the tracks again and followed them to the ashes of a fire—surprising a racoon that had been examining the spine of a fish. The ashes were cold. Horne poked around with a stick and turned up the charred corner of a K-ration box.

"How do you suppose he caught that fish?" Melvin asked. "He must have brought a hook and line along with him. I'm going to ask him when he gets back."

"When *we* get back, you mean," said Horne peevishly. "That skinny little Scotchman's probably checked in at the battalion office by now."

By evening of the second day they were beginning to regret having thrown away their Navy rations; none of them could stomach the pork or the spareribs, and even the cold fried chicken, which had turned clammy—beads of moisture had formed on the flabby, nodulated skin—even this chicken, which they had devoured so greedily, was becoming difficult to swallow. But the trip was nearly over: they were beginning to encounter more roads and they met other cadets whose course nearly paralleled their own.

On the third morning after leaving the barbecue stand they emerged from the woods within sight of the base, shook hands with each other, and split up, to arrive separately and at intervals. Melvin limped across the exact center of the parade ground with his head down and shoulders bent, his cotton jacket badly torn, stinking of swamp water, his face scratched and swollen, and paused deliberately in the middle, in view of the administration building, to remove his shoes, knowing that under any other circumstances his action would be suicidal and equally certain that on this one occasion he was privileged to insult the sensibilities of everybody from the captain down.

He reported to the battalion office and learned that the first cadet had arrived seventeen hours earlier. He was not surprised to learn it was Nick McCampbell.

At the barracks he inquired about Cole and Elmer and was told they too had checked in, quite a while ago; the cadet who told him this did not know where they were at the moment but thought they might be playing ping-pong in the recreation hall.

"How did it go, Isaacs?" he inquired, after a glance at Melvin's name tag. "We don't get ours till next month. I'm in the third battalion."

"Well, it ain't no picnic, brother," said Melvin wearily. "I'm going to hit the sack and stay there at least a week."

Just then Horne came striding up the corridor, naked except for a towel around his neck, with a bar of soap in his hand. "What the hell is this about a dance?" he demanded.

"That's right," said the third-battalion cadet, and pointed to the bulletin board. "They tacked up the notice yesterday."

Melvin and Horne walked over to the bulletin board and studied the announcement. On April fifteenth, at eight o'clock in the evening, there would be a dance in the gymnasium.

Finally Melvin asked, "Does it mean us?"

"Does it say anywhere it doesn't mean us?"

"Nobody ever gave a dance for us before. Why would they do it now?"

"I don't know," Horne said.

"It's probably a mistake."

They studied the announcement a while longer.

"If it isn't a mistake, it must be a trick."

"I think it might be real," said Horne. "I believe there's actually going to be a dance."

"Just for cadets?"

"Cadets and women, I expect. The Navy's queer enough without giving queer dances."

"If that's the case, you can bet they'll scrape up all the crows in Georgia. In fact, the more I think about it, the more I think it's just some kind of a cheap publicity trick. They'll take pictures for the newspapers to show everybody at home how well we're treated. Well, they're not about to trick me, because I'm not going! It doesn't say anywhere we have to go."

They looked at the invitation once more.

"It doesn't say anywhere you *don't* have to go. So that means you do have to go."

"That's tough," Melvin said, yawning. "I won't go, that's all there is to it."

However, when the day finally came, he decided to attend the dance.

They were in the barracks getting ready when the public-address system began to drone and sputter.

"Now hear this. Now hear this," came the weird metallic voice. "All cadets attending the dance in the gymnasium this evening stand by for a message from Commander Peabody."

The public-address system fell silent. A minute or so later the rasping hum was heard again; there was a mumble of voices in the background, the crackle of paper, and the commander said, "Good evening, men. It's a pleasure to speak to you this evening."

The cadets stopped getting dressed. The commander sounded affable, as though he were fond of them, and they mistrusted this. They gazed at the loudspeaker, or off into space, with remote neutrality while they listened. It took the commander quite a while to get his message across, at least to his own satisfaction, because he was ill at ease—a fact that was unmistakable to the listeners. Each time he seemed on the point of saying what he wished to say there would be the crackle of paper, sounding through the loudspeaker like an electrical storm, after which the commander would cough and clear his throat and drift from the text.

"Let's have it, let's have it," Horne growled, snapping his fingers. "Come on, you simple bastard, what have you got up your sleeve?"

"These lovely girls—these charming young ladies—" the commander was saying, and it sounded as though he had become excited. The paper crackled thunderously. "These—"

"Crows," Melvin said. "These crows. Go on, Peabody, we're right here. You got a captive audience."

"Ah," said the commander, "have been gracious enough—"

The point was, first, that the dance would open with a sale of war bonds and the commander earnestly hoped that each and every cadet would purchase at least one series E bond. Second, in order to encourage the sale, ten of the prettiest girls were to be auctioned. Here the commander sniggered; there was no question about it. He coughed; he shook the paper and went on. Each girl would spend the evening with the cadet who called out the highest pledge. Commander Peabody grew serious. He was very much concerned about this: he hoped none of the young ladies would be insulted by low bids, or, worse, by no bids at all. He hoped the cadets would not be stingy with their bids.

"I realize you men do not earn a great deal of money," he went on, but what he said next could not be heard because of the number of comments. The cadets earned $75 a month, but because of various deductions they never received that much, while the cheapest bond, as everyone knew, cost $18.75. Long before Commander Peabody had completed his address it was generally agreed in the barracks that nobody was going to bid on anything. It was agreed that the girls must be unbearably ugly.

"What have I been saying?" Melvin demanded in gloomy triumph. "I tell you people, there's no point in going to this rat race. It's just going to be pitiful. We'd be the only ones there."

Nevertheless, when his friends started for the dance he went along, heralded by a penetrating odor of bay rum and talcum.

The gymnasium was jammed with cadets. There was hardly room to move. There were about fifty girls in taffeta and lace, with ribbons, lipstick, earrings, silk stockings, necklaces, rings, and high-heeled shoes; they stood in a group near the orchestra platform, protected from any contact with the cadets by the presence of several officers in white duck uniforms, so that there was an open area like a fire lane separating them from the surging, muttering mob. The evening was warm, the ventilation was poor; Melvin scented the women the minute he came in the door.

To the surprise of almost everyone, and to the immense and obvious gratification of Commander Peabody, who was there in white, wearing two utterly inconsequential ribbons, the auction was a success right from the start. The first girl on the stage was bought for $75 in E bonds and the second girl brought the same price.

Melvin whispered to Horne, "What's the matter with these guys? Where do they get that kind of money?"

"What difference does it make?" said Horne. "It's just another deduction. There's nothing to spend it on anyway, except ice cream or a crap game. Then, too," he added thoughtfully, "they aren't spending it, they're actually saving."

Neither of them had taken their eyes from the stage, where another girl was up for sale.

"This could have a bearing on a board-of-review decision," Horne commented. "You know this goes on your record, how many bonds you sign up for, and if you need extra instruction at Pensacola, for example, the board might grant it if you'd bought a lot of bonds. Uh—*oh!* Give me five dollars worth of that," he exclaimed in a subdued voice. "Would you look! Just look at that flesh! Don't bother to wrap it up, Commander, just ship it to the barracks C.O.D."

"Stop slobbering," Melvin said. "People will think you're a sex maniac."

"I am," said Horne. "Just give me a chance."

A few minutes later Melvin whispered, "This stuff must be imported. I never saw anything like this around town. I looked everywhere, I even went to the YWCA."

"Put up your money if you want some."

"Not me! Not on your life. I'm saving my money. I mean I would if I had any—that game last night cleaned me out. These guys must be off their rocker." Another girl was going up the steps; she was plump, redheaded, with lovely blue eyes, and he said, "That one's worth a cool five hundred."

There was a stunned silence. He realized he had spoken louder than he intended. He saw Commander Peabody rise on tiptoe and search the audience.

"This is him!" cried a helpful stranger and lifted Melvin's arm. "He bid five hundred! I heard him!"

Commander Peabody was beaming.

"Will that lucky cadet please step up on stage to receive his prize?"

Horne was aghast. "Don't move!" he whispered frantically, looking from side to side. "Quick, run! My God, have you lost your mind? You haven't got a sou! Wait! *Don't go!*" But Melvin was already being carried toward the front of the gymnasium.

That night in the barracks just before taps, Horne came over and stood for a little while staring down at Melvin, who lay in his bunk with hands clasped behind his head.

"I never saw anybody in my life like you," he said, and there was a trace of wonder in his voice. "Is there anything I can do for you? I mean—well, hell, is there anything I can do?"

"Thanks," Melvin said quietly. "I'm all right. It's just that it sort of took me by surprise."

"What are you planning to do for the money? Peabody's got your name."

"It's just another deduction. It's just money, that's all."

Horne stared at him a while longer, and finally said, as taps came echoing through the barracks, "Well, good night." He seemed a little baffled.

"Good night," said Melvin. "Thanks again."

The world was full of surprises, or so it seemed, because on Monday morning Iron Mary announced, "Now hear this! Now hear this! Second Battalion. First Company. Platoons Able and Baker. Platoons Able and Baker muster in five minutes in front of the *Wasp* to be fitted for blue dress uniform. Carry on."

For more than eight months they had worn nothing but khaki, with the exception of a few snowy days in Albuquerque when they had worn green wool trousers and green mackinaws. Now they would have a blue uniform with gold buttons, and an officer's hat with a gold stripe above the visor. Anyone in the Navy would know by the narrowness of the stripe and by the absence of insignia that they were not officers, but there were a great many soldiers who would not know the difference and who would salute. It was, therefore, a day of some consequence.

Scarcely had the uniforms been distributed when cameras appeared. Horne, Roska, Elmer, and Melvin took snapshots of each other and of various other members of the platoon.

Melvin mailed some of the pictures home. He had not written to the family as often as he intended, and was embarrassed about this because they frequently wrote to him, though news from home was never exciting and he usually did no more than scan the letters. His mother worried that he was not getting enough to eat and asked repeatedly if his clothes needed mending, saying he should mail the clothing to her. Leah, now a freshman in high school, wrote about the boys in her classes and then one day mentioned that she had heard from Sergeant Kahn. Kahn had sent her a V-mail note; it did not say where he was, but she thought he was in North Africa. The name did not mean anything to Melvin. He knew his sister had been writing to several soldiers whose names she had gotten from the USO; he assumed Sergeant Kahn was one of them. The sergeant had also sent her a snapshot of himself, which she forwarded to Melvin with the understanding that it be sent back promptly. Louis Kahn was seated on the fender of a Jeep with a Garand rifle in the crook of his arm and a Montgomery beret on his head. He was massive and unshaven, with heavy-lidded, suggestive eyes. He was a powerful, virile, Mediterranean type of man with thick, juicy lips and a broad jaw. Leah wrote that the picture had been taken on his twenty-fifth birthday. Melvin thought he looked nearer forty, and when he returned the picture he commented that the sergeant probably wished to adopt her. One thing Leah mentioned which apparently fascinated her: Sergeant Kahn was heavyweight wrestling champion of his regiment.

As for his father's letters, he found them nearly impossible to answer. They were invariably the same. Melvin should study harder. Why was he having so much difficulty with communications and aircraft recognition? These subjects should not be difficult. Was Melvin keeping his nose to the grindstone?

In early summer the company, the surviving members of it, those who had not failed their ground-school examinations or taken sick from the dehydrated food, were ordered north to the Naval Air Station at Memphis for flight training in an open-cockpit airplane known equally well by three names—the Stearman, for the company which manufactured it; the N2S, which was the naval designation; or its familiar name, the Yellow Peril—with a provision of six days' leave between the date of detachment from Athens and the date of arrival at Memphis.

5

Melvin and Sam Horne both planned to spend their leave at home, and took the earliest train out of Athens. Melvin noticed that Horne was restless during the trip, and finally asked, "What's the trouble? Don't you feel well?"

"Mind your own business!" Horne shouted. "Get lost! Don't bother me!"

"Don't worry about that!" Melvin said, white with anger. "The minute this train reaches Kansas City you won't see me for a week! I've had to put up with your bad temper long enough!"

"*My* bad temper?" Horne asked in astonishment, and struck him on the arm. "Is that what you said? Did you say *I* have a bad temper? I never in my whole life met anybody who flies off the hook like you do." The more he thought of this, the more outraged he became, and he pounded his fist into his palm. "I'll tell you what the trouble is! I should have gone to Miami Beach with Elmer and Roska, that's the trouble! They asked me, but I said no. I don't know why I said no, but that's what I said. I could be on my way to Miami Beach now, but where am I headed? I'm on my way to Nebraska. I haven't got the brains God gave a chickadee."

"That's no fault of mine," Melvin said. "And another thing, I don't like being hit every time you get mad. You seem to think I'm a convenience of some sort."

"I really shouldn't do that, I guess," Horne said. "It's a bad habit of mine." He slumped in the seat and shook his head. "All my life I've chopped wood, and plowed, and milked, and slopped the pigs. Now I got six days to myself and I throw it away."

"Why don't you get off with me in Kansas City? It isn't Miami

Beach, but you could have a better time than you would on the farm."

"I just might," Horne remarked peevishly.

"We've got room for you at the house. The folks would enjoy having you. My father's asked about you several times in his letters."

"My old man's expecting me to help on the farm."

"Suit yourself," Melvin said rather crisply; his arm still ached from the blow. "I should think you'd be in a decent mood for once. *I* certainly am. I'm all ready to enjoy my leave. I'm going to cruise around Kansas City every night and sleep as late as I please. And I'm not going to salute anybody because I'm planning to wear civilian clothes. People will think I'm a 4-F," he added with satisfaction.

Horne didn't answer; his garrison cap was squashed on the back of his head as though he were a drunken Army private, and the muscle in his jaw was twitching.

At Kansas City Melvin got off and stood for a moment on the platform with his duffle bag balanced across his shoulder and looked up at Horne, who peered through the grimy window with an inscrutable expression. Then the train pulled out of the station and it seemed to Melvin that he himself was leaving.

After three days in Kansas City—during which he had worn civilian clothes once, for about an hour, feeling awkward and conspicuous—he did very little except sit on a stool in the kitchen with a pot of coffee and dully observe the birds hopping around the yard. The summer days were warm and similar and quiet; the postman came and went. Melvin took a dislike to the postman, waiting anxiously for his arrival each morning and going through the mail to see if there might be a letter addressed to him, but there never was, and, of course, he did not expect one. Who would be writing to him?

He thought of all the things he might be doing on the base. He could be in the gym playing basketball, or in the barracks lounge shooting pool, or merely lying on his bunk. He was very fond of his bunk. No matter where the company had been sent he had grown quite attached to it; whenever he was sick, or frightened, or bewildered, or frustrated, or exhausted, he would lie on his bunk and after a while he would feel a little better. The more he thought about his bunk the more he longed to be lying on it. Above him, usually, was the bulge formed by another cadet, and there was something inordinately reassuring about this. He could look to either side, and see other bunks and most of them would be occupied. He could not think of any place on earth he would rather be.

Or he could be in town looking for a girl. In all probability he would not be able to locate one. The mathematics of the situation had long since convinced him of this. Take a regiment of two battalions, for example, each composed of four companies, say, with four platoons to each company, thirty or forty cadets to the platoon. Situate these battalions in a town of possibly five thousand population. Assume, then, that of this five thousand about half will be female. Of this number there will be some three-fourths who are either too young or too old. Of the remainder there are bound to be fully ten per cent too ugly for consideration. And from what is left it is unlikely that any given cadet is apt to so much as lay eyes on two out of ten. Well, what is the result? One does a great deal of thinking.

The most satisfying thing about the base, however, was simply that if he were there he would be among his own kind. He would not have to explain anything. Nobody would ask what sort of food he got, or if he wore his coat when it rained. All the same, under no circumstances would he report to Memphis sooner than necessary, though he did not know exactly why, knowing only that he would take the last possible train and that he would then loiter downtown in order to catch the last bus to the naval base, and if there were still some time belonging to him he would stand outside the gate until the leave was completely over.

On the fourth day, desperate for something to do, he went to the zoo, which smelled as unpleasant as ever; to the art gallery, where his footsteps echoed eerily and somberly among the marble pillars; and at last, for lack of a better idea, he visited the Liberty Memorial. The Memorial stood on a hill across from the Union Station. It had been built after the First World War and consisted of a fluted shaft—from the top of which one might view the city—and two forbidding little buildings guarded by sphinxes. Inside one of these buildings was a replica of the table at which the Treaty of Versailles was signed in 1919. Around the table were

60

fourteen chairs, but no one was permitted to sit in them. There were murals, maps, and plaques referring to the "honored dead," as they were called. No one was in the room. Melvin began to feel depressed, there was such an aura of solemnity and portentous grace and the dreary chill of hallowed ground.

He walked across the mall to the other building and found it more interesting. There was a torpedo, tarnished by the years but still grimly impressive, with the sullen personality of a shark. There were a great many posters from the first war. The beckoning soldiers looked inoffensive, harmless, like actors in some amateur production. He studied the puttees and the curious, shallow helmets. ALL TOGETHER was the slogan on one poster. COURAGE, COMRADES, I'M COMING was another. He smiled and moved around the room. There were cases of medals with faded ribbons and faded flags in cellophane envelopes, and faded chevrons and faded photographs, and moldering streamers, and a gas mask with goggle eyes and a tube, and a pair of wooden shoes. He paused to look at a little German sign which had been translated and said: DRINKING WATER—WELL #295. There were some caps and spiked helmets, and a piece of stained glass from the ruins of the cathedral at Rheims.

Finally he rode the elevator to the top of the shaft and spent a while viewing the city, but was not particularly impressed; it looked very much as it did from the ground, and then, too, he had been to the top of the shaft several times when he was a child. His father liked to visit the Memorial on Sundays and had taken him there.

When he got home he found he had forgotten his key. He knew his father was at the office, Leah would not yet be home from school, and he recalled his mother saying that she would be away all afternoon. However, on the chance that someone might be there, and because he could think of nothing else to do, he rang the bell. A moment later he heard footsteps, the door opened, and there was Horne, with a drink in his hand.

"Hello, baby," Horne said. "I figured it was you. Come in."

Melvin walked in and looked around.

"Your mother got home earlier than she thought," Horne said, "but she had to go out again. Leah telephoned and wants to know if we want to go to a high-school dance tonight. Let me think—

there was something else. Well, I guess it wasn't important. You want a drink?"

"All right," said Melvin. "Do you mind if I mix it?"

"Go right ahead. I guess you know where the stuff is," said Horne.

That evening after supper they settled on the porch steps and Horne unwrapped a cigar. Over the lawn and around the trees night birds darted in search of insects, a rabbit hopped from the hedge, down the street some children were playing kick-the-can, the long June twilight slowly darkened. Horne smoked his cigar, Melvin chewed on a toothpick, and they solemnly watched a young housewife watering flowers.

"Who is that?" said Horne after a while.

Melvin said, "I don't know. She must have moved in while I was away. There used to be some people named Teefey who lived there. They had an airedale."

"Does she water those flowers every night?"

"I guess she does," Melvin said. "I see her every night about this time."

"She sure as hell makes a project out of it," Horne said. "I thought all the civilians were growing beets or some damn thing," he added reflectively.

"They grow beets in the back yard, flowers in the front."

"What does she do after she gets through sprinkling them?"

"She goes inside."

They watched until she had finished watering and gone inside.

"There's advantages to life in the city," Horne said. "That was a real nice little scene. On the farm you don't see your neighbors." He straightened up enough to loosen his belt, then relaxed and puffed on the cigar, blinking with good humor and occasionally turning his head aside in order to spit in the shrubbery.

"I couldn't find much to do here," Melvin said.

"I couldn't either," Horne said. "Soon as the old man let me off work I'd shower and drive the truck to town. I used to know a lot of people at the pool hall, but I guess they're in the Army or someplace. Civilian life seemed unnatural. They got us conditioned, the way I figure. Like the saltpeter in the chow—they got us right where they want us."

"Where who does?" asked Melvin, looking at him with interest.

"Why, you know," said Horne patiently, "the people who operate this circus. They condition us, see. Like you don't care about liberty any more, all you want to do is get back to the base. See?"

"I didn't say anything about liberty."

"Well," Horne said, and paused to think, "that's irrelevant. The point is, we're conditioned. It's one hell of a note. It scares me. As a matter of fact, I might as well tell you now, I'm thinking seriously of resigning from the program. I've about had it. It isn't worth the strain. Do you follow me?"

Melvin thought about it and then said, "No."

"Well, here. The point is, maybe we get through the program finally and receive our wings. So then what happens? They ship us off to the Pacific and we get shot down like ducks. What's the future in that? None! I think I may quit," he added. "I'm serious."

"Are you really?"

"Yes, I am. Nobody's going to play me for a sucker."

"But they'd just send you to boot camp and you'd wind up in the Pacific anyhow, as a seaman instead of a pilot. What would that get you?"

"I don't know," Horne said. "But I think I'll resign. I don't like this program."

"I don't know anybody who does. I don't think I'd like boot camp either, though."

"Listen, why don't you quit, too?" Horne said. "We could get out of this miserable program. All we'd have to do is fill out some forms."

"I don't want to quit."

"You don't want to quit?" said Horne, looking at him in astonishment. "You're always complaining about it. I never in my life heard anybody bitch so much about the program. Come on," he said eagerly, "let's quit, what do you say?"

"No, I don't want to quit. I decided I'd be a naval aviator, so I'm going to. I can't see any reason to quit."

"What better reason do you need than that if you go flying out to the Pacific you'll get your damn head shot off?"

"I might not."

"Might not what?"

"Get shot."

"You might not, but on the other hand there's certainly a good chance you will. We'd be fools to go on with this. Just look at the statistics. Remember what happened to those guys in Torpedo Eight? One man out of thirty comes back alive. Twenty-nine out of thirty get killed on a single mission! Holy smoke, what kind of odds is that?"

"You think that's a good reason to quit?"

"I swear there are times I don't understand you," Horne said after a moment.

"It's dangerous, I admit. The point is, we're at war. What if everybody quit? What would happen then? What if nobody wanted to fight? The Japs and the Nazis would be over here in a minute."

Horne was annoyed by this reasoning; he frowned and spat into the lilacs. A few minutes later the screen door opened and Jake Isaacs came out.

"Horne doesn't like the war," said Melvin.

"Who can blame him? Nothing on earth is more dreadful. We all pray to God it will soon be over. In the meantime you can take courage from the thought you are doing what I was not able to do—make the world safe for democracy."

"Sir, do you think that's possible?" Horne asked.

"Certainly! I have no doubt."

"You thought so in nineteen seventeen, didn't you, sir?"

"It was the peace we lost, not the war. That's invariably the way. Politicians lose the opportunity which was gained at such terrible cost. Let's hope things will be different this time. But first of all, we must win the war. Peace isn't negotiated until the battles are over. I remember my grandfather, years ago, telling me about the Civil War and how much everyone looked forward to peace, the same as today. The fighting then was just as dreadful. Our family lived in a small town called Lexington which was the scene of a famous three-day battle. I used to play on that battlefield when I was a boy."

"Is that a fact! Well, that must have been very interesting."

"Yes, indeed. I often imagined myself a Confederate officer."

"I remember Melvin once telling me you were from the South."

64

"Missourians, more properly. We've been here three generations. Lexington is only a few miles from Kansas City."

"I didn't realize the Civil War extended this far north."

"Definitely. My grandfather rode with the great Confederate general, Joseph Shelby. History books mention Jeb Stuart's cavalry riding around McClellan's army, but General Shelby rode around the entire state of Missouri with only eight hundred men, burning and plundering Union depots, pursued for a month by ten thousand Federal troops who were unable to stop him. It was one of the most amazing military actions of all time. Ten thousand Union soldiers were diverted from Chattanooga because of Shelby's raiders, who were instantly recognizable by the red sumac in their hats. I once saw the general when he came to visit my grandparents. Very definitely the war extended this far north. Tomorrow is Sunday. If you and Melvin have no plans I would enjoy showing you the battleground at Lexington."

"We haven't exactly got any plans," Melvin said. He turned to Horne. "Do you want to go?"

"I'd like to see it, hell yes. But what about gas rationing?"

"This is a special occasion. I consider it a privilege and a pleasure."

The next day shortly before noon they turned up the winding road to Lexington. It had been raining, but the sky was now almost clear. The river ran high, with a deep yellowish sheen, like chocolate or milky coffee, thick with silt. From the bottomlands came an odor of hay and livestock. A few birds soared in the summer wind above the cliff.

They drove through the center of the town, past the old courthouse where a cannonball was embedded in one of the pillars, and soon came to a field where two stone portals were linked by a rusty chain. No trees grew on the field, which was choked with briar and weeds.

"There should be a memorial here," Jake Isaacs said. "A plaque, at least." He pointed to a shallow gully nearly filled with brambles. "That was a trench. It was quite deep when I was a boy. I couldn't see over the top. But every year the snow melts, and then the rain—soon nobody will know what happened here. And the long ridge there! You see? Earthworks thrown up by Union

65

defenders for protection against cannonballs and grapeshot from Confederate guns down by the river." He picked his way through the field. Melvin and Sam Horne followed, and all at once found themselves on a precipice above the Missouri, which rippled muddily, reflecting nothing as it widened and flowed around the bend toward Jefferson City and St. Louis to join the Mississippi.

"There the Confederate boats were moored, by the willows. The soldiers came up this ravine, from bush to bush, under fire from the Union men where we are standing. Melvin, your great-grandfather was wounded here, shot in the throat as he crawled over the ramparts with his hunting knife. Two of his five brothers died on this field, one of them killed while trying to remove a thorn from his hand. A third brother was badly burned when a cannon exploded." Jake Isaacs did not say anything more for several minutes, but walked back and forth with his arms folded, looking down the ravine. Suddenly he turned and pointed to a yellow house which stood by itself on the other side of the road. "That was the Claibourne home. It's now a museum. It may be open to visitors. We'll see." He nimbly hopped over a trench and began to make his way through the thickets.

"So those were the good old days," Melvin said, and jumped the trench. An instant later Horne landed beside him.

They were met at the door by a woman of about forty who smelled of vinegar and beer and had a large mole on the tip of her nose. She was wearing an old quilted housecoat and carpet slippers, and with one hand she held a bath towel around her head. As they stepped inside the house she said without apology, "Washin' my hair, men." She nodded toward a long oak table where there was a visitors' register and a cigar box with a slit in the lid. "Twenty-five cents apiece," she said, settling the towel on her head. Carefully she watched them put the money in the box and sign the register. Then she began to speak in a shrill and remote voice; and her voice seemed to belong to the river, as though she had lived beside it so many years, and intimately observed it, and had known it like a husband.

"This here home was erected in the year eighteen and thirty-four with the funds of William Amadeus Claibourne of the famous hemp-growin' family, towards the end of his long life a gallant Confederate officer. There's an ell to the rear, as you'll presently see, and a gallery as well. Woodwork is of unpainted walnut. Each of the twenty-four rooms contains a fireplace. Yonder is the circular stair, entirely of walnut same as here, and we'll ascend shortly. Follow me, men." She shuffled into a room lined with display cases, on each of which was a hand-lettered card forbidding visitors to lean on the glass.

"Durin' the battle this house was first occupied by Federals, being some hundred yards west of the inner line of their entrenchments. Along about noon, September eighteen, this house was captured by a rebel detachment, being retaken by Yankees some two hours after, and captured once more by the rebels along about four o'clock. Both parties suffered severe loss of life and equipment in these attacks. Here, now, you see a device from the coat of a Federal captain, while in the cabinet by the hearth we are proud to possess the homespun suit wore on that day by a fourteen-year-old Southern boy mustered into service. The child's body was found doubled across the railin' in the central hallway, a Yankee dagger plunged full to the hilt in his heart. This coat is of homespun wool, the buttons carved of wood by the boy's nigra mammy, according to the family which still lives beyond the hill towards Waverly. Notice the stain on the coat, which was made by his life's blood."

She walked into the adjoining room and stood there feeling her hair and gazing across the river and the plains while they looked at the exhibits. She resumed speaking when they approached.

"Claibourne house was purchased by public subscription in the year nineteen and twenty-eight. Upper floor has not yet been restored. United Daughters of the Confederacy, as well as Daughters of the American Revolution, have been very helpful. We possess many types of souvenirs, such as furniture, pictures, guns, swords, countless flags and pistols, and much army equipment of all types. 'Tis said as how a hive of Italian bees was maintained by Colonel Claibourne on the attic floor, a hole being augered through the wall for their convenience."

She walked between two flags, through a door and into the central hall, giving an account of the battle over her shoulder as she climbed the stairs.

"This town, in common with other river ports, was captured

by Union troops to prevent the branches of the Confederacy from joining. In a valiant effort to break this chain of ports, immediately following the battle of Wilson's Creek, General Sterling Price marched his army upon Lexington. The Yankees was engaged in throwing up breastworks, visible to this day, when they was informed the Southern army was upon them."

She paused, breathing heavily, looked quite frankly and shrewdly at Horne, as though her thoughts had been on him from the beginning, and then resumed climbing the stairs.

"With troops on three sides of the entrenchments General Price demanded immediate surrender. However the Union man, Colonel Mulligan, did refuse, whereupon the battle for Lexington commenced. Firing took up on the morning of September eighteen and continued without cessation some fifty-two hours. On the morning of September twenty the Confederates constructed a movable breastwork of hemp bales saturated in water to withstand the heated shot, and taking cover behind them bales they did advance to within fifty yards of the Union line. The Yankee colonel's handwrit report of his men dying from frenziedly wrestling for water, and a-drinkin' it with horrible avidity, gives you all a glimpse of the nature of this battle. Come nightfall the situation was deemed hopeless and the white flag was raised. The battle for Lexington ended in a Southern victory. Needless to say, we was glad. Now follow me, men."

They had stopped on the second floor. She started up again, pausing several times to get her breath, and said "Whooee!" once and laughed.

At the top of the house, on the fourth floor, she leaned on the railing. "Right sorry," she said when she was able to speak. "Gettin' old, it looks like." She patted the rail for emphasis and led them into a corner where she bent and pointed to a gash in the wall. "Mark made by a bayonet after passing through a man's body. Smears of blood on the baseboard, as well as the fact that the mark is no more'n a few inches off the floor give indication the soldier was injured and lying helpless when mortally wounded by the bayonet."

She straightened up, adjusted the towel around her head, and dramatically pointed to a hole in the roof.

"Cannonball came a-crashin' through—*ho!*" she cried, and

clapped her hands. "Yes, sir. Come spang through yonder, eighty some years ago. Look sharp and you'll see how the timber inside is weather-stained from exposure to the elements. From the ravine it come. It was fired by the Confederate battery and it struck and bounced from directly overhead and then proceeded to roll down the staircase to the third-floor landing. We have it yet in the basement with other articles of similar nature."

She returned to the railing, which was disfigured as though a row of cigars had been left burning on it. "Fighting within the house commenced on the ground floor. Gradually the defenders was driven up the way we just come, up here into the attic. There are ninety-nine steps. Defenders contested every step without exception. After the struggle most of those who was captured alive was executed here, ropes being placed about their necks, and hands bound tightly behind their bodies. They was then lifted up by the victors and dropped. These marks you see is the burn of the hangman's rope. The victims went hurtlin' down and 'tis claimed they frequently did a somersault upwards with their necks broke. Most likely the landings and stairs was crowded with invaders resting after the terrible battle and watching the hanging. They was a few given a chance for life—they was let jump. Bayonets was placed upright on the floor, so not too many survived. Both armies alike treated prisoners in this cruel fashion. Look down the stairwell. Look down, men. Don't be afraid."

"I've been here before, thank you," Jake said. "I don't care to look again."

Melvin and Horne cautiously peered over the railing.

"See the bloodstains on the varnished boards? A lifetime they have been there, as dark as midnight, men, and fearsome as ever. 'Tis said all blood will flow again on Judgment Day."

It was late afternoon when they left the Claibourne house and drove along the Dover road, past sycamore and oak and silver maple and red ash trees, homes with mansard roofs and leaded casement windows, orchards and cornfields.

Jake Isaacs stopped the car in front of an abandoned Colonial farmhouse. It was the house where he was born.

The windows were broken, the front door stood half-open. The lawn was rankly overgrown.

69

"There was the apple orchard," he said, pointing into the shadows beyond the house, "and those crumbling walls on the other side of the fence were the slave quarters. From the roof of one of those cabins, Melvin, your grandfather, who was eight years old at that time, watched the Union and Confederate armies struggling for possession of the cliff. He always used to enjoy telling me about it. He was able to distinguish the flags and pennants tilting first one way and then another, and insisted he could hear the neighing of horses, the explosions, and the notes of a bugle whenever the wind veered, and long after the firing ceased could smell the burnt powder. What an experience for a boy! Watching the growth of a nation."

He walked across the lawn to the deserted house. Melvin and Horne followed.

The interior of the house had been stripped. The walls were bare and streaked. From the ceiling hung a chain; the chandelier was gone. The slab of marble which formed the mantel had been carried off. There was not a sound. Melvin looked through the twin arches toward what once had been the dining room and saw that the floor had rotted away. Weeds thrust between the moldering boards. Moss grew in the gloomy corners. He listened intently. A shaft of late sunlight entered obliquely through a window frame. There was everywhere the silence of night and decay; yet he had the impression that at any moment the crystal chandelier and the great marble mantel might reappear and a fire blaze on the hearth and the rooms fill with ghostly women and Confederate officers, and the vanished spinet would play a minuet while they danced and spoke of General Beauregard or the battle of Shiloh.

All at once Sam Horne stamped his feet and in the fireplace from between two cracked yellow bricks a stream of dust seeped, and then suddenly poured and quickly built a cone of earth-yellow powder on the hearth.

"It would be dangerous to enter the house any further," Jake said. "It's late. We'll drive back to the town for supper and then return to Kansas City. I hope you enjoyed the trip."

"Yes, sir, I did," said Horne. And later, on the highway to Kansas City, he added, "I can't explain why, but I feel a little better. Something about that battlefield—I don't know, sir, but there was a sort of purpose to it, if you know what I mean."

"The war was dreadful. Every war is dreadful, but sometimes we have no choice."

Melvin did not respond; he had not been able to eat much supper; he felt oppressed. It seemed to him that if there were a purpose to what he had seen it had been a senseless purpose, coursing perfectly as a torpedo and as indifferent to the consequence.

6

★

Melvin and Sam Horne left for Memphis the following afternoon. While they were boarding the train Melvin happened to stumble against an old woman with an evil temper who clearly disliked men in the service and who came near to hitting him with her stick. She was traveling with a lovely young girl whom he guessed, from a resemblance in the chin and brow, to be her granddaughter. That evening, on their way to the dining car, he bumped into the old woman again because he had been attempting to get in line next to the girl, and being exceedingly embarrassed he apologized, stepped backward, and tripped over a little boy who was eating a banana and who ran off screaming. The girl burst into shrieks of shrill, stupid laughter, Sam Horne clutched his head in despair, and Melvin hurried away trembling with mortification and excitement, unable to think of anything except the girl, whose rich auburn hair hung to her waist and whose skin, which was a deep golden copper suffused with tones of platinum and pink, seemed to absorb and reflect the light and give to her the immortal beauty of a figure in an oil painting. The more he thought of her the more it seemed to him that if he could not possess her he would go out of his mind: her throat, her arms, the slim and muscular elegance of her ankles, her pouting, childish lips, the eyelids so strangely experienced and mature, the simple-witted innocence, the half-conscious sexuality—soon he had stimulated himself to the point where he had ruined his appetite and could not do anything but walk nervously back and forth in the corridor while he tried to think up a plan for getting her away from the old woman.

Later that evening he managed to slip her a note, not knowing what would happen as a result, but so obsessed that he did not care; and in about an hour he got a note in return. Her name was Polly Ann Bergstrom, she was on her way to Memphis for the summer, and the old woman was not her grandmother, it was her mother.

Melvin wrote another note asking for her telephone number, but there was no response during the night or the next day.

He was standing on his seat trying to dislodge his duffle bag from the overhead rack when she came down the aisle looking neither to the left nor to the right, followed by her mother. Apparently she did not see him. But after they had gone through the coach he noticed Sam Horne, with a puzzled expression, unfold a chewing-gum wrapper which had dropped on the seat. On the inside of the wrapper was a number scrawled with an eyebrow pencil.

"That's meant for me," Melvin said, reaching for it.

Horne looked at the number again and frowned. He was reluctant to let go of something that might turn out to be valuable.

"It's no good to you," Melvin said. "Hand it over."

"I think I'll keep it," said Horne.

Melvin jumped down from the seat and said, "You don't even know her name. Besides, I saw her first."

"You give me her name and I'll share the number with you," said Horne.

"It belongs to me," said Melvin.

"If I can't have the name, you can't have the number," said Horne.

Melvin was enraged by this, but decided to conceal his feelings. "Well," he remarked in a superior tone, "to my way of thinking, that's disgusting, but of course—"

Horne grabbed him by the shirt. "*You* call *me* disgusting? Jesus, I've heard everything! No matter where we go you only got one thing on your mind. What happened to that broad in Iowa you thought you were in love with? Answer me that! You got the morals of a billy goat, but here you are calling *me* disgusting! That's a laugh! *Ha!*"

"You don't have to tear my shirt in half about it," said Melvin. "As far as I'm concerned, you're perfectly welcome to keep the number, since it means so much to you."

"I think I will," said Horne, and he tucked it in his wallet.

But the next afternoon, without a word, he flipped the gum wrapper onto Melvin's bunk.

In the weeks that followed they found they did not have much more liberty at this base than at any other, but what little there was Melvin spent with Polly Ann. The rosy bloom of her lips and the delicate, eternally altering contours of her shoulders and throat unbalanced and maddened him so that when he should have been thinking about his studies, or about flying, he found himself tense and congested with lust. On days when cadets had liberty he was the first one out the gate, the first one aboard the bus, and the only one who never hesitated when the bus unloaded in Memphis; he loped away toward the house where she was spending the summer with an aunt, her mother having returned to Kansas.

They went out for dinner, then he took her dancing, and then they began to argue: he wanted her to come to a hotel with him, but she would not. They had the same argument every night he came to town. He could not understand why she would not come with him, or, if he did understand, he claimed that he could not, while she insisted she could not understand why he kept asking the same question. He became exasperated, then sullen, and told her he was not going to see her any more, but they both knew he was lying. Clearly she was fascinated by his persistence. He was dimly aware of this and he perceived that because of it, because she was a little horrified by his demand, she could not resist him indefinitely. He redoubled his arguments. He became crafty; he spent hours thinking of ways to arouse her and weaken her. When they were together he always managed to have a hand somewhere on her; when she shrugged him off, or pushed him away, or glared at him, he would only grin and drift around to the other side. He gazed at her almost all the time, so that she was either pale or flushed, and after the first few evenings he made her so nervous that she was apt to drop things. He began to bring her gifts, mostly flowers and candy, and when she derisively called him old-fashioned he understood that he was not far from the goal.

It took them an hour or so to say good night. In fact, without either of them mentioning it, they began to end their evenings about nine-thirty or ten o'clock so there would be plenty of time to say good night. On the front porch of her aunt's home she would pat his cheek and then try to slip inside the screen, but he never failed to catch hold of her and pull her outside again. Then, after a long, whispered argument, she consented to give him a kiss. This led to another, and another, and after a while they would both be so excited and groggy that they were no longer able to stand up; he would stagger across the porch to the swing, dragging her with him, and there they would flounder around until the creaking chain or Polly Ann's sporadic resistance woke up her aunt, who would call softly from an upstairs window, "Dear, is that you?"

Polly Ann, rising from the swing with a look of terror, would call anxiously while straightening her dress, "Yes, Tanty!"

"Is there someone with you, dear?"

"He's leaving right now, Tanty!" she always answered, and then—for what reason he could never discover—she would deal him a painful blow in the ribs. At this he would give up and wearily stumble through the muggy Southern night to the bus depot with his uniform wrinkled and his collar smeared with lipstick.

Polly Ann put up a long and courageous resistance, for she was sixteen years old and played soccer in a convent, but eventually Melvin was too much for her. And so it came about that one sultry evening in July, after an especially grim and noiseless struggle on the porch swing, she gave an odd little sob, almost of luxury, and, leaning back, closing her eyes, struggled no more. Melvin, fiercely sprawled over her like a hawk on a rabbit, sensed the great nervousness leaving her body and he was electrified.

The next day she called the base and kept him on the telephone for half an hour, although, so far as he could tell, there was nothing in particular she wanted to talk about. She telephoned again two days later, and again the following day. Soon she began to call him at six in the morning or twelve at night, telling the switchboard it was an emergency. He was exasperated by these interminable, senseless conversations, and very soon grew sick of talking to her; but whenever he was summoned to the telephone he went, although he did not say much, and before long did not even listen to what she was saying. Whenever she paused he would mumble or clear his throat to prove he was still there. He could not imagine why she continued to call, since she abused him steadily, accusing him of all sorts of defects, and was apt to hang up without warning, after which he would stand quite still for a moment and gaze at the telephone in astonishment.

Then, in August, Polly announced triumphantly over the telephone that she was pregnant. With surly and vindictive relish she detailed her symptoms while Melvin listened, mute with horror, the receiver pressed tightly to his ear so the WAVE on duty nearby could not overhear. He had no idea what to do about this situation. Until now it had always been a joke. His first thought was to telephone his father for a suggestion, but a few moments of imaginary dialogue changed his mind.

Polly Ann called the base more and more frequently and challenged him to hang up before she finished. He never took the challenge. He had become very much afraid of her. He did not know what she might do if he antagonized her, nor could he imagine how the affair was going to end.

As if this were not enough, he began to have trouble in the air. The Immelmann turn bewildered him. In this exercise he was supposed to begin a loop, but instead of going all the way around he was expected to stop upside down at the top, just as the earth descended from where the sky was supposed to be, and roll the N2S right side up. If everything was done correctly he was flying straight and level in the opposite direction from which he started. Horne could do it, and of course any instructor could do it easily, but he himself could not. Time after time he stalled. Hanging from the safety belt, with dust in his nostrils and the blood collecting in his brain, he slowly dropped away into a disgusting spin. Down he went, cursing and whirling, and eventually, having straightened it out, pulled through the bottom of the dive with the goggles blown halfway off his face.

As he spiraled upward to try again he would brood over Polly Ann's condition. Her malice was staggering. She had become so vicious that he was more awed than hurt, and no longer made the least attempt to reply, partly because she instantly attacked whatever he said. If he observed that the weather at the station was pleasant she accused him of enjoying himself; on the other hand, if he said it was hot, she accused him of trying to make her feel worse. If he kept silent she berated him for not caring what happened to her. If he protested he had been worrying about her, she would become sarcastic and inquire what there was for him to worry about. Once he said, brusquely, for he had been made desperate by her nagging, that things would work out all right. She gasped; he seized this moment to hang up. It was the first time he had ever dared hang up on her and he felt frightened by his audacity, but also rather proud of himself.

Then, two days after this conversation, he received in the mail a large pink and blue card with a ribbon attached, congratulating him on the new baby. The card was signed Polly Ann. But the longer Melvin thought about it the more he came to suspect she had not sent the card, the reason being that it would never occur to her. She had no sense of humor, though she would shriek with laughter at a pratfall or a pie in the face. He did not know how anyone could have found out she was pregnant, he had not confided in anyone, but somebody knew.

He began to look sharply at his friends, convinced that one of them was taunting him, had crept up on him, so to speak, as Sam Horne had done in the forest. He did not think it could be Elmer Free, who was too dull, too slow, too simple. He thought it might be Roska, until he learned that years ago Roska had been in the same situation and even now did not think it was humorous. Then if it was not Sam Horne, and he knew somehow that it was not, who could it be? He suspected Pat Cole, who was clever and sardonic; and Nick McCampbell, who was so taciturn that nobody knew much about him. But neither they nor anyone else inquired if he had received any interesting mail or otherwise hinted, and he did not say a word.

As summer passed and the weather remained humid and disagreeable, Polly Ann's voice turned shrill, her features appeared to sharpen, and her complaints grew more querulous than ever. He was appalled by her increasing resemblance to the old woman and asked himself how he had ever gotten into this situation. No longer satisfied to beleaguer him by telephone, she began taking a taxicab to the air station and there she would have him summoned to the recreation center, on one pretext or another, for a monotonous, pointless, exhausting talk. He tried not to hear what she was saying because it was never of any importance; at least it was never anything new. She was simply taking advantage of a chance to humiliate and degrade him when in good conscience he could not strike back.

She demanded to see him each week end; he obliged, though he dreaded the sound of her perpetual whining even more than her stupid, vicious accusations. They would have dinner at the finest restaurants; she insisted on this. She did not bother to read the menu, but looked only at the prices and ordered whatever was most expensive. Melvin's heart sank as he listened to her telling him what she wanted, for he was already in debt to Sam Horne and to a lesser extent to McCampbell and Roska, and to a cadet named Ostrowski who always won a great deal of money in the dice games. He had been forced to borrow from them because the Navy was busily, impersonally, irrevocably, making deductions from his monthly pay check in order to purchase five hundred dollars' worth of war bonds, and what little was left of his check was quickly spent on Polly Ann. So it was that each time she ordered a filet mignon, or a specialty of the house, only to push it away after the first bite, his despair changed to hatred. He would take the plate away from her and eat everything that was on it, while she, seeing him wolf down her dinner as well as his own, would begin to weep and make a scene.

She wanted to know what he meant to do for her; he wiped his lips on the napkin, muttered, shrugged, and evasively asked what she thought could be done. Neither of them could think of anything. She liked to remark, caustically, that if he were half a man he would marry her, to which he replied with weary obstinance that aviation cadets were not allowed to marry. This was the first time he had ever found a Navy regulation to his advantage and to it he retreated as though it were a cyclone cellar whenever she brought up the subject of marriage. At the same time he sensed —though some instinct warned him not to mention it—that she

77

did not actually want to get married; she had just become seventeen and felt that she was too young for marriage. A girl of seventeen should enjoy herself before settling down.

After one of these dismal evenings he entered the barracks as taps was sounding and the lights were going out. It was too hot to sleep. There was no breeze at all. The long, yellowing, gray-green barracks smelled of perspiration. Most of the cadets lay wide awake on their bunks. Melvin stripped off his shirt and shoes and wandered along the aisle to the rear fire escape. Horne was outside sitting on the rail, dressed in gym trunks and a baseball cap; he was smoking a cigar while he watched the moon rise.

"You know, baby," he remarked a few minutes after Melvin had seated himself on the opposite rail, "I've been thinking a lot recently. Soon as this rat race is over I'm going to put in for my discharge and then take off for Europe like a big bird to study with Le Corbusier."

"I don't think I'll ever get married," said Melvin. But then it came to him that there had been no association between these two statements, and the name Le Corbusier extruded—so unexpected and incongruous there on the fire escape in the sweltering Tennessee night that he looked up and found Horne watching him attentively.

"Who? I guess I wasn't listening."

"He's an architect," Horne answered softly, and took the cigar from between his teeth. "A world-famous architect."

"Oh. You've talked about him before. Yes, I remember now."

Every once in a while Horne would launch into a discussion of such things as ferro-concrete pilings or elevated traffic ramps, and "space as related to form," and he had let it be known around the barracks that he meant to become an architect after the war.

"War means destruction," he was explaining. He sat on the rail with his fists on his thighs and glared a trifle absently at the moon. "The thing is this: I don't want to destroy. A person with my temperament ought to *build*. That's the sort of person I am. I've always been that way. For example, I'm up there among those thunderheads—there!" He pointed to a huge, motionless cumulus cloud. "Well, I don't necessarily look at it as a cloud. Sometimes I regard it as a building, if you follow me."

78

They looked at each other and Horne became embarrassed. He tugged at his baseball cap and spat over the rail.

"You must think I'm nuts. Maybe I am." A moment later he growled, "Christ, what a miserable climate! I'd like to know who organized this program, because he ought to get a medal for stupidity."

"You know this girl I've sort of been going around with occasionally?" Melvin asked. "Dark hair, and named Polly. She—oh, you've met her. She was on the train when we came here."

"I seem to remember."

"Well, her name is Polly Ann Bergstrom."

"I do vaguely recall, now you mention it," said Horne. "So?"

"Well, ah—it's just that it's kind of difficult to express, if you know what I mean, but you know once in a while things don't work out exactly like you thought they would. The way you planned. I don't know if that's clear or not," he added hopefully.

"It's clear."

"Really? Well, let me see if I can clarify it then, because—"

"Listen," Horne said, "do you know who you're talking to?"

"What do you mean?" Melvin asked, looking across at him with a wondering, miserable smile.

"You're talking to old Sam Horne. You know me, don't you? You know me from way back. I'm the one who gets you out of trouble on the average about once every two days. So let's go, baby, spit it out."

Melvin's head drooped. "It's nothing much, really. It's just that I'm sort of whipped. Things are pretty complicated."

"Let me put it this way," Horne said. "Let me be crude so we can get down to business. She's getting ready to have a little bundle of joy, is that it?"

"Do you mean you know?"

"Do I know," Horne inquired in a perfectly flat tone. He looked at the moon and muttered, "He asks do I know. Honest to God." He pounded his fist on the rail. "You haven't got the brains of a woodchuck! I sincerely mean that."

Melvin was too alarmed to be insulted. "Do you think anybody else knows?"

"Do I think anybody else knows?" He pretended to consider,

counting on his fingers. "Now let me see. I don't think the commanding officer knows. Outside of that I wouldn't be too sure."

"Tell me the truth! Do you think some of the other cadets know?"

"You poor, miserable, beat-up, ignorant slob," Sam Horne told him gently. "Why, you're actually out on your feet, aren't you? I don't think you know where you've been for the past two months." He went on more vigorously. "*Certainly* they know about it! *Everybody* knows about it! The WAVE at the switchboard knows about it. Your instructor knows about it. The whole battalion knows about it. I think nine-tenths of the personnel on the base know about it."

"Oh, you're just making this up."

"Oh, I am, am I?"

"How could anybody possibly know?"

Horne was exasperated. He sucked at his cigar and then hurled it away. "How the hell should I know how? What difference does it make? The only thing that matters is that if the skipper hears about it, or if some hard-nose junior officer gets wind of it, you'll be up at Great Lakes pushing a mop before you know what hit you. I swear to God, I don't know how you get in so much trouble. It's just one thing after another. I keep thinking it can't go on like this, but it does. One day you lose your recognition manual. Next day you forget to salute the squadron commander. Inspection day comes around and you've got your socks hung up to dry against the light bulb and there's an inch of dust under your bunk. You lose your necktie. You lose your toothpaste. The next thing, for Christ's sake, you'll probably step on some admiral's bunion. It wouldn't surprise me. I don't know what to do with you."

"There's no need to get excited about it."

"Who's excited?" said Horne grumpily. "It just beats the hell out of me, that's all." He jumped down from the railing and marched into the barracks; a minute later he came back outside with a package clumsily wrapped in tissue paper. He had not been able to manage the tissue very well; both ends of the package were criss-crossed with strips of Scotch Tape, and the red ribbon he had tied around it wore a grim little bow like a knotted shoelace.

80

Melvin looked at it suspiciously, afraid of a trick. "What's that?" he demanded, refusing to accept the package.

"It's your birthday, stupid. Happy birthday."

"Thanks very much," Melvin said. He accepted the gift and looked at it as though in admiration of the wrapping, and then clawed the tissue away, saying, "I'd almost forgotten this was my birthday. I got a package from my folks yesterday, as a matter of fact, that I haven't opened, I've been so worried. Well— a carton of cigarettes! That's swell. Thanks again."

"You're welcome," said Horne.

Polly Ann telephoned in the morning to wish him happy birthday, and though she meant well she was still unable to conceal her indignation over what he had done to her. Even so it made his day a little happier. It was the first time in weeks she had tried to say anything nice to him. He thought that if he could just make it to Pensacola everything would turn out all right. First, he would be within sight of graduation. As an ensign drawing flight pay, and counting benefits, he would earn approximately $250 a month instead of $75. Second, if he could reach Pensacola he would be a long way from Polly Ann geographically, and he could not think of anything that would please him more.

The day after his birthday he was summoned to the telephone. With a sigh he picked up the receiver and slumped against the wall of the booth, but an instant later stood bolt upright; it was Polly Ann, as he had known it would be, but the first thing she said to him was that she was going to have an abortion and would need some money. She was afraid to borrow from her aunt, who knew nothing of the situation; therefore she was depending on him. Melvin had difficulty controlling the exultation he felt at this news, for now, if all went well, they would never be forced to see each other again. He asked how much she needed and she told him the doctor would not perform the operation for less than three hundred dollars. He promised to give it to her the next week end, and with that the conversation ended.

He did not have three hundred dollars, or anywhere near it; the very thought of an E bond was enough to make his vitals contract. And borrowing from his father was out of the question. But Sam Horne had offered, in addition to a primitive kind of sympathy, his entire bank account. This account came to more than sixteen hundred dollars because Horne had been breeding pigs in Nebraska quite successfully.

So, carrying his friend's check, prudently addressed to "Cash," Melvin boarded the bus to Memphis to see his young mistress for the last time. They sat on the swing where it had all begun, and where it ended, and they talked for a little while. He offered her the check, hesitantly, fearful she might resume cursing him, slap his face, or burst into tears; she accepted the check as nonchalantly as though it were a potato chip, and he was taken aback once more by the incredible equanimity of women.

Summer was almost gone. High cumulus clouds drifted over the hangars and barracks, over the American flag above the administration building. Heat waves streamed from runways and from the paved streets of the air station, and at midday the telephone poles cast no shadow and the imitation shingle siding of the barracks was too hot to touch, and a dazzling meridian light shimmered through the network of white rafters above the swimming pool. Beneath the dark arched roof of the vast gymnasium with its gigantic sliding doors—through which it seemed a dirigible must issue, moored, towed by Navy tractors—the sound of basketballs was heard, and the thump of men on the trampoline, all the summer sounds. Yet summer was almost over, everyone knew. Soon the company would be ordered to Pensacola and after Pensacola they would move out to fight the Japanese, no longer as cadets but as ensigns or as Marine second lieutenants.

Melvin and Horne frequently lingered on the fire escape till late in the night and speculated on the future. So far only three men of the company had been killed—the Deacon the only one they had known very well—and not many had been washed out. But then, without warning, cadets were dropped from training. Evidently some sort of a directive had come from Washington.

A cadet named Callahan washed out. He had been doing well, at least he thought he had, but one day when he landed at the base he scraped a wingtip. He was brought before a board of review to account for his error in judgment. He claimed a gust of wind had struck his plane just as he was landing. Whether this was true or not nobody knew. The board would not accept the explanation. He was sent to Great Lakes.

A cadet named Vaughn, who bunked above Ostrowski and who was planning to be a priest when the war ended, drifted too close to another Stearman during a formation flight and although there was no collision the instructor in the lead plane was alarmed. Vaughn hurried to the chapel as soon as the flight ended, and that night he stayed up to read his Bible. Shortly before dawn Melvin awoke thinking a fly was buzzing around his ear, but it was Vaughn, kneeling in the aisle and praying aloud. The noise also wakened Ostrowski who rolled over and swore at him, but Vaughn, with tears streaming down his cheeks, continued to pray. He carried his Bible when he appeared before the board of review, but when he learned that the officers were going to dismiss him he flung it aside and began to scream obscenities.

More and more bunks were emptied, the mattresses doubled back. Voices echoed through the barracks. There was no waiting in line for a shower. Every day the platoons grew smaller; by the end of the month few of them were half the size they had been, and one platoon of forty men was reduced to nine.

Cole was amused by this. One day he said to Melvin, "Surely you don't believe the Navy cares what becomes of you. You are merely one of a certain number of cadets at NAS Memphis, as that Stearman over there is one of a certain number of Stearmans. You'll be junked as it will be junked, according to the whim of somebody at a desk in Washington. Just for fun I'll bet fifty dollars that you never make it as far as Pensacola. Neither you nor that imbecilic Elmer Free will make it."

But when the company at last completed the syllabus, both Melvin and Elmer were still around. Of one hundred and sixty who had come to Memphis, only thirty-eight remained. They talked of little else but Pensacola, repeating stories they had heard, which were concerned mostly with the accidents there. Crashes at Memphis had been infrequent and slightly ludicrous, even when somebody was killed—a cadet would hit a tree while practicing how to avoid the trees during an emergency landing, or, at night, mistake the lights on the water tower for the lights on the plane ahead of him in formation. But at Pensacola, so the stories went, there were high-speed midair collisions and the planes sometimes spun out of the sky like animals with horns locked together, and a wing or a piece of the tail might break off and drop stiffly for thousands of feet, or be caught by the wind and turn over and over, fluttering down to earth like the wing of a gigantic butterfly. A plane would disappear into the trees, a few seconds later the smoke came boiling up. If there was a crash at sea the plane would lift a steep, high shower of water and come to a queer, abrupt stop. Or, so it was said, a fast single-engine plane such as a fighter or a dive bomber might strike the water flat on its belly and skip across the surface like a coin or a rock until one of its wings hooked into a wave.

Furthermore, as though to prove they were advancing in the Navy, cadets killed at Pensacola were buried not in khaki, as had been the custom so far, but in blue. Melvin was somewhat shaken by this news: it was, so to speak, a form of promotion and he could not understand why the policy repelled him. He thought about discussing it with Cole but never got around to doing so.

The day before they were to leave for Pensacola he was sitting on a stack of parachutes just outside the hangar enjoying a breeze and feeling altogether contented. He was in debt so deeply that he would have no money for at least six months, but this was of little significance now that he had freed himself not only of his mistress, the very thought of whom was exhausting, but of the immediate threat of being dispatched to Great Lakes.

He reflected that henceforth he would be wise to profit by his adventures thus far: one should not merely accept life as it came along; it was important to evaluate, to be selective. He fell to thinking of the experiences he had had, and in a little while he was dreaming of how the Deacon died at Albuquerque, for this recurred to him persistently, at odd hours, when there was no reason to remember but every reason to forget. He recalled how absent-minded he had become during the days that followed the fatal crash, and how he had flown over the arroyo and peered down intently, as though there might be some explanation in the snow. It seemed to him that the war was ending, there was peace on earth; and the remarkable thing about this was that the war was ending not because one side was victorious but because both armies had discovered what they were doing, as though a mirror had been held up to them, one and the other, so that they were both stunned and amazed.

Melvin awoke gradually and found himself mirrored in the

practical eyes of an officer who asked his name and company number. Melvin understood, without having to inquire, that he had violated another regulation, though he had no idea what it might be—perhaps it had something to do with falling asleep on the parachutes—and that in consequence he would receive ten more demerits and four more hours of extra duty. He was not greatly disturbed by this. He had become accustomed to a certain amount of extra duty; it meant simply four hours of watering the gravel to keep the dust down, or sweeping out the hangars, or whitewashing one of the buildings when he might otherwise be playing checkers or volley ball. But he was horrified to learn he could not work off the hours until the following day. He rushed to the administration building where he argued his case, respectfully, though quite desperately, as long as he could without incurring an additional penalty. The officers to whom he talked were sympathetic but adamant: according to the regulations no cadet was permitted to work off extra duty on the same day the duty was assigned. This was the regulation. It was written down in case anyone doubted it and that was all there was to the matter.

As a result, Melvin's orders were changed and he was held over.

When his friends left for Pensacola they saw him climbing a ladder that leaned against the newly vacated barracks. He was dressed in gym trunks, tennis shoes, and a baseball cap, and even from the gate they could see that he was spotted all over with whitewash.

7

A week later Melvin arrived with the next draft from Memphis, and he felt more than anything else a vast sense of relief, as though at last he had escaped from the shadow of some threatening cloud.

Here, finally, was Pensacola. He walked all around the base staring at everything, dazed by the coastal sunlight, the roaring engines, and the ceaseless activity. Here were the blinding white sand dunes of interminable beaches, and causeways barely above the level of the water, and sun-drenched pastel buildings, and naval uniforms—green, white, tropical khaki, blue, gray, black shoulder boards with gold stars and gold stripes, multicolored campaign ribbons, and gold wings everywhere—and breakers crashing on the beach, and in the sky no matter where he looked were droning formations of Navy planes. He saw hundreds of cadets going in and out of various offices with folders and manila envelopes, and it occurred to him that they had completed training and were about to be commissioned as naval aviators. Their khakis were faded, their faces and hands were deeply tanned, and about them—the way they stood, and gestured, and laughed—was a look of experience which impressed him. He was eager to talk to some of them, but did not have enough courage. They appeared to be busy; he thought they would not want to be bothered. Often he stopped with his hands clasped behind his back and his face lifted to the radiant, glaring, burning sun while he listened to the engines in the sky and sniffed the warm Gulf breeze, and was almost overcome with nervous excitement. But he felt a little sad and lost to think he would not be training here with his friends. They would be one week ahead of him all the way. He would see them now and again, they might have liberty on the same nights and could meet in town, but it would not be the same.

He discovered that Pensacola was not a single base; it consisted of a large central station, referred to as "Mainside," and about half a dozen smaller bases within a radius of twenty miles or so. At this main station the new cadets attended orientation lectures for several days. Then, after drawing some additional equipment—textbooks, pamphlets, flight gear—they reported to the first of the auxiliary fields. From there they moved to another, and another, and eventually, if all went well, they would return to Mainside to be commissioned as naval or Marine aviators and assigned to operational training with a combat squadron.

On his second evening at the main station he had been lying

on his bunk for about an hour trying to decide whether to play billiards or go to the movies when he heard someone come striding down the corridor and stop at his room. The door was kicked open. Melvin rolled over and looked up. There stood Horne with his hands on his hips.

"What are you doing here?" Melvin asked.

"I figured I'd better wait for you," Horne said brusquely. "You'd never get through the program alone."

Melvin grinned. "You been telling me that for the past year, so knock it off. Listen, what *are* you doing here? I thought you'd be at Ellyson Field. That's where I go first, isn't it?"

Horne sat on the edge of the bunk, tossed his cap in the air, and caught it. "We all go to Ellyson together, day after tomorrow. Don't ask me why. We finished the orientation last week. All I know is, we got word that our draft and yours were going to be combined."

"You mean the other guys are still here?"

"Sure. Nick, Elmer, everybody. We're in the next barracks. Come on over and say hello. We sort of expected you'd look us up, but then I got to thinking and I figured you wouldn't have sense enough."

Melvin got up and put on his cap and followed Horne out of the barracks by way of the fire escape; it was longer that way but there was less chance of encountering an officer. They had not done anything wrong; all the same, it was difficult to predict what would irritate an officer so they made a habit of avoiding them whenever possible.

"What's the good word?" Horne asked while they were walking across the grass to the adjoining barracks.

"Since last week, not much. I got a letter from my father just before I checked out at Memphis, and he's pretty worried about sabotage and subversive activities. It was a real long letter. He says some congressman says there are twenty-seven subversive books in the Library of Congress."

"Is that a fact! Did he read them?"

"Who? My father? No, he mostly reads newspapers. That and detective magazines."

"The congressman! The congressman, stupid."

"Oh! I don't know. My father didn't say."

"Subversive books! I'll be damned," Horne remarked with a thoughtful expression.

A formation of twin-engine bombers roared over the treetops through the warm September dusk.

"Lot of stuff down here," Horne commented with satisfaction when the noise diminished. "New stuff, too. Couple of Helldivers came in the other day, and Ostrowski saw a whole squadron of F6's. He said he never saw anything so sweet."

Melvin nodded. "I don't doubt it, but you know, about the time we get through the engine syllabus it's going to be time to start over and learn how to fly jets."

Horne shook his head. "Those things'll never replace propeller-driven planes, not in a million years. They're fast, sure, nobody argues that, but they haven't got either the range or the maneuverability. They'll fade out of the picture, you watch."

"What makes you so positive? For now, maybe you're right, but the designers are going to improve them. They'll stay up longer and maybe get more maneuverable."

"As long as I've known you, you've been a dreamer. You don't belong in this outfit. You know that by now, don't you?" He hesitated, as though he had meant to keep his opinion to himself, but then went on angrily. "Look, it's none of my business, except that I think your old man is counting on you."

"What am I supposed to do? Get the Navy Cross?"

"Just forget it," Horne remarked. "I'm sorry I spoke." He trotted briskly up the fire escape to his barracks and Melvin followed. It was not quite dark. The breeze was mild, and through the pine trees came the odor of the sea. The evening star was glowing. High overhead a plane steadily reflected the sun below the horizon. Melvin hesitated, reluctant to go inside; he sensed that Horne felt the same.

"You know, it's queer," Horne said. He unwrapped a cigar and fondled it. "People can tell we're cadets."

"How do you mean?"

"Well," and with the cigar gripped in his teeth he straightened up and cinched in his belt, "like just the other day. Me and Elmer and Roska went to the beach. Now, you know Roska—he got drunk and passed out, so me and Elmer were lying there listening to a ball game on the radio when all of a sudden here come these two broads. I'm telling you, you should've seen them. They had one of these big striped umbrellas and they set it up, and pretty soon they started spreading this oil or lotion all over themselves. I swear to God"—he paused and frowned—"it's enough to drive a man wild the way they do that. You know how they do it—they sit there squeezing themselves and rubbing each other. So, anyhow, Elmer was for opening shop right there and the hell with the shore patrol and frankly I wouldn't of been one jump behind. But anyway—let's see, I'm getting off the subject. Well, there they were, pretending they didn't even know we were on the beach, though by this time we're practically breathing down their necks. So—ah, well, we hadn't been talking to them five minutes before one of them wanted to know if we'd come back to Mainside to get the bird."

"Get what?"

"The bird. That's what they call it down here—getting the commission. I don't know how it started, maybe on account of the wings. Anyway, the point is: they knew we weren't officers and they knew we weren't swabbies. But how? We didn't even have on GI swimsuits."

"Maybe the dog tags."

"Sure. Where does it say 'cadet' on your tags? It's mysterious," he continued, shaking his head. "We got some kind of a brand. Incidentally, over at the beach we can join the officers' club if we want to."

"That's what I heard. Is it worth it?"

"I don't figure it is. Most of our time in the area is going to be spent at auxiliary stations way the hell out in the woods. We won't be around here much."

"What's Pensacola like? The town, I mean."

"Me and Elmer went in the other night. There's tailor shops all over and they actually come right out on the sidewalk and try to pull you inside to sign you up for later. And there's some pretty fair restaurants. The bars are all jammed, you got to fight for a drink. And the streets are jammed. Everybody's selling something —if it isn't the Red Cross or the Salvation Army it's some kind of a sticker or a flower. Let's see—there's plenty of beer joints scattered around the edge of town, except we can't go in those,

89

and the whole area is lousy with shore patrol. That's about it."

"How are the women?"

"I wondered when you were going to ask that. The area's loaded, and no mistake, however the situation appears to be a little different from what we've been used to. These here look older, but—" He paused and pointed to a flight of planes breaking out of formation and spiraling down into the landing pattern. "You got a clear shot. Now, what are they?"

Melvin studied the planes until they settled behind the trees. "Those were either V's or J's. They look so much alike."

"Those were J's," Horne said. "SNJ's. That fin was just as triangular as could be. I honestly don't know how you could miss it."

Melvin leaned his arms on the rail of the fire escape and said, "Well, I honestly don't know how you could see it. Incidentally, does anybody get washed out on recognition here?"

"Nope. You're in luck. You don't get washed out for anything at Pensacola. The skipper told us that all but three per cent would get their wings. What a change from primary, huh? They slaughtered us there." He grinned. "Nope," he continued, "all you got to worry about is getting killed. As a matter of fact, though, come to think of it, I did run into one of those three per centers just the other day. He was leaving for the Lakes. He washed out of VB2—that's the land-based bomber squadron—and he was one sad sack. He was a Dilbert if I ever saw one. You can spot them. He just looked like one."

"What did he do wrong?"

"Led a flight over restricted territory. But unless you really dope off and do something stupid like that you won't get washed out here. All you got to worry about, like I say, is that you don't crucify yourself. If you smack up one of these machines they collect you on a shovel." He waved expansively and pounded himself on the chest. "I think, by Christ, we got it made!"

"Do you?"

"I do," Horne affirmed cheerfully. "I do, Ensign Isaacs, I do! Come on inside and say hello."

They stepped into the barracks and found everyone on the floor shooting dice.

A few days later they reported to Ellyson Field, the first of

90

the auxiliary bases, where they would spend several weeks learning to fly the SNV, an intermediate trainer known as the Valiant. It was a loose, roomy airplane, comfortable to sit in, but underpowered, like a two-cylinder limousine; even so it flew faster than the Yellow Peril. The two cockpits were enclosed by a long glass canopy with sliding panels known as the greenhouse; there were retractable flaps on the wings, and a variable-pitch propeller that could produce a shattering roar.

The SNV had one unusual feature: the wheels were set wide apart. This meant there would be little chance of ground-looping, which came about when an airplane swerved instead of rolling straight ahead. If it swerved, a wing would dip while the plane traveled in an arc, drawn by centripetal force, with increasing swiftness, toward the center around which it had begun to revolve. The accident customarily ended when the wing dragged the ground, since the friction was enough to stop the revolution. The pilot then found himself headed in approximately the opposite direction from which he had been going, with a scraped wing, in full view of the squadron tower and everybody on the flight line. It was not a dangerous accident, but it was humiliating; more than that, it was conclusive evidence that the pilot had lost control, and such was noted on his record.

Although it was theoretically possible to groundloop a take-off, this seldom happened. It was landing that caused the trouble, landing on gusty days, in a crosswind, and especially at night when the runways were invisible and the pilot was guided only by flares.

So it was that Melvin prayed for a bright, shining moon during his first night solo in the SNV; but on that night there was no moon at all, not even the stars could be seen. The sky was overcast, a brisk wind sprang up shortly after sunset, and the temperature dropped, which meant the possibility of ice forming in the carburetor; this, in turn, would mean a dead engine and a forced landing.

He stood just inside the hangar with a parachute slung across his shoulder and stared into the darkness of the field, which was lighted by a few flickering pots of oil. Hearing footsteps he turned around and saw his instructor, who, with false heartiness, slapped him on the back and asked how he was feeling. He answered that he felt all right, whereupon the instructor offered him a cigarette and remarked that, after all, this was not his first night flight; and Melvin, accepting the cigarette, agreed. He had been given a few hours of dual instruction in night flying at Memphis and the instructor knew it.

"Anything bothering you, Isaacs?" the officer inquired with a smile.

"Yes, sir," he replied, for he had expected some additional instruction.

"Got the jumps?"

"Yes, sir."

"You can handle it."

"Yes, sir," he repeated as he stared into the darkness.

"You can, can't you?" the officer asked, looking at him closely.

"Yes, sir."

They stood side by side, smoking and looking into the night, and at last the officer said, "You drew a black one, kid. I haven't seen a night this dark in months."

"It is, isn't it, sir."

"Isaacs, there are a couple of strands of high-tension wire on the downwind leg."

"I know where they are," Melvin said. "I know exactly where they are."

On top of the squadron tower the beacon was rotating, the green and white course lights bolting wildly across the station. Soon the night flyers would take off. Already the engines were starting: sputtering, expelling hoarse, roaring barks like sea lions somewhere in the night, while propellers kicked stubbornly back and forth and acrid fumes came drifting toward the hangar. Navigation lights blinked on—red, green, white. The air seemed to vibrate.

The instructor touched Melvin on the arm, and called to him above the roar of the engines. Melvin could barely hear what he said, but he knew it was time to go. He nodded and stepped on the cigarette. Perspiration had begun to trickle down his face.

The instructor shouted, "Watch out for propwash!"

Melvin read his lips and nodded. There would be ten or twelve SNV's circling the field to practice landings. They would follow each other closely and the air would be turbulent with their passage. He saluted, noticed how intently the officer was studying him, turned away, and began walking toward the flight line.

On the first landing as he was nearing the ground, banking cautiously over the high-tension wires, the left wing dropped. Instantly he pushed the throttle as far as it would go, saw the flares spiral toward him with a pitching motion as though he were on the prow of a ship; the wing flew up and the plane was momentarily level, rattling and howling. He thought it was going to crash; he expected to feel it twist away from him. It surged forward, the burning pots of oil flickered by like rubies beneath the wing, and he pulled up gradually into the circle and went around to try again.

By the time he had completed his final landing for the night he had been frightened so badly and so many times that he was no longer perspiring or trembling. His face was shocked and immobile. He climbed out of the airplane and wandered toward the hangar as though he had been struck on the head. He was not thinking of anything. He was aware that the flight was over; otherwise there was nothing at all on his mind.

The instructor was waiting. He had not been able to see the airplane except when it was on the runway rolling between the pots of oil, but he had followed it around the station by the navigation lights and by the flame of the exhaust. He had seen the lights tilt and dive toward the wires. He knew what had happened. It was nobody's fault.

The officer attempted to laugh, and called out, "Here comes the luckiest man in the world!"

Melvin heard him and tried to speak, but could not. He approached the officer, saluted, and made an effort to smile, but this was not successful either—his expression remained unchanged. Then, with the officer staring at him, he touched his face, because it felt numb, as though he had been in a blizzard, and realized he had not yet taken off his helmet. It was buckled beneath his chin. He shrugged jerkily, hiccuped, and very slowly walked toward the parachute loft to check in the equipment.

Horne was at the barracks getting ready to take a shower. He had completed his flight an hour earlier.

93

"Pretty rough night," he said when Melvin wandered into the room. "Must be a storm front bearing down. I thought I was on a goddam rolly-coaster."

Melvin didn't speak.

8

The next night they went up again, and Horne was nearly killed when an unidentified plane circled the field in the wrong direction; he saw the lights approaching and dove beneath them just in time. In the barracks he made a joke of it. When Melvin asked if he had not been frightened Horne shouted, "What the hell am I supposed to do, sit around and think about it till I get the shakes? You ask the stupidest questions! Of course I was frightened!" He tried to calm himself, and continued, "I was so scared I wet my pants, but I got through—I'm alive—I'm going to forget it. I really am going to forget the whole thing," he said, and pounded his fist on the desk.

"I wish I could forget that easily," Melvin said.

"Do you mean to tell me you're still hopped up about those high-tension wires? That was yesterday!"

Melvin was embarrassed. "I guess you're right. It's over."

"You think you had a problem there, just wait till we get to Whiting. Cole was telling me about some cadet who got so nervous under the hood looking at all those instruments that he went off his rocker and was crying like a little girl when they landed. They couldn't get him out of the plane—he wouldn't let go of the stick. They had to pry him loose. Yes, sir!" Horne added with angry satisfaction. "You want something to sweat about, just wait till we hit that instrument squadron."

In November they packed their duffel bags, climbed into a

Navy truck, and went bouncing over a new gravel road through the pines to Whiting Field. A mood of expectancy, of anticipation, overhung this base, which had a temporary look, as though the trees had been cleared and the runways poured and the buildings erected in a few days. There were, in fact, chinks in the walls of the barracks so that during certain hours a streak of sunlight would enter a room and creep along the coarse gray Navy blankets stretched taut on the bunks, and across the newly varnished desks. And in the middle of the night, or in a quiet moment at high noon, a fragment of plaster might drop from the wall or the ceiling. Roaches crawled through the showers and through the desks and the lockers. The paths between the buildings were deep with a fine, white, heavy dust as stifling as lime, which muffled the sound of the marching platoons. The cadets were accustomed to marching across broad, hard parade grounds drenched with sunlight, or to the sound of their heels on concrete and gravel, but at Whiting Field their shoes flopped in the dust, their voices were lost among the trees.

Quite early each morning they went swimming. The pool was outdoors. The water was so cold that after one length they were half paralyzed. It did not take them long to discover that no roll call was taken from the time they left the barracks until the time they returned, although an officer trailed the platoon from the barracks to the pool to make certain the cadets did not fade away into the forest. Once they arrived at the pool, however, this particular officer invariably seated himself on a bench, took out his pipe and a newspaper, and seldom looked around. So it happened that every once in a while as he lifted the newspaper to turn a page some cadet would draw himself swiftly from the freezing water and race to the fence. Over it he would go, like a monkey escaping from a circus, to be lost in the deep shadows of the pine forest. The officer was not ignorant of this, but he never said anything. He knew how cold the water was. So long as the entire platoon did not vault the fence he would not make life difficult.

Hours were spent in the Link trainer. A WAVE sat at a large desk beside each of these odd, stubby toys; she held a microphone and wore a headset to communicate with the cadet inside the Link. Jerkily, drunkenly, like horrible automatons, the machines veered and tilted. Across the desk a stylus moved, recording the pattern.

When they took off for actual instrument practice they climbed high in the air and stayed aloft for an hour or two, methodically executing the patterns in a brilliant windy sky. The flights were dual. An instructor taxied the plane to the end of the runway and made the take-off. Soon after leaving the ground he would order the cadet, who was riding in the back seat, to pull the hood over the cockpit; then in the sepia twilight, as though he sat inside a tent, suspended by the steadily throbbing machine, Melvin would examine the fluorescent lighted panel and wait for additional orders. Occasionally, as the instructor banked the airplane, the cockpit would grow faintly brighter or darker. Rarely, like the sun through a chink in the barracks, a slender stripe of daylight would find its way between the metal and the canvas. Except for this, and for the sound of the engine laboring or humming easily, there was no way to distinguish what was happening except by reading the instruments.

On each flight, as soon as the hood was drawn, he began to count the instruments. He did not know precisely how many there were, but if one included all the switches, knobs, pumps, primers, lamps, ventilators—whatever could be twisted, pushed, adjusted, or pulled—each of which had its own purpose and meaning, he estimated there must be something like ninety or one hundred. Counting them kept him occupied; it helped to control his anxiety. He never got everything counted; a few minutes after the plane was airborne the headphones would crackle and hum and he would hear the instructor ask if he was ready to take over. Then he would unhook the tiny black microphone, no bigger than a silver dollar, from its box and say, with dread and reluctance, that he was ready. Then the control stick wobbled, he took hold of it, and the lesson commenced.

Following instructions from the front seat he banked to the left—the gyro compass turned smoothly with him while the magnetic compass dipped and swung sluggishly, crazily, in the amber fluid—pressed the stick forward, and knew he must be entering a dive because the tachometer reading increased and the air speed increased and he could hear the wind rattling the canopy and flapping the taut borders of the hood; yet, despite

96

these proofs, his body insisted he was going up, not down. Or not down so steeply. Or was the plane level?

After a while his kinesthetic sense stopped functioning altogether: his body could not even estimate whether it was right side up, upside down, or sideways. He sometimes glanced at the safety belt to see if it was taut or slack; he trusted the belt, convinced it would not deceive him. But as for the instruments, he was not so sure; there was something malignant and unnerving in the absolute assurance of the dials.

He did rely, however, on one large dial in the upper right-hand corner of the panel: it was called the artificial horizon and consisted of two white horizontal bars, the shorter one representing the airplane, the longer one representing the horizon. When he was flying straight ahead, and level, there appeared to be only one bar, but the moment the plane began to deviate from this course—diving, climbing, or turning—the bars drifted apart: the horizon rose above the wing, or sank below it, or inclined precisely as the surface of the earth was inclined. If there had been nothing to do but fly the plane on an even keel one could do it with this instrument alone, but there were patterns.

The simplest pattern was called Able. Then came Baker. Then came Charlie, and so on. Charlie required about ten minutes. It included various turns, from 270 degrees to 450 degrees, at different speeds. It required gains and losses of altitude at predetermined headings within a specified number of seconds and at a particular speed. Melvin was continually busy, for no sooner did he correct one deviation than he discovered another. He scanned the panel anxiously, finding that a turn was poorly coordinated because he was heavy on the rudder, that the air speed was dropping, had already fallen two knots; now he was four degrees off heading. Time was running out: three seconds late at the beginning of the second leg. The tachometer was rising; he was banking at 35 degrees instead of 30, and now the plane was skidding. And he knew that all this time the instructor in the front seat was skeptically watching an identical panel of instruments. Often he could hear a clicking noise in the headset, caused by the instructor fingering the microphone button, which meant that the pattern was going badly and that the instructor was on the verge of telling him to quit and start over. Finally, completing the pattern, he was back where he had started ten minutes ago, an eternity ago.

Usually the instructor had no comment, or if he did speak it was only to criticize. At best he would remark that it was not as bad as yesterday. Then another pattern would commence.

On the way home the instructor released the hood. The canvas was attached to a spring and snapped backward so quickly that Melvin always jumped. The instructor in the front seat could feel him jump, and every day after this happened Melvin would see the instructor shaking with laughter.

In the barracks he discussed the patterns with Sam Horne and they analyzed the mistakes they had made, because, as always, when the syllabus had been completed they must convince a check pilot that they were qualified to continue.

McCampbell and Roska were the first to finish the syllabus and take the check ride. Both of them passed. Horne was scheduled for his last flight that same afternoon, and when he came down he was given a choice of flying the check immediately or waiting till the next day. He did not even stop for a cup of coffee. He went up again and returned to the hangar two hours later, saying the check was easy.

Elmer Free was the next to go up, and as soon as they saw him returning to the hangar they knew he had failed. The next morning he flew another check ride, and again failed. This meant he must appear before a board of review to request additional instruction. If the board refused to grant his request he would be washed out and sent to Great Lakes as an apprentice seaman.

So, with three of their acquaintances having completed the course and the fourth one about to be washed out, Melvin and Pat Cole wished each other luck. They were going up at the same time.

Melvin's check pilot was a lanky, taciturn lieutenant named Kennedy who had a bad reputation. Melvin found him sprawled on a row of gasoline drums in the shade of the schedule board. He was munching peanuts and flipping the shells toward a helicopter that had just landed. Melvin approached, came to attention, and saluted. Kennedy did not bother to return the salute; in fact he did not even look up. A pair of brogan shoes was in his line of vision, so he knew a cadet was standing there. He slipped another peanut between his teeth and absently said, "Where the Christ have you been?"

Melvin answered respectfully that he didn't know he was late.

"You bet you're late!" Kennedy snapped, holding up one arm so that Melvin could see his wristwatch. It was eight minutes before the hour. Cadets were expected to report to the schedule board ten minutes early.

"Well?" Kennedy demanded.

"I'm sorry, sir."

Kennedy spat out the remains of a peanut and languidly got to his feet. His coveralls were rotten with grease and perspiration. His eyeballs protruded. He breathed thickly into Melvin's face, glaring at him with impersonal hostility.

"You *cadets*," he said, and leaning down he grabbed a parachute by one strap and slung it across his shoulder. Without a word he snatched a piece of yellow chalk from the WAVE at the board, drew a diagonal mark in the box beside his name, tossed the chalk to her, and went slouching toward the flight line. Melvin hurried after him, keeping half a step behind.

The only thing the lieutenant said before they left the ground was, "You better be good."

At two thousand feet he turned over the controls to Melvin and ordered him to start at the beginning and go through everything he had learned.

It was a poor day for precision flying because the sky was filled with convection currents; the plane hit them with sudden jarring thumps. Some of the bumps were so hard that to Melvin, locked inside the canvas hood, they felt like solid objects in the center of the sky, like the bodies of birds, or ruts in a country road. He struggled with the patterns, but no sooner did he have everything organized than a current would destroy the heading, or the plane would abruptly drop fifteen or twenty feet and then bounce upward. In the front seat Kennedy was smoking; Melvin could not see him but he could smell the cigarette. Only once did the lieutenant speak. He slurred his words; it sounded as though he were holding the microphone too close to his lips:

". . . think you're *doing?*" he demanded. He was obviously exasperated.

"What do you mean, sir?"

". . . accelerate?"

"I'm sorry, sir, but I can't hear you!" Melvin answered with a feeling of desperation.

"I *said*, why the Christ did you *accelerate?*"

"I don't know, sir. I thought I was supposed to."

". . . *not!* Fly . . . second leg at *normal cruise.*"

"Shall I try it again?"

"*No!*"

Melvin went on with the maneuvers but Kennedy had taken the heart out of him. The plane struck another wild current and floated; he sucked the throttle back and carefully lowered the nose, but the altimeter continued to rise. Then he felt Kennedy touch the controls. Within a second or so the plane was again on course. The heading was perfect, the wings were level, the air speed no longer fluctuated. There was nothing to do but sit with his hands folded helplessly in his lap and admire the co-ordination of the instruments.

Presently they struck another column of air; the plane scarcely wavered. Kennedy completed the pattern and then the plane barrel-rolled. No sooner were they right side up than the throttle slid forward. Melvin knew something else was about to happen. He took hold of the braces beside the seat and waited. The air speed increased, the plane snapped over on its back.

They flew along upside down while he dangled uncomfortably from the belt and gripped the braces. His cheeks felt flabby and his brain was turning scarlet. The plane entered a dive upside down. He studied the instruments and was impressed to realize that the lieutenant was making inverted turns without skidding or slipping. He noticed, about this time, that they were getting rather low. He wondered how far above the trees they were; he wished the lieutenant would pop the hood so he could look out. He felt an attack of vertigo coming on, and soon, annoyed because he knew he was wrong, he became convinced that the plane was no longer inverted; his body told him it was in a leisurely, spiraling climb. An instant later he leaned to the right because he thought the plane was banking in that direction. All at once the hood flew open, flooding the cockpit with light. Melvin lifted his head, which was packed hard and heavily with blood, and

100

discerned what he thought was a solid, bluish-gray bank of clouds lying dead ahead. The plane was diving toward it, oscillating slightly, like a projectile. The clouds were curiously flecked with white, and he was struck, too, by the recollection that the sky had been clear half an hour before, and it was then he realized he was staring not at a bank of clouds but into the Gulf of Mexico.

Just as they were about to dive through the surface the lieutenant pressed the controls; the plane rolled right side up and flashed over the waves.

They skimmed across the Gulf for about fifteen minutes. Kennedy never said a word. Melvin remained absolutely motionless in the rear cockpit, arms folded, watching the spray flit over the wings; he was aware that he and the officer might be killed at any instant, but this thought did not worry him, partly because he did not think the officer would make a mistake but also because, if there was an accident, the officer, rather than himself, would be responsible. He knew that if they struck a wave they would never be found; the wreckage would sink in a minute and the Navy would never learn what had become of them, and, actually, would be apt to assume that the cadet had been the cause of whatever had happened. Yet this would not be the truth and he felt oddly secure in the knowledge that he was blameless.

He thought it might very well come to pass that they would crash, for he perceived that they were still closer to the water than before; it must be that the officer, for whatever reason, was seeking the ultimate risk. Once, in fact, he felt a bump as they raced over the crest of a high breaking wave and he saw Kennedy's head turn, ever so slightly. Melvin was dryly amused by this, and thought to himself that it might be just as well if the next wave caught them, for it seemed that the long months of work had been in vain. And it seemed to him, too, that the officer had not given him a fair chance—the air had been so turbulent. But he knew there was no appeal; he had failed, and now there was nothing to do but hope that somehow he would not be washed out. Discouraged and deeply resentful, he glanced into the mirror and met the lieutenant's acute, protruding, raisin-colored eye.

A moment later the plane arched steeply up, and up, rolled over and over again, and emerged on a straight and level course. Dead ahead lay the Florida coast. Kennedy wiggled the stick and mumbled into the microphone. Melvin accepted the controls and flew toward the base while the officer ate peanuts.

As they were approaching the traffic circle Kennedy took over again, cut into the pattern, landed, taxied swiftly to the parking line, and turned off the switches. He jumped out of the cockpit and started for the schedule board. Melvin expected him to say something, anything, but Kennedy slouched along, the parachute slung across his shoulder. He looked half asleep. Melvin walked not quite abreast of him and stared at the ground. They had not used the full amount of time; they were returning to the station almost forty minutes early.

When they reached the board Kennedy refused the chalk a WAVE held out to him; he picked up a stub that was lying on the concrete and crossed the diagonal with another to form an X showing the flight had been completed. Then, next to "Isaacs," he drew an arrow, tossed away the chalk, and began to feel around in the pockets of his filthy coveralls.

Melvin gazed at the arrow, which should have pointed down, not up.

"Any questions?" the officer inquired. He had split a match on his thumbnail and was picking his teeth.

"Questions?" Melvin said, unable to stop looking at the arrow.

"It was a rough afternoon. You made some nice recoveries."

"You mean you're not giving me a down?"

"You rather have a down?"

Melvin shook his head and continued to look at the arrow.

"That was a good flight," Kennedy said. "All you need is confidence."

The arrow was still there, pointing to the sky. It promised that he would fly again. It seemed to promise that he would be flying forever.

"You cadets," the lieutenant mumbled and slouched away.

Melvin hurried to the barracks to let everybody know he had passed, and there he learned that Elmer had appeared before the board of review and after a long interrogation had been granted two hours of extra instruction. Pat Cole had not yet returned, so

Melvin sat on the front steps to wait for him, and in a little while he appeared and mentioned as he strolled by that the check pilot had told him his flight grades were going to be among the highest ever recorded at the instrument squadron.

Melvin was impressed.

Cole hesitated, gave him a tentative smile, and said, "You're a nice kid, Isaacs. Too bad this is no place for kids."

The next morning Elmer began his additional instruction and on the following Wednesday he took another check ride. He was scheduled with Kennedy. He was up a long time and afterward was detained at the board while Kennedy talked to him. Evidently it had been a poor flight. At any of the previous bases he would have been washed out, but finally the lieutenant passed him. They were at Pensacola and for the first time the Navy was giving them the benefit of the doubt.

Before leaving Whiting Field they were allowed to order officers' uniforms. They had studiously ignored, out of jealousy, the fittings which went on every Tuesday in the barracks lounge, but now it was their turn, and while they talked with the different salesmen and read the slick paper brochures and wandered around fingering samples of cloth, trying on hats and gloves, studying themselves in the mirror, feeling the gold braid on the resplendent dummies, they were conscious that they were being scrutinized enviously and surreptitiously by cadets of the companies behind them.

Horne and Melvin planned to buy their uniforms from the same firm, but after visiting the display they were not able to agree on which firm should get the business. They borrowed some samples and went upstairs to their room for a private discussion.

"This is the stuff," Horne repeated patiently, holding a swatch up to the light. "Right here. This is it. This is Hazlitt and Lausch's stuff and there's no comparison. Feel it. Just feel it, that's all I ask."

Melvin felt the material and shrugged.

"You like Pettigrew," Horne went on. "What's Pettigrew got to offer? They got a fat little salesman with a waxed mustache. They got gold braid that'll fray and tarnish in a month. What's the matter with you? This is the stuff, I'm telling you!"

"Go ahead and buy it, I'm not stopping you."

"Oh, Jesus!" Horne exclaimed. "You got one of your obstinate days again. Here! Hold this up to the light! Look at that weave! Just tell me in complete honesty what you think, that's all I ask."

"It's fair. So-so. Nothing to get excited about."

They went downstairs after a while, not speaking to each other. Melvin placed his order with Pettigrew; Horne placed his with Hazlitt and Lausch.

Tuesday afternoons in the barracks lounge they stood motionless and erect while the nimble-fingered tailors crept around inserting pins, tugging at folds, marking with chalk, patting and smoothing. It was odd to find themselves in this position, to know they were so far along.

9

Shortly before Christmas the company was assigned to Barin Field for instruction in gunnery, strafing, and dive bombing. During the previous few months there had been so many accidents on this station that it had come to be known as "Bloody Barin." It was said that one week the mortality rate at Barin had been higher than that of any squadron in the Pacific.

Most of the rooms were for four men, but there were a few small rooms for two. Sam Horne, who was still the company commander, used his influence to obtain a two-man room for himself and Melvin. It was on the third floor at the rear of the building and gave a fine view of the water tank, the hangars and machine shops, the squadron tower with its tinted windows and revolving beacon, and the long rows of parked airplanes. But because it was at the opposite end of the corridor from the lounge where the pool table was located Melvin complained, and asked Horne why he had not chosen a room close to the lounge. Horne pointed out that there was a commissioned officer living in each of the barracks whose quarters were on the first floor in the front; their room, consequently, was as far away from him as possible.

And this turned out to be very sound reasoning, because the officer assigned to their barracks was a plump, foppish little ensign named Monk who had inexplicable fits of rage and hysteria during which he would gasp and sometimes shudder from an excess of emotion. Nobody could tell when he was going to become enraged, or why. The only sensible thing to do was to keep out of his way. Whenever he met a cadet who displeased him, Ensign Monk promptly looked at the ceiling, clasped his moist, pudgy hands behind his back, and cried in a shrill feminine voice, "Oh-*ho!* Oh-HO!" Then with a peculiar snuffling and choking like an animal—a pig, possibly, rooting through a trough of garbage —Ensign Monk would write the cadet's name on the pap sheet and give him the customary ten demerits and four hours of extra duty.

At Barin Field they would no longer be flying as individuals but as members of a team, in groups of six, and since they were permitted to form their own group Melvin and Horne invited Nick McCampbell to join them, then Roska, Elmer, and finally Pat Cole, after which they held an election to decide who should be the flight leader. There was a certain amount of prestige to being flight leader: on the ground he answered roll call and occasionally signed a paper of one sort or another. Otherwise the title was meaningless. In the air the actual leadership of the team changed from one to another. When the ballots were counted it was discovered that Horne had received six votes, which meant of course that he had voted for himself. So they reported to the squadron office where they were given a number: 487. They were the 487th group to enter training at Bloody Barin.

They had not been there very long when the uniforms they had ordered at Whiting Field were delivered. After the first look—the cartons unceremoniously ripped open, the so carefully folded tissue paper torn away with impatience—Horne and Melvin hurried upstairs to try them on. The uniforms were heavy and crisp, the fresh gold sparkling thickly on the sleeves. Once in a while, after that first day, they tried on the uniforms, saluted themselves in the mirror, and talked about being ensigns,

105

but for the most part the uniforms hung in the closet, the hat with the commissioned officer's insignia rested on a shelf.

Ground school continued, the subjects and the problems so familiar now that the cadets answered without thinking. In a dark, warm room on the second deck of the second hangar they spent an hour a day waiting for lantern slides to flash against the wall, and wrote down what they had seen. If it was a Japanese ship they knew its class, name, tonnage, speed, the thickness of its armor plate, and the location and strength of its batteries; if it was a plane they knew its wingspan, speed, armament, and maneuverability.

During the communications period each cadet sat quietly in a booth, listening through earphones to the frenzied, insistent code, and jotted down the messages: "Japanese convoy bearing zero-six-zero. Speed twelve knots. Heading zero-five-five. Attack immediately. Attack immediately."

Gunnery lessons took place in a Quonset hut in a device similar to the Link trainer. A motion-picture screen was set up directly ahead of the cockpit and an enemy plane flew wildly around the screen while the cadet attempted to shoot it down. The enemy flew over mountains and forest and across a beach and over the ocean while clouds floated by, puffs of anti-aircraft smoke broke all around, and the Quonset hut echoed from the noise of machine-gun bullets and the screaming, shrieking engines. The enemy dove through the clouds, diminishing, escaping, then seemed to increase in size, and if the wingtips spanned the screen the machine guns began clattering. Whenever the guns were on target the picture turned crimson.

If the cadets were not attending school they were at the flight line. But the winter rains had set in and there was almost no flying. One glance at the icy, sluggish, water-laden clouds settling over the base like seaweed and they knew the field would be closed all day. There were mornings when the clouds sank so low that the water tank was invisible—only the bottom of the trestle could be seen, while the powerful red beacon on the squadron tower was a dim, intermittent blur the color of rouge in a woman's compact —yet the company was required to muster in front of the barracks at the usual time every day and march down the narrow asphalt road to the hangars. There they had nothing to do. Everyone knew the clouds would not lift, but there the company was supposed to be, and there it was. The cadets played checkers and drank coffee, pitched pennies at a crack in the pavement, answered roll call every hour or so, and carried on long conversations with the WAVEs who worked in the parachute loft. They were not supposed to talk to the WAVEs except about the parachutes, but they did, and once in a while an officer would come around and run the cadets out of the loft and threaten the WAVEs, but a few minutes after the officer disappeared the cadets would come back; and it was here that Elmer Free got acquainted with one of the girls, whose name was Diane. Before the war she had been a dancer. Cole insisted he had seen her in a burlesque house in Chicago, but Elmer was not in the least offended. He chuckled amiably and replied, "Sho! You dog, Pat."

In a few days Elmer had become so interested in her that whenever the clouds did lift and 487 was scheduled for a flight he paid no attention to what he was doing. Whenever he and the WAVE got liberty together they would take the bus to Mobile and stay overnight. He soon began to talk about marrying her on the day he received his commission. But one drizzling afternoon about four o'clock, high up in the eternal twilight of the parachute loft, the WAVE removed her Navy blue coat and her shoes and placed them to one side and hanged herself. A rumor went around the base that she was pregnant.

After her death Elmer seldom spoke, and nights when he had liberty he did not go out.

On one of these nights he and Melvin were the only two cadets in the barracks. Everybody else had gone to Pensacola or Mobile. Elmer was lying on his bunk with his hands behind his head and Melvin was seated at a desk in the upstairs lounge with a blue band around his sleeve because it was his turn to keep watch. He had nothing to do all night except make an hourly inspection of the empty building. It was a dull job, and while he sat with his feet on the desk he thought about Elmer and wondered if there might be a way to cheer him up. Presently he noticed that he could see the cadet duty officer in the adjoining barracks. For a while this meant nothing; there was simply another cadet in charge of another barracks. Neither of them was doing anything. The other cadet appeared to be asleep. Then a singular thought occurred to

Melvin: he recalled that a cadet duty officer was responsible for the cleanliness of the corridors and the lounge. On nights such as this when everybody had liberty the barracks was a shambles. There were soda-pop bottles on the ping-pong table and on the floor, and there were cigarette butts and newspapers and tooth-picks and countless other artifacts strewn throughout the lounge and the corridors. Now, nobody had ever heard of an inspection taking place while all the cadets were on liberty, but it was not impossible. Melvin, pondering the terrible disorder of his own barracks, came to the conclusion that he could not get it cleaned up in less than two or three hours. Undoubtedly this same condi-tion prevailed in the barracks across the way. He took his feet off the desk and sauntered to the window. He stood there for several minutes, chewing his lip and thinking. Then he walked down the corridor to the room where Elmer lived with Cole, Roska, and McCampbell. Elmer was still lying in the same position on the bunk. His eyes were open, otherwise he looked unconscious.

"Got something to show you, Elmer," he said. Elmer obediently got up and followed him to the lounge while Melvin explained what he had in mind.

"I don't know, boy," Elmer commented. "What about Oh-ho?"

"Monk?" Melvin exclaimed with contempt. "That moron? Do you know what? He came up here about four or five hours ago and told me he was going to Fairhope. *Fairhope!* Can you imagine that? Not Pensy or Mobile for Oh-ho Monk—no, *he* wants to go to Fairhope! Who ever heard of Fairhope? I swear, he hasn't got the brains God gave a celluloid duck. And that name of his! Did you ever hear anything like that in your life? Every time I have to call him 'Mr. Monk' it's all I can do to keep from laughing. He's the stupidest officer in the Navy."

"Oh-ho's mighty sly," said Elmer dubiously.

"He's stupid! Why, when I think of some of the things he's pulled I just don't quite know what to say. Like running around on those cold rainy mornings looking for guys wearing unauthor-ized gear. I mean, how chintzy can you get?"

"Sho, he done give old Roska ten and four on account of wear-ing them two pair of socks."

Melvin grabbed Elmer by the arm. "Now listen. Oh-ho leaves his room unlocked and he's got a telephone in there. I'll call up the next barracks and disguise my voice and say that Commander Holt and Rear Admiral Magness have just come aboard the station and are making an inspection of the barracks. I'll tell him to expect them in fifteen minutes."

"Ain't no admiral would do a thing like that. A commander he might, but you better leave off the admiral."

Melvin gave him a crafty grin and stepped backward. "That's exactly what he'll think at first. But then he'll think again, wondering if it's a trick, and he'll decide that if it was a trick nobody would be stupid enough to say an admiral was coming. And so," Melvin concluded triumphantly, "he'll decide it's for real. It'll scare hell out of him. You watch."

"Maybe so, only you better not use Oh-ho's phone. You better use this one here."

"Who's afraid of Oh-ho?" Melvin cried, flung up his arms, and rushed away. It was a point of honor to use the officer's telephone.

The door to Ensign Monk's room was closed. On the chance that he might have returned Melvin tapped on the door. There was no answer.

"Sir?" he called. "Mr. Monk, sir?"

There was not a sound.

He took a deep breath, opened the door, and switched on the light. There was a disgusting odor of talcum powder in the room. The officer's soiled silken underclothes and black silk socks were lying on the unmade bed. Melvin picked up the telephone and announced an inspection. The cadet in the other barracks was so frightened he did not even bother to ask who was calling. Melvin put down the receiver and dashed back upstairs to the window. He noticed first of all that Elmer was laughing.

"Looky! Looky!" Elmer chortled.

The cadet was running down the corridor clutching his head. At the far end he tripped over something and fell. He was on his feet in an instant. They could see him hopping around, gathering soda-pop bottles. When he had all the bottles he could carry he came running frantically up the corridor and disappeared in a closet. He reappeared with a string mop and a pail and rushed into another room, and Elmer and Melvin leaned against each other and were faint with laughter.

Finally they had laughed so much that they could not laugh

any more, then they stood at the window holding their stomachs and painfully gasping for breath while they watched the cadet in the opposite barracks. He was still running around.

"Oh, me!" Elmer said at last. "You just got to let that poor ignorant cadoodler off the hook. My funnybone, it only stands so much."

"I guess so," Melvin answered, "but I sure hate to. That's probably more work than he's done all year."

Elmer chuckled and wiped his eyes with a handkerchief. "I know, only cadets don't hardly thrive on hard labor. You liable to kill him off like a old toadstool."

They discussed it a while longer as preparations for the admiral's inspection continued at full speed, and finally Melvin sauntered downstairs to Ensign Monk's room. The room was dark. The door was open as he had left it. He went in, picked up the telephone, and called the barracks.

"Look, Dilbert, you can knock it off," he said amiably. "It was a gag. We thought you ought to get on the ball for once." He could hear the victim panting; apparently he was too frightened or stunned to comprehend what had happened, because he did nothing except breathe hoarsely into the mouthpiece.

"Relax," said Melvin. "Don't let the program get you down." With a pleased expression he hung up the receiver. It had been a fine, successful joke. Nobody had been hurt and, at least for a while, it had made Elmer feel better. Then, all at once, his skin began to crawl. He knew someone else was in the room, and directly behind him he heard the little peacock cry.

There stood Ensign Monk with shining eyes.

The next day while marching off the first two hours of his extra duty, a rifle on his shoulder, from one corner of the barracks to the other, to and fro, Melvin watched the sun break through the clouds and saw the field come to life. The red beacon on the squadron tower was replaced by the flashing green and white course lights, mechanics hurried along the flight line untying mooring ropes, and in a short while the harsh cough of the engines resounded across the base and winter sunshine glinted on whirling propellers. As he came to one end of his route, halted, turned about, and prepared to resume marching, he could see the schedule board being trundled away from the wall.

Flight 487 was scheduled to commence high-side gunnery at four o'clock that afternoon. A few minutes before the hour they met the gunnery instructor, a Marine captain named Teitlebaum, who, after shaking hands with everybody, squatted on his heels and began to draw diagrams on the floor of the hangar with sticks of colored chalk while he explained the procedure. After he had completed his explanation he asked for a volunteer to pull the target, which was a twenty-foot nylon sleeve, but nobody volunteered. Captain Teitlebaum waited and the cadets restlessly shuffled their feet. The captain glanced up and happened to look first at Melvin.

"You volunteered, didn't you, cadet?" said the captain.

"Yes, sir, I guess so," Melvin answered reluctantly. "Is this a permanent assignment, sir?"

"It is not. Tomorrow you will be firing. Someone else will tow. This duty is rotational. What's your name?" he asked, standing up.

"Isaacs, sir."

"Pay attention, Mr. Isaacs. Watch yourself when you take off. When you hit the end of the cable you are going to know it. That air speed is going to drop. Do not stall out. If you do, ride the rudders and hold the stick full back because you will not have sufficient altitude to effect a normal recovery. Is that clear?"

"Ride the rudders? All the way down, sir? Won't I be up about forty or fifty feet?"

"You should be higher than that. I suggest you don't stall out."

He then inquired if Melvin knew where to rendezvous with the other members of the flight and Melvin said he did.

"All right then, Mr. Isaacs. On the double. We'll overtake you before you sight the beach."

Melvin saluted and hurried away to get his parachute. The tow plane, like most of the other planes at Barin Field, was an advanced trainer with the Naval designation of SNJ—the hump-backed, pigeon-toed J with the odd, triangular tail that Sam Horne had pointed out that first evening on the main station.

At the downwind end of the runway he swiveled into position for the take-off and pressed the brakes while a seaman wriggled underneath the fuselage to attach the cable. Melvin looked along the runway toward the trees. They were a considerable distance away, but not half so far as he would have liked.

The seaman reappeared, safely to one side, and gave the go-ahead signal.

Melvin turned up the engine enough to check the magnetos; finding the drop within tolerance, he took a deep breath, reflecting that it could be one of his last, stepped on the brakes as hard as possible, and shoved the throttle to the forward end of the slot; immediately he felt the control stick start to pull against him, and the tail seemed to be dancing an anxious jig. The SNJ was shaking and trembling from wing to wing. The brakes could not hold it; the plane was creeping forward.

Teitlebaum had given instructions not to drag the sleeve along the runway because the pavement would tear it apart. The idea was to jerk the sleeve all at once from the ground into the air and the way to do this was to fly the SNJ as high as possible in the shortest possible distance, which meant, of course, climbing at an extremely steep angle and holding this climb until the plane had lost its initial speed and was about to stall. If it stalled it would roll over on its back and crash. The fine point of the maneuver was to ease the airplane into a normal flying position before it was too late, but not very much before it was too late. It might be all very well for Captain Teitlebaum to suggest riding the rudders in the event of a slight miscalculation; it was a bit of advice the captain offered simply because this was a situation in which there ought to be some kind of advice. Nobody was deceived. The captain himself, as they were all aware, was not deceiving anybody.

Melvin let go of the brakes and the SNJ surged forward, gathering speed at a steadily increasing rate. For a few seconds there was nothing to do but wait. Then he knew the time had come; he drew the control stick into his lap and up he went, having left his entrails on the ground, his eyes fixed on the needle which registered the speed, groping delicately through some mysterious sensory apparatus for the very first of those faint vibrations which would be his ultimate warning.

He did not think he had felt anything, but suddenly, without question, he eased the stick forward, the plane began leveling off, and just then he did feel a distinct tug. The J seemed to be straining—the sleeve was off the ground—but it did not stall, though it was close; it continued to fly, and gradually accelerated.

112

He banked across the trees at the edge of the field and glanced over his shoulder: there was the sleeve, sluggishly roiling and twisting like a prodigious fish bent on swallowing the plane, the perfectly circular cloth mouth wide open.

He climbed to an altitude of about half a mile and set off for the rendezvous.

The clouds had dispersed, and below him the fields drifted by, green and lavender and brown and violet, occasionally a pond or a stream, giving an impression of immense fertility, and far ahead the Gulf of Mexico, shining in the sun. To the west a mile or so was another sleeve, level with him and on a parallel course. Some distance above it, farther away, motionless against the deep blue space, was another. Higher in the sky he could make out the gunnery formations, each hovering like a cluster of bees over a sleeve. And all this—the blueness of the sky around him, the globe of the earth, and the depth of the glittering sea—filled him with satisfaction. He began to think of the Deacon, who had been killed so accidentally, almost extemporaneously, as though some-one had decided only that morning to do away with him, and who therefore was not present to witness these things, to partici-pate in the afternoon, unless at death one did become present everywhere. He realized he did not know where the Deacon was buried, and all at once this seemed quite strange. And he reflected, too, that no one spoke of him any more, though only a year had elapsed. It had been last winter. He was gone, totally gone.

He became conscious of another SNJ flying alongside; he saw that the pilot was Captain Teitlebaum, who was holding a micro-phone in one hand. "That was a good quick rendezvous, Isaacs. Your heading will be one-eight-zero. Maintain constant air speed and altitude. Keep your eye on the chronometer. At exactly seventeen hundred you will reverse course and proceed to this check point. At this point you will alter course to the base and re-lease your sleeve in the alley. Have you any questions?"

Melvin shook his head.

Teitlebaum's SNJ abruptly stood on one wing—the underside vertically flattened against the sky, the small black wheels like buttons on a silver vest—and dropped out of sight.

Melvin banked a few degrees to be on course, trimmed the tow plane until it maintained heading and altitude of its own accord.

then lowered himself in the cockpit and loosened the safety belt because he had nothing at all to do for the next half hour. He felt around in the knee pocket of his coveralls. There was a stick of gum. He peeled off the wrapper and slipped the gum into his mouth. It had a sugary, fruity taste after the burnt coffee they served in the hangar and he sucked the juices greedily, blinking with pleasure. The cockpit had begun to grow uncomfortably warm from the rays of the sun on the glass, so he reached up and slid the canopy backward. In rushed a cool, sweet wind, the first of spring after the drizzling, gloomy winter. He yawned and stretched, almost overwhelmed by a feeling of luxury, and unzipped the top of his coveralls. He could hear Teitlebaum on the radio, some distance away because his voice was faint. He was giving instructions.

". . . full deflection. Sixty mils lead, not one hundred. Bear in mind that you people are after the target, not the man in the tow."

Melvin tugged the brim of his baseball cap over his eyes and squinted toward the sun, knowing they were up there somewhere, and thought he could make them out a short distance from the center of the glare. They should have been invisible, since he was the victim and was supposed to be shot down without even the knowledge of the enemy's presence. But he could just see them; they were a little out of position. Still, it was not bad, considering this was the first run, and then, too, the actual target was the sleeve and from there the echelon might be altogether invisible. It suddenly occurred to him that this would not be a theoretical exercise—above him were five SNJ's with loaded machine guns. He cranked himself higher in the seat and tightened the safety belt. He had no doubt his friends would attempt to hit the sleeve, but that, after all, was irrelevant. He remembered that Elmer seldom paid attention during gunnery lessons in the Quonset hut, and Roska usually shot too far ahead of the target. Then he saw the first plane bending down. It bore toward him with terrific speed, angling across the sun so that he was blinded. He stopped chewing gum; he waited tensely for the noise of the machine gun clattering, and glanced out at the wing, half-expecting to find a series of punctures busily stitching their way toward him, but nothing happened. He discovered the plane rising ahead of him; it had passed beneath him and was now climbing toward the echelon. The attack was already over.

He twisted around in the cockpit and gazed earnestly at the sleeve, wondering if it had been shot full of holes. The sleeve, which reminded him of a shroud, was yawing a little in the wind, the orifice gaping, the implication so sinister and somehow horrible that he felt sick at his stomach.

The second plane—for one instant he saw it—floated into the rainbow flame of the sun; he waited, listening, although he knew he would not hear anything, and a few seconds later it reappeared a hundred yards or so in front of him like the first one, returning to position. Just then he felt a tug and his plane lurched and darted ahead; instantly he rolled into a vertical bank and saw an SNJ spinning wildly toward the water with the sleeve folded across it. The canopy had been opened. The pilot was half out of the cockpit. Then the water exploded. The SNJ seemed to hesitate; near the center was an orange dot, vivid and motionless. Waves were rushing up the wings and over the fuselage and silently crashing into a raging, frothing tower from which one silver wing emerged diagonally; the wing gleamed in the light, slipped aside like the prow of a ship, and was gone. He thought he saw the plane beneath the surface, a shadowy cross, but he could not be sure; if for a few seconds it had been there it sank into the depths while he was watching, and he heard the captain on the radio give orders to return to the base and he obeyed.

Moments later, looking over his shoulder, he saw Captain Teitlebaum spiral down to the area where the SNJ had gone under. The captain would probably circle there until an amphibian arrived. And the men in the amphibian would circle for a while, an hour or so, scanning the area with binoculars, and perhaps land on the water if any wreckage came floating to the surface. But it was over. Nobody would pretend the pilot might be alive, or even that his body would be found. Here the Gulf was deep. The water was unscarred, there were no screaming birds; already the waves rolled powerfully, as they had before. On the floor of the Gulf the subterranean currents were flowing, bearing the wreckage toward some cavern or over some precipice where the coral grew.

All the way to the base Melvin stared at the column of planes, counting them again and again.

At the entrance to the traffic pattern he closed in on them, but suddenly drew back the throttle and lagged behind so that he could not recognize anyone. However, as they flew between the pylons and the leader tilted out of formation and dove toward the field he knew the pilot was Nick McCampbell—the J dropped so steeply and securely, curling toward the target as infallibly as a stooping hawk—and the second J was ready: the wings waddled left, right and down to the left it rolled. The pilot was wearing a red cap. Horne and Roska both wore red caps, but that had been Roska. Before the third plane dropped away Melvin shut his eyes and began counting aloud.

When he opened his eyes there was no one ahead, the pylons were directly below; he signaled his turn for anyone who might be following and dove into the pattern.

After he had landed and found a slot on the parking line he cut the switches and pushed aside the shoulder harness, but remained in the cockpit for a long time, leaning forward with his hands folded over the top of the control stick and his head resting on them.

When at last he entered the hangar he saw that somebody had marked the gunnery run complete, as though nothing had happened. He took off his coveralls, his cap, and his gloves, rolled them up as he always did, and placed them in the locker, and was about to close the locker when it occurred to him that all he had to do was examine the other bundles of clothing in order to learn who was missing. He hesitated, unrolled another pair of coveralls, and looked at the name inked inside the collar. They belonged to Roska.

Three bundles remained. He knew that one of them belonged to McCampbell; then he noticed in the bottom of the locker the casual, non-regulation shoes that belonged to Pat Cole. Cole always wore them when he was flying. Melvin slammed the locker and hurried away from the hangar in the direction of the barracks, but when he got there he could not force himself to go inside. He walked back and forth at the entrance and finally sat down on the steps.

When he entered the barracks it seemed to him strangely quiet.

The corridors were deserted. Usually there was somebody around, studying the announcements on the bulletin board or standing at attention in front of Ensign Monk's room or gazing out the windows.

He went up the steps to the lounge. One cadet whose name he did not know was lying on the leather sofa, smoking and reading a magazine.

Melvin walked through the lounge and up to the third floor and started along the corridor toward the room where he had lived with Sam Horne. He walked more and more slowly, and when he could see that the door was open he stopped. He could not hear any voices. Once again he was struck by the silence in the barracks.

Presently he sensed that there was no one in his room. He continued walking toward it, more rapidly, and by the time he got there he was positive. He looked in. The room was empty. He went in, lay down on his bunk, and put his head underneath the pillow, but almost immediately got up and went over to the wash basin to see himself in the mirror. He was surprised that he did not look any different than usual. There was no sign of shock or grief on his face. He put on his garrison cap and walked down the rear steps to the second floor, to the room where the others lived. The door was closed. He stood in front of it, with his arms folded, listening. He could hear bureau drawers being opened and shut; the closet door squeaked, footsteps pattered across the linoleum.

Melvin suddenly pushed open the door and saw Ensign Monk on his knees busily stuffing clothes into a duffle bag. The officer leaped nimbly to his feet, his pink face moist and swollen with emotion, clapping his hands and crying, "Out! *Out!*"

Melvin quickly shut the door, but he had seen that the linen had been stripped from Elmer's bunk and the mattress folded back.

10

★

Flight 487 was scheduled for the second lesson in gunnery at eight o'clock the next morning. Melvin had assumed they would be given a day or so of rest after what had happened, but Sam Horne nodded with approval when he saw the schedule. He said, "That's a good policy. They get us in the air again before we have time to think. That's the only way."

They met Captain Teitlebaum in a corner of the hangar where the colored chalk diagrams of the previous day were still visible on the floor; Melvin stared at the diagrams during most of the captain's lecture. Teitlebaum was very short and habitually stood with his thumbs hooked in the drawstrings of his life jacket. He always wore shoes with blocky crepe soles and every once in a while he would rise up on his toes and expand his chest. There would be, he remarked, a slight change in the procedure: they would rendezvous at the beach as usual, but would then fly out to sea in two two-plane sections instead of in echelon. The sections were more maneuverable and could save time. Roska was assigned to pull the target.

Horne and Melvin walked along the flight line together, and as they were nearing their planes Horne said, "Listen, don't get yourself on top of that sleeve. When you're diving, if you got a slow start, or if you aren't steep enough, it'll drift under you." He looked at Melvin, stopped walking, and dropped his parachute. "Will you listen to me?"

"All right, I'm listening," Melvin said.

"Stop thinking about yesterday. This is today."

"Nobody said it wasn't."

"All right!" Horne said gruffly. "I'm trying to be of some help. I'm trying to give you the word on what I found out. This is it:

about the time you're in firing range you may find out you're not ahead of the sleeve any more." He paused, demonstrated with his hands, sliding one hand gradually into the trajectory of the other. "You follow me? It slides under you if you don't dive steep enough. And then you try to correct, but you can't correct fast enough, and then—well, I don't know how to explain it. It's just one of those things you got to discover for yourself. But be sure you know what you're doing. You follow me?"

"Yes, all right," Melvin agreed, and went on, "I was just thinking that the only reference Teitlebaum made to Elmer was that today, with only four planes on the attack, we'd have more time to practice."

Horne looked at him in disbelief and all at once grabbed him by the coveralls and began shaking him; Melvin gasped and struggled to break away.

"Wake up, will you!" Horne shouted. His face was livid and his little blue eyes burned wickedly. With a gesture of contempt or of exasperation he let go, and said in a quarrelsome voice as he picked up his parachute, "Why don't you ever wash those stinking coveralls?"

Melvin was trembling with excitement and answered curtly, "They're no worse than yours!"

"They smell up the whole locker! They stink like a haystack full of mice!" Horne exclaimed. "Now come on, we're late enough as it is! God damn, wake up, will you?"

"I can look out for myself."

"You can? Is that a fact?" said Horne. "Well, that's news to me."

Neither of them said anything else until they reached the plane which had been assigned to Melvin; there Sam Horne muttered something—it could have been either an apology or a warning—and continued along the line.

Melvin said, "I'll follow you to the beach," conscious that Horne was already too far away to hear. He buckled on his parachute and got into the cockpit. A mechanic hopped up on the wing, inserted a crank in the cowl, and leaned heavily against it: a dull, protesting whine began to emerge from the interior of the engine and rose to a shrill scream as the crank revolved more and more rapidly. Melvin turned a switch: the propeller kicked, flung itself over, swung back, and vanished in a shining arc while smoke poured from the exhaust and the fuselage rattled from the vibrations. The mechanic, his faded blue dungarees whipping in the wind, skidded down the wing and jumped off. Melvin tuned in on the squadron tower, checked his instruments, and gazed around the station. It was only a few minutes after eight o'clock, but already the sun was hot. There was a strong sea breeze.

In a little while Horne came taxiing by, the brilliant orange rudder of the J swaying like the tail of a goldfish as he leaned rhythmically from side to side in order to see what was ahead. Melvin released the brakes and trundled forward, swung into the aisle, and followed him between the rows of parked planes into the cool rectangular shadow of the tower and into the sunlight again, where they joined the others weaving methodically toward the downwind end of the field.

Horne and Melvin took off side by side. The wingtips of the two SNJ's were only a few feet apart. It was against regulations to take off so close together, but they knew nobody would do anything about it unless they had an accident. If they drifted against each other and crashed, and survived, there would be a board of review and the probability they would be dropped from flight training; all the same they had gotten into the habit of leaving the field side by side. They did not know why, except that it was a tradition at Barin Field to take off and to land as close together as possible and they had come to feel a certain pride in doing so, just as they took pride in being able to say, when anyone asked where they were stationed, that they were at Bloody Barin.

They pulled up the wheels the instant they were off the ground and banked to the left, Melvin easing the throttle forward because he was on the outside of the turn and had farther to go, and in a few seconds they were curving over the pines on their way to the rendezvous, a puddle of soft aluminum sunlight slipping along the wings whenever they turned and reflecting from the glass canopies with a blinding flash.

Ten minutes later they hurtled across the beach. Behind them and several hundred feet above, hanging motionless in the sky, were Cole and McCampbell.

Down the beach the four planes roared, crabbed against the

off-shore breeze, passed above the tow plane where Roska hunched in the cockpit with his cap tilted over one eye, and arched out to sea—streaming over launches and sailboats, a few swimmers near the sandbars, slanting and twisting up and higher up. Far beneath them the gulls were diving after fish, and white flowers burst, smaller than daisies, when the birds struck the water.

Soon the SNJ's were out where the Gulf was dark, no longer mottled like turquoise with the shadows of caves and ledges below the surface, and Melvin, taking a moment to glance around, discovered Captain Teitlebaum flying close beside him. He had that disconcerting habit of materializing like some murderous little genie, a plump yellow cigar clenched in his teeth and a restless, malevolent glare in his merciless, violet eyes. Melvin stared at him and had no sensation of exchange; it was as though his look had been met by the insanely lucid and vigilant glare of some predatory animal. Nevertheless, whether man, wolf, or the emanation of a magic lamp, he was an officer and Melvin began to feel uneasy. So far as he knew he had not done anything wrong, but he had learned from experience that this was no excuse. Feeling somewhat harassed, he went on with his work, which, for the moment, was simply maintaining the position. Teitlebaum watched, said nothing, and in a little while sank out of sight and reappeared on Horne's wing. Melvin glanced across and was pleased to see the captain scrutinize Horne with that same implacable mistrust. Still without a word or a signal he whirled away.

Melvin next located him a quarter of a mile below them on the opposite side of the tow plane, from which position he evidently intended to observe the gunnery runs.

Horne had been leveling off and frequently turning around to his left to peer down at the target sleeve, and Melvin, flying on his right, moved in closer, for he supposed that Teitlebaum had been studying them to see if they were frightened by what had occurred the previous day and a tight formation should prove to him they were not afraid. Besides, the air was stable, there seemed to be no currents; and so he flew a trifle closer. He could not tell precisely how far the hub of his propeller was from the trailing edge of Horne's wing, but he guessed it might be eight or ten inches. He was tempted to ease in closer and was considering whether or not this would be safe, when Horne looked around to the right for the first time and his eyes bulged. Melvin saw him reach cautiously for the microphone and heard him say, not exactly with anger, but as though he were warning a dog that was about to spring at him: "Damn you, get away from me!"

Horne did not take his eyes off the shimmering propeller until the distance between the planes increased to about three feet. Then his expression changed; he blinked and swallowed. The color returned to his face.

"Go on!" he snarled. "Get out of there!"

Melvin eased back on the throttle and coasted a little farther away.

"Okay, hold it," Horne said. He looked beyond Melvin at Cole and McCampbell. "Now listen, you people, I'm leading this flight today, so will you please goddamit do me the favor of waiting for my signals? If I want you stacked up on my tail I'll give the word. Christ almighty! All right. Now. Here we go. Forget about yesterday. Make these dives clean and get back up here pronto." He was about to hang up the microphone, but looked again toward Melvin. "Don't push over too fast or the engine'll cut out on you."

"I know it," Melvin answered without bothering to use the microphone. They were still so near each other that Horne had no trouble reading his lips.

For a few more seconds they flew straight ahead. Then Horne dipped a wing to the left, dipped to the right, and curled down on the approaching target. Melvin flew on, counting aloud, and when he got to ten he dipped to the left, to the right, and pressed the SNJ out of formation.

Below and to the left he could see Horne firing at the sleeve, which was rapidly growing larger. Horne dove by the sleeve and out of sight.

Melvin hooked a finger around the machine-gun trigger and waited, guiding the sleeve toward the center of the ringsight. He noticed that the tow plane and the sleeve were drifting toward the bottom of the ring, so he steepened the dive. The sleeve was still drifting. He pushed the controls until he was diving almost vertically; but the nylon sleeve—much longer now, and much thicker—was being drawn under him, and then he understood that he was doing what Elmer had done. This was what Horne had been trying to explain. The sleeve was too big; he was past the point where he should have fired, past the point where he should have quit firing and gotten out of the way. It was much too big, still growing, filling the ringsight and extending beyond it. He could no longer see the ends of the sleeve. He got the control stick in both hands and forced it to one side. The wings wrinkled and something creaked as the airplane rolled; he saw the sleeve whip upward like a handkerchief flipped in his face.

As he climbed back into position the only thing he could think about was the terrible grade Teitlebaum must have given him. Teitlebaum could not help seeing how he had almost wrapped himself in the sleeve and undoubtedly would make a note of it. He expected to hear the captain on the radio, but there was not a sound.

The second attack was better, although the noise of the machine gun startled him. During the first run he had been so busy centering the target that he had not had time to shoot. Now, after firing one bullet, he stopped, afraid he had broken the gun. But when he touched the trigger again, to find out what would happen more than in hopes of hitting the target, there was another explosion just like the first. He concluded that must be the way a machine gun was supposed to sound. He drew the sleeve toward the center of the ring, fired several quick bursts as it grew larger, and was reluctant to roll aside when the time came.

The formation made two more attacks before the tow plane reversed course and headed for shore. Horne wasted no time establishing the new position, and as soon as the other planes were neatly behind him he dipped his wings and dropped away. Melvin followed almost immediately, with Cole flying third and McCampbell fourth. It was the best run of the day. They all knew it.

Teitlebaum was observing them from the opposite side of the target. The canopy of his SNJ was shoved back and the bill of his canvas cap was turned up, which suggested that he was in a good humor. He appeared to be grading each run on a tablet strapped to his knee, but in addition to watching them it was obvious that he was basking in the early spring sunshine. He was clearly visible a short distance outside the ringsight, unusually close to the target.

During the fourth run of the landward series the captain abruptly pulled up about five hundred yards and flashed over the cadet formation. Melvin, who had just finished shooting and was rejoining the echelon, watched in stupefaction as Captain Teitlebaum looped, flipped over on his back, dove, and emerged in a chandelle. The captain then rammed the propeller of his airplane into low pitch and spiraled vertically above the formation while they all gazed up at him in great wonder and alarm. Melvin thought the officer had gone out of his mind. Presently he materialized just a few yards to the side, opened the hatch, removed the cigar from his teeth, and, apparently berserk, flung it at Melvin, after which he snatched the microphone and gave orders for the formation to return to the base without delay, and having said this dropped out of sight.

They saw no more of him till they landed.

Captain Teitlebaum, without a word, inspected every gun belt to see what color the bullets were tipped. Melvin's belt was red-tipped, Cole's was blue, Horne's was orange, McCampbell's was green. The captain folded his sun glasses, slipped them into the breast pocket of his coveralls, and beckoned to Melvin. They walked out to the captain's plane. There were two bullet holes in the right wing not far from the cockpit. Around each hole was a trace of red paint.

That night Melvin said he did not feel like eating dinner; he had retreated to his bunk, where he went whenever he had been hurt or was confused, and there he lay absolutely motionless with the pillow concealing his face.

"You want me to bring you something?" Horne inquired. He was worried and so he pretended to be cheerful. "A pear? How about a nice pear?"

"I don't want a pear!" said Melvin.

"All right, if you're going to be that way, suit yourself. It certainly doesn't make the least bit of difference to me." He was peeved by this response to his attempt to be helpful. He snapped out the light and marched off to eat his supper. When he returned Melvin was still supine on the bunk, but willing to talk about the incident.

"I'm all through," Melvin said. "There's no hope."

"Teitlebaum say so?"

Melvin rose up on one elbow with a sardonic expression. "I hardly think it was necessary."

"So your aim was poor, so what? It could happen to anybody. I about beheaded Roska on that last run. Listen, if Teitlebaum was going to wash you out he'd have told you by now."

"No, I'll never make it," Melvin said. He turned over on his stomach.

"How about some pool?"

He shook his head.

"Table's empty. I'll give you a chance to win back that five dollars you lost last week."

"I'd only lose some more."

"Who is this I'm talking to?" Horne asked, gazing down at him. "I guess you are in a bad way. How about going to the lecture?"

"No!" Melvin shouted, pounding his fist into the pillow. But then, after a pause, he asked doubtfully, "What lecture?"

"That commander. That hot dog that scattered the Jap squadron over Tulagi."

"He did what?"

Horne became impatient. "How the hell should I know? He got the Congressional Medal, that's all I know. There's an announcement on the bulletin board telling what he did. It's been there for a month. Don't you ever read what's on the bulletin board?"

"What's he doing here?"

"Giving a talk, stupid, that's what he's doing. The Navy's got him touring these roach traps giving talks to get the cadoodlers all fired up. They want us to go out and do the same thing."

"Why should they want us to go out and give talks?"

"Oh, for Christ's sake," Horne muttered, clutching his head. "They don't want us to give talks; they want us to go out and shoot up whole squadrons of Japanese."

"I'm not a very good shot."

"Come on," said Horne, grabbing the pillow. "Come on, it'll do you good. Listen to a nice lecture."

"I hate lectures," Melvin said, but he got up and straightened his necktie and put on his garrison cap and the two of them walked over to the auditorium.

The commander was a good speaker and storyteller, but Melvin could not stay awake; he dozed off and woke from time to time with a horrified gasping noise that caused people to look around. As soon as the lecture ended he went outside and sat weakly on the steps while Horne remained in the auditorium to ask questions.

After a while Horne came out and sat down beside him.

"For a hero the commander's not so bad. He's a pretty nice Joe, in fact. Before the war he was a dentist in Wyoming. What a brawl that must have been over Tulagi! He knocked off five Jap bombers and two fighters." Horne stood up, looked around with an agreeable expression, and stretched. "Frankly, I'm glad the man plays ball on our squad." He took a deep breath and the khaki shirt nearly split. He looked down at Melvin and nudged him with his shoe. "So what's your problem, cadet?"

"I don't know. I think I'm sick."

"Everybody's sick. That's no excuse. How long have you been in this outfit?" said Horne, becoming frivolous. He clapped his hands and smacked his lips. "Yes, sir!" he exclaimed. "We got it made! This miserable program's a cinch. No strain! When I think back—no fooling, when I think back to what all we had to put up with! These crummy seamen giving us orders, honest to God! I'm telling you, though, it's practically over. Riding from one base to another in those moving-van buses with benches on each side and no windows like we were nothing but pigs—I'm telling you! Well, we're going to be out before much longer, we're going to be officers and officially gentlemen and by God in my opinion it's certainly about time!" He fell silent. He stood with his hands on his hips, scowling. "Well, I don't know," he said a few minutes later. "Anyway, though, we got it made."

Melvin pulled a thread from his trousers and said gloomily, "Maybe you have."

Horne looked down at him again. "Are you really sick?"

"I suppose there's nothing wrong with me," Melvin answered in a low voice. "I don't believe I'm physically sick, you know. It's just that—oh, nothing."

"You still in a sweat about Elmer?"

"Oh, I don't know. It's just that I got to thinking about this commander. He killed ten or fifteen people he never saw before in his life and received a medal. It's a little strange."

"*Ah!* So that's it. You're just now getting to that stage. Listen, stupid, if the commander hadn't broken up that formation there'd of been a pot full of Japs who got medals, that's for sure. What do you think they were headed for? A tea party? Remember, sweetheart, they were loaded for us!" Horne tightened his belt and grunted. "Come on, now. How about a game of billiards? You could get your five dollars back if you tried hard."

"No. I don't feel like it."

"Suit yourself. I'm not begging."

"Cole came by a few minutes ago and was looking for somebody to play."

"I don't play with that son of a bitch. You know what he did on that navigation hop the week before last? You know he was leading it and afterwards we all talked about how good it was, how we hit the check points right on the button? Well, I found out why. Somehow he got hold of the chase pilot's map and copied down the headings before we even took off. No wonder it was a sharp flight, and the bastard got a good grade for it. Always an angle. I don't think in all his life that guy has ever once played it straight. Like when we had combat last month, I was supposed to dogfight with Cole. So what happened? We went up to five thousand, scissored a couple of times, and then he quit. I got on his tail with no strain. He wasn't even trying. So afterwards I asked him why he didn't fight. You know what he said? He says with the dirty, superior smirk of his, 'I should risk *my* life?' Now I ask you, how do you figure a person like that? Cole's yellow. He's got no guts!" Horne spat through his teeth.

"I don't think I have either," Melvin said. He got up, walked a few steps and paused, and then continued walking.

Presently he realized that he was alone; he stopped with a feeling of confusion and looked around. Horne was nowhere in sight. He discovered, then, to his amazement that he was near the flight line. The hangar lights were on and course lights flashed from the top of the squadron tower. Out on the field the flare pots were blazing in the darkness. He stood with his thumbs hooked in his belt, thinking deeply.

When he looked up again he saw that he had reached the far

end of the line and was in the midst of the parked airplanes. He decided to sit in one of the planes. He listened for the security patrol, but could not hear anyone nearby so he climbed on a wing, slid open the greenhouse as quietly as possible, got into the cockpit, and pulled the glass over his head. He felt slightly nauseated, and his head was detached; it had been a grotesque, unnatural sort of day. And yesterday was so immediate, but at the same time so unreal. Death had come and gone as normally as a letter was delivered, Elmer was at the bottom of the sea, whatever was left of him, yet only the night before last in the barracks Elmer had been playing cards.

He became aware that the first night flight was going up. Mechanics with glowing, cherry-red batons were leading the pilots out of the line, waving them toward the runway. Awkwardly the planes trundled through the night while the colored navigation lights blinked alternately; and soon they were rising, one cluster after another, and drawing together in the distance. They returned and descended, more and more slowly, and had almost reached the ground when there was a screech. The lights bobbled stiffly, as though they had been frightened, and sped away through the narrow lane of oil pots flickering in the night wind from the Gulf while the roar of the engine diminished.

Melvin watched them land and take off for a few minutes, but then lost interest. He stared at the constellations, and after a while fell to thinking of a night when he had mistaken Mars for the tail light of the plane ahead of him and had obediently followed it, puzzled that it led him so far from the field but assuming, because he had grown accustomed to following whatever or whoever preceded him, that there must be some valid reason for the excursion. He remembered how he had followed it farther and farther without question or hesitation across the trees and over the beach and many miles out to sea before recognizing it for what it was. He had been shaken by what he had done, by the fantastic implications, and the next day had been astounded to learn he had not been alone. Behind him, one after another, came the others; and he had wondered then, as he wondered now, if they would have followed him on and on until they slipped into the sea like lemmings, betrayed by their faith, one and all.

Melvin opened his eyes, startled by the realization that he had drifted off to sleep and had dreamed he was in the mess hall where somebody at that very instant dropped a stack of aluminum trays; he sat straight up in the cockpit and was conscious that a huge, bulky object was falling from the sky. It crashed and exploded. A column of liquid fire spurted up into the night, burst and showered, silhouetting the squadron tower and illuminating the airplanes overhead. Another flame shot out diagonally with a dull boom that reverberated across the station, and he heard the rush of the wind. He stared at the blazing wreckage. Something else dropped out of the sky, bounced up and down like a joyous living thing, and then all at once, as though it perceived him there, came rolling swiftly forward. With unbelievable speed it rolled toward him and as it rolled by he recognized it as an airplane tire.

He found himself running in the direction of the barracks and knew from the searing pain in his lungs that he could not run much farther. His face was scratched and there was a bump on his head; he had no idea what had caused the scratches, though he had a vague recollection of springing to his feet while he was in the cockpit, and if the canopy was closed at that time, and he supposed it was, he would have hit himself. It was unimportant. He tried to stop running, but could only slow down to an animal-like lope that carried him rapidly through the shadows, gasping and choking and trying to cry out to someone. When he came within sight of the barracks he stopped and then staggered forward, holding out his arms to the cadets who were crowding the fire escape. He recognized Cole and Roska on the top step. They were carrying billiard sticks. They and all the others were gazing at the wreck, which lay near the center of the concrete mat surrounded by crash trucks. The fire had almost been extinguished; here and there a flame appeared for a few seconds as though a fissure had opened in the earth. A vast cloud of smoke had risen and obscured the stars.

The next day, which was Saturday, they learned that two cadets had been killed. It had been a mid-air collision. The first one burned to death in the explosion on the mat. The other one was not found until daylight; he had fallen outside the fence that enclosed the field. When his body was examined the doctor said— so it was rumored through the barracks—that he had lived for an hour or so and might have been conscious during that time. It was possible he had been listening to the men who were searching for him.

Melvin lay in his bunk all day, mute and terrified, with his hands clasped underneath his head. He stared at the ceiling and once in a while shut his eyes, but he was unable to sleep. He had not slept all night. Sam Horne was not disturbed by the accident, nor was he surprised; he had been saying ever since they arrived at Barin Field that the traffic pattern was too crowded.

"You'd think these moron officers would do something about it," he said as he sat at the desk and tried to sew a button on his trousers.

A few minutes later he continued. "It seems like every couple of weeks some guy gets clobbered. I'm glad we're almost finished. Those poor slobs that are just starting, I feel sorry for them. And those two last night, those poor guys! Well, it's their own fault, though." He threw down the needle in exasperation, and after glaring at it he sucked his thumb, which was bleeding slightly, picked up the needle, and resumed sewing.

"Night flying is pretty hairy. It is, for a fact. When that old ice fog drifts in and that manifold pressure starts to drop I say to myself, 'Sammy, you've had it tonight!' No, sir, I don't care for it. I'm glad it's over. Ah—but those two last night, they must have had their heads inside the cockpit. They're taught better than that. Even if the field is crowded there's no excuse for a mid-air. It was their own fault."

Holding the trousers at arm's length, he pursed his lips and considered the button. It was not quite in the right place, and it dangled, but he decided it was acceptable; he pushed the needle into the underside of the desk, where it was always kept, and swiveled around in the chair.

"Don't tell me you're still feeling bad!"

"Sort of."

"Go to sick bay, stupid."

Melvin shook his head. "They'd put me in the sack for a week and I'd miss some flights. It's just a touch of cat fever, I guess."

"I don't know what you're so worried about being in the sack a week for. You spend half your time in the sack anyway." He took his feet off the desk and walked briskly across the room to gaze down at Melvin. "You do look peaked, as a matter of fact. By God, you do!" Then, with no great concern, he added, "You look awful."

This irritated Melvin, who promptly got to his feet, glared straight ahead for a little while, and then slumped to the floor.

Horne picked him up by an arm and a leg and dropped him on the bunk. "I don't know, baby. I think you ought to log in at sick bay. You're sweating like a stuck pig."

"I feel fine," Melvin whispered. His eyes were glazed so that he could not see, sweat was rolling off his face, and his nose had started to bleed.

"Are you sure? Do you really feel all right?" Horne inquired. "You don't look very good."

Melvin rested a few minutes, licking his lips with a thickened tongue and shuddering as the chills swept through him, but finally managed to get up by clinging to the back of a chair. His skin was waxen yellow. His teeth chattered. He retched and dropped to his knees but indignantly waved Horne away and dragged himself up once more. He stood there swaying, trying to balance himself before the next attack of fever.

"Let's go to Mobile," he whispered.

Horne thought about it. "Well, I don't know. I guess we could scare up a couple of crows all right. If you're sure you feel okay."

Melvin insisted he had never felt better in his life. He was not able to walk alone, so Horne helped him to the shower and leaned him against the wall and turned on the hot water.

After about half an hour Melvin came lurching through the clouds of steam, feeling his way, as pink as a lobster, and claimed he was ready, so they put on their blue uniforms and went to Mobile.

11

★

It was raining in Mobile. Gusts of wind-whipped rain and interminable crashing rolls of thunder had followed the bus all the way from Barin Field; now the clouds were silent and the rain fell steadily. Once in a while the town echoed as though there had been an explosion far out in the bay; otherwise the only sounds were the occasional honking of automobile horns and the sucking hiss of tires on the pavement. Horne and Melvin stood just inside the entrance to a drugstore on Bienville Square and moodily considered the street. They had gone to the drugstore as soon as they got off the bus because it was where they always went first of all; it was where the town girls were apt to be, but tonight most of the booths and the soda-fountain stools were unoccupied.

"I guess we got here too late," Melvin said. He sneezed, rubbed his nose on the back of his hand, and resumed staring out the window.

"Yuh. We should've stayed at the field," Horne agreed. "Look at this rain."

A few minutes later Melvin said, "Maybe there'd be some stuff at the Rose Room."

"I doubt it," Horne answered finally. "Not tonight."

"Maybe you're right."

Horne took off his hat to scratch his head. "I got a couple numbers from Ostrowski. What do you think?"

"We're not doing any good here," Melvin said. "Might as well."

Horne cinched in his belt and strode across to the telephone. Melvin continued staring into the rain. The beneficial effects of the hot shower were beginning to wear away and he did not feel so well.

132

Horne came back from the telephone. "No answer."

"Neither one?"

Horne shook his head. "Stupid pigs. Jesus, they must go out all the time."

Melvin wandered to the tobacco counter and bought a package of cigarettes. Then he stopped a while at the magazine rack. When he returned to the window, Horne was peering intently at a woman in riding breeches and a red jacket who was standing under a store awning across the street.

"What's she doing?" Melvin asked. "Is she drunk?"

"She's trying to flag a cab. None of them will stop."

"I wonder why not. That's funny. She must be drunk. Let's go talk to her. Come on!"

"Oh, relax," Horne said. "Wait'll the rain lets up."

They stood side by side and thoughtfully studied the woman across the street. In a little while a taxicab stopped. She got in and the taxi drove away.

"We should have stayed at the base," said Horne bitterly.

"You know what I've been thinking?" Melvin said a few minutes later. "I told you about Monk wearing silk underwear, didn't I?"

"Yuh. It didn't surprise me."

"Well, I was thinking. He's probably got a whole drawer full of it."

Horne was not paying attention; he seemed bored.

"You know what?"

"What?" said Horne skeptically, and yawned.

"Well, what we could do is, because he always leaves his door unlocked, we could collect a few of those red ants that bite like hell and we could sprinkle them in the drawer. He wouldn't notice them if we only put in a few. But he'd notice them after a while, maybe on the parade ground, or some place like that!"

"You go ahead," Horne said without enthusiasm. "I'd rather get my wings."

The rain came steadily down.

"Oh, for the love of God!" said Horne with a heavy sigh. "What a night!"

About half an hour later they saw Roska hurrying along the street with his collar turned up and a package under one arm.

They buttoned their coats, flung open the door, and ran across the street, calling to him.

Roska was going to a party in a hotel. Melvin and Horne went along and found a suite of rooms crowded with cadets from Barin and Bronson fields, together with some Annapolis cadets who were on a Caribbean cruise and whose ship had put in at the Mobile yard for repairs, two Army pilots, some Mobile girls and several WAC's. McCampbell was sitting on a radiator beside an open window with the rain sprinkling his wrinkled face and the lace curtains floating eerily over his shoulder. There was a drink in his hand, but he had not touched it. Nobody was speaking to him; he stared into the night as though he were alone in the room.

"Aviation Cadet Isaacs reports for duty," someone said, and Melvin turned around. Cole was leaning drunkenly against the wall. His face was smeared with lipstick and his shirt was unbuttoned. "Pay your respects to the commanding officer," he said with a sardonic grin, and held up a bottle.

By eleven o'clock Melvin could no longer tell whether or not he had a fever, nor did he care. With his back to a mohair sofa he rested on the floor and impartially contemplated the carpet, stroking it with his fingertips, oblivious to the party which rocked along some distance overhead. He felt as though he were resting on the floor of the sea.

Horne sat cross-legged on the sofa, taking one cigarette after another and carefully mashing them between his calloused palms until the paper shredded and tobacco showered on the carpet. From time to time without a word he meticulously swept the tobacco out of sight.

He reached down, grasped one of Melvin's feet, and twisted it, forcing him to roll around on the carpet. "Scared are you?" Horne demanded, twisting vigorously. "So! You think *you're* scared? I could tell you a thing or two if I wanted. For instance, do you know who was right in back of him all the way to the Gulf? That was me, baby, *me!* I chased him down to the water, because I thought if I could dive underneath him I could bring him back up. Isn't that hilarious?" He twisted Melvin's foot again. "Laugh, why don't you! I had in mind to power-dive right under that J while it was spinning, and pick him up and carry him home like a kid on his father's back, and if I could have caught up with him I'd have done it, because that's what I was going to do. You know what would have happened, don't you? Don't you? We'd both be under the waves now, getting our bones picked by the fish. When you say *you're* scared, all I can do is laugh! Yes, sir," he went on a few moments later, gazing into space, firmly holding Melvin by the foot, "all of us are. What would we be doing here drunk as boiled owls if we weren't? Roska, for example, has got himself petrified. He's smart, old Roska is. He isn't thinking about Elmer, or about the old Deacon, or anybody at all. He's at peace, and he'll be that way till tomorrow. That'll give him a nice rest. That's what you and I should be doing. How do you feel?" he asked, almost tenderly.

"I'm all right," Melvin said.

"Did I hurt your foot?"

"Yes."

Horne looked as though he had forgotten what they were talking about. He frowned and sighed and after a while he said, "This is one fine town, Mobile. Any time it's too much, you just fog it over to Mobile and get squared away, except right now these miserable broads are getting on my nerves. Scream all the time and never make any sort of sense. I always knew women had jellybeans for brains. What we ought to do is get another bottle and take it back to the base with us."

"All right," Melvin said. "But who's going to buy it?"

Horne considered him with glassy, stupefied irritation. "You are! Who did you think? Cordell Hull or somebody?"

"I thought I bought the last bottle."

"Oh!" exclaimed Horne furiously. "If you're going to argue, forget it! I don't want to talk about it! Please forget I ever mentioned it!"

Melvin got to his feet, caught hold of a lamp, and gazed about the room. He hiccuped, rubbed his face, brushed some ashes from his sleeve.

"What time is it?" he asked.

"I don't know," said Horne. "Now go on out and get the bottle. Stop stalling around."

"Well, but what about the guard at the gate?" Melvin asked with a vague, apologetic smile. "Isn't it against regulations to bring whisky in?"

Horne was becoming impatient. He explained that the gate guard never inspected packages; all he did was ask what was inside. You lied to him about the contents and he told you to go on through. Everybody did it.

"But suppose he doesn't believe me?"

"He always believes you," said Horne. Then he corrected himself. "He never believes you. He knows perfectly well you're lying, but he doesn't care. He just has to ask the question because that's what the regulations say. All he wants is the answer and after that his job is finished. It isn't his responsibility if you tell a lie, see?"

Melvin leaned across the sofa, punched Roska in the stomach until he woke up, and asked him if what Horne said was true. Roska admitted thickly that it was. The gate guard never opened a package. All day Sunday, every Sunday, when liberty was ending, the buses from Mobile discharged cadets carrying shoeboxes full of whisky. At the gate the same question was invariably asked, the same answer given. That was the way it had always been and no one had any reason to suppose it would ever change: "What's in the shoebox?" "Shoes." "Go on through, Mister."

That was the formula. There was nothing to it. Roska would be taking his weekly bottle and offered to take another one, but Melvin refused. It had begun to seem like a challenge. He put on his cap and stumbled out into the rain.

After a long time he returned with a shoebox. Horne had disappeared and Roska was asleep. Cole stood in a corner with a dazed expression, drinking and occasionally shaking his head as though in disbelief. They looked at each other. Melvin's eyes filled with tears, and he stumbled into another room and fell across the bed, where he lay without moving.

Rain still beat against the windowpanes when he awoke. Beside him on the bed slept a cadet he had never seen before and a WAC who was wearing an Army officer's overcoat. He got up and wandered through the suite and came across Horne face down on the carpet with his arms outflung and fists half-clenched.

In another room Roska was reading a newspaper and sipping orange juice.

A little before noon Roska and Melvin started back to Barin Field. Horne, who was taking a shower when they left, had decided to remain in town that afternoon to see a movie about Navy flyers.

On the bus Roska fell asleep and Melvin, holding both shoeboxes in his lap, rode along with a vacant expression. His eyes were bloodshot and during the night somebody had burned a hole in his necktie. His white collar was limp, the blue uniform was wrinkled; he was generally damp and stained and smelled of liquor and perfume.

When they arrived at the gate the sky was lowering and the cold rain, which had stopped, was recommencing. The road was thick with muck. The cadets jumped out of the bus one after the other like sheep over a fence and hurried past the guard, who questioned everyone with a package. The guard stood under a shelter to keep out of the rain.

Roska, when his turn came, muttered, "Shoes," before the question had been asked. The guard waved him through, and Melvin, who had closely observed this scene, was astonished because it was obvious the guard knew Roska was lying. Now his own turn had come; he hesitated, then stepped aside. Other cadets went through the gate. At last he was the only one who had not been admitted. The guard waited for him to approach. Melvin squinted at the sky as though looking for something, and the rain streamed down his face. He decided to walk through the gate without paying any attention to the guard, but when he tried to do so the guard lifted one arm and asked what he was carrying.

Melvin grinned and blushed.

The guard pushed him back outside the fence and repeated the question.

Melvin studied the package as though he could not think how it happened to be in his hands. The bottle rolled to one side and the package tilted so that he nearly dropped it.

"That a shoebox you got there, Mister?"

Melvin agreed that it was a shoebox.

"Then I reckon you got a pair of shoes you bought in Mobile."

Melvin looked through the fence, hoping Roska had realized what was happening and was coming back to rescue him, but Roska, like the rest of the cadets, was far up the road to the barracks.

"You sound like a Southerner," Melvin said. If they could become friends the guard might let him through.

"Monroe, Louisiana," the guard replied, blinking. He was under shelter so he did not care how long the cadet wanted to stand in the rain.

Melvin tried to seem enthusiastic. "Monroe? I've never been there. What's it like?"

"Mighty nice," the guard said. "I live on Pecan Street." He unwrapped a plug of tobacco, gripped it in his teeth, worked a bite loose, and leaned against his post, chewing, observing Melvin solemnly and shrewdly.

"Looks good, that tobacco. Is it?"

Courteously the guard reached into his pocket.

"No thanks!" Melvin said. "We had a party in Mobile and my stomach feels like an antique shop." He lifted one foot and tried to kick the mud loose. "My name's Isaacs," he said wretchedly.

"Gorman," the guard replied.

"Glad to meet you."

"How do."

They shook hands.

"It's probably snowing where I come from," Melvin said.

Gorman eyed him suspiciously. "You from up North, hey?"

"Not quite. I'm a Missourian."

Gorman shifted the plug to the other cheek. "Never been up thataway. Buddy, how come you don't wear no overcoat in this here old storm? That's foolish."

Melvin shrugged. He was too discouraged to speak. He did not know what had happened to the overcoat. His shoes were filled with water. His head was throbbing, his stomach tense and unsettled, and he had begun to tremble. A chill swept over him; he shuddered and sneezed. He wanted more than anything else to take another of those marvelous, steaming showers and go to bed.

"Don't none of your buddies tote home these here packets?"

"All the time."

"What you reckon they got inside?"

Melvin suspected a trap. "They never say, so I couldn't be certain. It might be anything."

"Most generally," said Gorman, peering out his window to make sure no officers were in sight, "it might be liquor."

They looked at each other deeply.

"Now," said the guard, "how you figure they get that there liquor inside this here station?"

Melvin said he didn't know.

The guard considered him with scorn, but made one more attempt. "Looky here, Mr. Isaacs, I got me a job. The man say to me, 'Gorman, you got your instructions?' And I say, 'Yes, sir!' Do I let you through this gate without no question they might catch me, and buddy I ain't wild for no brig. Now what you totin' in that shoebox?"

"You want to look at it?"

"I'm willing to take your word. Just you tell me out loud what you got inside that box everybody puts shoes in."

"Well, I can tell you truthfully it's nothing very important."

"I know that, only you got to tell me. Just you mention me something, most anything at all. Nothing like no elephant, understand, only just something reasonable."

"How do you know the box isn't empty?"

"That there's the statement you wish to make. Is that it?"

Melvin shook his head.

Gorman was losing patience. "You want I should call up the OD and you explain this here foolishness to him? Then, buddy, make you a statement!"

Enraged and frustrated Melvin thrust the box at him and shouted, "It's whisky!"

Gorman delicately pushed the box away. "You sure it ain't shoes? What I mean, she's mighty damp today. Could be your tongue done slip while you intend to say shoes."

"There's one bottle of bourbon in there! Do you want it, or don't you?"

"Buddy," the guard answered with immense regret, "don't you know I can't allow you to hustle no bottle through this gate? Now, you know that."

"I bought it in Mobile."

"So I figured. Naturally. No cadet don't generally come rompin' home carrying no empty shoebox." He became plaintive, as though his intelligence had been insulted. "Mr. Isaacs, how long you been in this here Navy?"

"I don't know exactly. Sixteen or seventeen months, I guess. Why?"

"Lordy! Lordy! Longer than me. Some folks learn slow. You got to pay attention to what's going on, do you aim to succeed in this world. Now me, I keep me one eye hitched up yonder, and do I see a officer on the road I ain't chewing on no duty when he stops by." To emphasize the point Gorman pursed his lips and spat tobacco juice through the fence. Then he took the box away from Melvin, untied it, and examined the label on the bottle.

"You done bought the best. My pap, he always say to me, 'Son, don't drink yourself no cheap rotgut.' No, sir. Likewise, he don't drink only the best, my pap. He say to me, 'Son, always recollect a gentleman don't never drink hisself no rotgut and he don't wallop no woman without she done asked for it.' So, buddy, I'm obliged to confiscate this here fine bourbon whisky. Now you romp through most any time you please."

"Aren't you going to smash it? I thought that's what you did when you confiscated a bottle."

"Don't you worry about it," Gorman said, impassively chewing. And he added, "I'm real sorry."

"Oh, you got your orders. I'm not blaming you. I suppose in a way it's my own fault."

"You run have you a talk with some buddies. This one you count up to experience, and next time around you and me won't have us no fuss."

Melvin walked through the gate.

"So long!" the guard called after him.

Melvin nodded and waved. He stopped to scrape some of the mud from his shoes, then, with his head bowed, wandered disconsolately along the road to the barracks.

Horne did not get back until evening. He strode into the room and hung up his overcoat without saying a word. He tore off his necktie and hurled it into the wastebasket, pulled off his shoes, and sat down grimly behind the desk.

"Hot movie?" asked Melvin, who had been lying on his bunk all afternoon.

Horne scratched at an ink spot on the desk. He seemed to be meditating. Finally he said, "Great."

"I guess we won, huh?"

"Sure."

"We always do."

"Yuh. They had these SNJ's painted up like Zeroes with meatballs on the fuselage and some Hawaiians pretending to be Jap pilots."

"How do you know they were Hawaiians?"

Horne looked at him steadily. "I don't know they were Hawaiians. I just took a guess. For all I know, they were Peruvians. It was a waste of time," he went on. "It was miserable."

"So what did you expect? Did you think it'd be authentic?"

"I thought there'd be some big juicy broads."

"You mean there weren't?" said Melvin, looking at him with surprise.

"Oh, they had this one stupid blonde that looked pretty tender," he admitted, pulling off his socks and throwing them at the closet. He reached for a package of cigarettes and shook one out, but then, suddenly, half-rising from the chair as though someone had just called him, hurled the package at Melvin. They looked at each other soberly; Melvin rolled over and stared at the wall.

Horne remained at the desk, smoking and cleaning his fingernails with a pair of scissors. It was drizzling outside, the field had been secured for the night, every few seconds the red beacon flashed through the mist.

Horne kicked the desk and flung the scissors to the floor. "Well, by God!" he said furiously, "you did it!"

"Did what?"

"Oh, knock it off! Everybody on the base knows about that whisky."

Melvin lifted his head, oddly moved by the tone of Horne's voice, and gazed into the wicked little pink-rimmed blue eyes.

"You've joined the immortals," Horne said. "I always knew you'd do it, but I never thought it would be this way. By next

141

Saturday there won't be a cadet, or a swab jockey, or an officer anywhere within a hundred miles who doesn't know who Melvin Isaacs is. In a few days you'll be better known than the skipper. Just think! When anybody talks about it I can say, 'That's my roommate!' " He rocked back in the chair and stared out the window into the rainswept night.

"I don't see what's so funny," Melvin said.

"Funny? Who said it was funny? It's too incredible to be funny. It takes real genius to do what you did. I never heard of such a thing in my whole life. Already people are asking me what you look like, and do you gibber and walk on your knuckles. They'll be knocking at the door any minute to have a look at you. We should charge admission. What have you got in that shoe-box?" he inquired rhetorically. "What have you got in that shoe-box? And what does Isaacs say? He says he's got a fifth of bourbon in there. I never heard of such a thing! You must have drunk it on the bus. Is that why you had to tell the truth?"

"I guess I should have let Roska take it in."

"I guess!"

"Well, why are you so hot about it? It was just a bottle of whisky, that's all."

"You think that's the reason? I'll tell you something. I don't know why, but I kind of like you. I don't like to see you make a fool of yourself. That's why. Besides," he went on, because the admission had embarrassed him, "you're the first cadet in the history of Barin Field to have his whisky confiscated, and that ruins our record. Up until today we had a perfect score. It wouldn't surprise me if you were the first cadet in the whole history of Pensacola to throw away a fifth of good bourbon. Maybe in the whole history of naval aviation."

"Really? Do you think so?"

"It wouldn't surprise me a bit," Horne answered firmly.

"Oh, I think you're exaggerating," Melvin said. He sat up, lighted a cigarette, and began blowing smoke rings.

"You do, do you? Wait till tomorrow."

He was right. At breakfast Melvin noticed whispering and staring, and it was the same at the hangar while he was checking out a parachute. Even the WAVEs in the loft gazed at him curiously.

Cole thought it was hilarious. He was sorry he had stayed in Mobile; he wanted Melvin to re-enact the scene. But Captain Teitlebaum approached and they all came to attention.

While giving instructions the captain let it be known that a friend of his, an Army pilot, was visiting the station and wanted to observe a cadet flight. The Army officer would be riding in the back seat of his plane.

"Now, I am warning you people," Teitlebaum remarked. "You be on the stick today. If you go up there and behave like nincompoops I'll rack you. The entire crew. Now, when you come down that alley I want to know that stick is hard over and well forward. I don't want to see a Hollywood peel-off. You break out of there crisp and low and at the proper interval. Another item: this man is accustomed to Army landings. I want you people to demonstrate Navy three-point landings. I want to see five three-point landings in five seconds. I don't want that man to be able to see one inch of straightaway when you people come aboard. I don't want him to see one SNJ on level wings from the time you break formation until you roll across that mat. One warning should be sufficient. Do I make myself clear? Isaacs, you are leading this flight. These men will depend on you. Another item . . ."

Teitlebaum spent fifteen minutes warning them; the substance of his talk was simply that he wanted to be proud of his students.

Melvin, Horne, and McCampbell took off at the same instant, pulled up the wheels, and a few seconds later were banking away from the field, headed for the dive-bombing range; Melvin glanced down and noticed with a slight shock that his left wingtip could not be more than six inches from the concrete. The previous week a cadet from another flight had retracted the wheels too soon after take-off, the plane settled as the airflow was altered, and the propeller touched the mat. Melvin and Roska happened to see it as they were coming out of the gymnasium. It had looked like a pinwheel on the Fourth of July; the pilot was now in the hospital, and as soon as he recovered he would be on his way to Great Lakes as an apprentice seaman.

He glanced to the right. McCampbell and Horne were in perfect formation, tighter than he had ever seen them. He began to get excited, sensing that this was the day—a day he had not even anticipated, but now he understood that it was here and that he had been waiting for it. They had all been waiting for it to happen, waiting to become a unit instead of five individuals.

Confidently he steepened the turn and McCampbell and Horne rolled with him as though they were marbles in the bottom of a bowl, and they all three rolled out of it together and started climbing. He glanced back, aware that he knew instinctively where to find Cole and Roska, and they were there. They were coming up fast, beginning to slide toward their positions. There was no need to say anything. He looked ahead. There was nothing in the sky or on the watery horizon and for a few moments it seemed to him that they were somewhere in the Pacific, and that just beyond the horizon the enemy waited.

As the dive-bombing range came into view he picked up the microphone. "We're going to take number six. I say again: number six. Keep it steep. And it looks like there's approximately a ten-knot wind from the south, so be sure you compensate."

Four wooden stakes formed a square in the shallow water just off the beach. In the center of the square was another stake.

He led the echelon half around the target, feeling for the wind, drew the goggles over his eyes, and started down, steadily increasing the angle of the dive until it was almost vertical. He had the curious conviction he always had in a steep dive that the tail of the airplane had actually passed over his head, over the zenith, and that he was slightly inverted. The needle of the airspeed indicator was turning faster. He trimmed the plane, steadied it, and began to sight the target. Because the morning was cool he had worn his shirt and necktie under the coveralls. All at once the tie came fluttering out, blew around his chin, and then began hitting him in the face. He leaned to one side but the tie followed him, beating him over the nose and mouth and on the goggles like an infuriated butterfly. He wondered if he had time to let go of the controls long enough to catch it and stuff it back inside the coveralls. He looked at the altimeter, and at the water. The target was drifting; he eased the plane around, glanced again at the altimeter. At fifteen hundred feet above the water he was supposed to let go of the throttle, reach into the bottom of the cockpit, and jerk the bomb release. The necktie was flickering all over his face and he was afraid he was going to sneeze. He shook his head violently, shouted at the tie and tried to catch it between his teeth, took another look at the instrument panel, and was alarmed to see that he was beyond the point where he should have released the bomb. Not that this in itself made too much difference because he did not expect to hit the target anyway—on previous runs he had never managed to drop a bomb even reasonably close—but he was now so far below the release point that he did not know if he was high enough to pull out of the dive. He grabbed the handle, dropped the bomb, and dragged the control stick backward as fast as he could. The blood drained from his head so that he was blind, but half-conscious, and as soon as he felt the pressure lessening and saw his brain lightening in color he knew he was past the base of the arc and that the plane was starting upward.

He did not bother to scan the target area when his vision returned. The bomb had probably struck half a mile outside the square and he was so ashamed and disappointed that he wanted to forget about it. The flight had begun with such speed and precision. Now, all because of a necktie, the Army officer was no doubt trying to stifle his laughter and Teitlebaum must be furious.

He climbed toward the formation and as he leveled off behind the last man in the echelon, who happened to be Roska, he was surprised to see Roska turn around, grin, and triumphantly shake his fist. Cole had also turned around and was nodding as though in encouragement. Melvin began to feel touched by their loyalty. Somewhat discouraged, but determined to score a hit, he pulled off his necktie and tucked it between his thigh and the safety belt where it could not possibly get loose; and as Roska dove out of formation, leaving him again at the head of the echelon, followed now by McCampbell and Horne—with Cole rising swiftly toward them—he looked down at the bombing range and saw that the peg in the center of the target had disappeared. Apparently it had been broken by the concussion from nearby explosions and had floated away. He felt enormously relieved by this, for it meant the other members of the flight had partly redeemed him, and he was more than ever grateful to them. He watched Roska dive on the vacant square and place a bomb within it, not far from where the center peg had been, and his own failure seemed less important. What mattered was that the target had been destroyed, though he himself had been spectacularly unsuccessful.

Since the remaining target ranges were occupied by other formations, he led the second run against the same square and as he climbed away from it, twisting around in the cockpit to look down, he saw a puff of smoke burst within the boundary. It qualified as a hit, and he was thankful he had not missed again. He watched where the other bombs fell: McCampbell was inside the square, as he always was; Horne was in, as he usually was; Cole's bomb struck near a corner peg; and Roska's was a few yards outside. Of the ten bombs they had dropped, there must have been six or seven hits, and that was good. It was better than they had ever done before.

He signaled them to form in column behind him and led them down the beach to practice strafing on the driftwood. The sand kicked as the bullets stitched along, and sticks jumped like animals. He noticed an object riding in the waves a few hundred yards offshore, and turned carefully against it with his finger curled around the machine-gun trigger. It was a log, peeled and half-submerged and as fearfully pale as a body, and Melvin pulled up frantically swerving toward the shore.

On the radio Captain Teitlebaum called his number, ordered him to detach himself from the formation, and climb to an altitude of five thousand feet prepared for combat.

Obediently he went up to meet the captain. They passed each other once; then Teitlebaum's plane with the Army officer in the rear seat flashed by again so rapidly it seemed distorted, bending and elongating like something under water. Melvin kicked the controls, knowing Teitlebaum had already gained; moments later the captain's plane again flashed by, turning, having gained a little more, drawing into position to commence firing.

He tried everything he had learned, and flew desperately over the revolving sky, but there was no escape: each time he looked around he found the captain a little closer, and he understood for the first time how panic could overtake a man when death drew inexorably nearer. At last, trembling so that he could hardly manipulate the controls, defeated and drenched with perspiration, with the captain flying directly behind him, he dipped the wings in surrender.

Teitlebaum ordered him to rejoin the formation and return to the field.

Melvin lifted the goggles and let them rest on his forehead. He wiped his face, noticing that his hand was shaking badly, and spiraled down to lead the column home.

As they cruised over the pine forests, the country roads and the lakes and swamps, and at last came to the base and entered the traffic circle, he thought about the captain's victory because there had been something odd about it—it had been so unnecessary. Captain Teitlebaum had shot down eight Japanese fighters in the Pacific. There was no necessity to prove his superiority over a Pensacola cadet. And it had been so much more than a simple tactical demonstration.

One after another they peeled off, swung around the field, settled onto the mat, and taxied in. It had been a good flight. It had been a strange flight, but he knew that with the exception of himself they had flown beautifully and all together.

Captain Teitlebaum was not lavish in his praise; he commented that it had not been a bad day, and with that he dismissed them, except for Melvin. When the two of them were alone the captain took a cigar from the pocket of his coveralls and said as he was unwrapping it, "Are you positive you're in the right outfit?"

Melvin looked at the officer in confusion; Teitlebaum, rising on tiptoe, gave back that familiar bright and terrible stare.

"Here's what I'm getting at, Isaacs," the captain said. "The point is this," he continued, and put a match to the cigar. "I should recommend that you be dropped from flight training. Your grades are average, and occasionally, such as today, your leadership is commendable."

He hooked his thumbs in the drawstrings of the life jacket and narrowed his eyes, squinting across the hangar. For a while it seemed he had nothing more to say. At last he went on. "Your reactions are slow, but that is not the essential qualification for a military pilot. There is one characteristic of a military flyer, however, that you do lack. I don't know why. I don't know quite what is wrong with you. It isn't lack of courage. When that man was killed I thought you would break. You didn't. I liked that."

"He was sick, Mr. Teitlebaum. He was going around with that WAVE who hung herself in the loft and after that happened he never did know what he was doing."

"I am not ever interested in explanations. Free is dead. The Navy invested time and money in training him and that investment has been lost." He paused, returning to some earlier thought. "Four of you people are going to make fine combat pilots. The scrawny one who never says a word—monkey face with those beady little eyes—McTavish? Or McGregor? That boy is the sharpest I have encountered in this program. He should survive. Next, that tough towhead with the barrel chest and the broken nose—the one with the rasping voice. What's his name?"

"Horne."

"That's right. Horne. He's good material. Then those other two boys are fair enough. They'll shape up. I don't concern myself with those four. They belong. But right now, Isaacs, I'm going to tell you: naval and Marine aviation is the wrong place for you."

"Why is that, sir?"

"Because I am convinced you are unable to kill."

"You're washing me out," said Melvin quickly. "Is that what you're trying to say?"

"No. I am sending the five of you to pre-operational at Saufley. None of you will have any trouble there. The syllabus is nothing but a formality. Consequently, Isaacs, you will be commissioned. Now, that is not the end of your career; it is the commencement. You will later be assigned to a combat squadron and ultimately you will find yourself in the war. There will come a time when your existence will depend not only on your ability to fly, but upon your willingness to destroy other men. What your decision will be when that time comes I believe I can predict. Even so, you have chosen this course. Ostensibly you are succeeding. It is not for me to exceed the limitations of my duty, therefore I will allow you to continue. May God help you."

"Is there anything else, sir?"

"No. That is all."

Melvin saluted, the captain returned the salute, and they walked rapidly away from each other.

Horne was in the barracks, stripped to the waist but still wearing his garrison cap. The room stank of perspiration; it was evident he had been exercising, and Melvin, noting this, was astonished because he himself was exhausted and fell face down on the bunk and lay there without moving. He could not remember when he had ever been so tired; he was so overcome with fatigue that he felt no desire to go to sleep.

"What's the trouble?" Horne asked without showing much concern.

"I don't know," Melvin said. "I have a tired, run-down feeling and I have a nagging backache. I lie awake nights and suffer from loss of appetite."

"Want an asprin?" said Horne. He danced around the room, aiming swift blows at the furniture.

Melvin didn't answer.

Horne continued to box; he feinted, ducked his head, and jabbed at the gooseneck lamp that stood on the desk. "What you need is a big, fat—*ugh!*—juicy broad!" he grunted. He slapped himself on the chest and rotated his powerful, sweating shoulders. Then he paused. "You're always getting sick," he said, and the more he thought about this the more irritated he became. "Honest to God!" he cried hoarsely, "if it isn't cat fever it's the Aztec two-step or some other stupid thing! You don't eat right," he decided, although the two of them always ate together and had no choice about what they were served.

"Maybe so. I don't know what's the matter with me."

"Of course it's so!" Horne declared. "You don't eat a balanced diet and you drink too much coffee. You're always drinking coffee," he added righteously, somewhat pacified by this idea.

Melvin rolled over on the bunk and said without opening his eyes, "What's the word on this Saufley pre-operational? Teitlebaum says he's sending us on."

"You hear the same scuttlebutt I do. We're winning the war, not so many losses in the Pacific, so the program slows down. We got to lard around Saufley Field till somebody feels like giving us a commission. Fly a few hops in some old beat-up dive bombers, play basketball, good chow, no strain. Cole says a buddy of his who's over there now says they treat cadets almost the same as officers. I believe that when I see it. Even then I won't."

"What did you think of the flight today? How did it go?"

"Great! I sincerely mean that. You did a good job."

"I thought it was good, too, except for that first bomb run of mine."

After a pause, during which he seemed baffled and at a loss, Horne remarked, "I complimented you, didn't I? You did a good job, I said so. What more do you want?"

Melvin looked at him in bewilderment.

"You hit the peg," Horne went on. "Everybody saw it. You never did it before in your life and you'll never do it again, but you did it today and you couldn't have picked a better time. You blew the center right out of the goddamn target and that Army officer probably dropped his marbles when he saw it. Teitlebaum was so happy he was about to kiss you, I know for a fact. It was the last thing in the world he expected to happen. Now, is that enough? Are you satisfied? Or do you want me to get down on my knees and salaam?"

Melvin had been listening without comprehension; he understood the words, and he could tell Horne was not joking, but for a little while he could not believe what he heard. The bombs were so small, they weighed only a few pounds and had no more explosive power than a hand grenade. To have blown a stake completely out of the water the bomb must have struck within a few feet of it. He jumped up and began to walk excitedly around the room, gave a curious little skip, and seated himself on the edge of the desk with his arms crossed. But he could not sit still. He sprang off the desk and resumed pacing around the room with a mischievous frown, his hands thrust in his pockets. "Here's the thing," he said, attempting to control his excitement. "I hit the target, see? But it was luck. Pure luck!"

"I know it was luck. You know it was luck. Everybody, including Teitlebaum, knew it was luck. The only one who didn't was that Army pilot. He thought you did it on purpose."

"Yes! Exactly! But I did! That's what's remarkable, don't you see? Did I or didn't I? How can you say? Because I did precisely what I was trying to do! I was aiming for that peg—aiming right at it—but the fact that I hit it was an accident." He stopped, pinching his lip in concentration. "Now, should I receive credit, or not? Don't you think that's queer? Or suppose you take similar circumstances in another situation entirely—don't you see how unreal it could become?"

"It's queer enough. I'll queer myself if I hang around you much longer. They should've locked you up months ago."

"Do you think I should explain to Teitlebaum that it was a mistake?"

"That what was a mistake?"

"Why, hitting the target, of course. I don't want to be credited with a hit unless I'm entitled to it, any more than I'd want to be blamed for a thing if I wasn't guilty."

Horne had been tapping his fingers on the desk; all at once he jumped up in exasperation and shouted, "What's the matter with you? Just tell me!"

Melvin gazed at Horne blindly and did not even know he had spoken; he was thinking of what Teitlebaum had said. The day, which had started so well, seemed unaccountably shattered.

12

Melvin continued to think about what Captain Teitlebaum had said. From Barin Field the company was transferred to Saufley, and as the days went by it seemed more and more important to know if the captain had been right. Graduation was not far off. Every once in a while some cadet who had been in a battalion ahead of him would reappear on the station as an ensign or a Marine lieutenant and the enlisted men would salute. Several times Melvin saw this happen, and was filled with such emotion that he felt congested and a little dizzy. Soon he himself would be a naval aviator. He would be assigned to operational training and after that, in all probability, he would be ordered to the Pacific.

One evening after supper as he and Sam Horne were strolling across the base he said, "I've been trying to recall if I've ever known any Japanese, but I don't think I have."

Horne stiffened and took a deep breath. "All right," Horne said, obviously struggling to control his voice. "You don't know any Japs. Neither do I."

"I just think it's curious, that's all," Melvin said.

"I want to tell you something," said Horne, looking straight ahead. "We've been cadets a long time, right?"

Melvin agreed this was so.

"And it ain't been easy, right? All right! So we're coming to the end of the road. Let's enjoy it." Then he added vehemently, "This is the best base we've ever been at! For once we're getting a fair shake. The Navy's all right. I don't want to hear you knocking it, not at this moment."

"I'm not arguing. This *is* a good base," Melvin said.

Most of the rumors about Saufley Field had turned out to be true. The food was served on plates instead of aluminum trays, and the mess attendants used ladles instead of ice-cream dippers. The food was not only of better quality and properly cooked, but was made to look appetizing: breaded veal cutlets, for example, were attractively arranged in the pan, and there was hot gravy to go with them, whereas at every other base they had been stacked high and dry like cuttlefish in a Chinese delicatessen. At breakfast the beans were hot, toast was well buttered, and the eggs were fresh rather than dehydrated. Furthermore, they ate at a table with a tablecloth instead of at a bench, each cadet was given a cloth napkin, and when they had finished the meal they left their plates on the table instead of scraping them over a barrel.

Even the military officers, as distinguished from the flight officers, were not unreasonable. There was a junior grade lieutenant in charge of the barracks: when they reported to him for the first time he smiled and shook hands with each member of the company, and remarked on the length of the cadet program.

The company had a good deal of leisure, and it was spring.

The great rains of winter were over. Flowers bloomed and trees burgeoned and small red-tailed hawks soared in the Gulf wind.

On a grassy elevation in full view of the hangars and runways was the swimming pool. Here the cadets often gathered during the warm, sunny afternoons and long twilight hours. When the wind blew from a certain direction the traffic circle passed directly above the pool; then they would look up at the sputtering, smoking dive bombers; their eyes followed the landing pattern with intent, calculating, professional approval while the stubby little bombers came coasting around the final turn and plopped on the runway with a languid informality that characterized the entire station.

"All we got to do here," Sam Horne commented late one afternoon as a group of cadets was sauntering toward the barracks, "is keep from falling asleep."

"You'll never wake up if you go to sleep in an SBD," someone said.

"I could fly an SBD blindfolded," Horne replied. "Even Dilbert here," he added, thrusting an elbow into Melvin's ribs, "won't have any trouble."

Hundreds of the old dive bombers were parked on the field. Not many of them were used. They had been ferried back to the United States from the war in the Pacific and were tied down wherever there was room at Pensacola. On the ground or in the air they could be distinguished by the hoarse, thudding roar of the engine, and by the flaps on the trailing edge of the wing. These flaps split like the beak of a bird in order to decrease the speed of the airplane and provide greater stability during a bombing run. The flaps were perforated and these perforations could be seen almost as far away as the plane itself. In comparison to the trainers the SBD Dauntless was a ponderous, decisive machine—the first actual combat plane the cadets had flown.

There was a rumor that these particular SBD's had been condemned because of their age and because most of them had been shot up in the war; nobody proved or disproved this rumor, nor would it have affected anything anyway, but Melvin, after various calculations, wrote home that he was expected to risk his life for eleven cents an hour.

He had expected a week or so of dual instruction before attempting a solo in the Dauntless. He got only one brief ride in the gunner's ring while an ensign, who appeared to be about his own age, showed him the area around the base and nonchalantly displayed a few characteristics of the airplane. The ensign took the Dauntless up, pushed over into a shallow dive with the flaps split wide apart, and then decreased the angle of the flaps. The bomber immediately plunged vertically and almost irresistibly toward the earth.

When at last they came swooping out of the dive the officer looked into the mirror with a benign smile and asked if there were any questions. Melvin had no questions—the demonstration had been sufficient warning—so they returned to the base.

The runways at Saufley Field were long, but they were uneven, with ripples and depressions sufficiently pronounced to cast shadows in the early morning or late afternoon. The ensign pointed to one runway that had an abrupt rise at the beginning. Melvin noted this carefully. He had heard about it. Several pilots unfamiliar with the field had struck this hump, lost control, and crashed.

The ensign did not bother to mention a number of blackened swaths through the cornfields outside the fence, apparently because no mention was necessary. The swaths had been cut by planes that never quite managed to get into the air for one reason or another, or, if they did, came right down again; the engines detonated constantly, which gave the peculiar thudding noise heard from the ground, and occasionally stopped functioning altogether.

Later that afternoon Melvin went out for his first solo.

The taxi strip was crowded with torpedo bombers from a carrier that had dropped anchor off the coast during the night, and there was a landing signal officer in a fluorescent orange vest at the end of the runway to expedite the traffic.

When the last torpedo bomber had lifted sluggishly into the air and hung there, spraddle-legged, magically diminishing within a haze of acrid smoke, the LSO beckoned Melvin into position and twirled his hands overhead. Melvin pressed down on the brakes and eased the throttle forward. The handle felt thick, a large cool bulb on a metal stalk. The Dauntless began to tremble and dance.

154

The LSO—leaned forward, watching intently—suddenly spun around like a ball player and threw toward the far end of the field. Melvin lifted his toes and the shuddering old dive bomber trundled forward, grinding like a tractor, faster and faster.

In a few seconds he felt the tail wheel leave the concrete and the plane began to push against him, but he held it down, and forced it to stay down until he knew it was ready, and when he finally let it up it came up firm and powerful like the neck of a bull.

He flew straight ahead, scanning the instruments and listening to the engine. When he passed over the fence he started climbing. The control stick was heavily rigged to the cables and felt solid and squat and anchored deep inside the corpulent body. The finger grip was plump; it was pleasant to squeeze. In an SNJ the stick was a slender aluminum pipe that banged about in the cockpit like an old-fashioned automobile gear shift.

He flew the bomber up until he could distinguish the curve of the earth, and there he rode around, maneuvering cautiously but with increasing confidence, studying the instruments, listening, testing the way in which the Dauntless stalled and fell off to the side; and he gazed somewhat idly toward the Gulf twenty miles distant. The Gulf was hazy and devoid of much color. He slid open the canopy and the wind roared. He lifted his goggles and let them rest on his forehead. He dipped one wing and then the other, going nowhere, rocking along as though sunning himself on a raft. It was a fine warm afternoon. By his ears the high wind rushed and the engine thundered like the surf.

Presently he noticed a vee of basic trainers from Ellyson Field. They were about a mile below him. He spiraled down for a closer look, throttled back so as not to overrun them, and followed them a few minutes. He looked with amusement at the familiar turquoise rudder and at the squadron markings on the wing. It seemed long ago that he had been in basic training at Ellyson. He remembered that they used to call that plane the Vibrator because it rattled all the time, and at this he smiled. He remembered, too, that one day not unlike this day he had looked up and had seen a Dauntless high overhead, and had stared at it with envy and admiration. Since then much had happened and he was aware that he no longer felt the same.

The period was over, so it seemed, before he had fairly begun; regretfully he floated down on Saufley Field, radioed the tower for permission to land, and after permission was granted came in easily, guiding the tough stubby bomber as though he had flown it for years.

A few days later he was scheduled to lead a navigation flight. He had been expecting this, for it was part of the syllabus at every base, but he had not been expecting to lead anyone except cadets; now he discovered that two of the five men behind him would be officers. One was a senior grade lieutenant and the other was a commander. He asked if this was a mistake, very hopeful that it was, but it was not; the officers had returned to Pensacola for what was known as a refresher course.

The commander, an erect, white-haired gentleman about fifty years old with a crew cut, and a blue tattoo on the back of one hand, accepted Melvin's instructions for the rendezvous as though he found nothing the least extraordinary in the situation. Neither did the lieutenant find it incongruous.

When it was time to go to the planes Melvin did not know whether he was supposed to salute the officers or not, and decided to pretend—if they called him on it—that he had forgotten. Neither of them said anything as he walked away.

The flight went very well, except that the commander flew a loose wing position. The cadet on the opposite wing flew extremely close, as they all had done at Barin Field; and the second vee, which was led by Ostrowski, drifted around, appearing now on the left, and above, now on the right, but always symmetrical. The commander was the only one out of position. Melvin considered signaling him to pull in closer, but, after all, there was not much to be gained and there was, perhaps, quite a bit to be lost. The result was that they traveled the course properly, if not in perfect formation, and returned to the base on time, having had a pleasant and uneventful ride.

Melvin radioed in the usual manner: "Saufley tower. Saufley tower. This is Navy five-zero-five. Request landing permission. Six SBD's. Over."

An impersonal voice responded, advising him of the direction and velocity of the wind and giving the number of the runway which was in use at that time. They entered the pattern, circled the field halfway around, and settled on the runway one after another.

He had been in the barracks only a few minutes and was standing at the window thoughtfully folding and unfolding his garrison cap when Pat Cole sauntered into the room and mentioned that he had just returned from the main station, where he had watched the weekly graduation ceremony. Melvin nodded somewhat absently and remarked that in another four weeks their turn would come.

"Three weeks," said Cole with a quizzical smile. "As long as I've been acquainted with you I have yet to see you keep accurate track of the time. Invariably you're behind."

"I was thinking about something else. A very strange thing happened to me a little while ago. I was bringing in a formation, so I called the tower for instructions the way we're supposed to. And I got the instructions, and everything worked out right. Do you know what I mean?"

"No, I don't," said Cole.

Melvin went on with difficulty. "Well, it was as though I wasn't a cadet. It was as though I was a naval aviator."

"That's what you are," said Cole.

"Yes. But it's very strange, don't you think?"

And then Cole said, "Someday when you're not busy I'd like to have a talk with you."

"What about?"

"Oh, the war. Our situation. I may have the answers you're searching for."

Just then Horne strode into the room cursing the laundry which had pressed his shirts until the buttons cracked; and Cole, after helping himself to a peppermint, sauntered away.

"Liberty's been reduced to one night a week," Horne said. He crumpled the freshly laundered shirt and hurled it to the floor. "How do you like that! We might as well be back at pre-flight! One night a week! It's posted on the bulletin board."

"Did they give any reason?"

"They didn't post the reason, but the reason is the clap. Same old story. Sick bay full of guys with the crud they picked up in Mobile or Pensy and the skipper's disgusted. I suppose he figures if we can't get off the base we can't catch the clap."

"Well, he's right, of course."

Horne was furious. "You put fifty naval aviation cadets in a zeppelin and they'd come down with the clap! This is the stupidest stunt yet! This takes the cake! There used to be four liberty nights a week at this base. It was three when we first got here. Then two! Now we're down to *one!* The Navy's going to have a lot of fairy aviators if it doesn't change that policy."

"Maybe if they increased the Shore Patrol, that might help. I don't know how, though, the more I think about it."

"I don't know and I don't care!" Horne snarled, and gave his shirt a vicious kick. "I'm certainly glad we're almost through this dim-witted program."

A few days later, during which time Cole had made no further reference to whatever it was he wanted to talk about, an admiral visited the base. Just before noon a transport plane landed and the admiral was driven across the station in a black limousine with a four-starred flag fluttering from a mast on the fender. Melvin happened to be on the street when the limousine rolled by; he stooped a little and peered in. He saw, quite alone in the back seat, a shaggy, burly old man who resembled a gnome, with tangled yellow eyebrows and a penetrating but not unfriendly gaze. The admiral looked out just as Melvin looked in and Melvin straightened up quickly.

A familiar voice said, "How do, buddy?" and he turned around, and there was the gate guard from Barin Field.

"Hello, Gorman," Melvin said with a grin. "What are you doing here?"

"They done transferred me."

"The weather's a little better than last time we met. I was pretty soggy."

"You was a mite damp." An uncomfortable smile appeared on the seaman's face; he screwed up his eyes, blinked, spat tobacco juice into the grass, and finally remarked with an air of deep concentration, "Got me a old lady."

"You got married? Congratulations. Some girl from Monroe?"

"Naw!" He was amused. "Got me a little bitch I seen jitterbugging one night in the Yardarm."

"Where's the Yardarm? I never heard of it."

Gorman pointed in the direction of Mobile, and there was

approval in his knowing eyes. "Get you some real stuff there." He worked the tobacco around in his mouth, frowned, shuffled his feet, and said with reluctance, "Been doing me some powerful thinking, buddy. Been thinking about that liquor." He looked swiftly to see if Melvin remembered. An officer approached. They both came to attention and saluted.

"Didn't really figure to run into you no more," he continued when the officer had gone by. "That liquor, buddy, I drank her spang up," he added with a sparse grin. "Damn my everlasting soul if I didn't."

"Well, it'd have been a shame to waste it. To break it, or whatever you were supposed to do."

"Done cost you something, I figure."

Melvin realized with astonishment that the guard was intending to pay for the bottle. He had pulled up the bottom of his jumper to get at his wallet, which was folded over the waistband of his trousers.

"There at that gate all day long they lied to me. I know it. They know I knowed it. Then along come you, and you didn't lie to me."

"I tell you what," Melvin said. "You've been thinking about the whisky, I've been thinking about that tobacco. I've never tried chewing tobacco. Have you got any left? A good chew ought to square us for that bourbon."

The guard spun around, positive that someone had crept up to overhear the conversation, but there was nobody near them. "Generally that don't make sense," he countered, probing. Officers were his enemies, of this he had no doubt, he had never had any cause to doubt this, and a cadet would one day be an officer; at the same time he had heard that cadets, like enlisted men, were badly used. "You lying to me now, buddy?"

"You'll have to decide that for yourself," said Melvin.

Gorman squinted, pretending to look at something in the sky; then he bowed very briefly, the round white cap lay upside down in his hands, and in the cap, bent into an arch to fit snugly over his skull, was the plug. Melvin unwrapped it and put a corner between his teeth; he was not certain, when he felt something give, whether his teeth were still in his mouth, but he wrapped the tobacco and dropped it in the cap, Gorman bowed again and came up wearing the cap and a remote, mindless gaze. "Reckon she's chow time," he murmured.

Melvin nodded, unable to speak because of the juice spreading through his mouth. He thought he had a tongue full of pins, or sparks. Gorman, after studying him kindly, lifted a hand in a vague manner, in what could have been an incipient salute, did an about face, and was soon lost among a group of men near the recreation hall.

At the barracks Horne was lying on the bunk meditatively turning the pages of a thick, cloth-bound book. Without looking up from the book he said, "Lieutenant Caravaggio was here and just now left. Did you see him?"

Melvin walked to the basin and rinsed his mouth for several minutes before attempting to speak. Horne watched him curiously.

"Who?" Melvin said, wiping his lips on the back of his hand.

"What's the matter with you?" said Horne.

"Nothing's the matter with me. What does shellac taste like?"

"Shellac!" Horne echoed. "How should I know?"

"I was just wondering. Who did you say was here?"

"Lieutenant Caravaggio. Are you drunk?"

"I'm not drunk. Who's Lieutenant Caravaggio? I never heard of him."

Horne sat up and swung his legs over the side of the bunk, closing his book on one finger so as not to lose the place.

"Well, you act like you're drunk."

Melvin ignored him. He began to scrape his teeth with a fingernail. Presently Horne stood up and approached.

"What's the matter, baby? Are you sick?"

"Why should I be sick?" Melvin retorted. He glared at the book, which had no title. "What are you reading?"

Horne returned to his own bunk and sat down complacently, saying, "You wouldn't be interested. You're too young."

"Too young for what?" Melvin demanded.

Horne rolled over so that he faced the wall. In this position he turned the pages. Melvin angrily ran across the room to see what he was looking at, but Horne shut the book.

"Oh," said Melvin, "we're smart, aren't we!" He grabbed for the book and Horne slapped his hand away

160

"Go see the lieutenant."

"What lieutenant?"

Horne made a clucking noise and peeped into the book.

"Who cares what it is!" Melvin said in disgust, returning to his side of the room. He could still taste the tobacco. Horne's book annoyed him because it did not look exactly the way a book should look. He tried to peer across Horne's shoulder and believed he saw a female figure and sprang across the room to have a better look, and this time Horne did not hide the book, although he would not let go of it.

"How many are there?" Melvin whispered, watching greedily as he turned up one after another.

"I don't know exactly, but I think there's about six hundred and fifty."

"Did you get it at Ship's Service?"

Horne stared up at him and after a moment said, "Sometimes I don't know about you. What would a book like this be doing in Ship's Service?"

"Let me have it."

"No," said Horne. "Let go, it's mine. Will you kindly let go? Please! Holy cow, what's the matter with you?"

"What are you going to do with them?" asked Melvin, trying to twist the book out of his hands.

"I thought about pasting them on the wall or in the closet," said Horne. "Let go! You're ruining it!" He doubled up so he could use his feet to shove Melvin away, but Melvin slipped around and managed to get a knee on his chest.

"Where did you get them?" he demanded, leaning forward victoriously.

All at once Horne escaped and caught him in a hammer lock. "Drop my book," he ordered.

Melvin shook his head.

"Drop it, I say. I'm not fooling. I'll break your arm."

Melvin shook his head again and made a pretense of looking through the book although the pain was blinding him.

"Why don't you let go?" Horne asked. He was puzzled.

On his knees, with his forehead pressed to the floor, Melvin gasped in anguish and resumed struggling.

"Oh, Jesus," Horne muttered, letting him go. "I can't understand you. I ordered it from a place in New Hampshire, if that makes any difference. Now will you please let me have it? You can look at it all you want to after I get through."

"I want to look at it now," Melvin said.

"Well, I do too," Horne exclaimed, jumping from the bunk and catching him by the throat. They staggered across the room, hissing and snarling, and stumbled against the desk. The gooseneck lamp crashed into the wastebasket.

"Let go of my pants!" Horne shouted. "My other pants are in the laundry! These are the only ones I got!"

Melvin let go and at that moment his feet were kicked from under him and he came down flat on the linoleum with a blow that pumped the wind from his lungs.

"I just can't figure you out," muttered Horne. He picked up the book and discovered that one of the pages was torn. "Look what you did!" he cried pettishly. "I liked that one. That was one of my favorites. You simple clown!"

Melvin was lying supine on the floor with his arms outflung as though he had been crucified. He was not able to speak; he thought his vocal chords had been crushed. His lip was swollen and one of his teeth felt loose. The ceiling of the room had tilted and was continually sliding aside. He could hear everything plainly, but there was a singing and roaring in his ears. He was not able to feel his neck; it was as though his neck were made out of rubber and he thought it had probably turned black. He swallowed and made a gurgling noise.

"What's the matter?" Horne asked. He was trying to press the torn picture back into place.

Melvin feebly sat up, gazed at the torn page, and whispered, "Why don't you fix it with Scotch Tape?"

"There isn't any," said Horne, frowning.

"Desk drawer," Melvin said hoarsely. "Bought some last week."

"I used it all up yesterday," said Horne.

"You *what!* You used my Scotch Tape? Did I say you could?"

"You weren't around when I needed it."

"A man leaves his own room," Melvin said, "for about five or ten minutes, and some greedy slob not only uses his Scotch Tape, he uses it all up."

"By God!" Horne exclaimed, and jumped to his feet. "I'm sorry!" He slammed the book shut and strode out of the room.

Melvin lay on the floor tenderly feeling his lip and his throat, but after a few minutes, becoming somewhat lonesome, he got up and staggered along the corridor looking for Horne. He was at the door to McCampbell's room, squatting on his haunches and peeping through the keyhole. Melvin squatted beside him and listened. The noises were muffled—the chink of silver coins and every so often the patter of dice like the claws of a rodent scampering desperately across the linoleum.

Horne took hold of the door knob. Finding that it would turn he flung open the door; the gamblers, who knelt in a semi-circle against the wall, looked around in dismay. Cole was asleep on his bunk, dressed only in the polka-dot shorts he consistently wore in defiance of Navy regulations; his long, arched feet extended over the end of the bunk. Above him McCampbell sat cross-legged with a pillow behind his back and an aerology manual in his lap. The opposite bunks, which belonged to Roska and to a lean, agate-eyed Southerner named Dixon Kerdolph, were empty. Roska, Kerdolph, and five other cadets were gambling.

"You people are on report," said Horne. "Go down and sign the pap sheet."

"Shut up your mouth and close that door. And fix that blanket how we had it," Kerdolph said.

"I'll fix more than the blanket," said Horne.

"You ain't going to fix nobody, Mister. You want in this game, you're welcome. You don't, that's all right too. Make up your mind."

Horne stepped forward with his fists clenched and Melvin shouted at him, "Oh, for Christ's sake!" Horne was astonished by this; he looked at Melvin doubtfully, and then dropped to his knees to stuff the blanket against the door.

Some time later McCampbell, who had been studying quietly, said, "Do any of you remember Peter Tajitos at Barin?"

Melvin said he did, and added, "Why? What's his problem? One of the WAVEs overdue?"

"A friend of mine who's still at Barin telephoned this morning to tell me Tajitos hit the water tank last night."

"Was he killed?"

163

"Was he killed?" Horne echoed. "Of course he was killed! Roll the dice."

"I didn't know him too well," Melvin said. He felt dismayed and shocked by the news. They had been in the same company, although in different platoons, at the pre-flight school in Georgia, but Tajitos had caught pneumonia on the survival hike and had been left behind when the company was ordered to Memphis. Melvin straightened up and slowly shook his head and discovered, then, to his amazement, that he was not in McCampbell's room; he was in the lounge. How he had gotten there he had no idea. He was leaning against the cigarette machine with a packet of matches in one hand as though he had been about to smoke. It was dark outdoors. He vaguely remembered getting up from his knees and saying something to everybody who was looking at him, but that was all he could recall.

Thoughtfully he walked along the corridor and sat on the edge of his bunk. In a little while Horne came striding into the room and stopped, somewhat startled.

"What the hell are you sitting in the dark for?" he demanded cheerfully and switched on the lamp. He peeled a five-dollar bill from a thick roll in his hand and tucked it into Melvin's cap. Then he seated himself at the desk, licked his thumb importantly, and began to count the money.

Melvin took the bill from his cap and said with no interest, "I guess I must have won."

"No, you lost the same as usual. You were going great, but you lost."

"Then what's this five dollars for?"

"Go buy us some Scotch Tape. We're always running out. I don't know what we do with it all." Horne counted the money again, his chapped lips moving laboriously. His expression darkened. He counted it a third time with extreme care. After he finished he clasped his hands behind his head and said with no emotion, "Can you feature that? Can you imagine a thing like that?"

"What's the trouble?"

"Some friends!" said Horne. "Some friends! I'm telling you!"

"Who in particular?"

Horne went on as though he had not heard. "In all fairness, I ask you, did you ever in your entire life hear of anything like this? I ask you. Just what type of person do we associate with? It makes me sick. These are the people we fly with. We entrust our lives every day to this sort of person."

"What happened?"

"What happened?" said Horne. "I've been short-changed, that's all. Just simply swindled."

Melvin could not help feeling rather pleased. "Who did it?"

"Who would it be? Cole, naturally. He woke up after you left and wanted in the game."

"It's your own fault. You know you've got to watch him."

"I cashed a check for him, see? I mean I had already cleaned him out of all the cash he had, and did that make me happy! Well, so he wanted a receipt for his check. I don't know why, but being a nice fellow I said all right. So I was writing out this receipt, see, when he asked if I would take the twenty back and give him two tens—or, no, he said two fives and—well, anyway, I said sure. So then he said—"

"I get the idea. The point is, you were had."

"I can't understand it. Both of us counted the money. Well, by God, I'll fix his wagon. I'll get even and more."

"No, you won't. You'll never catch up with him."

"Oh, no? And why not?"

"Because he's too clever to suppose he's tricked you, even if you never mention it."

Horne appeared to be thinking about this. "When I first met the guy I thought he was wonderful. I could tell he was smart, and he had good looks and his old man's got dough, from what I hear. I thought to myself, I can use this guy. He'd understand me. So how wrong can I be?" The longer he considered this, the more it irritated him. He swore and slapped the desk.

"I know what you mean," Melvin said. "I could hardly believe it when I discovered that after flying with Teitlebaum for two months he didn't even know our names."

"He knew us."

"Not very well. That's what I couldn't believe. He knew our faces but he had to fumble for the names. I was sort of startled when I realized it. I'd supposed we meant more to him than that."

"What'd you expect—a dinner invitation? You think you're in college somewhere," Horne persisted, "where you go beer drinking with the professor after class? We're at war, something you seem to forget! Sure, we're nothing but faces, and names for a little while. Teitlebaum's got another bunch right now. He's taking them through the gunnery syllabus and in a couple more months they'll be gone the same way we're gone, and he'll never see us again any more than we should ever expect to see him again. And we won't see Monk again, either," he remarked with obvious satisfaction. "That's the way the system is set up and it couldn't operate on any other basis."

"Maybe you're right. I don't know."

"Of course I'm right." Horne stretched and yawned, and having nothing to do at the moment he picked up the book of nudes, licked his finger with a debonair expression, and began to turn through it.

"Who's this Caravaggio you mentioned?"

"Who? Oh, just some lieutenant."

"Well," said Melvin after a pause, "what did he want?"

"Frankly, I don't know," said Horne. "I just don't know."

"Did he come here to see me?"

"Yuh."

"What did he want to see me for?"

"I already told you, I don't know!"

"Well, I was just wondering," said Melvin. "Am I supposed to go see him?"

"I would, if I were you."

"Is he the chaplain?"

"Nope, he's line. He had a star on his sleeve. Ostrowski says he's the one who recommends changes in the duty orders if you don't seem fitted for what they assign you. I think we're supposed to have an interview with him before we go back to Mainside. He's supposed to find out if we've flipped. Personally, I don't think any man living could go through this program and not flip."

"It's odd he'd come over to the barracks. I wonder why he wanted to see me."

"For the last time, I don't know. The man came by. He asked for Cadet Isaacs. I told him you weren't home."

"If he can pull strings he should be worth meeting. I want to make sure I get a Corsair. I guess for two years now I've been waiting for the day when I could fly one of those."

"When my interview comes," Horne said, placing a hand over his heart, "I shall register a complaint in regard to the slop they serve for food. When I think back, I just don't know what to say!"

"What good will it do us now?"

"This is not for myself. I am deeply concerned about the welfare of the youth of America who happen to be following us through this crappy program."

Melvin threw a pillow at him; it struck the gooseneck lamp, which again crashed into the wastebasket. Horne picked up the lamp, straightened the neck, and twisted the cowl around before replacing it on the desk. Someone who preceded them in the room had painted a purple heart on the base of it. The lamp stood there in an attitude of weary patience, the cowl drooping as though exhausted by all the bickering.

On the wall not far above the lamp was a framed copy of the Navy flyer's creed, which Horne had clipped from a service magazine and framed and carried along from one field to the next. The pillow having knocked it askew, he straightened it. More and more often as the time of graduation approached he would lean back in his chair to contemplate this creed.

Covering the top half of the page was a picture of a pilot in summer flight gear: he stood on a wing and gazed resolutely forward. A propeller blade was visible, as well as a section of engine, while the Pitot tube was silhouetted like a lance against the cloudless sky. It was a dignified, inspirational photograph. The text below it was equally keen:

I am a United States Navy flyer.
My countrymen built the best airplane in the world and entrusted it to me. They trained me to fly it. I will use it to the absolute limit of my power.
With my fellow pilots, air crews, and deck crews, my plane and I will do anything necessary to carry out our tremendous responsibilities. I will always remember we are a part of an unbeatable combat team—the United States Navy.

When the going is fast and rough, I will not falter. I will be uncompromising in every blow I strike. I will be humble in victory.

I am a United States Navy flyer. I have dedicated myself to my country, with its many millions of all races, colors, and creeds. They and their way of life are worthy of my greatest protective effort.

I ask the help of God in making that effort great enough.

Melvin, too, frequently studied this creed. Again and again he read the concluding line; it reminded him of the inscription GOTT MIT UNS which he had seen on a German medal in a trophy case at the Liberty Memorial in Kansas City. It seemed the Lord was readily available.

Many copies of the magazine in which the creed appeared had been made available to the cadets. Melvin had sent one to his father, with the comment that he was enclosing a bit of propaganda. He suspected his father would not care for this remark, and waited with some curiosity to see if there would be a response. Very soon the answer came. His father wrote, "Is this a joke? Your sense of humor is misplaced. Is there something about the war that amuses you? Frankly, all of us at home thank God for the sentiment so wonderfully expressed in your creed. I'm enclosing a clipping regarding a speech made by your grandfather more than a quarter of a century ago. . . ."

Melvin had read the old clipping several times since it arrived; now he handed it across the desk to Horne, who was chewing a cigar and staring out the window with a look of boredom.

"This might interest you. My father sent it."

"You get ten times as much mail as I do," Horne said bitterly. He tilted back in the chair, put his feet on the desk, and unfolded the clipping.

LEXINGTON MAN IN ST. JOSEPH SCORES ROOSEVELT

Judge D. W. Isaacs Declares This Sedition Within America Is Costing Millions in Treasure and Blood of Countless Men.

St. Joseph, Mo., Jan. 25—David W. Isaacs, president of the Casque and Gauntlet

Club of Lexington, Mo., in a speech before members of the St. Joseph auxiliary
yesterday, mercilessly flayed ex-President
Theodore Roosevelt and those papers
which print his effusions, as well as other
critics of the government. He said in part:

"I care not whether the man who criti-
cizes be the pacifist, slacker, Congressman, a United States Senator, a newspaper, or an ex-President, the attacks being
made upon America from within our own
country are treason: nothing short of
that.

"And this sedition within America is
costing the United States and its allies
millions of dollars in treasure and the
blood of countless men of its citizenry.

"What sort of talk is being scattered
broadcast behind the German lines, in
Russia, in Italy and Roumania to make
the people of those countries believe that
there is dissension right here? God help
us if that sort of talk is not stopped in a
summary way.

"Constructive criticism of anything is
proper, but destructive criticism has no
place in our lives and should not be toler-
ated. It is our duty to stand behind the
government and the administration."

The address was one of the most scath-
ing and remarkable delivered in this city
since the outbreak of the war and was
accorded a standing ovation.

"As a matter of fact, that *is* interesting. It's very interesting,"
Horne remarked. "I didn't know they had the same problem in
those days."

"What problem?"

"People criticizing the war effort. They were in a war up to
their necks and—well, here, your grandfather says it—about sedition and treason. It's just like today."

"That's what my father thinks. Practically every time I hear
from him he's got something to say about espionage or subversion.
He acts like he was on the Un-American Activities Committee."
Melvin noticed that Horne was looking at him deliberately, quite

169

strangely. Feeling a little repelled by the strenuous events of the day, confused and discouraged and bruised from the fight, he held his head in his hands. He had begun to feel that some decision was required of him, but he had no idea what he was expected to decide. He rubbed his face with a distraught, anxious movement, and said, "You seem different lately."

Sam Horne gave a harsh laugh. "You're the one who's changing. Not me."

13

★

The next morning a few minutes before noon Sam Horne had his first accident. The brakes of a Dauntless locked while he was landing. The tail rose high in the air, the engine smashed into the runway with a grinding, searing noise, and for a few seconds it looked as though the momentum of landing would carry the tail over the top. This would have crushed him underneath the wreck. But the SBD did not quite tip over; it hovered in a vertical position and then rocked backward. The three propeller blades were twisted and the landing gear was bent, and the fuselage of the airplane sustained a certain amount of damage. Horne remained in the cockpit completely motionless until the crash trucks were halfway across the field; then, as if he had been sitting on a catapult, he was out and running away from the smoking hulk.

Melvin was at the hangar when Horne came riding across the field on a crash truck, gesturing wildly and insisting he was perfectly all right, and managed to talk with him a moment before he was taken to the hospital for a check-up. Melvin knew, though Horne would not admit, that if there had been less wind he probably would have been killed, for he then would have been traveling fast enough to turn over. The strong wind had diminished his ground speed. That he emerged from the accident alive and in relatively good condition had nothing to do, therefore, with skill. Horne had been extremely lucky, that was all.

So absorbed was Melvin in the contemplation of this that he ignored an officer who was passing by.

"Oh-*ho!*" piped a reedy voice.

He looked around in stupefaction, and there was Ensign Monk. He could not imagine what the repulsive little ensign was doing at Saufley, yet there he stood, with his paunch thrust out and his clammy hands clasped behind his back, obviously delighted at the opportunity to put Melvin on report again.

It had been quite a while since Melvin had been given extra duty, but he found that this time he did not mind the punishment; he had four hours all to himself, four hours in which to think. He marched up and down in front of the barracks with a wooden rifle on his shoulder and nobody spoke to him. It was as though he did not exist. He thought of Lieutenant Caravaggio, wondering what the officer had wanted. It was curious that an officer would come to see a cadet. Ordinarily, no matter what sort of business it might be, the cadet simply received an order to report to the officer at a certain time. But this officer, evidently, had left no such order. The longer Melvin considered this, the more irritated he became.

When the tour of duty ended he returned the rifle to the rack and walked across the station to the administration building. There he asked where he might find Lieutenant Caravaggio. He was directed to the lieutenant's office and found the door half open. Thinking Caravaggio might have stepped out for a moment, Melvin hesitated, took off his garrison cap, and then suddenly thrust his head into the office. The lieutenant had not stepped out; he was seated in a swivel chair at his desk with his hands folded and was leaning forward peering at the door, as though he had heard or sensed someone just outside.

"Now, who on earth are you?" the officer said.

Melvin came to attention and replied, "Aviation Cadet Isaacs, sir."

Caravaggio tipped back in the chair. With a doubtful expression he began to finger his lower lip.

"Very well, then," he murmured, "you may come in. Close

the door softly and have a seat, my good man." Melvin did as he was told, though he was already beginning to regret the visit. Caravaggio was looking him up and down.

"Let's have a cigarette," the lieutenant said. He had been swiveling from side to side with his feet off the ground so that the chair spun around almost in a complete circle, and as he rode past an open drawer of the desk he reached in deftly and snatched out a package of English cigarettes wrapped in gold foil. He tossed them in the air and caught them awkwardly, clutching at them with his fingers, like a woman, instead of catching them in his palm.

"No, thank you, sir," Melvin answered.

"Oh, come on now. Be friends."

Melvin shrugged. "Okay. I'll have one."

"I'm happy you stopped by," Caravaggio said, pushing the cigarettes, and then some matches, across the desk with the end of a ruler.

"Now," he went on, blowing a stiff cone of grayish lavender smoke, "what can I do for you, young man?"

"I thought you wanted to see me," Melvin said. He took a puff on his cigarette and gagged.

"I? I wanted to see *you?* What did you say your name was?"

Melvin got up and put on his cap. "I'm sorry, sir. Somebody's been playing a joke on me."

"Oh, sit down! Stop acting ridiculous. Really, Isaacs, come along now. Sit!"

"Is that an order?"

"Doesn't it sound like one?"

"Not like most of them, sir."

"You're implying I'm a poor officer. I could have your scalp, young man."

"I wasn't implying anything, sir. I only said—"

"Well, you're absolutely right. I'm a wretched officer. Will you please sit down? You're making me nervous standing there. What brought you here, Isaacs?"

"You stopped by the barracks, isn't that right? All right, they said you wanted to see me. So here I am."

"Did I leave word for you to report to me?"

Melvin looked around the office a little desperately. The perfumed smoke had begun to make him ill, and for some obscure reason he could imagine Caravaggio reclining voluptuously on a divan to the sound of flutes and tambourines.

"I don't know what this is all about," he began. "I guess it's probably my fault again."

"Nonsense, Isaacs, how could it be your fault? You've never done anything wrong."

"Listen, do you want to see me or not?" Melvin demanded, amazed by his own temerity. He had a premonition that he was about to reach across the desk and give the lieutenant a slap on the mouth. This thought was repugnant and fascinating; he pressed forward, biting his lip to keep from sneering or bursting into laughter. "Why did you stop by my barracks?" he demanded, choking with contempt.

"But, Isaacs, those aren't your barracks."

"Okay, okay, you know what I mean."

"You're the most insolent cadet I ever saw. Upon my soul!"

"How did you hear about me?" Melvin continued. He placed both elbows on the desk and stared at the lieutenant with aversion.

"What makes you think I heard about you? What a terribly odd thing to say! Really, Isaacs, you're quite odd."

Melvin straightened up with a confused and obsequious smile; he had been absolutely convinced that the lieutenant was intimidated, and yet the tone of Caravaggio's voice altered so subtly, with such a menacing undertone, that he did not know quite what to do.

"On your feet, Isaacs! Hop-hop! Snap to! Atten-*shun!* My, you look nice," he went on when Melvin stood in front of him with shoulders braced. "By the way, my boy, I did see you— ah, could it have been three weeks ago?—at the beach, where you were shining your wings in the sand. Did you shine them too industriously, Isaacs? Did you wear away the gold plate? What was underneath? Pray tell."

"Is that all, sir?" Melvin asked. "Am I dismissed?"

"Certainly not! You young monster. At ease. Sit down. Goodness."

"Look, I'm sorry."

"If there is one thing which infuriates me, it is an apology. Never recant, Isaacs. Never. Why do you suppose I wanted to

173

meet you? Be a man, for the love of heaven. We can destroy you, there's no disgrace, but don't be a twig." He took a pair of smoked glasses from his desk and slipped them on, his mouth fixed in a prim line. "I intend to be stern. You need expect no quarter from me."

"Why *did* you want to meet me?"

"You're dreadfully green. I'm almost afraid to bend you. But listen to me now. Is it true, Isaacs? Is it true?"

"Is what true, sir?"

"Oh, it couldn't be. Not even you! Now, do quit."

"Sir?"

"I'm warning you, Isaacs. I'm a dangerous man. Don't trifle with me or you'll regret it. Tell me, why did you shoot that Marine?"

"You mean Captain Teitlebaum? You heard about that?"

"Oh, my!" exclaimed Caravaggio, throwing up his hands. "Everybody has heard about it."

"Now listen, it was like this," Melvin said in a resigned but determined voice. He had told the story dozens of times without being able to convince anyone that he had simply missed the target. "So you see, Mr. Caravaggio," he concluded, "it really didn't amount to anything at all, just a couple of little bullet holes in the wing."

"Oh."

"Listen," Melvin went on patiently, for there had been an infinite amount of sarcasm and disbelief in the lieutenant's tone, "it was an accident, I tell you."

"Are you able to prove it?"

"I don't have to prove it."

"And that, my boy, is where you are wrong. You're in a very bad spot, I don't mind telling you. Your dossier fascinates me."

"My *what?*"

"Why do you look so astonished? Don't you realize that your government takes a personal interest in you? It wants to know not only what you do, but what you have said and what you believe." He formed a steeple of his fingers and began singing, half aloud, with a crooked smile, from the Navy hymn: "E-*ter*-nal Father, strong to *sa*-ave, Whose *arm* doth bind the rest-less *wa*-ave," but then, after humming along and rocking in the chair, he nodded, as if in confirmation of something he had suspected, and sang the conclusion in globular bass tones: "O hear us when we cry to thee, For those in *per*-il on the sea!"

Some SBD's were landing; a glass of water on Caravaggio's desk was trembling from the vibration of the engines; he watched it for a while and then picked up the ruler and tapped the glass smartly. "The wind must have changed," he said. "Isaacs? Oh, Isaacs?" he whispered.

"Sir?" Melvin had been scowling at the floor and twisting his garrison cap.

"You're perspiring."

"I have a right to," he said, not looking up. He was frightened, although he did not know why. The only thing he was positive of was that Caravaggio was mocking him, taunting him.

"Goodness," he heard the lieutenant murmur, "what a volatile young man. I'm afraid to strike a match." At this Melvin looked up with such an expression of hatred that Caravaggio swiveled around in the chair and laughed. "Nothing but a little joke, Isaacs." With a sultry smile he continued, "For some reason I make people nervous. Now tell me, how many more flights do we have?"

Melvin held up one finger, afraid to rely on his voice.

"Well, imagine! Our final flight. When are we scheduled? Tomorrow. We know all about each other. And then we'll be finished. Won't that be a relief? No more check rides, no more ground school."

Melvin gave a brief nod and sat on his hands because he was afraid that he was losing control of himself and might lunge over the desk. He heard the SBD's, thudding and coughing, fly lower and lower; they were landing not far from the building; he could hear a screech as each one touched down on the runway.

"Tell me, Isaacs, was this a difficult program? Truthfully now, you young treasure."

Melvin took a deep breath; he felt shaken and exhausted and wondered if he was going insane. He wiped the perspiration from his face.

"Do I have permission to put it in my own words?"

Caravaggio, with a skeptical air, nodded.

"Sir, this program," Melvin said, gazing with blunt hostility at

175

the doubtful lieutenant, "to be perfectly honest about it, is a twenty-one jewel self-winding son of a bitch."

"*Ex*-cellent! Oh, how *marvelous*, Isaacs! I'm proud of you. That is exactly what the program was intended to be. The Navy has no use for half-baked aviators. We're quite proud of our men who wear the wings. We like to think they're the finest. Now tell me—the men who have gone through training with you. Are they good?"

"Some of them are fairly hot, sir. Sam Horne is good."

Caravaggio looked disappointed. "But he's such a weather-cock, Isaacs. How can you abide him? Why, the moment I laid eyes on that young man I knew all about him. You shouldn't trust him."

"No, you're wrong," Melvin said, stubbornly shaking his head.

"Wait and see. La-dee-da! Wait and see, my boy. Oh! Here, I have a gift for you." He held out a miniature enameled American flag, which Melvin accepted.

"I know him, Mr. Caravaggio. You're absolutely wrong."

"Proceed," the lieutenant said, and he sighed with a limp, airy wave as he rocked back in the big chair. "Someone else. That gnome whose uniform simply does not fit one iota. Surely they must have something in his size."

"Oh, McCampbell, you mean. Actually—now you mention it —his uniforms don't fit, do they? I mean, they do sort of bog and draggle. But he looks better in his blues."

"You tell McCampbell to get acquainted with his uniform before I scalp him."

"Okay, sir, I'll tell him. He's one of the best flyers I ever saw. He's better than some of the instructors."

"Quit! That's utter rubbish. Tell me something else. No more of this 'I swear it was an accident' claptrap, I warn you. Speak to me honestly or you'll regret it as long as you live."

"All right," Melvin said. "What do you want to know?"

"Why in the name of sense did you offer a drink of gin to the guard at the entrance to Barin Field?"

"Oh, what's the use?" Melvin asked gloomily. "No matter what I do, somebody always has to distort it."

Caravaggio grimaced. "But that's absurd!"

"Well, you heard me," Melvin remarked. He had noticed soon

after coming into the office that the lieutenant had a distinct musky odor, like a fox or an unhealthy house dog, and this odor disturbed him; it occurred to him that he had never met anyone quite so insignificant and loathsome as this officer; and all at once he became positive that Teitlebaum had come to Saufley Field to talk to Caravaggio.

"Captain Teitlebaum was here recently, wasn't he?"

Caravaggio appeared to be confounded. "What? What?"

"And he talked to you, didn't he?" Melvin persisted, looking at the officer with disgust. "He did, didn't he? He came over here and told you what we talked about in the hangar after that bombing run."

"My dear boy," Caravaggio said uneasily. "I despise Marines and I haven't the—"

"Oh, shut up! Don't lie to me! I've been lied to for so long I don't know what I'm talking about."

"Mr. Isaacs, please remember that you are nothing but a—" Then Caravaggio stopped with his lips parted, gazing at Melvin, who had leaped to his feet. Melvin, noting the consternation on the officer's face, was enormously gratified; still he was intent on learning exactly what the captain had said.

"Now stop that!" Caravaggio whined, gesturing, and Melvin realized that he had been nervously twisting his identification bracelet. He had bought the bracelet only a few days before, a link silver chain with a pair of miniature gold wings soldered to the centerpiece, and it felt heavily strange on his wrist.

"Mr. Teitlebaum has received a promotion. He is now a major."

"Is that so," Melvin said.

"I understand you don't like to fly after dark. Is *that* so?"

"Well, yes. But how did you know that?"

Caravaggio smirked. "Don't you have the sensation of an abyss somewhere beneath you? Do you descend into that stygian limbo with perspiration trickling down your face? Isn't the fleece lining of your helmet a bit clammy, my lad? Oh, yes— *He! He! He!*" Caravaggio laughed, but then stopped with a look of distress, as though something had made a tremendous impression on him.

Melvin looked at him in stupefaction, convinced the lieutenant was insane and that he was not a naval officer but an impostor who had managed to escape from an asylum and steal a uniform.

"Umm . . . my son did this," he went on, tapping the ruler against the rump of a crudely formed ceramic animal which resembled a hippopotamus. It was glazed a brilliant blue and he had been boosting it around with the ruler and a pencil. "Posh, I'm exhausted! Utterly and simply exhausted. But wasn't it a grand day!" he continued, and taking off the dark glasses he twirled them with a look of idle good humor. "Well, now, let me think. Where were we? Oh, yes! Yes. Well, Mr. Isaacs, Mr. Ancient Pistol, you're just the type our Navy needs. You're made to order for this life, so admit it. Don't be ashamed. Admit that you enjoy taking orders from a superior." He began to amuse himself with a box of paper clips, pushing it back and forth while he hummed the Navy hymn, and Melvin, staring at him, could not think of anything to say.

"Now stop!" Caravaggio said. The plaintive lilt of his voice did not match the groping intelligence in his face. He suddenly tossed the paper clips in the air, but missed catching them; in fact, although he extended one hand as if meaning to catch them, he made no attempt to do so. The box dropped to the floor and the clips sprinkled everywhere with a variety of interesting little sounds. He bent down behind the desk to gather the clips. The swivel chair seemed to be moving by itself. The officer's face appeared above the level of the desk, gorged with blood, round as an olive. They looked at each other.

"Did you get it?" Melvin asked.

Caravaggio held up the box.

"Isaacs, it was you, wasn't it, who hung a Nazi flag out the barracks window? You might as well admit it, because I have inside information that you did it."

"I didn't do it."

"Yes, you did. I know you did."

"No, sir, I didn't do that."

"Hmm," Caravaggio said, fingering his lip and closing his eyes. "But the flag fits in so perfectly. Well, then, who did it?"

"I don't know."

"Can you prove your innocence?"

"I don't have to."

"Wrong again, Isaacs. Consider the evidence. First: your flight record is blotched like a Rorschach. Second: whether it was accidental or not, you did open fire on Major Teitlebaum. Third: you were caught red-handed attempting to smuggle whisky into a United States Naval Air Station. Fourth: you had an extraordinary number of telephone conversations at NAS Memphis with an unidentified woman while two of the Navy's newest interceptors were being overhauled on that station. Why so amazed, my boy? Don't tell me you didn't know. Fifth: your navigation instructor at Albuquerque has made an allegation, the substance of which is that when under a condition of stress, the stress of extreme concentration, for example, you have been observed to draw a swastika. Several of your navigation examinations had a meticulous row of swastikas along the margin, despite the fact that you had attempted to erase them. Sixth: upon arrival at— Shall I continue? Isaacs, are you listening? It would not be difficult to interpret your actions as those of an unstable personality. You have no idea what can happen to the truth when it falls into the hands of the unscrupulous. However, that is neither hither nor yon; I am endeavoring to point out in the most elementary terms that your officer aptitude is low. Very, very low. Is it illogical to assume that you were the one who hung a Nazi flag from the barracks window?"

"No, I guess not."

Caravaggio folded his hands in satisfaction. "I am waiting for you to confess."

"I can't confess, because I didn't do it."

"I'm perfectly aware you didn't, you goose. I'm trying to teach you a few things. You're utterly defenseless. What's going to become of you? How long was that flag hanging out the window before anyone noticed?"

"Before the cadets noticed it?"

"They knew about it right away, I imagine."

"Yes, sir. You mean the officers, I guess."

"Yes. How long was that Nazi banner flying on the station before an officer saw it?"

"Oh, I don't remember exactly," Melvin said. "I guess it was about a week."

"Where on earth did it come from?"

"Somebody's brother in Europe sent it to one of the guys in another barracks. At least that's what I heard."

"This is bizarre. Really, do you know what I mean?"

"We all thought it was sort of bizarre, sir. We wondered how long it would take an officer to discover it, but I guess they were thinking about more important things. That could be the reason. Then, too, the officers usually look at the ground when they march us somewhere. I don't know why."

"Yes, I've noticed that, too," Caravaggio murmured, lifting his head. "Well, thank you for volunteering some information. I couldn't have endured it if you'd been smart with me about that flag."

"You're welcome, sir. I don't want to hurt anybody."

"You hurt more people than you think. Did the enlisted men know about it? I suppose they did."

"Yes, sir. They knew."

"Hmm! Are you a coward?"

"I don't know, sir."

"Come now. You must know."

Melvin shook his head stubbornly. "All I know is I'm not too keen about fighting. Maybe because I usually lose."

"What about this liberty-or-death business?"

"What do you mean?"

"So much tripe, isn't it? Very odd. Yes, indeed. Consider. If it were true that men preferred death to the loss of their liberty, would you be good enough to explain to me why our prisons are not replete with suicides? Various patriots sing various songs; isn't it queer how the tenor rings flat to the sensitive ear? All the same," he went on, touching his eyebrows, "we must continue with our war. Once more unto the breach, dear friends, once more. In peace there's nothing so becomes a man as modest stillness and humility, but when the blast of war blows in our ears, then imitate the action of the tiger: stiffen the sinews, summon up the blood, disguise fair nature with hard-favored rage; then lend the eye a terrible aspect: let it cry through the portage of the head like the brass cannon; let the brow o'erwhelm it as fearfully as doth a gallèd rock o'erhang and jutty his confounded base, swilled with the wild and wasteful ocean. Now set the teeth and stretch the nostril wide, hold hard the breath and bend up every spirit to his full height! So we can't simply quit, do you understand?"

All at once Melvin felt on the verge of an important discovery. "What do you want?" he asked, trembling with fright, and saw the lieutenant start back in surprise and look at him acutely. "What are you trying to make me say?" Melvin demanded and pressed forward. He did not know what to say next or what to do.

Caravaggio had recovered himself; he sighed, and resumed swiveling and picking at the gold stripes on his sleeve. He had plucked loose a corner of the upper stripe and when he was engrossed in speaking or thinking his fingers would stray toward this corner as though to verify what he had done.

"I'm quitting," Melvin said with absolute composure. Then he sat down, wondering what had come over him. "Have you got some forms for me to fill out?" he asked uncertainly.

"But, Isaacs, weren't you listening?" Caravaggio asked, leaning forward and delicately clasping his hands. "Not one moment ago I explained why you can *not* quit. It's *impossible*. It isn't being done."

"Maybe so," Melvin said, laughing. "I'm not arguing. Just hand me whatever forms are necessary."

Caravaggio sprang to his feet and went striding toward a large map on the wall. Melvin noticed that he walked in a highly military fashion, with his shoulders back and his paunch withdrawn. He picked up a long wooden pointer, and after tapping it against the floor he cleared his throat and began to trace the front lines of the American defense in the Pacific.

"Isaacs, when you enlisted we were in a desperate situation. The Japanese were advancing on virtually every front. We had been pushed entirely out of the strategic Philippines. Wake Island had fallen to a fanatical enemy. You know about these things, I'm certain. Let me put it this way: in the old days when a captain needed men for his ship he dispatched his crew with orders to recruit men from the streets, by force if necessary—with clubs, gunny sacks, Lord knows what all. And unfortunately, Isaacs, the United States Navy found itself in a similar circumstance. We needed you. Desperately, believe me. And we still need you, quite desperately. Never doubt for a moment that the Navy is proud of you. You have one more flight, Isaacs, after which you will have successfully concluded the most rigorous training program ever devised. You will have come through it with flying colors. Your difficult, somewhat sophormoric moments will be forgotten, I assure you. Thereafter you will be known as Ensign Mel Isaacs of the United States Naval Air Corps. Do you have any comprehension of what that means? You should! A glorious tradition surrounds you. The hands of the past rise to salute you —*Ensign* Isaacs! Ta-tum-te-*tum!* I see the hand of Captain Kenneth Whiting, USN. Commander Theodore G. Ellyson. Lieutenant Louis T. Barin. Lieutenant, junior grade, Richard C. Saufley. These are among the greatest names in United States Naval Aviation, my boy."

"I know they are."

"And you want your friend Horne to be proud of you, don't you?"

"Yes. But that's up to him."

"You're not responding to this," said Caravaggio. He frowned. "Well, Isaacs," he said in a slightly modulated tone, "I am not supposed to reveal this, but I will, because you have been honest and straightforward with me. Now pay attention: your orders have arrived. What do you think of that? Shall I tell you your assignment?"

Melvin hesitated. He swallowed and passed a hand over his head. "No. It doesn't make any difference. I'm through."

Caravaggio had been looking at him deeply, squeezing his protruding, purplish lips. Now he dropped his hand and turned away, saying, "Has the wind shifted again?"

Melvin listened to the distant coughing of the engines.

"Yes, sir. They're landing north by northwest."

"Isn't that the dangerous runway?"

"Well," Melvin began speculatively, "if you've got your head stuck up your—"

"Yes! Yes!" Caravaggio interrupted. "That'll do, Isaacs. Now what was it you wanted to fly? I have your preference somewhere in here." He pulled open a drawer and looked with distaste at the mass of papers.

"An F4U."

"Well, what on earth—oh! I know. The F4U is that charming Brunswick blue machine that resembles a seagull. Yes. My, you have good taste. The F4U is grand."

182

"It's a good-looking plane," Melvin admitted. "I wanted to fly one from a carrier."

Caravaggio appeared to be shocked. "Are you insane? Have you ever been aboard a carrier? Of course you haven't. But I have, and I can promise you you wouldn't like it a bit. I became ill."

"I was planning to request night fighter duty."

"But *why?*"

Caravaggio was posturing again. Melvin could feel, nevertheless, the merciless thrust of someone else behind the mask.

"I couldn't think of anything more dangerous."

Caravaggio gazed at him in stupefaction, momentarily confronted, as though they had come upon each other unexpectedly after wandering through a labyrinth of mirrors.

"Would you mind running through that again?" he asked.

So Melvin explained why he had chosen the most dangerous service he could imagine—piloting a night-fighting Corsair from a carrier. "You see, sir," he concluded after several minutes of trying to clarify it, "even when there was no enemy it would still be frightening, so that way I could test myself."

Caravaggio looked deliberately into his eyes, and asked, very slowly, "Are you trying to tell me that was what motivated you to enlist as a naval aviation cadet?"

Melvin grinned and nodded. He had lived with the idea for so long that it seemed quite normal and reasonable to him; he was puzzled by the consternation on the lieutenant's face.

"Isaacs, by my immortal soul, it's conceivable that you actually are mad," said Caravaggio, gliding away through the mirrors. "Well!" he paused, squeezing his lip and frowning. "Where are we now? Really, Isaacs, I could skin you."

"That Teitlebaum," Melvin said, "he isn't afraid of anything. He sure is one tough egg."

"Now listen, my dear child," Caravaggio said hastily, "you and I are surrounded by tough eggs. Naval and Marine pilots are merciless, expert killers. They are blasting the Japanese Air Force out of the sky and they are enjoying the work immensely. Your friend Teitlebaum is not a man; he is an executioner. He has come down to us from the Dark Ages. Furthermore, you live in a barracks filled with his apprentices. Your dear companion Horne is a perfect example. Now, let me see. Ah—hmm! Well, Isaacs, I'm sorry but you can't have it. But here is what I *will* do for you: I'll give you the best assignment of all. How would you like to be a primary instructor? Only four men in your entire graduating class drew that. It's positively the juiciest thing we offer. I'll give you one of those four positions. You spend perhaps two months at the instructors' school in New Orleans, and then you teach cadets to fly the Yellow Peril. It's marvelous! You don't know what sort of life a primary instructor leads. This will interest you. He goes up for two or three hours a day and rides around in the back seat of a Stearman looking down at the scenery. He shouts through the gosport tube, 'Keep your goddamn nose up!' or, 'What the hell are you trying to do? Kill us both?' And then he comes down and he eats a lovely dinner of lamb at the BOQ and catches the bus to town. That's what he does! Now how would you like that?" He tilted back, pulling at his hairy fingers one after another until the knuckles cracked, and studied the untidy desk as he rode around in the chair. All at once he unbuttoned his coat and began patting himself rhythmically on the belly.

"Our Navy needs you. In nineteen forty-one we suffered appalling casualties. We found ourselves in a most hazardous situation. To this call the youth of America gallantly responded. You are one of these brave youths. The grateful people of the United States will not ever forget what you did here, you and the others. I don't suppose they'll ever forget. Maybe they will. Oh, of course they will! Why should I try to deceive you?"

He brought his chair forward and stood up. There was not a sign of recognition on his sulky face. "Everybody has troubles. I wish I could do something, but unfortunately I can't. Why should I feel sorry for you? Do you feel sorry for me? Of course not. You don't even like me. Go on, get out. I'm unusually busy right now and I can't help you about that resignation claptrap." He pretended to study his wrist watch.

Melvin stood up and opened his mouth to speak.

"*What!*" Caravaggio shouted, placing his hands on his plump hips. "What did you say to me? You're a cadet, so get out of here!" He hurried to the map on the wall, where he stood with his head going busily up and down to prove he was searching for something, but when Melvin did not leave the room he suddenly shrugged out of his coat, came around the desk with deceptive speed, and flung the coat over Melvin's shoulders. His officer's hat lay on top of a filing cabinet; he grabbed the hat and jammed it on Melvin's head. "Magnificent," he murmured, stepping backward with clasped hands. "Take it. Take it! It's all I have in the world."

Melvin laid the coat across the desk. The hat gave him some trouble, but finally he managed to pull it off and placed it on the coat.

"Oh, cut that out," Caravaggio was saying. "If you ask me one more time for the forms to fill out, do you know what I'll do? I'll give them to you. You wouldn't like that. You came here for sympathy. I know your type. You wouldn't like being a sailor. Bell *bott*-om trousers and coats o' *Na*-vy blue! You'll climb the *rig*-ging like your *dad*-dy used to do! Not you, Isaacs. You're like me. You want the best. Anyway, that's how it goes, young man. You cadets are all alike. Because a man has a stripe or so, you're positive he can be duped. I could tell you a few things, but never mind." He blew through his lips with a weak, popping noise and collapsed into the creaking chair. He shuffled through a stack of papers on the desk and muttered, "The fun's over." Then, with a sigh, he dropped the papers and relapsed into a gloomy silence, twisting a gold thread that dangled from his sleeve.

Melvin gazed at him for a little while and then stumbled out of the room. He felt weak and sick. He thought he heard Caravaggio call to him as he walked along the corridor, but he did not stop. He could not understand what had happened, and when he emerged from the building it was as though he had wakened from a ridiculous but terrifying dream. I've thrown everything away, he said to himself; he knew this was true, but he could not explain why he had done it. It was as if he had been hypnotized, or drugged.

While he was crossing the station he saw two mechanics at work on an engine, and it occurred to him that before long he might be doing similar work. Hesitantly he wandered a little closer, studying their faded blue dungarees, the skivvy shirts, and the white caps perched on their heads. One mechanic was straddling the cowl while his partner was kneeling on the wing handing him tools.

"How's it going?" Melvin inquired.

The mechanics glanced at each other. Neither of them spoke. He understood that they regarded him as an officer; they assumed that in a few days, a week or so at most, he would be commissioned. Consequently they would volunteer nothing and would respond only if asked a direct question—which, in fact, he had asked, yet with such negligence and with such absence of authority that they did not feel obligated to reply.

"I've been washed out," he remarked. He thought this would draw some kind of response.

The mechanic on the cowl quit work and studied him with no particular sympathy, but without the courteous exclusion of a moment before; he was neutral, lenient, mildly interested.

"Holy God, fellow," he murmured. "That's rough."

The other mechanic had also paused and was watching Melvin, and he asked, "At *this* base? *Here?*"

Melvin grinned, and felt foolish, as though he had been boasting. Both the mechanics were surprised, he could tell that, and word would soon spread among the enlisted men that a Saufley cadet had actually been washed out; but he could see that at the same time, though he had given them a bit of news, they were not concerned. What was vitally significant to him did not affect them any more than if they had heard of some distant relative who had met with a catastrophe. Their eyes were fixed on him. They were thinking about him, and about what he had told them; he was dimly stirred by the realization that he was on the verge of communicating with them, as if, at this instant, he were infiltrating an intricate, mystical defense. He found that he was extremely anxious to tell them how it had all come about.

He took a step forward, looking at them eagerly, first one and then the other; but to his disappointment he could see them withdraw. "It was my own fault," he explained. "It isn't official yet." And he went on hurriedly, hoping to hold their attention. "It's confusing, but I've made up my mind. I'm positive about this. Let me see if I can clarify what I've said."

186

They retreated farther; they observed him from a vast distance. He did not know if they could hear him now even though he shouted.

He turned and wandered away, and heard the clink of a hammer as the mechanics resumed work. He thought of the family, the effect his decision would have on them. His parents would be puzzled and bitterly disappointed, especially his father, who would bring up the fact that he had served in the First World War. How many times Melvin had heard about the AEF and the first war with Germany he did not know, but he did not want to hear of it any more. It was an old war, without meaning. The battle of the Marne had been important, according to history books, but that was a generation ago. The shadows over Ypres and Verdun were as long as those cast on Kings Mountain or Shiloh. He reflected that soon this war, like other wars, like those of his father and of his grandfathers, and of their fathers before them, would pass equally into history. Before long there would be men who would think of Hitler and Mussolini as he himself thought of the Kaiser with the withered arm. And the bawdy marching songs would come to seem as quaint as Mademoiselle from Armentières. And they might hear from their grandfathers of Tokyo Rose. Nor would it be long till Rabaul and Salerno rang strangely on the ear, and Garand cartridges found their way into museums beside the corroding minie balls his father had dug from the earth at Lexington. He opened his fist, aware that he had been clutching something, and discovered the miniature enameled flag the lieutenant had given him.

When he returned to the barracks he found Roska in the room wearing the uniform of a Marine second lieutenant; he was studying himself in the mirror. Horne, stark naked, lay on the bunk munching an apple with his eyes screwed up as if the apple was sour. Melvin sat down at the desk with a despondent expression and tried to think of a way to occupy himself. It seemed to him there was nothing to do: there was no longer anything to worry about, nothing to anticipate. There were no plans to be made.

Roska, who could not get enough of looking at himself in the mirror, took a moment to glance at Melvin and asked if he had gotten some more demerits.

"You let Inscrutable One alone. He's got problems, he has," said Horne.

Melvin stood up and started for the door.

"Now just look what we did," said Horne to Roska, and pitched the apple core into the wastebasket. "Come on, baby, talk to your old buddies. What've you done this time? You got the skipper's wife in trouble?"

Melvin left the room without answering and went for a walk around the station. He could not get over a conviction that he had no more future. He was to be taken care of by the Navy; he would be fed at certain times, given clothing, a little money, and not much would be expected of him. The world had suddenly, inexplicably, grown socialistic.

He stopped at the recreation hall to drink some coffee, and while there he decided he ought to send a telegram to the family to let them know what he was going to do. This turned out to be more difficult than he had thought: after throwing away one telegram after another he wrote, simply, that he was resigning from the aviation program.

The WAVE at the desk, having read this message, briskly counted the words and informed him that he was entitled to five additional words at no extra charge. He thought he might as well make use of whatever he was entitled to, so he added, "This is a good base."

The remainder of the afternoon he sat on a gasoline drum in the hangar; he sat on the drum and swung his feet and looked at the airplanes and the people passing by; he knew his father would call Saufley Field as soon as the telegram arrived and he did not feel like talking.

That evening after supper and a movie he reluctantly went back to the barracks and found a sheaf of telephone notices. There were also two identical telegrams from his father saying he would arrive in Pensacola the next afternoon.

14

★

In the morning he went to the hangar at the usual time, because there was nothing else to do, and found that he was scheduled to fly. He had assumed Caravaggio would notify whoever made out the schedules that he was quitting. It occurred to him, as he stood in front of the board, that he could accept this flight if he wanted it. Probably, because he had informed Caravaggio that he was resigning, to do so would constitute a violation of naval regulations; the longer he thought about this fact the more he felt like taking the flight. He looked around with a guilty expression. Nobody was paying any attention to him. He picked up a piece of chalk, drew a diagonal mark beside his name, and hurried off to get a parachute. Then, slightly puzzled that nobody had even questioned him, he changed into his coveralls, took his gloves and muffler from the knee pouch, and with the parachute slung across his shoulder started walking along the line of parked bombers, looking for the one which had been assigned to him.

A cool, salty wind was blowing from the Gulf, carrying a few clouds like puffs of cannon smoke. The wind blew through the pines and swept over the endless rows of rusty, blue-gray airplanes, the stumpy flat-bottomed SBD's that had swarmed on the Japanese carriers at Midway and had sunk the *Shoho* in the Coral Sea. Now they were rusting away in the humid air of Pensacola.

At the eastern end of the field he found it. Even from a distance—when he could just make out the A-156 painted on the fin—he could tell it was one of the oldest planes on the field. As he came closer he saw a quadrangle of Japanese flags stenciled on the fuselage beside the cockpit and he wondered where the plane had fought. It might have been over Truk or the New Hebrides; it might have been a part of what was now a legend. It might well have flown over the jungles of Guadalcanal.

He climbed onto the wing and stood beside the cockpit as he put the parachute on, buckling the straps around his chest and thighs; then he straightened up, looking more closely at the plane: long metallic scratches glittered like strands of a spider web through the camouflage, and the wing was actually dented as though somebody had been dropping rocks on it. He noticed, too, that a spot of rust was eating away the white star beside the gunner's ring. He stepped to the forward edge of the wing and looked at the battered, corroding cowl. He leaned over far enough to see one of the tires; it was worn smooth, and a network of white fabric was visible through the black rubber.

Melvin frowned, jumped off the wing, and walked around the disintegrating old Dauntless. There was a hole in the rudder. The tail wheel was almost deflated. Obviously this was one of the condemned planes which would soon be demolished for scrap; he knew he would be foolish to fly it. He did not even know if the engine would start; assuming it did, there was no way of telling if the plane had enough power to leave the ground. It was evident that somebody had made a mistake; the SBD was unsafe and should never have been assigned. He looked back along the line of parked planes and saw that no one else had come this far. He thought, then, he might have misread the number on the schedule board; in any event, it did not matter whether the mistake was his own or that of someone else, here was a situation in which a decision was required. The intelligent thing to do, assuming he did want to accept this flight, was to return to the schedule board and request another airplane. This SBD might catch fire when the engine was started, or, for that matter, perhaps there was no gas in it; and at this thought he felt relieved and went around to look into the tank. If the tank was empty the problem was solved; he could not possibly fly the plane. But the tank was full.

The Gulf wind ruffled his hair and pulled gently at the white silk muffler while he tried to decide what to do. He considered the clouds drifting high overhead and listened to the waving boughs of the pines nearby, and he became convinced that the wind and the sky and whatever godlike agent did exist—these were urging him to come and join them where they were, nodding and beckoning and summoning him.

Melvin found himself on the wing again, attempting to slide the hatch open, but the metal had oxidized. And when this happened—when he found himself locked out—he remembered how often he had wanted something and had been denied. With both fists he pounded on the hatch, and because it continued to resist him he kicked at it with his heavy government shoes until he had broken the rust and at last was able to force the canopy backward far enough to squeeze inside.

He had no trouble with the engine: it started to cough and spit, the propeller blades jerked, and soon, with a roar of hoarse authority, the blades dissolved in a shimmering wheel. While he spoke to the engine in an encouraging way, as he was in the habit of doing, he listened with his entire body to the pulsation, and the sensation of oscillating life within the cylinders seemed convincing. If trouble developed it would probably be in the fatigued metal of the wings, or in the tail structure, or in the hydraulic system.

The radio had begun to warm up, filling the earphones with the drone and crackle of electricity, and from far away came a few melancholy notes of music: pressing the phones against his ears he heard and recognized a few Spanish words which told a story of love's anguish, of meeting and fulfillment, and of a departure for some unknown land beyond the sea, and though he had no sense of being especially loved by anyone the lyrics were appropriate, for he was departing and did not know if he would come back.

He cranked the handle around in search of the Saufley squadron tower.

". . . Zero. One. Zero," came a voice through the sputtering void, and faded as he went beyond, but it had been so near as he went by, as though someone had spoken from the adjacent plane—and it had been a woman's voice—that it could only have been the Saufley tower. He reversed the handle, cranked more slowly through the crackling droning emptiness and came gradually to the voice, saying, "North by northwest at—" and as it faded he again reversed the crank, reducing the arc each time until her voice came over the phones ungarbled and he could almost hear the people in the background.

He noticed, with more curiosity than alarm, that his hands were unsteady, and recalling how he had pounded on the canopy he began to wonder if he was somewhat out of his head. This idea was vaguely irritating. He had forced the airplane open; there was no reason he could not force himself to do whatever he wished. He placed his fingertips between his teeth and bit them until the pain was so intense that the trembling ceased; then he unhooked the microphone and asked the WAVE in the tower for permission to take off. She soon announced the runway number and wind velocity and granted take-off permission.

He released the brakes and went fish-tailing along the lane toward the downwind end of the field. Several other SBD's and a midnight-blue Corsair were ahead of him. The big fighter swung back and forth with ponderous grace as the pilot tried to see ahead, and with every change of direction the stubby SBD wallowed and dipped in the blast from the Corsair's four paddle blades.

At the end of the taxi strip the planes parked, one after another, in an oblique line and waited. The first SBD trundled ahead, swung around facing the wind, and began to shudder as the pilot tested the magnetos. Soon, in the tower, a green light winked on. The bomber rolled forward, faster and faster, the sunlight sliding along the wings. For a moment or so its pudgy wheels dangled uselessly in the air, then folded inward and flattened against the belly. Already the second bomber was in position.

When the Corsair swung around, Melvin could see the pilot hunched inside the bubble like a captive insect. The tapering wings waved gently against the insistent rhythm of the engine, and a few seconds later the Corsair was past the tower and over the trees and floating toward the clouds.

Melvin taxied into position on the runway. The green light shone straight in his eye. He pressed the throttle ahead, holding the brakes with his toes until the SBD was quivering, lifted his feet and felt himself drawn forward, and could feel the pavement speeding beneath the wheels. When the horizon rose above the cowl he knew the tail of the Dauntless was in the air; the control stick had gradually come to life and now stood erect of its own accord, turgid with strength. A gust of wind tipped the wings; the Dauntless swerved, bounced once, and thundered away from the earth. Two solid thumps as the wheels folded into the belly told him that the hydraulic system was operating.

He was well off the ground before reaching the center of the field, and thought he might have a look at the WAVE who was directing traffic, so, instead of holding the Dauntless low to gain speed, he pulled up steeply and turned his head as he flew by the tower. He saw her there, holding a microphone to her lips as if she were about to speak, a stocky, broad-shouldered woman in a wrinkled seersucker uniform with that peculiar flowing necktie poets wore a hundred years ago. As many times as he had seen those ties he could not get over a suspicion that there had been a preposterous error in the supply department. For a second or two they looked at each other. He was close enough to distinguish the insignia on her sleeve and to note that she did not have a wedding ring. She was watching him without much expression. He nodded pleasantly and looked ahead.

When he left the traffic pattern he discovered another SBD cutting inside the arc; he looked again and saw it was not one but two planes in tight formation and they were obviously intent on joining him. The pilots were McCampbell and Roska. He shook his head and banked away. This was to be his last flight at Pensacola. He wanted the time to himself.

He rolled out of the turn alone, trimmed the plane for climbing, and settled more comfortably into the cockpit. And all at once it seemed incredible that he was the pilot of a dive bomber. It must be a dream, or a hallucination—he had not the faintest idea how to fly an airplane!—and a bemused thrill of terror swept through him. He looked at the parachute on which he was seated, and even this familiar canvas package appeared strange—he wondered how it was meant to be used. So fantastic indeed was the illusion of unreality that, though he knew he could destroy it when he wished, he could not bring himself to do so; and while the dive bomber steadily spiraled higher, pulsing and thundering, growing from the earth with brainless mechanical conviction, he brooded over this curious circumstance, aware that when the time came for him to assume control he would do so with no hesitation, with no doubt.

He asked himself the meaning of this, but was at a loss for an answer. He did not know how he had gotten into such a situation. It had all come about as a result of the attack on Pearl Harbor, that much he knew. Although, of course, it could be traced farther and farther backward in time to Manchuria, or Commodore Perry, or farther, as each event in human history was antedated by another, and from it developed. Still, for ordinary purposes, the war opened on the island of Oahu that Sunday morning; consequently it was inevitable that he should now be in one military service or another, and as he had chosen the Naval Air Corps there was, most plainly, no mystery.

He could hear, as remote as though she were in another state, the voice of the WAVE in the tower, and peering down he discerned the field and the miniature rectangular building where she was.

He unhooked the microphone and in a muffled voice he said, "Saufley tower. Saufley tower. This is the Green Hornet. Do you read me?"

There was a pause.

A man said, "Green Hornet, this is Saufley tower. We read you loud and clear. What is your number? Over."

"Saufley tower, this is the Green Hornet," Melvin said. "My number is Fond du Lac 6-4125. If a man answers, hang up."

There was another pause.

He waited, peering down in high glee. He knew that by now the squadron tower was swarming with officers armed with binoculars. There were dozens of planes in range of the tower and there was, so to speak, a price on the Green Hornet. The Hornet was a tradition, a symbol of defiance who transferred immortally and anonymously from one battalion to the next, a goading voice from the sky. Every so often he addressed one or another of the Pensacola towers.

"Green Hornet, this is Saufley," responded an unusually affable voice, a voice that should be considered genial and kindly, or even more—positively eager to be regarded as a good friend. "Hello there, Green Hornet," said this amiable Christian voice, "Do you read me? Over."

194

"I read you," Melvin answered. "Can you give me the bearing and distance to the Mark Hopkins hotel in San Francisco?"

With suave good humor, in fact with a jovial chuckle, the voice replied, "Operations is plotting that course for you, Green Hornet. Please waggle your wings if you can hear me."

"Well, thank you, but, no thanks," said Melvin. "I'm the Green Hornet, however I'm sure not that green."

He hung up the microphone. But then he reflected that he had nothing to lose by identifying himself. He was through anyway. He was not going to be commissioned, he was going to Great Lakes as an apprentice seaman and could not possibly be broken any lower. It might be nice, somehow, rather gratifying in a way, to remember during the long disagreeable months ahead that he was not apt to be forgotten by the cadets, or, for that matter, by anyone at Pensacola. They might forget his name but as long as Pensacola endured—and as long as it did endure there would be a Green Hornet somewhere overhead, calling down his desperate taunt—they would remember there had once been a Green Hornet who was not afraid to identify himself. So he dipped the wings, and though he was high above the field he knew the movement could be recognized, and that, when he descended, one way or another they would have him bracketed.

The tower was speaking. He could not hear it distinctly. Another station was interfering. He began to hear, with increasing clarity, what must be a Cuban news broadcast—a delirious gabble with the words *guerra* and *muerto* recurring constantly, and having had enough contact with the world below he unplugged the radio. The sky had become a deeper blue. From the ground it had looked cerulean and warm as the Gulf water. It was now a thin, chill indigo and the clouds were far below. He gazed around, yawning. Except for the monotonous tremble of the engine he thought he might have been asleep.

Abruptly he shivered from the cold, and glancing at the altimeter he was astounded to find it registering close to twenty thousand feet; only an instant ago when he looked at it the needle indicated fourteen thousand. Immediately he sat up, pinching and slapping himself and whistling, and quickly strapped the oxygen mask across his face, watching the gauges and the little rubber bellows to make sure the apparatus was functioning.

Yet, in a while, despite himself, reminding himself he should pay attention, he had resumed gazing into the cold and gaseous void that varied only when the icy gray cowl of the bomber floated slowly by the sun, appearing to bow a little with each revolution, as if in obeisance to some higher deity; he went around and on around and around again, undisturbed and fascinated. And he fell into a dream, then, so absorbed and lulled was he by the whole vessel of the universe; and all through and among those invisible stars whose miraculous opulence was blinding it seemed to him that he was journeying, and he did not doubt that he could see around the earth entirely—far beyond the swamps where De Soto wandered, beyond the Western plains to where the lace-white surf came feeding on the California shore, and to the volcanic islands of Hawaii and rain-drenched valleys of Samoa, and New Guinea, and the lost pyramids of Siam. Beyond the Ganges to the high plateaus of India, and the waters of the Red Sea and Algiers, and Portugal, westward to the Azores and to the jeweled Antilles, and to the Florida keys.

The motion ceased. The Dauntless swung and dipped at anchor. The air was thin. The controls cold as ice, useless. He plunged the pedals to the bottom, one and then the other: the Dauntless barely responded. He unlocked the shoulder harness so that he could twist around in the cockpit and look backward while he kicked the pedals again, and he saw the tall blue rudder swaying to the left and to the right with a sonorous clang that echoed within the hollow fuselage like church bells in a corridor. The plane nosed mildly back and forth. He looked at the instrument panel and found that the altimeter was stationary. He could go no higher. This was the summit.

Lazily the bomber slipped away, gyrating like some heavy indolent bird, while he relaxed with his hands folded in his lap. Far, far beneath him the earth was enveloped in a planetary haze; even so there was an impression of solidity to that harmless tufted ball, and while he was descending he contemplated the broad, soft arc of the idly whirling horizon and felt near to it, yet not altogether a part of it, though it was the one home to which he must return after each absence, and he thought he might lie down on it soon to rest for a little while. Without fear he considered it, with the same benign indifference he used to feel as a child when he studied the whole world from the steep gilded saddle of an undulating stallion on a carousel.

Steadily the earth came nearer.

He accepted the plump stick that stood between his knees and disdainfully pressed it forward until it grew rigid and the wind hissed jealously at the cracks in the canopy. He pulled the stick into his lap and rolled to his left and to his right and rolled over completely in joyless abandon, came up again higher and higher, and the plane somersaulted off the track over the top into loose space and fell clumsily, with no direction or meaning, like a broken kite.

Down he went, on down, but pulled up savagely with the blood half-sucked from his brain. The canopy rattled and the engine shook, the cowl dipping like a porpoise diving through the waves, until at last it stalled and sank aside into a mushy, sickening spin. He pushed the lever that set the flaps to opening, and watched the trailing edge of the bomber's wing split wider and wider apart with the awesome precision of hydraulic machinery. The harness cut through the coveralls into his shoulders, and the safety belt— he tapped it with one finger—had become as hard as a board on his lap. He pushed the stick forward to the instrument panel, but the speed did not increase very much, nor the degree of inclination: the Dauntless was traveling about as fast as it would go, unless the flaps were closed. He remembered what he had been told about retracting the flaps in a dive; he remembered the partial demonstration, and the fact that a year or so ago some lieutenant from another field had done this, probably by mistake. No one saw him come down, but not far away there was a crew of lumberjacks who felt the ground shake and thought a meteor had struck the earth.

The flaps closed smoothly. The safety belt gradually relaxed and the shoulder straps hung limp. His head rested comfortably on the hard leather cushion while he gazed ahead, lost in meditation.

And the great globe of the earth rushed up to meet him.

Melvin blinked and stretched; he knew he had been dozing again. The wings of the Dauntless were hissing in the wind. He saw that the compass was gyrating senselessly in the amber fluid and he realized that he had neglected to lock it. With dreamy indecision he was speculating on whether the dive would damage the compass when he understood, without quite knowing how he understood, that the plane was about to break apart. He was certain he had heard nothing more than the sibilation of the wind and the shriek of the engine, nor had he observed anything remarkable, except a few extreme instrument readings, or scented smoke or gas or oil, or felt the knowledge through his body, and yet the plane was going to disintegrate. He knew this, and he knew he was not mistaken.

Casually rolling his head across the cushion, he fixed his eyes on the radio mast just outside the greenhouse. At that instant the mast broke off. He scarcely had time to see what direction it went, although he knew it had been left behind, or, since the Dauntless was in a vertical dive, the mast would now be high overhead, perhaps a quarter of a mile overhead already. He thought the mast had struck the fin, although the impact he felt could have been caused by something else snapping off. It was possible that the entire tail section—the rudder, the fin itself, and the elevators—had broken off completely. In that case he was riding to his death—of this there could be no question. He tried to twist around and peer over his shoulder, but he did not have the strength. He could barely lift his arms. He could not even sigh; the pressure on his chest was inexorable. And he could not make up his mind what to do: whether to die or to struggle against this impersonal, relentless, and diabolic power. The day must come when he would die. It might as well be now. This would be a satisfying death, free of thought and pain. There was nothing to do but remain as he was, and muse on what might have been, until the end. Then he would exist no more, although he might be remembered with a certain awe by everyone who had known him, and by those who heard the story. But if he lived and worked for half a century, what could he achieve? Who would care what he said, and who would repeat to strangers the opinions he held? He would live in obscurity until, on a day that would be remarked for some other event, he died.

Melvin had been sitting in the cockpit with his arms crossed, prepared for death—it seemed so reasonable—but then his right hand of its own accord began to grope for the control stick. He could not prevent it; he watched his hand fumbling for a grip and understood that his life or death depended on the success or failure of his hand. He noticed that the fingers had an arthritic look and that some intense power was forcing them to encircle the stick. They went around it and tightened, and he saw the stick begin to move backward, but he could not tell whether the hand and wrist were straining from the effort or whether some convulsion made the tendons appear rigid and the flesh of the hand sunken like the hand of a cadaver. He watched in fascination to see what would happen next. The needles were still traveling around the dials and the wind screamed outside the canopy. He noticed a movement in his left arm; the hand opened deliberately, reached forward, and joined the other. As soon as he saw this he suspected that the tail of the airplane had not broken off; if the elevators had broken away the stick would be attached to nothing but a few cables whipping in the wind and it could be moved easily with one hand. An immense pressure must have caused him to take the stick with both hands. Just then he discovered that a strip of black rubber which protected a seam on the wing where the dihedral commenced had disappeared. He was certain the strip had been in place when he left the field. He glanced at the opposite wing and saw the rubber on that side breaking and snapping out of sight a few inches at a time and he realized the rubber had crystallized. Two little holes, like bullet holes, were suddenly visible in the seam, then another, and another—rivets were popping out. He waited and watched, expecting the rest of the rivets to break, and then the wing to tear away, but nothing else happened.

It occurred to him that during the dive his mind had become separated from his body, and the more he thought about this the more convincing it became. Proof of it lay in the fact that while he had resigned himself to death his body had not, and was, even now, attempting to save itself. He considered his hands and his wrists; they were straining to draw the control stick backward and he wondered if he should help. He did not want to assume the burden; it seemed to him that he was entitled to relax. A great deal had happened since he joined the Navy, the experience had been tiring, and he only wanted to use whatever time remained in thinking the matter over; and yet, as some part of him did so earnestly hope to continue living, he thought it would be selfish to ignore that fanatic struggle which was proceeding so silently but with such devout passion only a few inches away.

The altimeter registered eight thousand feet, but the needle lagged—he did not know how much; he might be nearer to seven thousand, which meant that if he intended to do anything he would have to do it in the next few seconds. He surveyed the wings; one of them appeared to be all right. He looked at the altimeter again and was shocked to see the needle dropping below five thousand; stunned by the speed, he followed it around the dial: four thousand. It was as though somebody were setting a clock, turning back the hours, the longer needle overtaking the shorter one again and again, and when the two stood straight up at noon the dive would be over.

He looked through the windshield. Plowed fields and a country road were twirling toward him. The fields were green, umber, henna, purple, variegated and tumbling like crystals in a kaleidoscope.

He took a deep breath in spite of the pressure on his chest and tried to pull the stick backward, but he could no more pull it back than he could have pulled up a sapling by the roots. He had not expected this. Tears crept into his eyes and his chin quivered. He did not know what to do. He had thought his decision to struggle for his life would entitle him to succeed, but apparently it did not make the least difference.

He loosened the safety belt and managed to get both feet on the instrument panel, thinking he could obtain more leverage this way; then, with the veins standing out on his neck and tears rolling down his cheeks he tried once more. In a little while his vision grew dim. He could not see his hands. The dials on the panel slipped out of focus and came floating toward him like wandering black halos merging and separating and merging again. This meant only one thing: the course was changing. But he thought he had waited too long and braced himself for the impact. He expected, for some reason, to ricochet at least once before the final crash, like a stone skipping across the surface of a lake, and then through the noise of the wind and the howl of the engine he distinguished a grotesque sound—it sounded to him like the terrified baying of a mad dog. He rolled his head toward the mirror. Why the mirror was turned down into the cockpit he had no idea, but there he saw the reflection of himself. His mouth hung open, saliva drooled from the corners. He wore a helpless, earnest look, a pleading look. After that he could not see anything, and lost all knowledge of himself.

When his sight returned he could not, for a moment, think where he was, but he had the feeling that he was older. Then it came to him that he was about to die. He thought of the road, which he remembered had been just in front of the engine; he glanced ahead, expecting to catch a glimpse of the road as it came smashing through. Instead, amazed, he saw nothing but the milky sky. The control stick was drawn all the way back between his legs and the SBD was soaring majestically upward, on its fin like a dolphin in the Florida sunlight. The airspeed was diminishing; in a few seconds the Dauntless would stall again, this time so close to the earth that no recovery would be possible.

At the last moment he brought the plane over and sank forward as though returning to the sea. He discovered that his feet were still on the instrument panel. Several of the dials were broken. He had crushed them beneath his heels.

The bomber was ruined. There was a jagged rip near the tip of one wing. Whether it had been the body of a bird, or a meteor fragment, or only the wind, he did not know, but something had torn the metal surface as though it were tinfoil, and part of the aileron was missing so that the plane would no longer fly straight ahead; it flew aslant, crabbed, and he was obliged to hold the stick to one side to prevent the wing from dipping and the plane from spinning down around it. The crack in the opposite wing had lengthened where the rivets had burst and the seam was gaping. The engine was vibrating so heavily that he guessed the propeller blades had been twisted out of alignment. The vibrations were passing over the entire airplane; he could feel them through the soles of his shoes and through the parachute pack on which he was sitting. He began to smell gas. The Dauntless was ready to explode. Even if it failed to explode it would not remain in the air much longer.

Something trickled over his lips. He put out his tongue and tasted blood and immediately looked in the mirror and saw that he was bleeding from both nostrils. He wiped his nose across the back of his head, looked in the mirror again, and saw the blood reappear. He did not feel sick or faint, so he concluded it was nothing serious. He was being pricked in the throat, however, and discovered splinters of glass in his muffler, which he cautiously picked out. The glass must have come from the broken dials on the instrument panel, but he did not know how it had gotten into his muffler. The cockpit was now thick with smoke and gas fumes. He could not see any flames streaming from the cowl, as there would be if the engine had caught fire, nor was there any heat, but there was a strong odor of burning oil which made him cough and choke. He tried to fan the smoke away, but it was too thick and seemed to be getting worse. Soon it was inside his goggles, so that his eyes watered and stung and he was almost blinded.

He tried to think what he should do, but it was difficult to concentrate because the plane was shuddering so badly and the wing continued to dip. Everything was breaking apart, and he thought the plane might dive after the ruined wing at any moment. He could feel the vibrations from the throttle and control stick pass up his arms to the base of his neck and he discovered that unless he kept his jaw clenched his teeth rattled; this struck him as so preposterous that he grinned. Then the Dauntless gave a sickening drop like an elevator slipping a cable and he grew sober and again tried to decide what he should do. He could fly back to the station, or as far as he could go in that direction, and attempt to land. If permission was refused because of the condition of the airplane—if an attempt to land would endanger the lives of other people—then he would obey whatever orders the tower gave him. The next step, providing he got out alive, would be to confess what he had done. And he had knowingly, willfully, violated instructions. He had been told quite explicitly what would occur when the flaps of an SBD were closed during a dive. He had even been shown a movie of the khaki-and-blue wreckage in the woods where the lieutenant had crashed, and often since then he had thought of the lumberjacks who paused in their work to hunt for the meteor. But he had done it anyway; he had closed the flaps in the middle of a dive and the result was now in his hands. The Navy would expect him to return to the base without delay and accept the consequences.

There was one alternative. He could head for the Gulf of

Mexico. When he flew over the beach he could lock the controls and use the parachute. In a few hours, if it held together that long, the Dauntless would be over deep water and out of gas. There it would crash and sink and the wreckage would not ever be recovered for examination. Meanwhile he could be making his way back to the station, and when they asked what happened he would swear that the engine failed in an area where there was no possibility of effecting a safe landing. That would be a form of truth because the engine would fail over the Gulf, although it would be a lie and he would always know it was a lie. And when they asked where the plane went down he could swear, not only that it had gone down at sea, but that he had sent it there in order to protect the lives of civilians who lived in the vicinity.

These were the courses before him, diverging sharply. If he chose the first, returning to the base, he must accept the judgment, however unreasonable, of other men; he would be washed out, and thereby forfeit whatever slight dignity there might be in quitting. In addition, there was a reasonably good chance he would be dishonorably discharged, or discharged without honor, or however it was they elected to convict him. He had destroyed government property, and what the sentence or punishment for that might be would depend, he supposed, on whether they adjudged the destruction accidental or intentional.

But if he chose the second course, abandoning and concealing what he had destroyed, he had only to judge himself.

He studied the sky, shading his eyes and squinting, searching for the glint of sunlight on metal or glass, but the wind had carried him far beyond the usual practice area. There was not another airplane in sight. He was alone. A cynical smile came to his lips and he began a careful climbing turn in the direction of the Gulf of Mexico.

While heading for the beach he rehearsed his story, and it was absurdly simple. He went through it again to be certain there were no mistakes, and nodded with satisfaction. Never before had he been in a situation where he could lie without literally telling a lie, and as he thought about this he understood how useful it might be to develop such a faculty.

So he leaned from side to side as he flew along, because he was afraid to bank the ruined plane, and he looked down and found that the land below him was an unearthly, sulphurous green—he was over a swamp. The hoarse cough of the engine disturbed a great blue heron that came flapping up from the stinking water and swung away to the east, and this big solitary bird that flew so easily with its feet withdrawn and its head thrust forth as if in contemplation, this heron seemed to be saying that no other living creature had come that way. No one would discover the mendacity which would be his salvation.

He was pleased. He grinned as he looked ahead. There lay the Gulf. Soon he would be parachuting toward the beach while the Dauntless thundered out to sea, hour after hour, until at last it came down and left nothing but a brief scratch on the water.

He began to get ready. He took off the earphones and turned up the bill of his baseball cap. Then he reflected that the cap would blow off when he jumped, so he rolled it up and stuffed it into the pouch of his coveralls. The oxygen mask was hanging around his neck; it had slipped off his face when he pulled out of the dive. He unsnapped it and hung it on the panel. He pushed the radio cords aside so there was no chance of getting caught in them. Everything seemed to be ready. But all at once he realized he had forgotten the safety belt: he was still strapped to the seat. If he could forget that, what else had he forgotten? There was not much time. He fumbled anxiously at the hasp of the belt and finally managed to throw it open. Next, working furiously, he stuffed the shoulder harness behind the seat. He could not find anything more to do, so he practiced grabbing the ripcord handle. He felt restless and impatient; he wanted to jump into space and hear the boom of the parachute. He had never heard a parachute open, but he thought it must sound like a cannon and fill the air with a voluptuous shock.

The Dauntless was tilting more ominously. He had already trimmed it as best he could; now he was obliged to lean against one wall of the cockpit in order to sit erect. The engine was not going to last much longer; but he was only seconds away from the beach, and if the plane would fly out to sea for just two minutes it would go down in deep water where nobody would ever locate it.

Then he grew a little sick because he knew he was not thinking lucidly: he had carefully planned his escape without once thinking about the canopy. It was closed and locked. He would have butted his head against it when he tried to stand up and might have knocked himself unconscious.

He let go of the throttle and grabbed the release catch. The hatch slid open easily, though he could feel the metal edges grinding through the corrosion. It occurred to him that for the past few minutes he had been doing everything more violently than usual. He recalled how much difficulty he had had getting the hatch open at the field, but now it had been simple—he had not been conscious of much resistance. And he had noticed, too, how the halves of the safety belt flew apart and banged against the walls of the cockpit, but had not thought about it. Suddenly he understood it was terror that had given him such strength. He had heard of this happening to people, but it had never happened to him. He felt a surge of elation, a furious joyful urge to demonstrate this power while it lasted; he glared around for something to attack—anything—it did not matter what, so long as he destroyed it, while the disintegrating bomber, tilting always a few degrees more steeply, thundered nearer to the Gulf.

But then he became aware of the damaged engine, which frightened him so that he forgot everything else. When the canopy was closed he had not been able to hear much except a distant roar, and sometimes the wind; now he heard the broken thudding and clanking. He leaned forward, ready to let go and dive over the side. Nervously he licked his lips, but the crust made him ill and he was panic-stricken by the idea that he might faint. Oil was seeping along the cowl, drops were blowing against the windshield. He tried to wipe away the streaks, even though he knew this was impossible because the oil was outside the glass and he was wiping the inside. Again, unable to stop himself, he reached forward and wiped frantically at the glass. He could barely see through it, but he was able to make out the beach and the combers rhythmically crashing in the sunlight.

So, at last, the time for which he had been waiting was at hand. This was the moment to stand up, cross his arms on his chest, and escape. No longer was there anything to prevent him. Nothing bound him. And yet, with a truculent expression, he went riding out to sea.

A few minutes later the small gray bomber commenced a

cautious climbing arc and headed landward, bearing directly for the station.

As he approached the practice area he was mystified to see a number of airplanes converging on him. In amazement he watched them angle toward him from every direction.

He plugged in the radio and called the tower for permission to make an emergency landing. He was answered by the WAVE, but a male voice interrupted, advising him to fly over the field so the damage could be assessed.

"Negative," Melvin replied. "I don't think I've got time." He looked at the aileron, which was about to fall off, and then he looked to the other side to see if the crack in the wing had gotten any wider. He screamed—he did not know what—into the microphone. Ashamed of himself for having become hysterical, he stared at the wing and spoke again, calmly, but in an urgent voice. "Request permission to land on first approach."

No one answered.

He repeated the message, adding, "First approach imperative. I say again. *Imperative!* Do you read me? Over! Over! Come in Saufley tower!"

After a long silence the tower responded, "Read you loud and clear."

"All right, let's go!" he shouted. "What about it? I've got to come in! I've only got a few seconds!"

There was another pause.

The Dauntless was listing steeply. At any moment it would wheel and fall. He was pressing the right rudder pedal to the floor in an attempt to hold a direct course toward the field.

"You got a fire truck out there?" he called.

The tower answered, "Crash wagon standing by. Come ahead."

Someone cried in a piercing feminine voice to get the asbestos ready; he was not sure whether the voice had come from the tower or whether it was his own. He realized he was panting with excitement.

"Fire apparatus standing by. Take it easy, cadet. Everything's going to be all right."

"That's what you think!" came the wild feminine scream, and he suspected himself. The tachometer needle was bouncing back and forth across the dial. Most of the gauges were broken. Fluid was dripping from the bottom of the instrument panel. The engine stopped, caught, missed again, caught, and kept going.

"Navy one-five-six. Navy one-five-six. This is Saufley Field. From which direction will you arrive? Over."

"From which direction will I arrive?" Melvin gasped. It seemed unbelievable they would ask such a question when he was about to crash. He was furious with the officers who were in charge of the situation; they must be incredibly stupid. They were not doing anything right. He choked and coughed, wiped his eyes, and began talking to them, but stopped in consternation when he realized he was chattering and that he could not recall what he had just said. He coughed again and rolled his head feverishly from side to side trying to find enough air to breathe.

"Say again, one-five-six. Your previous message was garbled. We do not read you. Say again. Say again, Navy one-five-six. Over."

Melvin did not answer. There was nothing anyone could do for him. He placed the microphone in his lap, watched the oil stream across the windshield, and waited for the crash.

Another SBD was drifting toward his left wingtip; he looked at the pilot and was not greatly surprised to see McCampbell, and he knew, then, even before he looked to the right, that Roska would be there. And there he was, with his curious egg-shaped head slightly tilted and a look of cautious estimation on his face. He floated in, judging the distance. The dinky salmon-pink baseball cap was cocked low over his emerald eyes. Roska had tried to wash the cap but it had shrunk and turned that ridiculous color.

The two of them were already flying a tight formation, but they were intent on coming even closer. Melvin knew it was dangerous for them. If his plane should give out, as it was ready to do, he could not help sliding into one of them, perhaps both of them, and they would go down. He glanced at the altimeter; it registered ninety feet. At that altitude nobody would have a chance. He knew they were aware of the danger. He was particularly puzzled by Roska who had always disliked and feared formation flying even at a safe altitude, and then it occurred to him that they were closing in to demonstrate their faith in him, their belief in his skill and in his courage; and because he had never thought of himself as being skillful or courageous, he was deeply moved by this. He wanted to let them know how he appreciated it, but what they were doing was so insane that he bared his teeth at them and furiously motioned them away. Neither paid any attention; they did not even bother to read the signal, which was so extraordinary that he was dumbfounded. He saw that their eyes were fixed on the diminishing space between his plane and their own. Already they were so close that he could have stepped from one wingtip to another. He wondered if they meant to lift him up and carry him forward to the field the way Sam Horne in his madness had tried to save Elmer.

He believed, then, that he was going to be killed. Their presence convinced him of this; it was as though they were priests who had come to administer the final sacrament, and, seeing them, he gave up hope. He had no more will to live, but was filled with resignation. Death seemed not so terrible. The others who had been killed, wherever they were—and he accepted without doubt that they must be somewhere, unchanged, in their own bodies as before, with their own prejudices and ambitions not in the least affected by death—wherever they were, all those uncountable billions he had never met, and his own few friends as well—the Deacon, Elmer, a few more here and there whom he had known by name or face—if they were watching him now, and he assumed they were, they must be amused at his predicament.

The engine of the Dauntless was knocking and thudding, but it was still going; it should have quit long ago and the fact that it continued to operate now began to annoy him. This airplane was to be the cause of his death, and having at last submitted to the idea that on this day at Pensacola, in this bright pleasant hour a little before noon, he Melvin Isaacs, aviation cadet whose home was in Missouri, son of Jacob and Hannah, brother of Leah, would meet his death in a training accident, and, dressed in a blue uniform, would be shipped home for burial, and then, gradually, as one day followed another, be forgotten—amenable at last to this grotesque and senseless termination of his affairs, he could not help resenting the intractability of the machine. He looked at it stupidly. It was destroyed, but it kept going.

Presently he noticed that the wings were not vibrating quite as heavily, and the list was no longer increasing. The plane appeared to have stabilized itself, almost as though it were alive and were fighting to reach the field.

Melvin felt his throat constrict, and a wild, frantic, useless hope brought him half-erect in the cockpit. He wanted to live. There had never been anything he wanted so much. But the plane was descending. He had already pushed the throttle to the forward end of the slot; he knew he could not push it any farther. However there was nothing else to do, so he tried, and bent the steel handle. He had never heard of anyone doing this and felt proud of his strength, but also rather foolish and embarrassed. He signaled to McCampbell and Roska that he was going to split the landing flaps to try for some additional lift, then he saw the water tower rising above the trees and quickly signaled that he was altering course.

The three SBD's banked to the right, glinting in the sunlight, and roared slowly over the pine trees.

The field came tilting into view.

From the tetrahedron and the tower lights Melvin knew he would be going in downwind, but there was nothing he could do about that. He had no time to make the usual circular approach to the upwind runway.

The tower was calling. He could hear the message although the headset was in his lap. The tower was advising him that one of the wheels had failed to descend. He was ordered to gain altitude, cross over the field at a minimum of fifteen hundred feet, and attempt to shake the wheel out of the fuselage.

Briefly he considered the fantastic command. He had been flying at full throttle for ten minutes and had not been able to maintain altitude, but the Navy had just ordered him to climb fifteen hundred feet above the field. He was going down and the Navy was insisting that he go up. With a gasp of rage he snatched the microphone and tried to throw it out of the cockpit, but he had forgotten to disconnect it. He grabbed the cords, wound them around his hand, jerked them loose and threw everything out—the microphone, the cords, and the headset.

Now his friends were leaving. He watched, a little sadly, as they drifted higher and higher above him. Or so it seemed, although he knew this was an illusion. They were not climbing any higher; it was just that he was sinking into the trees.

Once more he was alone. Sick with apprehension, he watched the air speed diminish. The SBD was not far from the stalling point. At any moment it would go. He knew exactly how it would feel: the mushy, passive settling, and a wing dipping, and the bulky little bomber rolling belly-up like a dead fish. Then he would be in the trees, the metal wings grinding and breaking off while the fuselage plunged ahead with mindless determination. There would be an explosion when the plane struck the ground, and he would be somewhere inside the explosion, perhaps alive enough to be aware of it.

He watched the crash trucks leave the parking area and drive in a leisurely way out the taxi strip. Then someone must have radioed further information about the approaching bomber, because both trucks stopped and turned around, stopped again, one of them backed up, and finally both trucks drove across the grass to the edge of the landing mat. They looked out of place there, oddly shaped, painted red and white. Melvin could see the drivers as he came flying through the treetops, and he could not understand why the drivers failed to see him. But it was obvious they did not; they had stopped again and backed away, off the pavement, and apparently were going to park and wait for additional orders.

Then they saw him. They lurched forward, throwing mud and clods of turf from the wheels, and swerved onto the mat. The smaller truck almost tipped over, but righted itself and came speeding toward him with a horrible flashing of lights. He could see the hulking form of a firefighter in a white asbestos suit clinging to one side.

Now the time had come. Oil was pouring from the cowl, a dense green rain spattering the windshield—he could no longer see through it—and the stall had begun. He eased the stick forward, hoping for another few seconds of flight, but the trees were rising around him; he pulled the stick all the way back and held it there. When he felt the Dauntless start to roll he cut the switches and flung up his arms to protect his face while the stubby gray bomber broke through the branches like a boat on a choppy sea, bounced crookedly into the swamp grass and weeds at the edge of the runway, and slewed across the concrete in a high metallic orange shower of sparks.

210

Even before it had come to rest, there was fire on the engine, and smoke boiled sluggishly from the cowl. A wing of the bomber had broken off; the wing had turned over twice and lay upside down on the scorched pavement, showing a large white star on a blue panel and the letters U.S.

The crash trucks stopped not far from the wreckage. The man in the asbestos suit lumbered powerfully forward, crushing the glowing skeletons of branches, and vanished like a medieval apparition in the smoke and flame.

15

Melvin woke up in a hospital bed and asked if the plane had caught fire. A nurse told him it had, but that he was not burned. He next asked what time it was, because he was supposed to meet his father that afternoon and was afraid of being late; she told him that his father was at the field and would be admitted for a short visit in a little while. Then he stared at the ceiling for some time and went back to sleep.

When he woke up again he was alone. He felt better, much stronger, but was unable to recollect anything beyond the moment when he had flung up his arms to protect his face. Most vividly he could recall the oily windshield and how frantically he had pushed the throttle while the SBD was going through the treetops.

He found a bandage around his head. He explored it with his fingers and located a tender spot. Otherwise, excepting an extremely stiff neck and the general impression of having been in another fight with Horne, he thought he was uninjured. He decided he should telephone the barracks because Horne would probably be interested in hearing about the wreck, so he swung his legs over the side of the bed, stood up, and started through the ward to the corridor, but he had not walked very far when a young nurse—a chic, sweet, English-looking nurse with neat auburn hair and a mole like a little button on her cheek—intercepted him. She asked what he was doing out of bed. He explained about telephoning the barracks. She took him by the arm and they started walking back toward his bed. He was mortified by the nightgown somebody had put on him while he was asleep or unconscious and, as he looked at her, he wondered if she had put it on him. He leaned against her; she glanced up at him suspiciously. The odor of her crisply starched white uniform and the thought of his own nakedness began to arouse him, so that in a few seconds he was obliged to bend forward in order not to hook the gown. She said nothing about this odd posture; in fact there was no change whatsoever in her expression, which implied that she had guessed the reason for it.

"I have a sort of a cramp," he explained.

"My, my!" said the nurse.

He decided to let it go at that. She was difficult to deceive.

"Like I say, I was only going to call the barracks," he repeated, climbing into bed while she held the covers open. "I wasn't going to stay up long. What's your name?"

The nurse tucked in the blanket. "Ensign Sullivan."

"Let's forget this ensign business," Melvin said. "I'm in a bad way. I've just been in a wreck and I'd like to be friends. What's your name?"

"Go to sleep," the nurse said.

"Where are you going to sleep?"

She looked down at him curiously, as though she could not quite believe what she saw. There was a pure antiseptic odor about her, a strangely virgin quality; Melvin's eyes began to shine and a lump came into his throat. He thought of how narrowly he had escaped death. He rolled swiftly to the edge of the bed and stared at her substantial, white-stockinged legs, and was surprised by the size of her feet, they were so small. Her little white shoes belonged on a child.

"Well," said the nurse, "I declayah!" She was smiling a little.

"Where are you from?" said Melvin.

After a moment the nurse said, "Why do you want to know?"

"Because you're no Southerner."

"Why, I am so!" She was still smiling. "I'm from Delaware, to tell the truth. But, honey, I'm jus' lulu 'bout the way they talk down heah. Now, y'all go to sleep."

He made an awkward grappling lunge for her knee and without hesitation she smacked his hand. He attempted to sit up; she deftly pushed him flat, the bed squeaked, she caught her underlip in her teeth and turned around to see if the other patients were watching.

"Sit down here," he suggested. He patted the bed.

"Mistah Isaacs," she began, and all at once he sensed good fortune tapping at his door. He heard in her tone the eternal promise of womankind. For a month he had been at Saufley Field without having seen this nurse. That was regrettable but couldn't be helped; the thing to do now was to look ahead. He expected to be released from the hospital in a few hours, since there was nothing wrong with him, and a number of days must elapse between then and the time the Navy sent him to Great Lakes. During that interval he would not have much to do, and the custom was that cadets who had been washed out were given quite a bit of liberty.

"You relax now," she was telling him. "You be nice a little while."

This sounded so familiar. Be nice, be nice now. How they loved to say that when they had made up their minds to abandon themselves. Melvin looked at her significantly.

"Lie down, lovah bun," said the nurse.

He did so. She tucked him in and left the ward.

He thought she might be going to arrange a private room for him. He considered getting out of bed and following her. They could have a smoke together and make some definite plans. But while he was debating this idea she returned with the doctor, a muscular man of about forty who was totally bald and who was wearing an expensive gabardine khaki uniform with the three full stripes of a commander.

"There will be no indiscretion here," the commander remarked as he picked up the chart which hung at the foot of the bed.

Melvin started to ask what he meant, but thought better of it and remained silent with his fingers laced on his chest.

"How do you feel?" the commander asked.

"Fine, sir. How soon can I leave?"

"Possibly tomorrow. That will depend."

"But why can't I leave now? I feel swell, sir."

"So I have been advised, Isaacs. May I suggest you obey orders until you are discharged from sick bay. Otherwise you will have cause to regret your audacity." Followed by the nurse he visited the other patients, and after writing something on a chart at the far end of the room he walked out.

In a little while a delegation of visitors entered. First came his father, then Horne, Roska, Kerdolph, McCampbell, and Ostrowski, and several other cadets. They gathered around the bed and looked at him. Melvin was embarrassed. To his father he said, "I suppose you've already met these guys, huh?"

"Yes, in the waiting room. How are you feeling? Don't answer —you are supposed to be resting. I spoke to the doctor. He informs me there is nothing wrong with you. What a shock—this accident! How did it happen? I'm not letting your mother know, she would be worried."

"I'm all right," Melvin said, and looked from one to another of his friends. He saw that they were ill at ease. None of them had much to say. It was evidently a courtesy call; they had heard he was not seriously injured, which was all that mattered, but they had felt they should stop by and appear solicitous.

"There's an inspection Thursday," said one of them.

"Oh? Well, that's bad news," said Melvin.

There was a pause.

Kerdolph suddenly rubbed his mouth and Melvin saw that he was trying to conceal a grin.

"Hell," said Kerdolph apologetically, "I know it ain't funny. You just about got killed. But it was sure humorous—you trying so hard to keep that heap aloft, and chunks of it dropping off."

"At the moment it doesn't strike me as funny," Melvin said. "Maybe in about ten years it will."

"We got to run along," said another cadet, and looked at his wrist watch. "We're cluttering up the joint and you need sleep. Take it slow, man. See you at the barracks."

"Sure. Thanks for stopping by," Melvin said, and they all trooped out, with the exception of his father and Sam Horne.

"Cole said to tell you he'd try to get over here to see you, but his grandmother is in town."

For some reason this sounded implausible. Melvin was perplexed; he looked at Horne and thought Horne was lying. He could not make any sense of what was going on; he felt sick and exhausted.

"It doesn't matter," he said. "I'm tired. It was nice of everybody."

"You're all right, aren't you? You're not really hurt, I mean?"

"I don't know. I'm fine, I guess."

"Okay, listen. I'll see you at the barracks in the morning. Between now and then you keep your trap shut. We'll figure out a story. I don't know how you can get so screwed up, but don't say anything until you've had time to tell me what happened. We'll get you out of it some way."

"Everything's been figured out."

Horne clenched his fists on the footrail of the bed. "We'll talk it over tomorrow, I said! I don't think anybody's going to bother you till you get out of here, but if they do you just play it tight. I know a yeoman in the ad building. You're going to get a board of review, sure as God made apples. Oh, well—skip it for now. I don't want to upset you. You want anything?"

Melvin shook his head.

Horne stared at him, and attempted to be sympathetic. "You're still groggy. You'll be all right tomorrow."

"As landings go, it was a little rough."

"I guess! You were lucky. I hope you know that."

"Yes, I know that," Melvin said.

Horne made a clucking noise, put on his cap, and strode out of the ward swinging his arms.

"Draw up a chair," Melvin said to his father.

"I am too nervous to sit down. Thank God this accident is not serious. I have never been so shocked. But explain about the telegram. What does it mean? Are you in trouble, and if so, of what sort? What does your friend mean by a board of review?"

"I'm in no trouble. If I wanted to get commissioned I'd be in a hell of a lot of trouble, but it doesn't make the slightest difference now because I'm quitting."

"Come and have lunch with me tomorrow in Pensacola. Can you be excused from the base? We will talk about everything. Everything. You're not in pain? You're recovering?"

"I'm all right. That commander is keeping me in the sack here just to prove he's a big shot."

"Do whatever he says. In the meantime, do you need anything? Money? I'll give you some money."

"I haven't even got my pants. What would I do with money?"

"All right! It was a question. Something I could do for my son. Will you please be good enough to tell me why you are always in so much trouble?"

Melvin said after a pause, "I do get fouled up sometimes. I don't know why."

"I'm going now to telephone Kansas City, to let the family know there is nothing to worry about. I won't mention the accident. Terrible!" He lifted his hands. "There's nothing I can do for you?"

"They feed me. I guess I'm all right."

"How long has it been?"

"Has what been?"

"Since I have seen you."

Melvin had begun to feel nauseated. The memory of the time when he expected to die came back to him. He gazed at the ceiling and made no attempt to speak.

"Excuse me," his father said, touching the pillow. "I don't mean to interrogate."

"I know you don't. It's just that you do."

"We will talk tomorrow. Have a good rest. Obey the officers."

After his father had left the ward Melvin lay quietly in bed considering the past few days. So much had happened. His head was filled with thoughts and impressions which bounded over and under one another like tigers in a circus, so that he felt besieged and dispirited and finally came to the conclusion that he wanted nothing so much as a long period of time to himself. It seemed to him that if he could be alone for a while he might possibly manage to organize his experiences and benefit from them.

About an hour later Pat Cole sauntered in. He sat on the edge of the bed without saying a word. He was carrying a book, as he often did.

"Well, hello," Melvin said.

"Hello," said Cole.

"I didn't think you'd be over."

"Why?"

"Horne told me your grandmother was in town."

"I haven't seen Horne all day. When are you going to wake up?"

"What do you mean?"

"Horne's an ass, and twice the cheat I am, or ever could be. However, that's irrelevant. No doubt he concocted that story on the assumption your tender feelings would be bruised if I didn't show up."

Melvin looked at him doubtfully.

"If you had the intelligence of your convictions," Cole went on, pinching the tip of his nose, "you might amount to something. For better or worse, however, you're too obsessed by your personal problems to exert much influence on the citizens of this grand and glorious republic. Or should I say, loyal subjects of this great oligarchy? In any event, this morning you demonstrated once again your really impressive inanity." He hesitated, pursed his lips as though he was about to whistle, and finally said, "You did this on purpose, but frankly, I'm damned if I know why."

"Did what? I'm not sure I know what you're talking about."

Cole crossed his legs, shaking the trousers up so that his knees would not ruin the crease, and then rested his chin in his hand while he appraised Melvin in a cool, knowing way. "Yes," he continued softly, and seemed to be amused. "What a shame that in every other respect you're mediocre. If I had what you have, say, or if you had what I have, there'd be the holy devil to pay. But the motivation, the motivation! You wrecked that SBD on purpose, you imbecile. Why didn't you talk to me first? I tried to get hold of you once before. Now it's too late." His eyes still fixed on Melvin, he straightened up and drew a cigarette case from his breast pocket; then, conscious of being in a hospital, he replaced it. "Why are you threatening the Romans?" he asked, and laughed shortly. "Because when you do that you threaten me as well. The paradox is that you are not even conscious of the extent of your revolt." He made no effort to say anything further. He began to examine his fingernails.

"Do you have any idea what kind of duty you'll get?" Melvin asked finally.

"Primary instructorship."

"You sound so positive."

"Why shouldn't I be positive? It was arranged six months ago. Commodore Lehigh and my father have been close friends for thirty years."

Melvin had never heard of Commodore Lehigh. "So you go first to New Orleans to the instructors' college, is that it?"

"That's right. Then I'll be assigned to the primary station at Glenview."

"Where's that?"

"Right outside Chicago. I'll have my car there. I'll be able to drive home every night. The base is about twenty minutes from my home."

"That's been arranged?"

"Yes."

"Well, all I can say is, you've sure got the gouge on this program."

"You and your suicidal independence," Cole murmured. He was still cleaning his nails.

The nurse stepped into the ward to announce that visitors must leave. At the far end of the room was an elderly couple; they and Cole were the only visitors. He stood up and without saying good-by he sauntered away.

A few minutes later the nurse came to Melvin's bed. She asked how he was feeling.

"Let me show you," he said and again reached for her knee, but she was alert; she dodged, and her eyes flashed. He was not sure whether she was angry or just exceptionally vivacious. Then he realized that she was holding a hypodermic. He was alarmed by this and started to sit up; she slapped one hand against his chest and shoved him down so vigorously that he bounced.

"Now, listen here," he said, "I'm sick! You can't treat me that way. I don't feel good."

"You jus' flip ovah and close them luscious big brown eyes," the nurse said without a smile. She pulled the sheet away from his chin, but Melvin caught the sheet and held on.

"I don't need a hypodermic," he said. "The commander didn't say anything about giving me a hypodermic. And even if he did, that needle's big enough for a horse. I don't want it. I won't take it, see. I refuse!"

218

"Cadet, I don't care whether you want this or whether you don't. You'll take it one way or another."

"I want to talk to the commander," Melvin said, hoping that he had secured for the night, but as soon as she placed the syringe on the table and started for the door he waved his hands and muttered, "Okay, okay."

"Roll over and make it snappy," she ordered. He turned on his stomach, she pulled up the nightgown.

"No Southern girl would do a thing like that," he said.

"Hereaftah, lovah man," she remarked as she swabbed him with alcohol, "you have mo' respec' fo' yankee ladies," and with that she inserted the needle.

Melvin grunted. "Now, about us," he resumed when the needle was withdrawn, "What time do you get off duty?"

She pulled down the nightgown, drew the covers up to his chin, and after collecting the equipment on the table she left the ward.

He meant to stay awake and talk to her further because he did not believe she was as uninterested as she pretended, but then he discovered it was morning. The other patients were waking up and there was an elderly nurse on duty. Seeing that he had come to life she walked over and slipped a thermometer in his mouth. A few minutes later she stopped by to read it, and after giving him his breakfast she brought his clothes.

Outside it was clear and warm with a fresh Gulf breeze, and Melvin was struck by the splendor of the day; he paused on the steps of the dispensary to look around. He felt rested and confident, more certain of himself than he had ever felt before. It seemed to him as he emerged from the shadow of the ward that a great change was coming over him and that he would never be the same. He drew a deep breath and started walking across the base.

Horne sat on the front steps of the barracks playing with a pair of gold wings. He was holding them up to the sun and trying to shine the reflection on his breast.

"What kept you?" he asked, squinting at the cloudless sky. "I figured you'd be out of there at dawn. Sick bay gives me the creeps. I can't stand to be sick. You feel okay?"

"All right," Melvin said. "Except I'm stiff."

"I ran into Kennedy. He wanted me to tell you he hoped you weren't spooked."

"Who's Kennedy?"

"That moldy lieutenant at Whiting, the peanut-eater. The instrument check pilot."

"Yes, I remember him now. What's he doing here?"

"Search me," Horne answered. "He was walking out of the ad building with a WAVE and recognized me and said he'd heard about the wreck."

"Is he still teaching instrument at Whiting?"

"I don't know. I don't run around poking my nose into an officer's business."

"I'd like to have seen him."

"I don't know where you think you are!" Horne cried, jumping up. "You certainly don't act like you were in the Navy. The Green Hornet! What in God's name is the matter with you?"

"Nothing's the matter with me. Not any more."

"Oh, no? Suppose we take a trip to the hangar. There's something you might like to see."

"Well, now, ah don' mind if'n I do," Melvin said, and he whistled cheerfully through his teeth as they walked along.

Already the swimming pool was crowded, beach towels spread on the grass embankment. On the basketball court a few officers and some cadets were choosing sides for a game; it would be a leisurely game. Overhead an echelon of SBD's was breaking up—one after another spiraling down with the plump black wheels unfolding and acrid blue smoke streaming from the exhaust; he watched them coast out of sight behind the administration building and felt the shadow as one passed between him and the sun.

"You must have looked gorgeous," said Horne in a hostile, embittered voice. He shook his head in disgust.

"Like a bird," said Melvin, grinning.

"Nick told me he spotted you two miles away. What were you doing near the Gulf?"

"Joy-riding. How did he recognize me two miles away?"

"By the smoke, of course," Horne said, stopping to look at him. "He thought you were a stove."

"Smoke? What smoke?"

"What smoke," said Horne, rolling his eyes. "Baby, they could have seen you from Mainside."

"Was there that much? I thought it was just in the cockpit. Why didn't anybody tell me?"

"What would you have done if somebody did tell you?"

"I don't know. Bail out, maybe."

"You have any idea how low you were?"

"That's right. I was fairly low."

"And besides," Horne went on, "they took up ten of those parachute packs the other day and threw them out and four of them didn't open."

"Really? I bet those girls in the loft caught hell."

"Have you seen what you came home in? Were you conscious when they pulled you out?"

"No," Melvin said. "It was still in the air the last I remember." And he added, thoughtfully, "It's probably sort of beat up after that landing. I did the best I could."

"Beat up," said Horne. "They had to scoop it up. They unloaded it in the hangar. You want to look, or not?"

"I don't care. I guess so. Why not? Sure, let's have a peek."

A rope had been strung around the SBD to keep everyone away. Both of the wings had broken off; the second one had fallen off while the wreckage was being dragged across the mat. The stack of metal was twisted and oily and scorched. The paint of the fuselage was blistered and the tires were punctured, and one blade of the propeller was bent at right angles to the other two. The entire hangar smelled of gas and burnt rubber.

"Listen," Horne said after a while, "I don't know what frequency you're on, but nobody else is tuned in. But nobody! Nick asked me the other day what was eating you. Look, I haven't asked too many questions. Maybe you've got problems at home; maybe you're worried about letting your father down. It's none of my business, only it seems like you're up on a cloud somewhere twiddling your thumbs and observing the situation. Did any of us hurt your feelings?"

"No."

"Then what gives?"

"Nothing."

Horne took a deep breath.

"I hate to tell you: the squadron commander phoned the barracks. You're to appear before him at two o'clock this afternoon."

Melvin was standing with his hand on one of the posts that supported the rope and he was looking intently at the ruined airplane. It seemed incredible that yesterday he had been five miles above the earth in that pile of blackened junk.

"I'll be there," he said at last, lifting his hand from the post, turning away from the wreckage. "Tell the commander not to worry. I'll be there at two o'clock."

"What's the matter?" said Horne. "Tell me."

Melvin smiled at him, and suddenly understood how a woman some day would fall in love with him. He wanted to put his arms around Horne and for a little while to hold him close.

"Nothing," he said. "Why should anything be the matter? Don't be miserable. It's me, not you who's in trouble. Next week you'll be an ensign. You've done it, don't you realize? You beat the program. You're a success."

Horne was angry and puzzled. "Sure, I beat the program. Except I got beat in the process. I'll be an officer, but still I'll be afraid of officers. I don't understand what they've done to us." He was fondling the gold wings, nervously turning them over and over and squeezing the clasp. "Listen, there's a chance you can talk your way out of it this afternoon. Try, will you? For almost two years I've been looking forward to the day when we'd march up those steps, one right after the other, and get those wings and have the old man hand us a diploma. You don't know how much I've wanted that. I don't think you ever really cared about it, not the way I did. But up until the war I never got much fun out of life. I lived on a farm and bred pigs. You don't know anything about that. You've lived in a city all your life, but on Saturdays my brother and I'd get dressed up, all gussied up, and we'd drive to North Platte to raise hell. You can't raise much hell in North Platte. You just can't. Once in a while we'd take out for Lincoln or Grand Island. Twice in my life I got as far as Omaha. Baby, you don't have any idea what kind of a life I had. When you and I went through Kansas City on the train I was twenty years old and that was the first time I'd ever seen skyscrapers. But now—and I'm not fooling—I'm going places! I'm a naval aviator and there's nobody better. You think you sweated it out? Didn't you ever wonder about me? You thought because my grades were higher that I didn't have trouble? There were nights you sawed wood for eight straight hours while I sat up in the sack wringing my hands and trying to figure out why I goofed on some recognition exam, or on some instrument pattern. But I got through, and I've got the right to wear those wings, and I'm going to wear them. I never worked so hard for anything in my life. Because I never spoke about the Deacon getting killed at Albuquerque, or about Elmer, you thought I'd forgotten? Run through that one again, baby."

Horne was trembling with emotion. He pointed at the ruined SBD. "There's no excuse for that! You dove that hulk too fast. You should have known better. These planes are old but they won't fall apart at normal diving speed. How fast were you going?"

"I forgot to look," Melvin grinned. "I was moving, though."

"I guess! And I'll tell you another thing: some enlisted men were offering six to five odds you'd blow up. Ostrowski heard them."

"Is that so? I wish I'd been there."

"Why?"

"I'd have given a lot better odds than that. I didn't think I had a Chinaman's chance."

Horne threw the wings violently against the floor of the hangar and turned on him with a ferocious expression. "Don't talk to me like that!" he shouted. He stopped and waited until he had recovered himself, then continued in a strained voice, clenching and unclenching his fists, while perspiration trickled down his face. "Listen, who are you talking to? Don't you recognize me any more? I'm your old buddy, Sam Horne. We've been together a long time. We understand each other, don't we?"

"Sure," Melvin said.

"Talk to me!"

"What about?"

"Just let me know what's eating you, that's all. Maybe I can help a little bit."

"I'm fine," Melvin said.

"You're lying," Horne said gently. "You're lying, that's what beats me." He took another look at the devastated airplane and turned away quickly, hitting his palm with his fist. "I hate to say this, baby, but you're through. You haven't got a prayer. You don't have one single prayer."

16

★

Melvin telephoned his father that it would be better to have lunch earlier than they had planned because he had to be back on the station by two o'clock. After this he showered, dressed in his cadet blues, and started toward the gate. Near the administration building he saw Lieutenant Caravaggio.

"Isaacs!" the officer called, hurrying down the steps, "I must talk to you!"

"I have to meet my father in Pensacola," Melvin answered without stopping, and without saluting.

Caravaggio skipped along beside him. "Will you talk to me when you get back? I could make this an order, you know."

Melvin shook his head.

"What's this accident? I hadn't planned on that. You're confusing me, damn you!" He stopped, breathing heavily, and Melvin walked on.

"Good-by!" he called.

Melvin did not answer. At the gate he glanced back, afraid Caravaggio would be watching, but the officer was nowhere in sight.

On the bus he took from his wallet some snapshots of his friends. He looked at them while the bus rolled along the highway to Pensacola. There was a picture of Horne grinning, posing with truculent confidence in front of a Dauntless; in the same picture, crouched like an Indian in the shade of the wing, with his chin strap dangling and his head almost touching a propeller blade, was Nick McCampbell; on the opposite wing stood Roska. Cole was supposed to be in that picture, too, but he had become bored, Melvin remembered, because there had been some difficulty with the camera, and had walked away and had not come back. There were snapshots from Ellyson and Whiting and Barin. And when he came to a photograph of Elmer in the cockpit of an SNJ it seemed to him that a great deal of time had passed since then, though it had only been a few months. Elmer had been killed the day after the picture was taken; Melvin remembered how reluctant he had been, because of this fact, to get the films developed.

And while the Navy bus rolled on and on through the deep pine forest, bursting into the bright noon light and into the shadows again, he fell to thinking of all he had experienced. So much had occurred so inexplicably, too rapidly, yet no one worried; it was as though they had tacitly agreed to participate in a play which had no beginning and no climax, which was so mysterious that no one understood the plot.

Now that it was over he could reflect on it with something like pleasure, which was not quite pleasure, really, or satisfaction, or pride; he did not know, in fact, just how he did feel about it all, but he knew he would not forget what he had seen and what he had done. He would not forget his friends, though he might never meet them again after they received their wings; or the nights of liberty in Mobile; or the particular nature of each station—the light filtering through the trees, the shape of the barracks, the muggy, long summer nights or the dry, cold winter nights, the sounds and odors of the mess hall, the bulletin boards, moving pictures, the billiard tables, the public-address systems and the auditoriums and the textbooks. But most of all, and with a feeling as near to gratitude as to anything, he thought he would not be apt to forget what it was like to fly—to be a flyer.

It seemed to him that he was able to hear once more the steady reassuring tremble of the engine and to feel on his ankles the warm, constant breath of the heater, so like a cool morning on the beach, standing barefoot at the water's edge and listening to the faraway thunder of the breakers while the Gulf eddied and washed along the sand with a soft gurgling and lapping. The sky, the sea, and the splendor of the earth—these he would not forget.

These could not be taken from him no matter how humbly he was dressed, or how menial the services he performed. He did not think he would ever quite forget the awesome flash of the green and white course lights illuminating the night sky like an electrical storm, or the coughing, barking engines like sea lions somewhere in the darkness, while fumes drifted through the hangar on a sweet evening breeze, and the screech of tires far out on the landing mat. If he listened he could hear, and if he looked diligently he could still see the moon behind the long-legged water tower, the water tower with its absurd Chinese hat. A tire fell from the sky and it had come bouncing toward him while a great diagonal flame shot up and the dull boom rever-berated over bloody Barin Field, and he remembered the crash that preceded the boom like the grinding clash of trays in the mess hall and the way his heart was palpitating as he raced for the safety of the barracks while smoke boiled up in the sky and obliterated the stars.

He shifted restlessly, tipped his hat over his eyes, folded his arms on his chest. The bus swung around a curve, rattled across a wooden bridge, and swayed along to Pensacola.

The bleak and gaseous silence of the upper air, the miracle of being separate from the world—a solid, miniature world, and really very like the painted cardboard globe mounted on a cheap brass base which he used to spin interminably when he was a child—green horizons lower down where the air was warm and thick with human voices and where the trees emptied of birds as he came nearer while the mirrored sun went walking with godly freedom across the tapering aluminum wings. And how the echelon hung unmoving in the opal light, angling down the beach against the off-shore breeze, and swept beyond the speedboats and the swimmers, and curved fanatically up and up and up like scimitars—leaving the birds below and the splash-flowers opening on the vibrant blue glass of the Gulf, until that warm water did seem deep and devoid of mercy, and the cockpit assumed an entity, totally enclosed, as a solarium, or as a very small and ascetic studio with a skylight arched against the universe, until the canopy slid open and winter vanished into spring and he became aware of the coveralls damp with perspiration, stuck to his shoul-ders in the hot enclosure, the coveralls zipped to his throat, or unzipped to the waist, and the straps and strings of the parachute and life preserver—the stainless metal nub of a carbon dioxide capsule—designed, developed, manufactured under certain rigid specifications for the preservation of his particular life, which was valuable to the nation at war, this impersonal metallic capsule, as integral and as different as the sugary, fruity taste of the gum he was chewing while he idly fingered the nub and considered what might happen if he inflated the life jacket, for no better reason than that he had worn one every day and had never used it—and twisting about, gazed at the mouth of the long white sleeve, the voracious oral beginning, swimming eagerly over the trees and over the water and after him wherever he went. And shortly afterward the tow plane lurched. An SNJ was falling, out of control, caught by the sleeve. The impact where it struck. How the water unexpectedly flowered.

The bus bumped along the shoulder of the highway, slowed and stopped. There was some obstruction, and a junction. Melvin gazed at the road crew; they were putting down their picks and drills; it was time for lunch. Brown paper bags, Thermos bottles; the sun must be directly over the bus, because he could see no shadow. Somebody had sat down beside him and in a moment he smelled perfume; he glanced at the woman as the bus started up, was uninterested, and resumed looking out the window.

The terror he had known as he witnessed those petals of water close on the sinking plane, and the powerful, incomprehensible emotions he had felt as he followed the echelon toward Barin Field—these he could summon up, yet they had no greater meaning now than at the time; they meant no more than the black necktie fluttering around his lips, or the vision, as he drew back on the controls, of his own brain compressed so fearfully odd and solid, and pink as a muddy salmon. On the deserted beach the driftwood animals jumped when the bullets struck, rolling over and over from the impact, and those lying half awash went floating out to sea, to the deep water, and how or why they were so unmistakably animals, he did not know. And he remembered clearly the horror he felt as that skinned white log he had centered in the ringsight of the gun turned over in the water like a human body.

Soon—for already they were in the suburbs—they would be at

the terminal, and then he must have lunch with his father and try to explain what had happened. There was no way to explain it. It had just happened, he did not know quite how; he did not want to think about it.

He decided to think about Whiting Field, for there were no unpleasant associations to the instrument squadron; at least there had been no accidents, only a laborious, methodical, interminable procedure and the sense of having been harassed, suffering from vertigo, obliged to do too many things in too short a period of time; three hands would have made it easier, and with four or five hands and an additional brain it would have been simple to create some orderly pattern from the chaos in the unnatural fluorescent light—that lavender-white funereal light which dis-colored his skin in the gloom of the canvas hood, reminding him inexplicably of water and space and of the iris of a woman's eye. The radio beam's shrill unending whine—dash-dot, dash-dot when the plane drifted—a startling cone of silence above the transmitter, throbbing along, bumped by currents of air from fields and roads a mile below. The compass imprisoned in amber liquid sluggishly dipped and crazily swung from south to south-east as the bus swung on the highway.

There was, too, the winter in Albuquerque; he hoped that dur-ing the future, a future which held no promise, his memories of the west mesa buried in snow, and the vastness there, and all that went with this, might sustain his spirit. There would be, for in-stance, the rasp of Lycoming engines like bumblebees on the con-crete apron, and the cadets in mackinaws with their backs against the sunny side of the hangar and their hands tucked up their sleeves, while snow on the box toes of their government shoes softened and trickled away. There would be the memory of frozen ruts the color of Indian pottery, and the way the airplanes bobbled across the ruts, and how he felt himself lifted from the earth by the December wind into an immense primeval silence.

And he thought, then, as he rolled along toward Pensacola, that it would be wise not to begin too soon, not to spend this day in-dulging in dreams. There would be time. There would be enough time to recall how the birds wheeled open-mouthed through the dust-blue Georgia twilight, the cottonwood trees beside the Rio

228

Grande, and the humid melancholy of a Memphis summer. There would be time enough and more.

In the hotel lobby at Pensacola he saw his father pacing back and forth, slapping a rolled newspaper into his palm with an expression of determination.

"Ah! There you are!" he exclaimed, rushing across the lobby. "I thought you weren't coming. How do you feel?" he asked in a voice filled with emotion.

"I'm all right," Melvin said. "Let's eat."

They walked into the dining room. The windows were shut. The fans were not operating. Melvin took off his blue coat and hung it over the back of a chair.

"Is that permissible? It doesn't look nice, to be frank. A naval aviation cadet."

"I don't know if it's permissible or not," Melvin said. He loosened his necktie and rolled up his sleeves while he looked at the menu. "I think I'll have chicken à la king with peas."

"That won't be good. Try the steak. The steak should be all right."

"I want chicken à la king and peas."

"Small hotels don't know how to prepare delicacies. Eat the steak. That's what I'm having." When the waiter came to their table he ordered two steaks.

"One steak," Melvin interrupted. "One chicken à la king with peas."

"Whatever you wish, don't say I didn't warn you. And a bottle of nice wine," his father remarked to the waiter. "Domestic. I leave the selection to you."

The wine the waiter brought to them was cool, it was roseate, and Melvin called on it frequently during lunch. The more of this wine he drank, the more he became convinced he had been neglecting one of the finer things of life. In a little while he scarcely knew he was drinking this wine, it went down that graciously. He swore to himself he must remember this wine, and, to make certain, he kept the bottle so close at hand that his father was impressed and ordered another.

He did not know at what point during the meal he became aware of the objects on the table, but there were a drop of lead

229

from the Argonne forest, a faded ribbon of the Rainbow division, an Iron Cross, a number of old photographs—his father had taken them from an envelope and was insisting he look at them.

"Here I am, beneath the Arch of Triumph, wearing puttees. You never had to wear puttees. Look, do you see? This is I, here, beneath the arch shaking hands with a Frenchman. That's the Arch of Triumph, a famous French monument. We marched through it, down the boulevard, I'll never forget. See this picture? The tomb of Napoleon! I am the second soldier from the right. Here is a theater stub, to a Paris theater. Very interesting. Next, this is part of my railroad ticket, look at that! Read the date. Right there. Nineteen eighteen! Amazing." He looked into the envelope again. "Ah! I have been planning to tell you more about the family, our ancestors." He held up a photograph showing a group of people on a brick veranda. "The man in the cavalry hat is your great-grandfather who rode in the Civil War with General Shelby!"

Melvin nodded. Whenever his father stopped talking he nodded. The thought of the impending board of review had begun to frighten him. He did not know what he was going to say to the officers. If they only wanted facts it would be simple, but if they asked for explanations he had no idea what he could say. He drank some wine and poured another glass. The wine and the muggy tropical air made him dizzy and he thought he would like nothing better than to lie down in a cool corner away from everybody and go to sleep. He started up, and realized his father was shaking him by the arm and was holding out an old newspaper clipping for him to read. Melvin accepted the clipping and dizzily read it with his head in his hands while he tried to keep from falling out of the chair.

DAY OF PATRIOTISM

War Indorsed

Crowd Hears Patriotic Program And
Speech By David W. Isaacs—Bond
Campaign Launched

Saturday, Apr. 6, was a day of patriotic renewal for the county. The ringing of bells in the morning startled many people and a few thought peace had been declared or a decisive victory gained. The bells rang again and whistles blew at 12 o'clock and at six o'clock in the evening.

Towards noon the city band played patriotic airs and banners spelling out the words "Buy Liberty Bonds" were hung around the courthouse square by Boy Scouts, who then staged a tableau representing the familiar Leyendecker bond poster. Each scout held a "Can the Kaiser" pennant, with a tin can tied to the end of the pennant.

The courtroom was decorated with bunting for the meeting, with the allied flags on either side of the speaker's table. Truman T. Morris presided. After the invocation by the Rev. L. R. Borland, Miss Sarah Borland, accompanied by Miss Angela Mert, sang "What kind of an American Are You?"

Judge Isaacs, principal speaker, opened his address with a statement of the war preparations already made by the United States.

"The time has passed for mollycoddling," Judge Isaacs went on. "The fact is that the enemy is not 3000 miles away. He is in our very midst. It would not surprise me in the least to learn that there is a paid German agent in this very audience." A wave of murmurs swept through the audience as he said this. He cautioned his hearers to guard against the work of incendiaries, especially around the oil refineries.

Two incidents he told especially touched the audience. They were the story of a French family just rising from poverty into comfortable circumstances, and their happiness at going back to fight the horror in whose shadow they had lived; the other of the eagerness of a young recruit to join his seventeen relatives in the Army.

After Judge Isaacs' address Mr. Morris

asked for loan subscriptions and there was a generous response from the audience.

"What time is it?" Melvin said as soon as he finished reading. "My watch is slow. We'll ask the waiter. In every war, I'm trying to point out, our family has devoted time and effort—our lives, in fact—to making the world a decent place. Your ancestors, Melvin, fought in the Revolution for independence. Doesn't that mean anything to you? Their children fought against the Mexicans, and against the Spaniards, and so on. I myself had a very close call during the First World War. I have a trunk filled with souvenirs in the attic in Kansas City—a trench knife with metal teeth on the hand guard, a spiked German helmet, old uniforms. I even have a bayonet on which it is still possible to see traces of blood."

Melvin finished off the wine and wiped his lips. "I have to be getting back to the base."

"What are you expected to do this afternoon? I understand it's to be an investigation. The officers are going to inquire about your accident. Request another opportunity. You can make good, if you try. Apologize for the accident. It doesn't matter whether you are to blame or not. Merely apologize. Ask for another chance. Promise me. Is that too much?"

"I can't promise anything," Melvin said irritably. "I don't know what I'm going to do or say, so how can I make a promise? I have to think about things. Now I've got to go. I'm probably going to be late for the board as it is. Not that it makes much difference, except that as long as I'm going to appear I might as well try to be there on time."

"Of course. But first, we've been telling people we were coming to watch you graduate. Now what will we say? You don't seem to care! Think of your mother and your sister! How are they going to feel?"

"Things just didn't work out. I don't know why."

"An explanation is the least you owe us. You've told me nothing. You send a telegram that you are resigning. That's all we know. It doesn't make sense!" There were tears in his eyes.

"Let me alone!" Melvin cried in a choking voice. He got up

232

from the table, but staggered and quickly sat down. He wiped his face, drank some water, and after a few moments he stood up again. "I think I'm all right. It's so hot today. I know you're disappointed. I'm sorry. I tried. You don't believe me, but I did try. I did!"

"It means so much. After so long, success means so much."

Melvin looked down at his father and for a few moments was not able to speak, but finally he said, "The war is going to end someday. I can't wait any longer," and with that he picked up his coat and hurried away.

The bus was disappearing around a corner as he came within sight of the terminal. It was thirty minutes before he got another bus, and when he reached Saufley Field and entered the commander's office he saw that he was almost an hour late. The board of review, however, was still in session; in fact, he had not even been called. Apparently they were going over all the material that had accumulated about him since he first applied for admission to the training program. He sat on a bench in the corridor holding his hat in his lap and waited. Twenty minutes after he arrived they sent for him. His uniform was rumpled and there was dust on his shoes. His necktie hung askew. His gaze was vague and he reeked of wine.

The officers requested his account of the wreck; he told them what happened as though he were reciting a narrative he had memorized; he spoke in a monotone, paying no attention to their reaction, but paused frequently to correct himself over some insignificant point such as that he might possibly have climbed a few hundred feet higher than his preliminary estimate, or that he might have emerged from the dive in a westerly rather than a southerly direction.

The officers did not ask why he had brought the damaged plane to the field instead of abandoning it in the Gulf. He had hoped that one of them would ask about this. He had no answer, he would have made no particular effort to supply an answer, and yet he wished someone would ask; it would mean that they were concerned not only with what had happened, but why it had happened. However, no one asked.

The inquiry did not take as long as he had expected.

17

★

He thought he might find Horne and the others waiting for him in the corridor—but it was deserted—or outside the administration building, for he was sure they were anxious to know the results of the board of review, but the only person he encountered as he left the building was an elderly chief petty officer who was tacking a notice on the bulletin board by the front door.

The sky was clear, planes were flying. He walked across the station with his hands in his pockets and a dejected expression. Nobody noticed him.

At the barracks he found everyone getting ready for the trip to the main station where they would be commissioned. Horne was squatting in the middle of the room with his hat on backward; he was cursing monotonously and without much conviction while he rammed books and clothing into his duffel bag. When Melvin entered the room he glanced up, scowling, and hit something inside the bag with his fist. Melvin sat down on the bunk.

"Well?" Horne growled after a few minutes.

"They kicked me out. I knew they would."

"Who didn't!"

"It wasn't their fault," Melvin said mildly. "They were doing what they thought they had to do."

"Did you just stand up there like Little Red Riding Hood with your thumb in your mouth and tell them the truth?"

Melvin grinned and nodded. Horne considered him and then resumed packing the duffel bag. Melvin began to look around for a cigarette; a package smacked against the wall beside him.

"There! Have a cigarette, George Washington."

"Oh, relax," Melvin said. "It's over. It wasn't bad."

The next morning the company left Saufley Field. Melvin helped throw the bags aboard the truck, shook hands all around, and promised that if possible he would visit Mainside for the designation ceremony. As the truck went through the gate he waved, and some of the cadets waved back.

When he could no longer see them he wandered around for a while but at last returned to the barracks. The building was vacant and quiet. Most of the doors to the rooms were open. He sauntered along the corridors looking into the rooms at the doubled-up mattresses, the shades half-drawn, and the dust settling through the beams of light, a little surprised that it was hard to remember who had lived where. The name plates had been removed from the doors and the rooms were so similar.

Later that afternoon the new company arrived from Barin Field and a lanky, leathery cadet named Burl Atcher was assigned to Horne's bunk. Atcher was full of questions about the flying characteristics of the SBD, and he was nearly overcome when he discovered that Saufley cadets ate not from aluminum trays but from plates, the same as civilians. Then Melvin told him about the napkins. Atcher found it hard to believe.

"Shucks, buddy boy," he muttered. "Cloth napkins!"

"That's right," Melvin answered, lying on the bunk and trying to wiggle his toes one at a time for lack of anything better to do. "No more paper. They're made out of linen and you get a clean one for every meal."

"Shucks," the new cadet said. "I ain't had me a napkin since Ponca City."

"This is a pretty good base," Melvin told him. "You're going to like it here."

Eventually the conversation got around to why Melvin was alone in the barracks. He had hoped Atcher would not inquire, but knew the question was inevitable.

"I've been washed out," he said, and waited.

Atcher frankly stared.

"It's the truth," Melvin said. "I'm waiting for my orders. In a few days I'll be going to Great Lakes."

"Your buddies gone to Mainside?"

Melvin nodded, reluctant to talk about it. All of them were at the main station now, polishing their shoes and getting their uniforms pressed. Next Tuesday their names would be announced over a loudspeaker and they would march across a platform to receive a diploma and shake hands with the commandant of the base. "They left a little while ago. They were pretty excited about it."

Atcher suddenly sprawled on the bunk that had belonged to Horne. "Shucks, buddy, I guess! I tell you for dang sure, I'm looking forward to that day."

"It won't be long," Melvin told him, and he could not help hating Atcher a little, not for anything he had said, or done, but because he had appropriated the desk, and the lamp, and the closet —everything—that had belonged to Horne.

Atcher propped himself up on one elbow. "I'm dang sorry. I sure am. A good buddy of mine got washed out at Albuquerque for no reason at all. Spang!" he exclaimed, snapping his fingers. "Like that! They didn't give him no reason at all. Just out he went."

"So you were at Albuquerque," Melvin said, although he was hardly conscious of Atcher. Ever since his friends had left the station he had been unable to think clearly; he kept seeing the row of officers at the board of review and kept hearing the courteous, irrelevant questions they put to him. He saw the gray epaulets and the midnight-blue epaulets with the stripes and the star, and the wings above the immaculate quadrangles of campaign ribbons, and the battle stars. They had not known anything about him except what was written on the record. He half heard Atcher talk about the various bases he had gone through; Atcher had arrived at each base—Iowa, Albuquerque, Athens, Memphis—an hour or so after Melvin left.

"Say," he was asking, "did you ever meet up with that crazy cadoodler?"

"The program's full of them. Which one?"

"The one that shot down that gyrene colonel."

A familiar sense of discouragement came over him when he heard this, but at last he said, "The guy was a captain, not a colonel. He wasn't shot down—he just got two bullet holes in the wing. It was an accident." He intended to let it go at that, but knew that sooner or later Atcher would suspect the truth. He decided to get it over with. "His name was Teitlebaum. He was

236

my instructor. He was closer to the target than he should have been and my aim was bad. He wasn't injured; just plenty mad. That's the story."

Atcher was chewing a match, eyes narrowed. "Buddy boy, was that you?"

"It was. Amen. Yes, it was," Melvin said.

Atcher needed a while to get used to the idea that he was actually talking to the cadet who had shot his instructor. At last, placing stress on it, and concluding with a heavy wink, he said, "Some accident!"

Melvin became uncomfortable when anyone winked at him; he winked back just as deliberately and said in an irritable voice, "Strictly between you and me, friend, it was no accident."

"Dang!" Atcher called, and sat erect with an expectant grin.

"Yes, that's right, but keep it confidential," Melvin went on. "You see, I never did like that son of a bitch and he rode me once too often. I doubt if he'll bother me again." It had been a long time since he had lied to anyone and he had forgotten how refreshing it could be. The ideas began to flow; he felt as though he could talk for hours, and as one lie danced after another he became alert, cheerful, and often gestured with expansive good humor. "What's more," he continued, chuckling, "if I could get Captain Teitlebaum in front of a thirty-caliber one more time—" he snapped his fingers, flung his arms apart, and fell on the bunk. "Listen, pal," he resumed, sitting up, "too bad you weren't here the other day to see what I did. I wrecked an SBD. What do you think of *that!*"

Atcher, removing the match, studied him in grave surprise. "It was *you* done cracked up that old Dauntless?"

"You mean you've heard about it?"

"Surely did. Only didn't nobody at Barin reckon it was the same cadoodler."

"Friend, are you trying to tell me Barin Field has heard about that wreck?"

Atcher was unable to keep from staring at him as though he were an object on display; he resented this, but for the moment he was so startled that all he could think about was that if Barin Field knew of the wreck, so must every other auxiliary station.

"She didn't burn you none?"

"No. I wasn't burned."

Atcher seemed disappointed. "We done heard how she cooked you like a strip of bacon."

"Just a bump on my forehead," Melvin replied, and touched the bandage.

"Buddy," the cowboy said, "I been hearing about you all the way through this here program, only I didn't know it was you." He came shambling across the room with one hand extended.

Melvin understood that he was being congratulated; for what reason he could not imagine, however he accepted the hand, which was callused and scaly and reminded him of a lizard.

In the next few days he spent most of his time drinking coffee in the recreation hall or at the hangar, watching the planes take off and land, or observing the enlisted men—how they responded to officers, what they did when they were off duty—and he often contrived to overhear their conversation, which now seemed to him singularly fascinating. And because he was at liberty until his orders arrived he went to Pensacola or Mobile every evening, as much to avoid his new roommate as for any other reason.

Since he had not yet paid for his uniforms he called up Pettigrew's and explained that he had been washed out and asked if he could return them. Pettigrew's said he could not, and that he would be expected to pay for them.

On the day his friends were to become officers he took a bus to the main station and hunted up the barracks where they were quartered. More than two hundred cadets from various squadrons would graduate that afternoon and the barracks echoed with shouting, singing, and laughter. Cadets rushed in every direction, back and forth through the corridors, up and down the stairways and from one room to another. Melvin did not see anyone he knew. He was standing uncertainly at the top of the stairs with his cap over one eye and his hands in his hip pockets when he heard a hoarse bellow of rage and frustration halfway down the corridor and the crash of an object hurled to the floor or against a wall. He walked toward the noise, looked into a room, and found Horne dancing about in an agony of indecision and glowering at himself in a full-length mirror.

"Oh, it's you," Horne said. "Did you ever in your life see such a miserable uniform? Honest to God, the money I paid that quack tailor! It shrunk when I had it dry-cleaned. I wanted to get rid of that new look, you know, so I had it cleaned, see, and by God it shrunk! It's too tight!"

"Tailors aren't quacks," Melvin said, "they're hacks. You're thinking of doctors."

Horne tore off the blouse, swore at it, and trotted out of the room with his fists clenched.

Just then Pat Cole wandered in. "The all-American boy seems to have a problem," Cole remarked as he tapped a cigarette on the back of his wrist.

"He's excited."

"As usual."

Melvin smiled. "I suppose you've received your orders by now."

"Oh, yes. Yes, I have them. We all do."

"Judging from your attitude I'd guess you received what you expected."

Cole glanced at him in a friendly way, as though Melvin had complimented him. "Yes. Two weeks' leave, after which I report to the instructors' college at New Orleans. Incidentally, my parents are here. I'll introduce you, if you like. My pater tells me the Glenview assignment has also been arranged. He spoke to the commodore the last time he was in Washington. All in all, I have no complaints." He tossed the lighter nonchalantly in his hand. "Do you know, for the past three days, Melvin, they've had us out drilling in the hot sun—right face, left face, left oblique —the entire syllabus, as though we were apprentice seamen. A Marine corporal has been our drill instructor. This was the Navy's final gesture of humiliation toward us; it was altogether deliberate. There was no need to abuse us, but the Navy did it, and this porcine Marine concurred with obvious delight. He stood in the shade, mind you, in that grotesque, licentious way Marines are taught to stand, with their hips thrust forward, and from there he bawled the orders, switching his thigh with a stick. I gather he is allowed to do this every week. I suspect he has erotic dreams about it. Well," said Cole with an absent smile, "he has a gift coming from me, although he isn't cognizant of it yet. He enjoyed himself with Aviation Cadet Cole. However, as soon as the designation ceremony concludes, Ensign Cole is going to the

Marine barracks—for a 'chat,' should we say?" He looked around; Horne was just coming into the room. He bowed sardonically, murmured, "Adieu, gentlemen, adieu," and sauntered away.

Horne scowled after him. "I'd crucify that clown if it was worth the effort."

"It isn't. What duty did you draw?"

"Fighters. Operational at Jacksonville," Horne muttered. He was powdering his jaw with talcum. "They call these new 4U's the ensign killers. A fellow I ate breakfast with was telling me two ensigns got it last week at Jax, stalled on the final turn and went down like sheep in a slaughterhouse. I was hoping for an F6—that's what Kerdolph drew."

Melvin walked to the window where he stood looking toward the area where the ceremony was to be held. He could see a rectangle of collapsible chairs and a platform with a lectern and microphone, and flags to either side. Some enlisted men were unrolling a long red carpet.

"Come look at your reward," he said.

Horne came to the window. "I'll be damned! It actually is a red carpet. Well, it's no more than we deserve, after what they put us through."

A few minutes later Roska dashed into the room and demanded in a menacing voice, "All right, you people, where is it?" He smelled of bay rum and cleaning fluid.

"Is what?" Horne replied mildly; he was straddling a chair and was trying to sew up a hole in one of his socks.

"Don't get smart!" Roska shouted.

Horne, lifting the black silk sock, examined it critically while the needle and thread swayed back and forth. "If you wish us to assist you, sir, you've got to be more specific."

"Oh, hello," Roska said, seeming to recognize Melvin for the first time. Then he threw back his head and called, "Now hear this! You people! Whoever stole my bourbon bring it back on the double!" Then, as if he had remembered something, he clutched his head and hurried down the corridor.

"What are—" Melvin began, intending to ask what Horne was going to do after the ceremony, but stopped because several cadets he had never seen before were in the doorway arguing about the number of wings that could be worn. One cadet had a row of wings pinned to his shorts.

"So what was that all about?" Melvin asked when they had moved along.

"Same old story—women. You'd think the Navy was commissioning a bunch of goats, the way these people go after it. That guy with all the wings, he doesn't think about anything else. Night before last we went into town and he laid a bet he could make a WAC, a WAVE, a BAM, and a civilian before liberty expired, and by God if he didn't! I never heard of such a thing," Horne added piously. "It was revolting."

"How do you know he did it?"

"Ostrowski hid in the closet."

"That must have been some party."

"Yes, it was," said Horne. "It was quite an evening."

After a moment Melvin said, "I still don't understand about the extra wings. What's he wearing so many for?"

"He figures it'll make it even easier. Whenever he runs into a stubborn broad he'll give her a pair and say they were the ones he wore when he was commissioned at Pensacola. He figures she'll be so flattered she'll hop right into the sack."

"But why is he actually wearing them? There's no way of telling whether or not a pair of wings were literally worn during the ceremony. He could hand out a pair and merely *say* they were the ones he wore."

"I don't know," said Horne. "But it's certainly sickening." He had wetted a new thread and was attempting to poke it through the eye of the needle.

Melvin watched for a while, and then said, "After the war where do you plan to study architecture? Once you mentioned going to Europe." During the past few days he had almost stopped thinking about the Navy; it seemed temporary and unimportant.

But Horne paid no attention; he was restlessly brushing his coat, brushing around the wings and ignoring the rest of the coat. He decided he had pinned the wings too high, so he took them off and tried again. This time he pinned them too low. Now he was concerned about the number of holes he was punching in the cloth; he licked his thumb and pressed at the holes, and scratched them with his fingernail, and finally blew on them in hopes they would disappear. At last he got the wings where he wanted them. He put on the coat and buttoned it up and stepped in front of the mirror. Melvin handed him the gold-braided hat. He put the hat on straight. Later, after he had been an ensign for a little while, it would be worn at a slightly rakish angle; he would not remove the grommet in order to crush the crown and sling the hat on the back of his head as Army pilots did, and he would not do this because he was a Navy pilot. He would no more mash his hat than he would wear crushed leather boots and twirl a key chain as he walked along the street, yet in the wearing of this hat he would contrive to let the civilians know he was no amateur.

He saluted himself in the mirror, clicked his heels, tried to see his own profile. He barked a few orders. "Get the hell back in ranks! Get the hell off your can! Get the hell up when you see an officer approach!" He thrust his head forward until the visor tapped the mirror with a dry click. "On the double now. Jump! Get the lead out!"

"Terrifying," Melvin said. "How about trying it with your pants on?"

Horne flexed his hairy, muscular thighs. "Maybe I'll go get the bird this way. Give the folks a treat, huh?"

"Is your name Horne?" somebody asked, looking into the room.

"That's me, Buster. What's your problem?"

"You're wanted on the phone downstairs. Long distance. Nebraska."

"Is that a fact!" Horne said. "What do you know, my old man squandering a buck! Well, what do you think about that? Hogan's goat!" he muttered, and went trotting down the hall.

McCampbell stopped by with a letter from his sister. She was a WAC who worked in the Pentagon, and he had a snapshot of her; she was about forty years old and very plain. Horne returned, and Roska appeared with a paper cup of whisky, and Kerdolph and Ostrowski and two other cadets in ensign's uniforms whose names Melvin did not know, but whose faces were familiar from somewhere. Then all at once it was time to go, and still fumbling with buckles and buttons they crowded into the corridor and down the steps and began milling around outside the barracks.

Melvin stood a short distance away and looked at them. The uniforms, being new, had not taken on the characteristics of the owners, with the result that the ensigns were almost indistinguishable from each other. Cole was so tall and erect that Melvin located him, and McCampbell, being small and curiously lopsided, was standing near him; and because there were only four Marines, resembling birds of paradise in their dress uniforms, he was able to find Roska. But Horne had vanished among the other two hundred officers. Melvin knew him so well, knew his stance and his every gesture so perfectly, that he was puzzled by the way Horne blended with the crowd, and edged closer trying to find him, but could not.

A lieutenant trotted down the barracks steps with a silver whistle on a lanyard around his neck and Melvin knew the cycle was now complete, for he recalled a summer day and a crowd of young men at a train station. There was a Navy truck parked at the edge of the platform and there was a lieutenant with a whistle who ordered them to throw their baggage aboard the truck and fall into ranks, and then they had gone marching beneath the elm trees of an Iowa town where locusts sang through the late afternoon.

The lieutenant brought the company to attention and made a tour of inspection. He straightened a few neckties and here and there pulled down the visor of a hat that was cocked. He gave the command to right face. He took his place at the head of the column.

"Forward," he called over his shoulder, and Melvin closed his eyes, again in the Iowa town, hearing the gears of the Navy truck and feeling the afternoon sun on his neck.

"*Harch!*"

"Eee-yo-lep," they chanted, tramping along, "eee-yo-lep, yo-right, yo-lep."

"Pipe down!" he called. And then there was only the cadence of their shoes on the gravel, on the hard packed earth, crossing the street, and on the grass.

Melvin trailed along with his hands in his pockets. There were no clouds in the sky and there was no sign of a Gulf breeze. The cadets marched across the base with their arms swinging in unison and the lieutenant never stopped calling cadence.

Overhead the planes were flying. This was not only a day of celebration for Pensacola, but another day of business as well. A formation of SNJ's broke up, gleaming in the sunlight, and swept over the water tower with engines howling. High above the J's, so high that it hardly moved, and so high that the thundering engines were inaudible, a giant patrol bomber was flying out to sea.

"Mark time," the lieutenant sang. "Mark!"

The bus to Ellyson Field went by on the way to the gate. The Whiting bus went by.

"Forward," he called, "Harch! Pipe down back there."

They went on through the shade of the trees and crossed over the road in the sunlight. A white-haired captain with a briefcase in his hand stopped, smiling, to let the column go by. When they came to another street they found that all traffic had been stopped because of them.

"Column right," the lieutenant shouted, stepping aside while they marched ahead.

"*Harch!*"

An echelon of Corsairs arched overhead, tilting on the axis of slender gray wings, and streamed over the trees like gulls. The shadow of one Corsair darted along the marching men. Some of the ensigns glanced up, knowing the pilot had seen them and was wishing them safety and an honorable career.

Near the platform they came to a halt, were dismissed, and filed into a section of chairs which had been set up for them. On the platform were the senior officers of Pensacola and a visiting admiral.

After the speeches and the chaplain's benediction, an officer began reading the names into the microphone. As each name was called, one of the graduates walked along the carpet to the platform, climbed the steps and marched halfway across, came to a halt, turned to his right, and saluted. The commandant handed him a diploma. Next he was congratulated by the admiral. Then he descended and another ensign took his place.

There had been no breeze, the afternoon was still, but just as Cole marched across the stage there was a rustling in the trees, and while he and the admiral were shaking hands the American flag majestically unfurled. The sky was as blue as the sky on a recruiting poster and there was a burst of applause.

When it was Horne's turn he hopped to his feet and was in such a rush that he overtook the man ahead of him and was obliged to wait a few seconds at the bottom of the steps. When he got on the stage he expanded his chest, lowered his head, and stepped forward as though he planned to assault the admiral. He kept going until it appeared he would not be able to stop, but he did, and the click of his heels carried through the public address system. The admiral said something to him as they were shaking hands; Horne grinned, saluted, and marched away.

All at once Melvin became aware that someone nearby had been furtively watching him; he turned and saw a young cadet dressed in clean, starched, neatly-pressed khaki. The cadet's cap rested squarely on his head.

"You must be new," Melvin said.

The young cadet did not answer.

"Welcome aboard. What's your name?" Melvin demanded with his hands on his hips, conscious that his own khakis had faded to a tawny color.

"Simms," the newcomer replied in a shy voice. "You must have been here quite a spell."

"How do you know?"

"You look like you have. I can tell." He smiled, and suddenly became confidential. "Isn't this base gigantic? I've been exploring all day. I walked as far as the ruins of the old Spanish fort."

"My first day here I did the same thing."

"Pensacola! I can't believe it!"

Melvin was a little embarrassed by the enthusiasm and could not think of anything to say. The sun was beating down and he did not feel like talking any more. He shrugged and continued watching the graduation. In a little while McCampbell appeared on the stage. He looked shriveled and inadequate, sidling across with one shoulder lower than the other, his wrinkled head cocked to one side like an inquisitive midget. The Navy would commission him, but he would never be on a poster. As an officer he was somewhat irregular. But Melvin, watching him accept the diploma, remembered certain afternoons over the Gulf when McCampbell's SNJ sliced out of the blazing sun and seemed to fasten itself to the target, tearing at it like a shark; and later, when the sleeve was stretched out on the pavement while they crawled over it on hands and knees counting the colored bullet holes, there had been times when McCampbell scored more than the rest of them together.

"Are you stationed at Barin Field?" asked the young cadet.

"I was," Melvin answered. "Down here, though, friend, we refer to it as 'Bloody Barin.'"

"I've heard about it."

"You're going to hear a lot more."

Roska was standing up. Melvin watched him march crisply along the carpet, mount the steps, and cross the platform. Nothing betrayed the amount of whisky he had drunk that day, unless the admiral was able to smell his breath.

The young cadet asked what type of duty Melvin was expecting.

"Let's put it this way: I don't know for certain. I could be assigned to almost anything."

"I'll bet you're proud."

"Yes, indeed I am," said Melvin. "You have no idea."

They talked a little longer and then, as the ceremony was concluding, Melvin wished him luck, warned him about the high-tension wires at Ellyson Field, and quickly worked through the crowd until he was close to Horne—who was peeking at his diploma while the chaplain prayed.

The instant the ceremony ended Melvin called, "Congratulations, sir!" and saluted.

Horne was startled. "Where the hell did you come from?" he asked as he rolled up the diploma.

"Come on, return my salute," Melvin insisted, grinning.

Horne's face grew red and he frowned. But several people were watching, so, with obvious reluctance, he acknowledged it.

"Now the dollar," said Melvin.

"What dollar?" Horne cried. "What's the matter with you? Get lost, will you!"

"You know what dollar, don't hand me that line. The first salute an officer gets costs him a dollar, and I got you first so I want my money."

"You going into the business?" Horne gestured at the enlisted men who were darting around the edge of the crowd saluting every ensign and lieutenant they could find. "How disgusting can you get! Jesus, you've come to prey on the ceremony. Oh, all right," he said, and took out his wallet. "I only wish I had a hundred rusty pennies."

With the dollar in his hand, the money touching his fingers, Melvin realized he did not want it; he had not even thought about the dollar except as a joke, but the dollar itself was not quite a joke, it was disagreeably real.

"Take it back," he said.

"Take it back?" asked Horne. His face assumed a turgid, furious expression. "Keep your damn money, it's what you wanted!"

This was how their fights began; it had happened before. Horne was outraged and Melvin, the longer he considered this, could feel himself growing angry. He crumpled the dollar and threw it on the grass. Horne shut his eyes and gritted his teeth.

Melvin nodded toward Cole, who was talking to his parents, and said with an effort, "I think I'd better go congratulate glamour boy."

"Go salute him! He's loaded with money!" said Horne. "Never mind, I didn't mean that," he added, wiping his lips on the back of his hand. "You took me when I wasn't ready. I don't know how this got started."

They left the dollar where Melvin had thrown it and walked through the crowd and were introduced to Cole's parents. Dr. Cole was a stout, pink-faced man of about sixty with a white mustache and penetrating gray eyes who was wearing a tight linen suit; he shook hands without speaking and then walked away a few steps and stood looking at the patrol bombers taking off and landing on the bay.

Mrs. Cole was cradling a drowsy chihuahua in her plump, freckled arms, petting the dog while she talked. "I've heard so much about you boys," she remarked, and presently, noting Melvin dressed in khaki instead of blue, she said, "And of course you must be the Marine we've heard so much about, and I—"

"No, ma'am," Melvin interrupted. "I'm the one who washed out."

"How unfortunate. I do hope you boys will drop in on us when-

247

ever you are in Chicago," she continued, smiling at Horne. "The doctor and I are usually at home in the evening."

A few minutes later they were gone. They drove away in a creamy Cadillac convertible with Pat and the dog in the rear seat.

Already the flags had been taken down. The public-address system was being dismantled, a crew of enlisted men were collapsing the chairs, a truck was backing up to the platform.

"Well, I guess that's that," said Melvin. "You know, I've been thinking we ought to get together tonight for a party in Mobile. We can find Roska, and Nick must be around somewhere. And Kerdolph, and some of the other fellows, and we can get a case of champagne and rent a suite. How does that sound?"

"That's a good idea," Horne answered. He shuffled his feet and scratched the tip of his nose. "You scare up Roska and Nick and those fellows."

"What about you?"

"As a matter of fact, there's supposed to be a party at the BOQ."

"You'll have plenty of time for BOQ parties in the future."

Horne was fretful. He seemed anxious to get away. "I've been planning on this."

"Did you promise anybody you'd be there?"

"Look," said Horne, "maybe it would be all right if you came along. It's going to be a free-for-all. I doubt if anybody would notice you there."

Melvin turned away, shaded his eyes, and squinted across the bay. "Well, thanks, but I don't know. I was thinking about town. This should be a good night. We could find Roska, you know. Listen, if Mobile is too far, how about Pensacola?"

Horne pretended to be enthusiastic. "Why don't you come along to the BOQ? I doubt if anybody would bother you."

"I think I might hit Mobile once more. There's a cashier in the drugstore that looks ready."

Horne didn't say anything. He looked at his wrist watch. The sun beat down on the grass which yielded up faintly the odor of summer.

"This breeze is a little stronger," Melvin said. "Maybe a storm tonight."

Horne shrugged, and stretched elaborately. "Could be. When do you—do the—?"

"My orders? Any day, I guess. I'll check out as soon as they get here. There's nothing left for me in this area."

"Great Lakes, huh?"

"Sure. Where else."

"Chicago's a red-hot liberty town, they say."

"That's what I hear."

"You could look up the Coles."

"Yes. She'd love to see me."

"Yuh," Horne replied absently. "I've got to run along. You know how it goes. Last night ashore—wine, women, and stuff. Wild blue yonder."

Melvin knelt on the grass to untie a shoestring and tie it again, quite slowly. Horne looked down at him.

"When do you shove off?"

"Tomorrow," Horne said.

"Stop by Saufley before you go. We'll have breakfast together."

"I'll do that."

He was edging away; he was nervous and was snapping his fingers. Melvin followed him. He knew Horne wanted to leave and he felt ashamed of himself for trying to prevent him from leaving, but all at once the poverty of his situation seemed more than he could bear and he did not, above all else, want to be alone this afternoon and this coming night.

"Take it easy, baby," Horne said, and he kept backing away. "You got roughed up in the program, but you're not hurt."

Melvin stopped. "No, I'm not hurt."

They shook hands, Horne muttered something, grinned insincerely, and went trotting across the field toward the officers' barracks, running faster as he got farther away.

18

★

The sense of dejection, the lassitude, and apathy, that overwhelmed him during the final tedious days at Pensacola persisted through the course of indoctrination at the Great Lakes Naval Training Center and was still upon him, more onerous than ever, when he was ordered to report for duty at the Naval Air Station in New Orleans. He was a seaman. He felt awkward and preposterous in the skin-tight jumper and bell-bottom trousers and he blushed when anyone stared at him. His rump felt strangely exposed, and his feet, as he gazed down at them, seemed remote and exceptionally large. He much preferred the dungarees which were his work uniform, because they were cut more conservatively and they were, in the harshness of the cloth, not unlike the khakis he used to wear as a cadet.

He remembered that Pat Cole had received orders to the New Orleans station and might still be there; consequently he went to the officers' barracks as soon as he arrived and learned that Cole was living there. He was not in, so Melvin left a note.

But the days went by and Cole made no attempt to get in touch with him. It was summer by this time, the middle of June, and the air was unpleasantly hot and moist. The temperature stayed in the nineties.

The air station was across the road from the beach at Lake Pontchartrain, and there it was apt to be cooler than anywhere else; Melvin often walked across the road in the evenings and lay down on a stone wall at the edge of the lake. He would lie there for hours, motionless, with his head cradled in his arms, staring up at the constellations, the night birds, and the meteors, and listening to the modest splash of the waves and to the people who waded in the shallow, tepid water in search of prawns or whatever else was edible

Nights when he was restricted to the base he usually sat on his bunk. He could hear music from the amusement park and he could see, through the fence, an arc of the Ferris wheel; he would sit on the bunk in his shorts, eating a candy bar and looking at the Ferris wheel while his feet crept back and forth on the board floor as though amusing themselves. Late in the night when he decided to lie down, because there was nothing else to do, he seldom managed to sleep. The sluggish air weighed on him, and congested his lungs. One hour passed after another while he perspired and waited to become sleepy. There were times when he was still awake at dawn, the sheets soggily twisted around him.

Seldom did he go into the city. In the streets, the hidden courtyards—everywhere he went it was hot and muggy, even more so than at the base; and dressed as he was, conscious of his failure, he could not bring himself to enter the night clubs, hotels, and restaurants for which New Orleans was celebrated. He did not think he would be admitted even if he tried.

He did not know anyone at all in the city. He began to take morbid pleasure in the fact that he had no desire to meet anybody, although with an expression of drowsy and sullen fatigue he stared at the women in their summer dresses, and desired them with a hopeless, tiresome ache. But he did not have enough energy to go after them, it was so hot all night. And he thought they would not want anything to do with him; there were so many service men around.

So he only watched, and observed the women, and lapsed into a weary and languorous stupor, feeling more disheartened every day. Occasionally, when in the city, he stopped at the USO, though it was a chore to climb the steps, and there he played a lethargic, jaded game of ping-pong or checkers, usually losing; and once he attended a dance where he remained all evening in a corner by the electric fan, blinking and yawning. Most of the dances in the city were for officers.

He sometimes thought about the war, which was still going on, and with an air of boredom he read of American victories. It had become evident that the Axis would lose; he was glad enough of that, but found himself hoping the war would drag on a while, because as soon as it ended he would be obliged to begin thinking about the future. The end of the war would mean he would be discharged and would have to find something else to do. He did not have any plans. For a while after leaving Pensacola he had thought he might apply for medical school as soon as he could manage to get out of the Navy, but as the weeks and months went by the idea began to seem somehow like a dream—so much study, so much hard work would be necessary. He considered transferring from the reserves to the regular Navy; that way he could stay where he was, or in some similar position. He would be fed and clothed, given directions as to what to do, and would have a little money to spend on week ends.

One sweltering noon as he was listlessly emerging from the enlisted men's mess hall into the blazing sun he stumbled against a tall, lean officer with a bristling mustache. The officer, an ensign, was wearing dark glasses which gave him the expressionless half-human look of a homosexual, or a child's doll, and Melvin promptly saluted, for he had gotten into the habit of saluting whenever he found himself in a threatening situation.

"Damn you, watch where you're going!" the ensign snarled.

"I'm sorry, sir," Melvin blurted, standing at attention and squinting up at the officer. All he could make out was a peaked garrison cap silhouetted against the glare of the sun and the ominous robot sockets of the polaroid glasses.

"So it's you," the officer said after a moment of silence.

Melvin was still blinded by the sun and could not see the officer's face, but he recognized the voice. It was Cole.

"You never did know where you were going," Cole went on. "How have you been?"

"All right," Melvin said, and stepped to one side in order to be able to see him. "When did you grow that?"

Cole twisted the ends of his mustache and grinned, and it seemed to Melvin that he was actually pleased they had run into each other.

"Did you ever get that note I left you at the BOQ?"

"Of course I got it. But what have we to talk about? We live in different worlds now, you know that."

"I know," Melvin said. "I just wanted to say hello, and I wondered if you might have heard from any of the other guys."

252

Cole shook his head. "I don't expect to hear from them. What are you doing? Do you work in the mess hall?"

"No. I'm a sort of flunky in sick bay. I run errands and sweep up."

Cole laughed, and with curious sobriety remarked, "That's what sustains you, I believe. You can't understand that you're defeated. You're a total, unmitigated ass. I don't know where you belong—on a street corner, perhaps, gesticulating and admonishing. Look at you: two years of hard work and you're lower than when you began."

"You don't have to remind me of it," Melvin said. "Incidentally, there's something I've been wanting to ask you. Back at Memphis I got a card congratulating me on a new baby. I was—"

"Yes, I sent it."

"I suspected you did."

"I know. I used to catch you gaping at me." Cole smiled. "I knew that eventually you would conclude I must have sent it. But, ye *gods*—after all this time!" He stroked his chin, laughed, and then touched Melvin lightly on the chest. "You're not intelligent—no doubt you realize that—but you compensate by utilizing faculties the majority of people neglect. You've reached the evolutionary level of, I would say, a fairly competent bird dog."

"I guess I'll take that as a compliment," Melvin said after thinking it over.

"You might as well," said Cole, regarding him somberly.

"Listen, could I bum a ride some day when I'm off duty?"

"You haven't had enough flying?"

"I never had anything against the flying itself. I always loved that."

"All right," Cole answered with none of his usual malice. "What morning are you free?"

So, one humid, cloudy morning of the following week, Melvin clambered into the rear cockpit of a Yellow Peril, the rickety biplane in which he and Cole had taken their primary training at the air station in Memphis.

With his toes just resting on the pedals and one hand touching the throttle and the other on the stick, he studied the once-familiar cockpit and looked down at the earth while Cole practiced the various acrobatics he would be teaching after he had graduated from the instructors' college. A gosport tube stretched between the cockpits, and Cole's voice emerged from the tube with a muffled, intimate quality that reminded Melvin of a telephone he had made out of string and two tin cans when he was a small boy.

"What we do here is not dissimilar to our old primary syllabus. We learn a few additional maneuvers, such as the cloverleaf and the inverted Immelmann; the principal thing, however, is to learn to speak. To elucidate during the actual course of the demonstration. No doubt you can recall the S turns to the circle, and how, no matter what, we were determined to hit that circle. I can clearly recall a day at Memphis when I rolled into a steep bank on the final turn, possibly ten yards above the ground. At the time I thought nothing of it. Not until I got here did I fully appreciate the danger."

He spoke rhythmically, with a pleasant intonation, as though it were a recitation; it was evident that he meant to become a conscientious instructor, which surprised Melvin a little, for, without thinking much about it, he had assumed Cole would be no more concerned about his students than he had been about anyone or anything else, except his own self.

The Yellow Peril went spinning noisily along, the engine sputtering in the heat and the wind whistling through the struts. There was a patch on the underside of the top wing, a ludicrous X of adhesive tape.

"I loiter around the BOQ every night drinking Manhattans and playing the slot machines," Cole was saying. "Sundays I customarily go dancing in the city, shoot a few holes of golf if the weather isn't unbearable, swim, fool about on the pistol range squandering the tax-payers' money. By the way, try those Sunday affairs. Les Rebelles and another group known as the Mademoiselles both do it up quite nicely, magnolias and punch and that sort of thing. There's a certain graciousness to the life down here."

"They wouldn't let me in the door."

Cole laughed. "That's right—they wouldn't. See what I mean about different worlds?"

The Yellow Peril gradually entered a shallow dive, the engine sinking below the horizon, and then rising as the plane started rolling—over it turned very slowly, the rudders altering—and came up the opposite side. The maneuver had been executed with style and assurance. Cole had bored a perfectly horizontal hole in the sky, and Melvin complimented him.

"I used to have a great deal of trouble with those," Cole replied. "I slipped and lost altitude and heading. It seems remarkably simple now." He rolled the plane again, remarking as he did so, "I enjoy this life. I enjoy being a pilot and an officer. I enjoy being respected, Melvin. All of us do. You should give it some thought."

"I don't doubt a word you say. I've wished more than once that I had your knack for—"

"Knack!" Cole interrupted. "So you think it's a knack! Small wonder you failed."

The Yellow Peril rolled over again and Melvin looked at the great delta of the Mississippi twirling beneath his head; then they were right side up and the sun was burning steadily into his shoulders and against the back of his neck. A yellow wing went up, the tail sank, and with sickening speed they slipped toward the river while the altimeter needle drifted backward around the dial. In the channel he could see a number of rusty merchant ships; a brightly painted excursion steamer whose top deck was crowded with sightseers was approaching a wharf.

"Do you hear from anybody?"

"The other day you asked the same question. Are you so discouraged that you've taken to living vicariously? As a matter of fact, I did have a card from Roska. He was beached in San Diego and didn't think he would be going anywhere. Apparently he continues to drink himself into a stupor every night. He also mentioned—or should I say he *did* mention, since he didn't specifically observe that he stupefied himself every night—that McCampbell and Horne passed through on their way to the Pacific."

"Were they headed for combat?"

Cole drew the plane out of the slip before answering. He glanced in the mirror, patted the top of his helmet, and jerked his thumb backward.

"All right, I got it," Melvin said, taking over the controls. There was a metallic *clunk* and the airplane rocked as Cole pulled the lever of his seat adjustment and dropped to the bottom of the cockpit.

"I wouldn't know where else they would be headed," he remarked dryly.

Melvin had not been aloft since crash-landing the Dauntless, and it had been a year since he had flown a Yellow Peril. Already it felt strange—the pressure of the wind against the surfaces, and the way the pedals sank to the floorboards. The instrument readings were unfamiliar; he stared at the manifold gauge for a long time, thinking it was too low, but did not want to ask Cole.

"Well, Horne in combat," he said and flew along. "When he runs out of bullets he'll probably begin throwing his shoes. But he'll get through all right. Nick will, too."

"If they're lucky," Cole said. He had taken off his helmet and was running his fingers through his hair.

"I get the feeling you never liked any of us."

"I didn't dislike you. It's simply that I thought and still think you are credulous—the four of you—gullible. Your prissy patriotism outraged my sense of reason. When I overheard you telling one another about the malevolence and perfidy of the Japanese, in toto, as though they were less than human, you insulted my intelligence."

"If you're that cynical why'd you get in the Navy? You could have pretended to be a conscientious objector."

"Frankly," Cole said, with a laugh, "I didn't think of it until too late. America raped me while I was a babe. America the beautiful. Like a woman, she concludes that whatever she wants, she should have. Now you're wondering how I can masquerade as a naval officer," he suggested, looking into the mirror, there in the sunlight high above New Orleans—gold bars pinned to the collar of his short-sleeved tropical shirt and wings pinned to his breast, handsome, sun-tanned, with curly hair and a mustache and quizzical, amused eyes—a Navy flyer not much different from others Melvin had seen many times at other air stations.

"Seriously, though," he went on, "I don't pretend. I'm honest, believe it or not. I'm not a conscientious objector; consequently I would never take refuge in that. I never deceive anyone, and most certainly not myself." He loosened the gosport mask in order to light a cigarette and then held the mask to his lips whenever he was not smoking. "You consider me a hypocrite. How so?" he asked.

"You accepted a commission, and you accepted all that training, but you never had the slightest intention of going to war."

"You have a high-school education, possibly one year at some local college or state university—the actuality doesn't interest me," Cole said patiently, "and on the basis of that *you* presume to evaluate *me!* This is absurd. What do you know of intellectual discipline? Your dialectic is as specious as that of the common man, which, essentially, is what you are. For example, how intensively have you dialyzed the Synoptic Gospels? What can you tell me of Aristotelian morality? What exegesis could you offer of the Samaritan Pentateuch, let us say, or the books of the Apocrypha? You do not know what I am talking about, yet you—*you* undertake to censure *me*. This is ridiculous!

"There's no need to look so abashed," Cole went on. "I'm not trying to hurt your feelings, nor would I ever say to you in public what I have just said. Cynical?" he inquired after a pause, "No. No, Seaman Isaacs, I am not cynical. I am sincere, I am altogether genuine. Hitler must be destroyed, and there is, consequently, a necessity for human cannon fodder. What you interpret as cynicism on my part is nothing but the fruit of elementary reasoning. Thus: twenty years from today no one on earth will know or care what I did during this war, any more than you or I really care what our fathers did in their war. And whether I, myself, in person, go off to fight, or whether I pass the time in the suburbs of Chicago, will not materially affect the course of events. Assume that I went into combat and was killed. What then? I would be dead, dead and absolutely nothing more. The war would end as it will end, whether I live or die. What is a man profited, if he shall gain the whole world, and lose his own soul?"

"You are willing to exchange your soul for the world, then."

"Quite the contrary. I shall keep my soul. I shall keep it."

"Well," Melvin said, "it's no mystery why you were more or less unpopular. That isn't exactly what I mean," he added with an apologetic glance in the mirror.

"Popularity. Popularity. Let us now cast our votes for the most popular corpse."

"Sometimes your sense of humor doesn't amuse me."

"I am not attempting to amuse you. After all, I'm not a clown."

"I suppose you think I am?"

Cole seemed to be considering this. "Yes," he said finally, "but I've never held that against you. You don't mean to be a bumpkin. You do your best, really. That's one of your most engaging traits. I don't believe I've ever known anyone who tried as hard as you do. You remind me of someone who believes in the truth of Horatio Alger." He shrugged, and looked down at the city. "If only you had more sense. You'll get killed if you aren't careful."

"It's a good thing you weren't assigned to combat," Melvin said irritably.

Cole grinned. But when he began to speak he was serious. "Now pay attention to me, Melvin. The imbeciles killed in battle are invariably characterized as having heroically given their lives for their country. That's a lie. They seldom give their lives; they are driven to it by the very real fear of being thought cowardly, and their deaths, by and large, occur when they are attempting to kill someone else. I would be inclined to call this poetic justice, if it were not so pitiful." He buckled on his helmet. "Don't allow yourself to be deceived. Don't ever believe in the integrity of a government. No government ever existed which honestly cared about the individual. Ours is no exception. It is opportunistic, militant, and does not comprehend the meaning of remorse. Ever since this nation was founded the government has spent approximately five-sixths of its entire income on purposes associated either directly or indirectly with war. From seventeen seventy-five to nineteen twenty-three, for example, our military forces engaged in more than one hundred separate conflicts comprising almost nine thousand battles. Yet the citizens of this country insist our wars are defensive and have been brought about through the wickedness of other nations. For a century and a half we've been involved in an average of sixty battles per annum. Still we claim to be a peaceful country. On this assumption we arrive at the conclusion that a nation, isolated by geographical accident from the rest of the world during a large part of its life, can fight nine thousand defensive battles. Anyone who thinks so has a slight case of patritis."

"Of *what?*"

"Inflammation of the patriotic gland," said Cole. "And speaking of popularity, Mussolini was made an honorary member of the American Legion and was invited to address the annual convention in Boston. Listen to this: 'Every male brought into existence should be taught from infancy that the military service of the republic carries with it honor and distinction, and his very life should be permeated with the ideal that even death itself may become a boon when a man dies that a nation may live and fulfill its destiny.' That sounds like Mussolini, doesn't it?"

Melvin nodded. "Yes. Mussolini or Hitler. But I didn't know he addressed the Legion convention."

"He didn't. The invitation was later withdrawn. And I wasn't quoting Mussolini. That statement was from an article by Douglas MacArthur in the *United States Infantry Journal*."

They flew along in silence for a while. Then Cole said, "The Russian attack on Finland was, according to President Roosevelt, 'unprovoked aggression' by a 'brutal despotism second to none on earth,' but not so long afterwards we began to supply Russia's war machine. Yet *you*, who do not find this outrageous, if indeed you ever reflected on it, can imply that *I* am a hypocrite. Perhaps you're right, after all. Who knows? The paradox of our century is the aphasia of the moral man, and am I not an example? I think myself moral, yet do I speak out against the jingoes—the gory butchers with their star-spangled cleavers? I do not. Why not? I don't fancy myself as a sacrifice. I wash my hands." He went on in a moment. "While you and your apoplectic friend Horne were poring over government manuals to discover the wing loading of an obsolescent dive bomber I was doing a little research of my own, curious as to why we were in the Navy. Nobody ever got around to telling me wars were fought for economic reasons; I was under the impression we were resisting an aggressor."

"Japan attacked America. You know that."

"Ah, so! Did it? Long before Pearl Harbor the Allied blockade shut off three-fourths of Japan's normal imports. What were they to do? What would any nation do under those circumstances? Burn incense and hope for the best? Yet how sanctimonious we became when they decided they must fight or starve. A day of infamy, we labeled it. It was that, it was indeed. But how can we absolve ourselves? Nevertheless this absolution was accomplished by the United States, as nations have accomplished it since antiquity.

"Let us assume, though, that we are at war; regardless of the genesis, we are at war. I demand to know why I, personally, am served up like a pig on a platter to the Axis gunners. Why have *I* been granted the privilege of defending good old Mom's gooseberry pie, and why is *my* life being risked to defend the right of a co-ed to lie around cramming a cedar chest full of silverware? What privileges are these? I am here because I was given no choice. And I tell you this: if there is one thing which infuriates me, it is coercion." He paused, looking into the mirror without a smile. "More than once, for instance, I have gone a considerable distance out of my way in order to cross a picket line. Do you hear me?"

"I hear you," Melvin said.

"Not to avoid crossing a picket line, I say, but to breach it—to rupture it!" he exclaimed with a rising voice.

Melvin had never heard him speak with such emotion; very quickly Cole became aware of this and continued in his usual restrained and sardonic tone, "Essentially it is that pickets symbolize organization, which is pure force, and all my life I have thought force despicable." He did not say anything else for several minutes, but then lifted the mask once more to his lips. "Just the other day in the mail I received a circular from my alma mater—I should have brought it along to read to you. They are raising funds for a memorial to be erected after the war honoring us who have died, or are about to die, although that fact is phrased with admirable discretion. The gall of it, really! They tell me it is my privilege to contribute. They will erect a carillon on the campus, and around the base of this carillon there will be inscribed on bronze the names of those who gave their lives in service. They point out that the site is ideal. Someone has calculated the number of persons who will be able to hear the bells."

"Are you going to contribute?"

At this Cole studied him in the mirror and burst out laughing. "Do you think I should?" he asked.

"I don't know," Melvin said. "Most people would."

"Not a dollar! Be certain of that. The Memorial Fund Committee poetically concludes that the bells will peal forth the names of our honored dead and the hill winds will remember them. Bells peal forth no names, nor does the wind remember, and I dare say the memory of man is but slightly superior. No, I will not contribute. Nor will 'Patrick Cole' be inscribed on any bronze plaque. The patterns of behavior which have worked for better or worse over the course of some thousands of years are rapidly becoming lethal. The survival of mankind depends on whether or not we are able to pierce the thought barrier erected by homespun minds over the course of centuries, a barrier which prevents the man with the hoe from observing that superior force cannot be the final arbiter of disputes." His eyes narrowed as though he were smiling behind the mask. "In any event, each morning before getting up I ask myself, 'Pat, where are you?' And if I can answer myself rationally, 'You are in the United States Navy, friend, and you will not get out today,' then I know I will be all right." He took another cigarette from the breast pocket of his shirt and leaned forward, hunching his broad, loose shoulders.

"Have you ever considered," he asked while smoke streamed from his nostrils and whirled out of the cockpit, "the possibility of American suicide squadrons? You assume the *kamikaze* is peculiar to the Japanese. We all do. And so it is, but for one reason only: as yet America has not been obliged to resort to such tactics. I doubt if we will hear of them in this war, because we seem to be winning, and because at present the Americans are not psychologically oriented to suicide, but there may come a time when we will begin to hear of the Minute Men, for example, or, let's say, the Pilgrims. They would wear distinctive uniforms —just think of the possibilities! Boots, epaulets, a star-spangled neckerchief, perhaps a tri-cornered hat. Now let's continue: they would have carte blanche, as do the condemned. It could be made quite attractive economically—a handsome government annuity for the widow and children. Then, too, it would be the ultimate challenge, and youth does love a challenge. With the full weight of government propaganda behind it, such a program would gradually be regarded as not unnatural. After all, these posters we now see in every post office—the ones which portray a man charging with a fixed bayonet while in the shadows behind him we see a charging football player—we accept this utterly preposterous analogy. Is war a game? War games, indeed we call them. A *game!* Fancy that! And the slogan beneath the poster, what of that? It was conceived in some advertiser's hollow head to ring out as one enunciates it. Slogans are generally alliterative because alliteration plugs the holes of slovenly logic. For instance: Courage! Confidence! Cooperation! Now should anyone stop to reflect, which, for better or worse, the poster cannot prevent one's doing, it becomes apparent that this exhortation is valid for whatever one has in mind, whether it is winning a war by bayoneting the enemy, robbing a blind man, or decapitating the little wife.

"Consider the euphemisms for aggression. They change like a menu; all that truly matters is that they titillate the simpleton's palate. Prior to assaulting a nation it is only necessary to disseminate the information that the invasion has become an 'obligatory assault' or is a form of 'remedial pacification,' or that, we'll say, in order to insure freedom, with the usual ecclesiastic blessings, we intend to forestall aggression by means of a 'preventive war.'

"We were, as you know, itching to enter this one. Not long ago I discovered that our naval vessels in the Atlantic received orders—two months *before* Pearl Harbor—to destroy any German or Italian naval or air force encountered. And several days prior to the attack on Pearl Harbor our Pacific forces received orders to sink any Japanese ship they encountered. By the purest luck our warships encountered no Japanese. But what if they had? What then? How would history read? I'll give you another fact: in September of nineteen forty-one, three months before our declaration of war, we destroyed two Nazi weather stations in Greenland and killed several Germans. The necessity of this I am not arguing either way—it is the hypocrisy I resent."

Presently he went on. "Haven't you learned that we are never told the truth until such a time as the truth can no longer affect the course of events? A generation ago our fathers went raging off to destroy the Kaiser because he was maiming Belgian children. Not until long after the war were our fathers informed that no such thing ever happened—it was a fable created to stimulate enlistment. By then, of course, what difference did it make?"

"But atrocities do occur."

"The reply of a slipshod mind. Certainly they occur. And America, like every other nation, is guilty. How many thousands of prisoners have been shot in the back by American troops too lazy, or tired, or angry, to honor the terms of surrender? Yet, for the moment, that is irrelevant. A generation ago this nation was outraged by the news that one hundred and fourteen Americans had gone down on the *Lusitania*. What else was aboard that ship? Nobody could find out—not until the war was over. Only then did we learn that it was packed with munitions for the British: two hundred tons of rifle ammunition, two thousand cases of cartridges, eleven tons of black powder! The *Lusitania*, furthermore, was a British ship, not an American ship. The German high command was guilty only of a tactical error, that error being that the destruction of the ship did not quite compensate for the subsequent entrance of the United States into the war."

"Then you have no interest in defending the United States?"

"In an extremity I would assassinate whoever or whatever threatened me, without the slightest compunction. But when it was over I would not genuflect in the expectation of being commended by God and bemedaled by the nation, for if there were a God surely he would not hesitate to strike me with lightning."

"But won't it bother you to be training cadets? I mean, knowing you were training them eventually to kill other people?"

Cole cranked himself up in the seat, took over the controls, and swung the airplane around a billowing cloud. Far below them the Mississippi gleamed in the noonday sun, and there was the city of New Orleans and the vast, shallow lake, and the field with its flashing beacon and swastika-like complex of runways.

"I impart to them my skill," he said. "That is all they receive from my hands. If, then, they commit murder, how can you hold me culpable?"

He landed the plane smoothly, and as the Yellow Peril rolled along the runway, he said, "How about giving me some assistance on the brakes? They get pulpy in this hot weather."

263

So, working together, pressing the brakes in unison, they taxied in.

A few days later Melvin was assigned to another job, cleaning the officers' barracks. He was sorry to be removed from the dispensary because he was beginning to enjoy it, but there was nothing he could do about the assignment. He thought of asking Cole to intercede; he might have some influence, despite the fact that he was only an ensign, but after thinking it through Melvin decided not to ask. For one thing, he had not seen Cole since their flight together, which very strongly implied that Cole had no interest in seeing him again. Then, too, there was a possibility Cole might have had something to do with having him transferred, although this was so utterly pointless that he could not take the idea seriously.

He dreaded cleaning up Cole's room. Each morning as he approached, working his way along the corridor, he was hoping the room would be empty, but one day when he knocked, instead of silence he heard the bored voice call, "Yes? What is it?"

Melvin steadied himself and opened the door and walked in, holding up the mop and the pail.

Cole was lying on the bed smoking a slender, ladylike cigar with a long, zinc-white ash. It gave off a pleasant but rather sugary aroma. He was reading the sports section of the newspaper. He lowered the paper to his chest and watched Melvin go around raising the shades.

"Put the shades back the way you found them," he said.

Melvin was about to begin mopping the floor; he leaned the mop against the desk and lowered the shades.

"That starboard shade was almost touching the sill," Cole murmured. "Let's see you fix it."

Melvin dropped the mop on the floor and jerked the shade a few inches further down.

"Square it away," Cole said evenly. "I said, square it away. There, that's better," he added, "But it's still a trifle high. I don't like the glare from outside."

"It's good enough the way it is."

"On the bureau you'll find my nail file. Bring it to me."

Melvin ignored him and commenced mopping the floor.

264

Cole folded the newspaper. He tapped ashes on the wet linoleum.

"I've about had enough," Melvin said. "I've got a bellyful, so look out."

"Are you disobeying an order?"

"You know what you can do with your orders."

"Have you any idea what I could do to you for that remark?"

"I've been in this business as long as you have," Melvin said. He slung the mop around beneath the bed. "Be careful, Pat. I'm warning you."

"Is that the way you habitually address an officer?"

"Since when are you an officer?"

Cole raised himself to one elbow and looked at Melvin with an expression of boredom, or negligence, in which there was only the barest curiosity, and said, "You can't do anything, can you? Not *anything!*"

"How would you like a poke in the nose?"

At this Cole gave a wan smile and placed the cigar delicately between his front teeth as though he might nip away the butt.

Melvin continued working, but the silence became oppressive, so he said, "Any new word from Roska?"

Cole made no attempt to answer, nor even indicated that he had heard; he was watching, turning the cigar around in his smiling lips with his little finger hooked as though he had hold of a teacup.

"Suit yourself. Don't answer. It doesn't make a damn to me. How much longer will you be here?"

Gradually Cole relaxed on the bed and crossed his arms over the paper. He looked at the ceiling with a whimsical air and replied, "You can hardly wait for me to shove off. Isn't that so?" He flipped the burning cigar through the doorway into the hall where the clean-up cart was parked and waited to see what would happen.

Melvin began to twist the filthy water from the mop; he did not know quite why, but this part of his duty was particularly odious, more so than emptying garbage or surgical waste, and he looked at the pail with aversion, conscious that Cole was aware of his extreme distaste and was amused.

"As a matter of fact, now that you mention it," Melvin said, while the water dripped from the strings, "maybe it won't really break my heart when you do shove off."

"I have one question. I'm not requesting an answer. I do suggest, however, you take a few minutes some day after I've gone to reflect on it." He shook open the newspaper so that his face was concealed, and asked, "How do you think it makes me feel to see you doing this?" And he was never again in his room when Melvin came around.

One morning several weeks later, while the swimming pool was unrestricted, Melvin was stroking along under water when he bumped into a pair of pale, slender legs and the first thing that came into his mind was that these legs belonged to a WAVE; he popped to the surface with a look of buoyant anticipation but was confronted by a dripping mustache. Cole appeared to be equally startled.

They were near the deepest part of the pool and in order to talk they were obliged to tread water. After the first contact and recognition they had each backed away so that a few yards of water separated them.

"How's it going?" Melvin asked, determined to be civil.

"I bought a convertible," Cole said. He pushed the hair out of his eyes and squinted into the maze of white-washed rafters overhead.

They rode high in the water, which reeked of chlorine, their legs churning as though they were on unicycles.

"What happened to your fiancée who was supposed to come to the graduation with your folks?" Melvin asked.

"She married a 4-F."

"Oh. I'm sorry. I remember you talking about her even back at Albuquerque."

"You're sorry?" Cole inquired with a mocking smile. "I'm touched."

"All right, just skip it," Melvin said, controlling an impulse to spring at him and hold him under until he drowned. He was surprised that Cole did not swim away. They had nothing in common any more. What had seemed a genuine and permanent bond was due simply to the fact that circumstances had placed them in the same barracks and classrooms for a while. They had

266

become accustomed to each other, as they had become accustomed to abuse, uncertainty, and fear throughout the cadet program, as they had become accustomed to obstacle courses and curious instructions and philosophical acceptance of the fact that it was to result in peace, subsequent to the usual damage, waste, mutilation, death, fire, wrath, and havoc.

"Why is this water so dark?" Melvin inquired, peering down. "Have they painted the bottom?"

"Somebody told me it's from an artesian well."

This sounded like a reasonable explanation. Melvin tried to see his hand a few inches beneath the surface. "I didn't know artesian water was black."

"Well, you think about it," said Cole; he put his face into the water and snorted, and came up dripping. "So long," he remarked briefly, filled his lungs with air, and dove out of sight. He reappeared at the shallow end of the pool, where he climbed the ladder, picked up a towel and dark glasses and baseball cap, and went outside to the sun deck. Melvin could see him preparing to lie down on a gymnasium mat.

Not many days after this, when he entered Cole's room at the usual hour he found it vacant. Linens and blankets were heaped on the mattress and the bureau drawers were open. The desk drawer was on top of the desk, as though he had become impatient with the details of packing and had perhaps just emptied his possessions into his cruise box. Paper clips, pencil stubs, some old literary magazines, an almost empty gin bottle, and a book or two—these were the mementos on the floor, and in the wastebasket a few of the slim, sweet cigars.

There was such finality in this disorder that Melvin paused, and though he had no desire to meet Cole again he wondered where he had gone, and felt somewhat restless. He recalled that at Pensacola Cole had been quite certain of an assignment to Glenview after finishing the instructors' college. Curious as to whether he had in fact been able to manipulate the machinery of the Navy, Melvin walked over to the administration building that afternoon and asked the WAVE on duty if she could let him know where Ensign Cole had been sent. Somewhat to his surprise she got up without hesitation and went to a filing cabinet; in a few moments she came back and said Ensign Cole had received orders to report for duty as a primary instructor at the Naval Air Station in Glenview.

"Old Dead-Eye Dick," said Melvin, and the WAVE looked at him uneasily.

September brought no relief from the breathless, stagnant heat. Melvin occasionally rode the bus into New Orleans. There, for an hour or two, he wandered up and down Canal Street and through the French Quarter in the hope that something rare and unforgettable would occur, but nothing ever did. Ordinarily he ended each night at the USO. Listless and sticky in his tight white uniform he played checkers with a gravely discouraged expression until it was time to return to the base.

In October a card arrived from Sam Horne. It had been forwarded from Kansas City. Horne was in Honolulu. He had gotten married the previous summer, about two months after leaving Pensacola. His wife was still in the United States and they expected their first child a bit sooner than was customary, probably around Lincoln's birthday. Horne was confident it would be a son.

On receipt of this news, concluding that he had been left behind in every possible respect, Melvin went into New Orleans and hastily drank himself into a stupor. The Shore Patrol came across him lying in an alley with neither wallet nor shoes; they picked him up by the hands and feet and started carrying him to the wagon. On the way he woke up, and was not displeased to find himself being carried, but began to struggle in order to prove that he could not be handled so unceremoniously. The door banged shut on his protest and he relapsed into a state of aggrieved rumination. Everything considered, it was an ignominious way to salute his best friend, and while he was riding back to the base with the other drunken sailors he reflected that his dossier by this time must resemble that of a confirmed bolshevik.

Having been in the service of the United States Navy for what seemed to him quite a long time he wrote to his father that he would get a leave at Christmas, but he didn't. He was not able to understand this, and went to the administration building determined to look into naval regulations governing his situation, but could not get in to talk to anybody. Then, in January, he was detached from New Orleans and was sent to a base in central Texas. He rode on a train filled with soldiers, and, knowing that he had not been a particularly valuable piece of property so far, began to wonder if the Navy had somehow contrived to trade him to the Army.

19
★

On the day he reported for duty aboard his new station a chief petty officer with gold hash marks led him around to the rear of a low, white-washed adobe building where there was a flagstone patio. On this patio were a number of wide-backed chairs and glass-topped tables shaded by beach umbrellas, and at the far end there was a barbecue oven. There was also a row of little buckets.

"Tell me your name, son," said the chief in a kindly tone. He was a grizzled old man whose hands sometimes trembled and whose head nodded.

"Isaacs," Melvin said, looking suspiciously at the buckets.

"That's fine, son," the chief said, and patted him on the shoulder. He opened the screen door of the building and stepped inside. When he came out he was swinging a golf club. "This here," he said, "is a golf club, son. Club to play golf with."

Melvin nodded. The club was a brassie.

"You got her so far, boy?"

"I think so."

"That's fine," the old chief petty officer said. "You won't have no trouble, provided you listen close and do like I say. Them little bitty buckets over yonder, you see them buckets? Go get me one of them. They is full of balls."

Melvin walked across the patio, picked up one of the buckets, and brought it back to the chief, who had waited silently in the shade.

"That's fine," the chief said. He waggled the brassie a few times, cleared his throat, spat on the flagstones, and beckoned the new seaman to follow him.

They walked without haste through the glaring light, past the barbecue oven, and stepped off the patio and continued across the dusty earth until they came to a bunker. They climbed to the top and here, all at once, Melvin got his first view of the Texas prairie. It was concave, studded with gopher holes and pearl-gray sagebrush, and gave the impression of being solidly packed with dust. A telephone line which was attached to the adobe BOQ went straight out and kept going and finally, miles away, disappeared over the horizon—the poles diminishing regularly with stark, geometric purpose. Melvin stood on top of the bunker holding the bucket of golf balls, limp with astonishment. The distant telephone poles rippled in the drifting waves of heat. Nothing else moved. There were no birds in the stupendous sky, and the sky appeared to be everywhere except directly beneath his feet. There was no sign of life. The earth sagged and baked in the light of the roaring sun, like the floor of an evaporated ocean.

"Now here," the chief was saying. "You see this?" He pointed to the withered grass that covered the mound.

"What?" Melvin said, touching himself on the forehead. He had begun to feel dizzy and could not hear very well.

"I'll show you everything you need to know," the chief replied. "I like a boy to ask. Shows he's a thinker. Now, son, let me have that bucket. That little bucket of balls. Right there she is. You got her in your hand."

Melvin handed him the bucket. Carefully, as though it might explode, the old chief set the bucket down. Then he squinted across the prairie toward a succession of tin signs spray-painted to resemble rainbows, and with a look of mild good humor he shook his club at them. Each sign had been stenciled with the distance from the tee.

"This grass," he said, bending over a little stiffly to place a ball on a tuft, "you got to sprinkle two, three times each day, especially on extra warm days like today." He waited, half-bent over, to see if the new man was paying attention.

"Two or three times each day."

270

"That ain't all, boy," said the chief with some asperity. "Especially on extra-warm days like today."

"You don't look clear about it. Something puzzling you? Speak up. Anything you want to know, make sure to ask."

"I'm all right," Melvin said. "There's nothing wrong with me."

"Well, now, that's fine," the old chief said. He placed one hand against his spine, grunted, hesitated, and at last straightened up.

Suddenly Melvin asked, "How long have you been here?"

But the CPO was examining the brassie and did not hear.

The noonday sun was burning through Melvin's blue shirt and dungarees and he thought the top of his head was missing—he removed his cap and touched his hair. It felt curiously slick and scorched. He blinked, cautiously put on his cap, and wandered around in a circle. "Will you explain this whole thing again?" he demanded in a loud, wild voice. "The whole damn business? From the beginning to the end?"

"Of course I will, son," remarked the kindly old chief. "You fill up a can full of water from the hydrant yonder and keep this here grass wetted down so's she don't burn. The sun burns up the grass. Dries her all up. You got that so far?"

"Who's buried here?"

The chief was shocked and stepped backward. "Why, this ain't no grave! They ain't nobody buried here. Whatever in the world give you such an idea?"

"Oh, I don't know," Melvin answered, putting his hands in his pockets and staring, in spite of himself, into the miles of undulating heat. "What happened to the guy who used to have this job?"

"That boy was transferred not long ago," the chief mused, thinking back. "And he was a good boy, too. I don't know where he went. Yes, I do, come to think of it. He went to New Orleans. They give that boy orders to some aviation unit back in New Orleans, Louisiana. Now, son, would I be standing on this grass if they was anybody buried underneath?"

Melvin shook his head.

The chief rebuked him gently. "Of course not! Pay attention to me here now." He spat on his palms, waggled the club, and having considered the ball for several seconds with a look of extreme gravity, he took a swing at it, but missed.

"Son," he said, "will you squuunch up that grass? The ball appears to be a little hid."

Melvin sat on his heels and squeezed and twisted the grass until it would support the ball.

"You're a fine boy," the chief said. "Now step aside. Out the way."

He assumed a new stance and raised his head, the better to see over the plains. His lips trembled. His pale eyes were lusterless and cast with film. He stood that way for a long time with a gentle, benign smile. Then he remembered what he was doing. He lifted the club as high as he could and swung again. After a long silence he asked, "Which way did she go, son?"

Melvin quietly stood to one side with his thumbs hooked in his belt, unable to think of an answer.

"Must have been a right high one," the old man muttered, shading his eyes and moving his head from one side to the other as he searched the blue heights of the sky. After a while he looked down and he located the ball on the tuft of grass. He was neither perturbed nor ashamed. He examined the ball, bending down to make certain it was not some mean illusion. Then he straightened up swiftly with a ruthless expression and swung again. The ball trickled off the tee. It oscillated a few yards through the alkaline dust.

"Fix me another!" he ordered vigorously, stamping his feet. "Thirty-six years I been in this man's Navy! I was in China before you was on this earth! Why, son," he said, and he was breathing heavily, "I sailed around the world! Around the entire world! I could tell things you ain't never dreamed about. Things you ain't never heard of. Someday I'll tell you all I seen and done. You're a fine young fellow."

Half an hour later, when the pail had been emptied, the chief inquired if he understood what had happened so far, and Melvin said he did.

"All right, sonny boy, hop to her!"

"What am I supposed to do?" Melvin asked.

"Why, run out there and shag them balls!"

Melvin took another look at the prairie where the balls were winking out of sight in the heat and reappearing like planets or moth balls at the bottom of a hill. He picked up a pail and started walking toward them.

But the chief called after him, "Son? Come here! Son, you can't do that. I told you three, four times already. You'd ought to pay close attention. I like a boy to think."

"Can't do what?" said Melvin, and his own voice seemed to arrive from a distance.

"Them gunny sacks, boy. You wasn't listening. You was *daydreaming!*"

"Gunny sacks?"

"It's all right this time. Only from now on you'd ought to keep on your toes. I'll tell you once more. Them gunny sacks is piled up behind that first sign and that's where you squat down to wait. The officers, they'll let you know when it's time to shag the balls."

"All right," Melvin said. "Let me see if I've got it right. First of all, I'm out behind the sign while they're shooting."

"Now you got her. What else, boy?"

Melvin took a guess. The CPO had not given any instructions about the gunny sacks, but they could be there for only one purpose. "After the officers give me the word I'm supposed to collect the balls and put them in a sack? Is that right?"

"That ain't all."

"No?"

"You got to hustle back here on the double and fill up them there little buckets so's the officers don't never run shy of balls to play with. Them officers love to play ball." The chief paused and lifted his hat to scratch his head.

"Extra buckets is inside the BOQ, right behind the door, and there's where you stand up the clubs in the corner when the day is over. Now I raised a blister here on my thumb, otherwise I'd give you a bit more practice." Thoughtfully he studied the new seaman. "You won't have no trouble. Recollect to keep your head down like I told you. Don't go sticking your head up over that sign or you're liable to get beaned. Them balls is hard. Mighty hard. Feel of one. Knock you silly, boy."

"I think I'll sit down behind the two-hundred-yard marker," said Melvin. "They couldn't hit me that far away."

"You can't do that."

"I can't? Why not?"

"I'm going to tell you just once more. Them gunny sacks, I told you four times them gunny sacks is piled behind the fifty-yard sign. You sit on them sacks to wait for the signal."

"Yes, I know. I'll carry them out to the two-hundred-yard marker."

The chief was patient, but he was firm, and it was evident that he had begun to lose confidence in the capability of the new seaman. He said, "Son, now hear this. You can't do that."

"Well," replied Melvin, growing angry, "why not?"

"Because," the chief said, and he paused after each word, "they is not behind the two-hundred-yard sign."

Melvin took a long time to think it over. Up to this point the Navy had taken moderately good care of him. No matter in what difficulty he found himself, no matter how illogical the situation, the Navy had presupposed it and had formulated a procedure. For this reason, a little unwillingly, he had come to trust the Navy and to believe in its omniscience. It had no sense of humor and it had no soul. Being in the Navy was rather like being in church, its attitude benevolent and its comportment mildly bizarre. Knowing it meant him no harm he had accepted the occult dogma, but now, at last, the wild roots were exposed. Still, after further reflection, he decided not to struggle. The system was too big. Certainly it would overwhelm any one man.

"You're right, chief," he said. "I hadn't thought about that."

The CPO was enormously relieved that the new seaman finally comprehended the situation. Before leaving Melvin in charge of the tee he observed, in the gentle dignity of his nature, "You'll get along fine, son. Something puzzles you, you come ask. You know where to find me."

Melvin promised to do this, and when the elderly chief had walked away, mopping the band of his hat with his handkerchief, Melvin collected the golf balls, which had been sprayed in a broad arc, and then filled the pail and sat down on the patio to wait for his first customer. The afternoon was remarkably quiet, the spring sunshine debilitating.

When an hour passed without a sound he took off his shoes and put his feet on a table. In this position he fell asleep.

He was wakened by a hard kick on the soles of his feet. He had been dreaming, though he did not know about what, and the kick coincided with the climax of the dream; he opened his eyes and found himself looking up at three identical, incredibly tall lieutenants, whom, from the wind wrinkles around their bleak, unflinching, desert eyes, and by the flowered leather boots they wore, he judged to be Texans.

"How'd you like to go on the *re*-port?" one of them murmured, and Melvin, not yet fully conscious, suspecting they might be three evil brothers from his dream, nodded drowsily.

"How'd you like thet?" another said, chuckling. "How'd you like thet?"

Melvin awoke, then, and put on his shoes as fast as possible. Without bothering to tie the laces he grabbed the gunny sack and fled over the prairie to the first sign, where he huddled with his head tucked down between his knees while the balls came whistling by and soared away in space. One after another the balls came howling by, searing the wind.

"Out theah, hey! You theah! Wake up, you!" the Texans called.

Melvin sprang to his feet with the sack in both hands and saw them standing on the bunker, standing in a row like characters from a myth of the Western frontier.

"Get goin'!" one of them called.

He turned around wretchedly and for a minute, seeing no balls, thought he was still asleep—but the balls were there, far, far out on the prairie, out among the rippling telephone poles.

"Le's go! *You! Le's move!*" the Texans cried in remote, yodeling unison.

Melvin started walking, knowing it would take a long time to reach the balls, and then he began to trot and then he began to run. Out where the crop was thickest he looked toward the patio and could just make out three lank figures beneath an umbrella. They seemed to be on a level with him but he knew they must be higher because of the distance they had driven the balls; the floor of the prairie sloped down to where he was, and he saw, as he bent to pick up the balls, that some of them were still moving. The balls would stop, trickle a few inches farther, hesitate, and move on, and for a moment he was overwhelmed with panic and began gathering them frantically or they would lead him onward and downward forever. He was out so far that there were cracks in the earth, and dust, or volcanic smoke, seeped ominously upward, swirling around him so that there were times when the entire base was obscured.

After he had delivered his sack to the patio the officers sent him out again.

Not until the middle of the afternoon did they get tired of playing; then they lounged in the shade of the striped umbrellas and drank and talked while he crouched on the prairie with the sack over his head to defend himself from the sun.

Toward evening several other officers emerged from the BOQ and fired a few rounds. A breeze had come up and, occasionally, as it shifted, he was able to hear the clink of ice in the glasses, and once in a while he would hear a word or two, or faraway laughter. In spite of the chief's advice he had taken to crouching behind the two-hundred-yard marker. This offered a number of advantages. For one thing, the balls bounced and rolled so far that even the weakest drive carried almost two hundred yards and some of them were still fairly well up in the air when they passed overhead. For another thing, he felt less confined well out on the prairie; he was no longer quite the vassal he was when close to the patio. But the principal advantage, as he had suspected from the beginning, lay in the safety of the outer ramparts. Occasionally a ball would carom off the sign where he had concealed himself and if the range was fifty or a hundred yards the concussion was paralyzing; it was as though a fire engine had run over him, or somebody had crept up and exploded a paper bag next to his ear, and the hair stood up all over his body.

He reported for work at nine o'clock each morning and spent the entire day behind a sign, or collecting balls, or sitting on the patio ready to leap to his feet when the screen door creaked. Despite the winter declination of the sun, his blue dungarees faded almost white, while his skin began to look like pemmican, and from a distance, except for his dangling arms and flat-footed Midwestern stance, he resembled a Comanche who had brazenly outfitted himself in material stolen from a settler's wagon.

The CPO, a solicitous man, often stopped by to ask how he was getting along. Melvin would invariably say all right. Then the chief would caution him to keep his head down so as not to get hit.

One day Melvin asked, "When the war is over, chief, do you think we'll ever have another one?"

But the CPO was staring at the tee. "Son," he muttered with a worried frown, "I give you instructions to sprinkle this grass."

The officers, too, had observed that the grass was dying, for which reason Melvin was put on report. However, he was in splendid physical condition from so much running and scarcely minded the additional work. He was, in fact, growing rather fond of his job. He had a great deal of time for meditation and relaxation—during the hours he spent alone on the patio he had taught himself to juggle—and, so affected was he by the magnitude of the earth, that he had been moved to draw some pictures of it: cached in a depression behind one of the signs was a pencil and a tablet, and often, while the officers took their exercise, he would be sitting with his back to them, the tablet on his knees, sketching gophers and sagebrush, or the line of the horizon.

During certain ineffably quiet afternoons when the telephone wire hummed in the desert wind, when the sagebrush bent low to the earth and tumbleweed spookily bounded over the flag-stones and struck the adobe wall without a sound and bounded on and on until it was lost from sight, compelled to wander through all eternity, it seemed to him that from beyond the horizon someone was whispering to him, and he grew restless and was filled with a sweet yearning. Then it was that he went shuffling around the patio, his arms swaying from side to side, pausing now and then to cock his head to the unutterable tidings of he knew not what, until, unable to remain, he sprang over the wall and slunk away, looking across his shoulder with a guilty expression in which there was, yet, the hint of a crafty grin, and went trotting over the dust-packed primeval earth with his head lifted, eagerly sniffing the wind. There were times when he would lope a mile or more across the plains with the conviction that he would never stop, and he considered the idea of subsisting on wildlife, for he was sure that before long he could learn to catch gophers and jackrabbits and would locate a water hole. More than anything else he liked to squat on a ridge about a mile southwest of the buildings and passionately think over his life while studying the horizon. Three years or so he had been in service—time was less meaningful now and he had difficulty remembering. But such cogitation soon exhausted him; mildly addled, as though he had been smacked on the nose with a folded newspaper, he would stretch, get to his feet, stiff-legged, and trot a little farther.

In the enlisted men's barracks whenever he listened to a news broadcast, or read a paper, he half-expected to come across the names of his friends. When the American forces attacked Iwo Jima he wondered if Sam Horne had been there in a Corsair, or if Nick McCampbell had come hurtling down like an avenging monkey on Mount Suribachi. And once, after calculating the time differential, he was struck by the fact that General Schmidt's Marines had been running across the beach at Iwo at the precise instant he himself was reporting for duty on the golf tee. He offered up this information to the man who bunked above him, a hulking pock-marked half-breed named Dawes; but Dawes, who was picking his teeth, did not respond.

Letters he received from his father in Kansas City grew longer and more ebullient with each assault on the Axis, and shortly after the twenty-seventh of April, when news was radioed that the Russian and American armies had joined on the bank of the Elbe northwest of Dresden, he received a letter which so extolled not only the contribution of the Russians to the Allied cause but the excellence of virtually everything Russian, that he became somewhat uncomfortable and sought to recall if it had always been this way, or if, a few years previous, his father had been hostile to Russia. But he could not be certain; he had been so young at the time, and had not paid much attention.

He received this letter after a particularly hard day at the tee, a day in which the heat, the space, the ill temper of the officers, and the surging ethereal balls contributed to a sense of confusion; which, he reflected, was why the lines of his father's letter had blurred and intermingled as he attempted to read, and why, after a few minutes, he had lain down dizzily.

The officers by and large were unexceptional golfers, but he had come to the conclusion that the three hazel-eyed Texans in their tooled and flowery boots were professionals before the war. One thing, at least, was certain: they aimed at whatever sign he was using for a shield, so that by sundown almost every day his

278

head spun and his eyes bugged as though he had been roped to the clapper of a cathedral bell. He heard, no matter where he was—at meals, in the shower, or in his bunk—a distant click. Then, stiffening, he waited, and counted the seconds, and presently the ball hissed by and he relaxed, or there was a shattering crash. He could not accustom himself to this noise, nor banish the impression upon opening his eyes after each concussion that the prairie had caught fire, and all he had learned during four months of service at the tee was to take the chewing gum out of his mouth whenever the three lieutenants appeared—otherwise he was apt to swallow it when one of them hit the sign.

In the sunset, as he returned to the enlisted men's barracks with his lips parted in a smile of dull stupefaction, the half-breed would gaze down on him from the upper bunk with affable concern and tell him that he ought to request a transfer, and he would nod in agreement. But after he had rested for a while in his bunk with his hands crossed on his chest and a damp towel over his eyes, the echoes would diminish and he would begin to defend his job. It was the first outdoor position he had ever held and he thought it was beneficial. He had begun seeing coyotes and enjoyed racing after them when he was not busy retrieving balls, and he recognized various creatures who burrowed in the range and he thought, he was almost positive, that some of these little animals now could recognize him. Then, too, the prairie air was so invigorating that cigarettes tasted unpleasant; he seldom smoked, and felt odd when he did. And, in a sense, he was free; whereas Dawes, who waited on table in the officers' mess hall, merely went from the kitchen to the table and back again as though attached to a chain or a leash.

On liberty the two of them went to a movie. The movies were imbecilic: the love stories reeked, and those which dealt with the war were so buttered with propaganda that Melvin occasionally shut his eyes and put his fingers in his ears. However, that was the way movies were made, no one had a right to anticipate anything better, and besides, there was nothing else to do, except drink beer. He had never cared much for beer, but, after the movie, he and Dawes would drink some. The town swarmed with glossy, greenish-black flies the size of beetles that circled interminably with a deadly buzzing noise which could be heard for half a block in the desiccated air; these monstrous flies now and then would drop like molten glass or bullets to the rim of the bottle and with obscene frenzy crawl through the sticky foam, and Melvin, holding his head in his hands, would concentrate on happier times.

So, in this way, the weeks went by.

And the CPO remarked on one occasion, after surveying him with clinical, professional approval, "You're holding up better than them other boys."

One morning in May he reported for duty as usual, and a day of profound isolation it promised to be. He strolled around scuffing dust into gopher holes and trying to stamp on lizards, and when at last an officer appeared on the patio he settled himself behind his usual sign and opened the drawing tablet.

After a while the golf balls stopped bouncing by; he closed the tablet, ready to go to work, but, because he did not hear the customary halloo, he remained where he was. Fragments of conversation floated out to him, the morning was so quiet. He heard what sounded like "Europe." Something or other must have occurred in Europe. He turned on his side, peered around the edge of the sign, and saw that the patio was crowded with officers. They had glasses in their hands, tall glasses, no doubt frosty, such as one would use for gin, lime, and ice. Melvin's throat began to constrict. With his cheek pressed against the edge of the sign he gazed wistfully toward the crowd. He could tell they were celebrating. He decided to collect a few balls and use this as an excuse for going in to be near them, to watch them enjoying their drinks, and to overhear whatever they might be saying to each other. But he had no more than gotten to his feet and opened the gunny sack when he heard a shout. He did not bother to look around; he dropped the sack and lunged for shelter, hearing a thud right where he had been standing. He threw himself flat on the ground and buried his head in his arms. Moments later the sign rang from a direct hit.

When, at last, he heard the all clear he sat up, brushing the dust from his clothing. Then he got to his feet and staggered away through the sagebrush, dragging the sack behind him. He could see where he was going but could not hear anything other than a high, singing whine. He ran his fingers uncertainly through his hair, trying to think where he was, and a cloud of dust came

280

sifting down. There was dust inside his dungarees, on his lips, and in his nostrils. He thought he felt all right, so long as he stood erect and kept walking, but each time he bent down to pick up a ball it formed a double image so that he often found himself groping for a hallucination and could not entirely rid himself of a sensation that he was careening through space.

At the patio, having filled the buckets, he folded up his sack and then, fearfully, approached the lowest-ranking officer—an ensign whose collar bars were so bright that he could not have been commissioned more than a few weeks. He was dressed in a gray work uniform and was standing a little to one side as though he did not know anybody and had, perhaps, just recently arrived on the station. Melvin came to attention in front of him and saluted.

"What do you want?" the young officer inquired, looking at him in surprise and amusement.

"Sir," Melvin began, and stopped; he had not addressed an officer for so long that his voice quavered. "I wonder if you can tell me what's going on in Europe."

"What makes you think there's anything going on in Europe?"

Melvin stared at him in bewilderment. "Why, ah—sir, I heard you talking and I was curious."

"Is it any concern of yours what we talk about? What's your name and rate?"

"Isaacs, sir. Seaman, second."

"A bit of advice, Isaacs. Mind your own business."

Melvin saluted and turned away.

Crossly the ensign commanded, "Come back here. Maybe I'm upset today. What is it you want? You want some information?"

"Yes, sir. If it isn't too much trouble."

"No trouble at all," the ensign said. "Do you care about the war?" he asked, looking at Melvin humorously.

"Yes, sir. Very much. Naturally."

"Hmm! Well, grab one of those buckets and follow me," the ensign told him, and selected a club from the rack. "Now why should you of all people concern yourself with the war?" he continued as they were walking toward the bunker. "Look at you," he went on while Melvin was teeing a row of balls for him to hit. "Five thousand miles from the front lines," he said, and touched

Melvin's knee with the tip of the club. "What possible difference can it make to you?" He assumed a stance, drew back loosely but powerfully, knocked a ball high into the wind, and watched it slice over the markers and lift a distant puff of dust. "That always reminds me of tank warfare in the desert. I've never seen it, but that must be what it looks like."

Melvin said nothing.

"Well, anyway, I met a man," the ensign resumed while he was addressing the second ball, "I met a man, a man who knows quite a lot about war. Told me some fascinating stories, this man did. Said to me that the Nazis conceived a few rather novel atrocities, such as putting an ape in a cage. What do you think of that?"

"I don't know, sir," Melvin replied. "What did they do to the ape?"

"The ape? They didn't do a damn thing to the ape! They merely let the beast into a cage with a woman. She was stripped. Yes, that's right," he murmured, and hit the ball. "And it seems apes are smarter than we think." He took off his new gray garrison cap and slapped dust from it, put it on again, and neatly tucked in the corners. "Seems it didn't take those apes long to get the idea." He waggled the club and hit another ball; shading his eyes he watched it climb through the milky Texas sky.

"Know much about war?" he asked.

"No. Not much," Melvin said. "Nothing, I guess, really."

"Remote, isn't it?"

"I guess it is. Yes, I guess it really is. I think I see what you mean."

"When you enlisted in the Navy didn't you expect to cover yourself with glory? Silver Star and so forth? Fancied yourself sporting a decoration or two, didn't you? Maybe you used to wallow in that old sack and dream about the day you returned from foreign waters. Have you been overseas?" he asked, glancing at the faded dungarees.

"No."

"Never been out of the States?"

Melvin shook his head.

"Where are you from, Isaacs? Didn't you say that was your name?"

"Yes, sir. Isaacs. I'm from Kansas City."

"Missouri or Kansas?"

"Missouri."

"That's something I never did understand," the ensign remarked after a pause. "But never mind. Used to picture yourself coming home. Photograph of you on the front page of the Kansas City paper—whatever the hell the name of it is—local boy, some dignitary, the mayor, shaking you by the hand. Flash bulbs. Reporters. You, modest, reluctant to describe the battles—Midway, Coral Sea. That's how it was, wasn't it? Tell me the truth."

"I don't know. In a way, maybe," Melvin said uncomfortably.

"But it didn't work out. Suppose you tell me what it'll be like when you do go home. People will ask where you were. What will you say?"

"Say I was here, and if they want to know where else I've been, I'll tell them."

"Be sure to watch their reaction."

"Now look, I didn't ask to be sent here five thousand miles from the war! There was nothing I could do about it! I was ordered here, you know that," Melvin retorted, and wondered why it was that of all the normal, reasonable, decent officers in the Navy, of the thousands of officers who would simply have answered his question and been done with it, he had the bad judgment to pick this one.

"Sure, sure," the ensign remarked with his unpleasant, toothy grin. "But only one thing will matter when you go home. The fact that you didn't get into combat. You didn't shoot anybody and nobody shot at you. That's the yardstick. Frankly, how *did* you get here, Isaacs? How did you manage to be stationed as far from the fighting as a man can be? You know you couldn't be farther from the action if you were in the antarctic."

"Well, it's a long story, sir. I was an aviation cadet for a—"

"You were *what?*"

"I was in the V-five program, but I got washed out at Pensacola, then they shipped me around the way they do and I wound up here."

"Am I being given to understand that you were an av-cad at Pensacola?"

Melvin was puzzled by his tone and looked at him stupidly.

"Well!" the ensign breathed, leaning on the golf club with

both hands. Then he tossed the club in the air and caught it as it fell. With his thumb he pushed the garrison cap back on his head and grinned.

Melvin understood, then, that the ensign had once been an aviation cadet; they glanced at each other and both of them were grinning.

Melvin said, "Well, I'd about decided I was the only one in the world."

The officer wagged his head: "No, no! Lots of us. Lots. I got the ax at Bunker Hill. In my company thirty-nine out of forty-two washed out. Damnedest thing you ever saw. Directive from Washington—too many cadets being trained, get rid of them, miscalculation. Familiar story. Governments can multiply, but don't know how to add. It was like a plague, Isaacs." Thinking about it seemed to summon an old resentment; he snapped his fingers and sighed.

"One after another we went, bunks emptied. Every day or so another wash-out. Don't know why, but it began at the far end of the barracks and spread toward me. Mattresses turned back, duffel bags missing. Upper bunk, skip one, upper bunk, lower, upper, skip one, coming right toward me. I couldn't believe it. So methodical, like a crazy roll call. Buses left for the Lakes twice a week. The plague skipped over me, thought I had it made, then. They got me on the last flight. Chase pilot said I didn't signal clearly enough. Board of review. No extra time. Not a chance. Wasn't the chase pilot's fault; he had his orders. Get rid of us. Hell, you know how it was. But I'll never forget the last day. I was out, but my orders to the Lakes hadn't arrived, so I watched the lucky ones start for Pensacola. *Three* from a company of forty-two. *Three.* They lined up in regular formation: company commander, platoon commander, one man in the ranks. Company commander accepted the orders from the exec, saluted, about-face, exchange salutes with platoon commander, repeat orders, platoon commander saluted, about-face, bawled orders to the ranks—that one man. I saw them marching toward the depot. Three of them. Company commander bawling cadence. Damnedest thing in the world."

"We didn't lose quite that many at Memphis. I've forgotten by now what the percentage was, but it seems to me that no more than seventy or eighty per cent."

The officer nodded. "We heard Memphis was easy."

"Yes, but you ended up with a commission anyway."

"My uncle's a senator. After I fouled up at Bunker Hill and went through the Lakes he recommended me for ground officers' school. I'm what's known as a ninety-day wonder."

"Well, the situation doesn't bother me as much as it used to," Melvin said, and was prepared to tell his story; but the ensign, once more squaring the corners of his cap, had begun to frown and was plucking at the golf club with impatience and disapproval.

"What was it you wanted to know?" he demanded curtly.

"About Europe, sir."

"What would you do," the ensign inquired picking at the lacquered string which bound the head of the club, "if somebody told you the war in Europe was over?"

"I don't know." Melvin shrugged. "Nothing special."

"Wouldn't you get drunk?"

"There's no reason to."

"Is that a promise?"

"Sure. I mean, yes, sir."

"Suspect that could be why they're so pleased?"

Melvin glanced toward the other officers, who had formed a circle with their arms around one another's shoulders and were singing and clinking glasses.

"Yes," the ensign whispered, bending down and pounding on the prairie with the dusty club, "*Yes! Yes!* I didn't help, but the war in Europe is over!"

Melvin thanked him and wandered away with the sack tucked underneath his arm.

So the war was over. In Europe the war was over. The Germans were again defeated. This meant that when the Japanese surrendered, as they must, and the armies and navies once more disbanded, he, Melvin Isaacs, would be released.

That evening when he returned to the barracks he found the CPO describing to a group of men how the war had begun at Pearl Harbor, how he had been climbing a ladder of the *Arizona* after eating breakfast on the morning of December seventh when the first bomb fell. He had not thought it was a bomb; he had been arguing with a machinist all through breakfast and he thought the machinist had run after him and struck the stanchion with a length of pipe. The concussion blew his hands from the rail and he dropped to the deck of the battleship, bleeding from the nose and the ears.

Just then Melvin was summoned to the telephone. His father was calling from Kansas City.

"Wonderful news! Thank God! And it means Japan is doomed, thank God! The Russians will march through Siberia, I am positive. Vladivostok. They have submarines, a magnificent air force, trained pilots and bombers vastly superior in every respect to the Japanese, which are imitations of American models. I am too excited to say much, however we are anxious to have you home. It will all be over soon. I cannot bring myself to think of the past. How soon will you come home?"

Melvin replied that he did not know.

"As soon as possible, don't forget. Request to be discharged from service. We are expecting you. It is not too late, you can become an attorney. Nothing will be more logical; one day you will be inheriting my practice, a select clientele. Some of the finest people in the city, I am happy to say. A gentleman, recently, from the Plaza district, with considerable holdings, came to me on a confidential matter. I was surprised, with large offices in competition, but delighted, I assure you. I'm requesting information from the University of Missouri, undergraduate studies nicely designed leading to the school of law. You will have to study with diligence. Tuition is low for residents of the state, in addition you will be able to come home on week ends."

"I'm not going to be a lawyer," Melvin interrupted. "You might as well get used to the idea. I'm not sure just what I want to do, I'm thinking over various professions. But I don't want to be a lawyer. I'm sorry—I know you've counted on it—but my mind is made up and I don't feel like discussing it now."

A letter postmarked about an hour after they had talked on the telephone referred not only to Melvin's future career but to Pensacola: the family was still disappointed that he had failed to graduate, and, he surmised, they would not ever quite overcome their embarrassment. He did not think his naval experiences would be a topic of much conversation when he returned to Kansas City.

20
★

In August the war with Japan concluded. As soon as the news was announced Melvin hurried to the administration building to see about obtaining his release from the Navy. A number of weeks went by, however, before his application was finally approved, and not until one evening in late autumn did he arrive in Kansas City.

With his duffel bag balanced on his shoulder and his sailor cap on the back of his head he made his way through the crowd in the Union Station and out the door by which he had entered three years previous. Across the street and up the hill, on top of the fluted column of the Liberty Memorial, the traditional fire was burning, the flames bending in the night wind like the beard of Barbarossa. He stopped a moment to look at the Memorial, and wondered if another shaft would be erected at the opposite end of the mall to honor those who died in the Second World War. With two additional wars the mall could become a rather attractive quadrangle.

The city, as he gazed around, seemed unchanged: the billboards overlooking every corner, the barren park, the streetcars and automobiles passing continually over the bridges that spanned the railroad pit. The streetcars were olive green, he noted, looking at another. He tried to recall whether they had been painted that color before the war, or whether someone in the family had written about it; they had been a cheerful orange-yellow when he was a boy, and he had been quick to see them when they came rocking around a bend. These had a wartime look, as though they belonged in England or Germany.

In the taxicab on the way home he could not get over a feeling of discontent, which seemed to grow stronger as he came nearer. He tried to distract himself by observing the city, and noticed that the elm trees which lined the boulevard were nearly devoid of leaves. This, too, this knowledge of the long, impending winter, disturbed him and contributed to a sense of dissatisfaction.

There was a light in the kitchen. He was surprised by this, because it was almost midnight, and concluded it might be Leah home from a movie. But it was his father who answered the door, a newspaper clutched in one hand, very much startled to see him there. And within a few minutes Melvin understood why he had not notified anyone that he was arriving, and why he had been ill at ease during the journey. The reason was that he dreaded the conflict with his father.

"Your application for admission to the University of Missouri is in my office," his father said. "Tomorrow at ten in the morning come downtown, sign it, and I will personally take care it is mailed to the registrar. We will send it special delivery. In addition I happen to have a client, very influential in these matters, who will be delighted to write a recommendation to the chancellor."

"You're too late," Melvin replied, shaking his head and clasping his hands behind his back.

"Too late? For what, if you please?"

"While I was in Texas I sent for an application form to the University of Kansas. I filled it out and I sent it in. And what's more, they're going to accept me."

"The school of law at the University of Kansas, I don't—"

"I'm not going to law school. I'm entering the art department."

"Department—*what?* Of what? What did you say?"

"That's right," Melvin said. "I've decided I'd like to be an artist. I have the GI Bill and I'm going to study art."

"So you have decided you would like to be an artist! Excuse me, nothing is so simple as a decision. I could decide I would like a seat on the Supreme Court. Perhaps I am mistaken, but would you be good enough to explain to me what you know of the fine arts?"

"I don't know anything about them and I don't want to discuss it. I made up my mind, that's all." He had been walking nervously back and forth while they talked, and now went to the window where he peered out into the night. "How is everybody? The last letter from Mother said you're worried about Leah."

"That's a fact. Where is your sister at this moment? Out. Out where? She doesn't tell. I should be firm, she is too young to be out so late. She gets around me, wheedling, pleading, then at times a furious temper. She should be spanked, but she is too big. I don't know what to do." All at once he fell silent as though struck with an idea, walked rapidly out of the kitchen, and returned a few minutes later with an old, warped, black buckram scrapbook with D.W. ISAACS stamped in gold on the binding. The scrapbook was packed with clippings from local newspapers. The pages were dry and brittle. The penciled dates were scarcely legible.

"I'm not attempting to give orders, Melvin. Do whatever you wish," he said, turning through the scrapbook. "It's your life. Nobody is more aware of this fact than I am, however I am hoping you will become an attorney. I've been planning on that, but do whatever you wish. It seems to me you have never been conscious of the past, of history, obligations. Ah—here's a sketch of your grandfather as a young man, wearing a wing collar. Notice the pearl stickpin, which was the fashion in those days. He was going to Jefferson City on this occasion to speak to the governor. I might as well be frank—nothing would please me half as much as knowing that one day you would join me in the office. I haven't mentioned it, because I wanted you to make your own decision, but I've been planning on this for years. I'm positive, too, that your grandfather, if he were still alive, would be pleased to know the tradition would continue. I'll never forget how proud I was the day my name was lettered on the door beneath his. In a few years we could put your name beneath mine. What would you think of that?"

"I'm sorry," Melvin said. "I've already decided. There's no point in talking about it. When do you think Leah's going to get home?"

"I told her to be home early. I was expecting her two hours ago. She has begun to imagine she is the queen bee. And I'm putting a stop to this soldier she writes to. He's now in France, and letters are flying back and forth. I don't like it. He's old enough to be her father. What does he intend to do—stroll into my home, tip his hat, and stroll away with my daughter? He is in for a surprise. I am going to have him arrested! I've warned her that's what I'll do. She should be interested in a boy her own age."

"Won't she listen to you?"

"To be perfectly honest about it, Melvin, no."

"What does she say? What sort of argument does she give you?"

"There's no argument. She's like her mother. Neither of them argue with me. They do as they please. It's amazing! I can't believe it. Both of them ignore me. It's too much! I've been thinking I might go away on a little trip and see if they appreciate me then."

"They'd love you in Baghdad."

"It amuses you to tease people. I don't mind. Except that there are times to be serious. Fine arts, what kind of a life is that, will you be good enough to explain? Artists starve to death. Think of all the starving artists. Think of Millet living in a little hut. During the first war in France I took a Sunday trip to see the hut where Millet lived. It was awful. Think of that."

"I've thought about it," Melvin said. "The last year or two I've had plenty of time for thinking."

"You can't be serious."

"I never was any more than I am now."

"I refuse to believe you! Years ago your grandfather said, 'I am not a very good liar myself, but I appreciate good lying when I hear it.' What makes you think you could succeed as an artist? Do you have any talent? So far you haven't shown it. Nothing but difficulty would result from attempting to become an artist!"

"You'll wake up not only Mother but all the neighbors if you keep talking that loud."

"Your mother, whom I love very much, would sleep through an air raid. As for the neighbors, who cares? Painting pictures, everyone will think you are too lazy to work!"

Overhead the floor was creaking. In a little while Melvin's mother solemnly entered the kitchen. She was hunched and wrinkled. Her gown had come open at the throat; the folds of her skin filled Melvin with deep surprise. She was trembling. He sensed that the obstinate, relentless nature of his father had all but consumed her and that she would not live many more years. For the first time he wondered what she had been like when she was young. "How have you been, Mother?" he asked, pressing her hands. Then he looked away from her and could not think of anything else to say.

"Mama, run back to bed, it's late. Your son will be here in the morning. We are discussing matters which would not interest you."

"I'm interested," she replied, without taking her eyes from Melvin, "in whatever concerns my son."

Jake Isaacs shrugged and resumed walking back and forth with quick, stooping steps. He looked at the floor as though searching for something. He shook his head with a birdlike jerk and stopped at the back door to try the latch. Melvin, watching these nervous, anxious movements, realized that this was his father's home and that he himself could no longer live in it.

"Naturally we were disappointed by the unfortunate conclusion of your career in the Navy. However, that is all in the past. It was a disappointment, frankly. All the same, the war is over."

"That's probably the only thing we agree on," Melvin said. "Because I'm going to study where I want, and what I want to."

There was a long silence while his parents stared at him.

"Buy a new sweater before you go," his father said in a strange voice, and tucked several bills into his breast pocket, "leather patches on the elbow don't look good. The porch light I'm leaving on—your sister will turn it off when she comes home."

"I know. I remember. I haven't been gone that long."

"Some things are easy to forget. Good night. We are pleased you are home."

Melvin remained at the kitchen table with his head in his hands until he could no longer hear his parents moving around upstairs. Then, without paying much attention, he began to turn the pages of the scrapbook, but gradually he became interested in it. He remembered that when he was very small he used to enjoy sitting on his grandfather's foot, with both arms tightly wrapped around his grandfather's leg and his face pressed to his knee; in this position he would be taken for a ride, backward, through the rooms of the great red brick house in Lexington with a curiously comforting motion unlike anything else he had ever experienced. Up, over, and down he had gone; up, over and down, through one room after another, and it now seemed to him that his entire life had been like this.

All at once a draft of night air swept through the kitchen. He smelled perfume and heard the rustle of a woman's clothing. Leah, carrying her shoes in one hand, bending down to kiss his forehead, was drunk, silken and plump, almost fat, with a moist warm mouth and mascaraed green eyes as feline and meaningless as the eyes of a lynx. She had grown several inches taller and her body gave an impression of massive delicacy, and of immense depth and weight which reminded him of sculpture. He noticed that she was eying him speculatively, with an intelligence born of some vegetative instinct but nothing more; she seemed to be trying to locate his thoughts, with no effort, like fungus seeking the dark.

"Oh!" she murmured, "why, you nasty creature!" and blinked, ducked her head with an expression of low cunning, breathing through her mouth. She straightened up with the clumsiness peculiar to her and stared at him vacuously, smiling a little, blinking stupidly and swaying in voluptuous pleasure. All at once she gave a wild, hissing noise and reeled across the kitchen to look into the cookie jar. She stood there on one foot, enjoying her drunkenness, trying to balance her unfamiliar woman's body by wiggling her toes, clutching a large woman's shoes with the dimpled hand of a child, and leaned forward and plunged the opposite hand into the milk-blue cloisonné jar, but it was empty, except for some crumbs. She muttered unintelligibly, tossing her hair over her shoulders, and licked her fingers, then dipped into the jar again with an intent smile, her fingers scratching the enamel as though there were a squirrel inside.

"Dear brother!" she announced. "Louis is coming home! Christ, help me! Sweet God!" Tears rolled down her cheeks. She gasped and bit into her lower lip and collapsed on the floor with the full, harsh length of her unbound hair dragging over one fat, taut, glossy knee; she lay on the floor as though she had just been beaten, shaking her head and sobbing. Melvin had jumped up, shocked, and did not know what to do; he gazed down on her with a feeling of awe and dread. One of her shoulders had slipped out of her dress. He was fascinated by the cool platinum sheen of her skin, and the swarthy gold and olive shadow the dress cast over her breast. He discovered that she was looking at him with no expression.

"You'd better go to bed," he said, turning away from her. "You drank too much. You aren't old enough to drink."

She yawned noisily and he had the feeling that she was amused. He sat down at the table and rested his chin on his fist.

"Tell me about this sergeant," he said, turning the pages of the scrapbook. Leah did not answer or make any sound and the silence filled him with alarm, so that he continued speaking, teasing her; but then, thinking she must have fallen asleep, he glanced around. She was watching him through narrowly glittering eyes, and there was still that ominous absence of any human expression.

"Get up!" he said urgently, and he himself got up. "You can't lie on the floor."

She tumbled heavily, luxuriously, with her hair drifting across her face, but would not get up. It occurred to him that for some reason he did not understand she wanted to remain on the floor at his feet. He stepped back, sat down uneasily, and could not prevent himself from staring at her. He recognized her as his sister, and yet she was someone he had never known. She was wearing a sheer crimson dress of silk or satin or jersey—he did not know what it was, except that it had a liquid appearance and had been very popular with the prostitutes in the French Quarter of New Orleans who would wear a black velvet choker for emphasis. Now the dress was twisted around her body, strained until he could make out the indentation on her protruding belly. She had grown so large that her head looked a trifle small; her neck too long and thick, yet the disproportion was alluring, and the quick enormous swell of her thighs amazed him steadily. He thought of an afternoon several years before when he had been looking down at her in this same position. They had gone swimming together and she had been sleeping in the sun when he came to tell her it was time to go home.

"Please don't lie there," he said, and nudged her with his foot.

"I despise you," she murmured, and thrust out her tongue.

But in a little while she got up and tiptoed out of the kitchen; soon she was back, leaning through the doorway to pick up her shoes. She hesitated, sucking her lip and looking at him with a crafty, petulant expression as though she were about to play a trick; then she giggled, patted his cheek, and disappeared.

Later, as he was about to replace the lid of the cookie jar, which she had left overturned on the stove, he became aware of the persistent hum of the electric clock on the wall and he glanced at the pointer sweeping inexorably around the dial. It reminded him of the altimeter needle which marked his descent before the crash—so rapidly and convincingly it moved. He recalled how he had folded his hands in his lap while the Dauntless plummeted toward the earth, and how extraordinarily difficult it had been to rouse himself even though he had known his life depended on it. He watched the pointer sweeping around, and fell to thinking of Elmer Free, whose life had been stopped with such curt brutality, and how, on a tropical morning, he had vanished forever into the depths of the water, and how quickly the explosion subsided and the whitecaps jigged along toward the distant shore. Now, at the bottom of the Gulf, bright striped fish were swimming through the half-opened cockpit of the SNJ, streaming by the engine, while primitive, spiny sea creatures crawled laboriously over the wings, scuttled between the cylinders, claws rattling in the midnight as though to communicate with whatever remained of him, these mindless ancestors—a few scraps of still brilliant orange rubber and a metal valve, some nylon webs, a buckle, a fractured length of mossy human bone. So he is gone, he is gone, Melvin reflected. So many have gone and disappeared, and have no life but that life imparted to them by the sea and the jungle.

Becoming conscious that he had repeatedly and painfully pinched his lip, he jerked his hand away with a distraught expression; yet soon, subdued as deeply by the long night silence as by his own meditations, his fingers strayed nervously forward, crept over and around his lips as if to pluck forth some secret knowledge; and it appeared to him that life might not be a transitory thing, as he had always supposed it was, and he was greatly puzzled by this. He remembered how, at Albuquerque, and at Pensacola, at all the various stations where he had been, he had contemplated his life and had attempted to solve the problems that bewildered him, to perceive what he ought to do in order that his life should be full and satisfactory, and how it ought to be done. And he recalled how he had become disheartened by the immensity and the complexity of life, and had been unable to justify the simplest opinion, so profound and disturbing were the considerations involved. Now he thought about these matters again, these questions which had beleaguered him and left him helpless with doubt, and they did not seem so formidable; perhaps, after all, there was at work in the universe a divine purpose, some ineffable moral providence or law. If so, if this was true, then whatever happened must be worth while. War, for instance, which appeared so catastrophic, was not that at all.

He stirred uneasily and discovered that he had been listening, but for what he did not know. He cupped his hands like seashells beside his ears and was able to hear, as plainly as ever, the revolution of the earth, and another noise to which he listened a while and found to be the warm, positive beat of his own heart. It seemed to be delivering a message of tremendous importance.

21

Shortly after Christmas the new semester opened at the University of Kansas, in the town of Lawrence about forty miles from the city, and Melvin registered for as many courses as he was allowed in the Department of Fine Arts. He noticed that the students who had not been in military service were younger than he was; they looked very young indeed, the more he looked at them. This surprised him because he was not aware of having grown any older, only that he now shaved every day. But still, if he studied himself closely in a mirror, provided the light was unflattering, he perceived a few fine lines, like threads or the structural veins of a leaf, at the corners of his eyes. At the same time, despite these proofs of age, he experienced a curious feeling of youth, as though he had somehow regressed, and concluded this was because he was surrounded by students. In the Navy he had belonged to a more factual world where the fundamentals were men and women and death and business as usual.

He very soon discovered that he preferred the company of other veterans, whom he could identify, as they could identify him, by their clothing, which almost invariably consisted of brogans, khaki shirt or trousers, and a Navy peacoat or a leather jacket with some insignia, a row of bombs and an eagle, perhaps, painted on the back.

One of these veterans was also studying art, and within a few days after the commencement of classes Melvin learned that his name was Kip Silver, that he belonged to a Greek letter fraternity, and that he had been a bombardier on a Flying Fortress. He had taken part in raids against many of the German industrial centers —Emden, Münster, Cologne, Frankfurt—and had a number of medals and citations. He was a sturdy little man in his middle twenties, sway-backed, with sloping shoulders and a rump like a Hottentot's. His face was underslung, the jaws resembling a muzzle, an impression accentuated by a silky cocoa-colored mustache which flowed with sinister implications around the corners of his protruding, purplish lips and descended into a neat goatee. He looked, to Melvin, not like a man quite so much as an orangutan which found nothing exceptional in masquerading as a man, particularly on cold days when he would put on a black-brown leather helmet and buckle it tightly under his chin. On sunny days he wore a large French beret.

They had been acquainted only a few weeks when Melvin received in the mail a card inviting him to dinner at the fraternity house. He accepted, but with surprise, for he had supposed Kip Silver spoke to him on the campus or when they passed on the street only because they happened to attend classes together. He was still more surprised to receive a second invitation, which he also accepted, and then, that same evening, to be asked if he would like to pledge. This would mean living in the fraternity house, eating at the community table, attending parties, and in general living a sociable sort of life. When they asked him he did not

296

know what to say, because he had never thought about joining a fraternity, but they were waiting, and being afraid that they might think he was discourteous he thanked them and said he would feel honored to be a pledge. He meant that he was grateful and that he would think it over, but they misunderstood: one of them seized him by the hand while all the others crowded about offering congratulations and patting him on the back. He realized that they were making a mistake, but it seemed to him that it was his own fault and he therefore felt obliged to go along with the idea.

A few minutes later he was in an upstairs room, seated beside a table on which there was a candle and an opened book—his right hand lying on the book; Kip Silver, the sponsor, stood behind him with fingertips resting on his shoulders. He listened without comprehension to one of the members, who had donned a billowing livid purple gown with a mask and a peaked hood, define the nine articles of faith and fourteen perpetual obligations which he, Melvin Isaacs, now assumed.

The next day, wondering if it would be all right to ask if he might listen to those obligations once more and possibly get a copy of them, he moved into the fraternity house, assisted by Kip Silver and several other members. He had been living in a drafty boarding house that smelled of gas and cabbage, so it seemed like a wise move. He did not have many belongings: books, clothes, some phonograph records, a sea shell he had picked up on the beach at Pensacola, a potted cactus, a box of raisins and one of shredded wheat, for he customarily got hungry at night, a jar of powdered coffee which tasted watery no matter how it was brewed, a bullfighting poster, and a bottle of sour-mash whisky his father had given him. There were a few other items, but he was packed in about fifteen minutes, the whisky rolled in a sweater at the bottom of his duffel bag because he had a feeling that if it were seen he would be expected to share it with everybody in the fraternity house.

He was assigned an exceedingly small room at the end of the third-floor corridor. This arrangement suited him; he felt fortunate that he had no roommate, except that a telephone was fastened to the wall beside his door and rang every little while. He hung a blanket on the wall to see if this might muffle the bell and the objectionable voices; it seemed to, slightly, but he was apt to swivel around from his desk and shoot paper clips at the blanket while someone just outside was talking—usually to a sorority girl, to judge from the inanity of the conversation.

And it was on account of this telephone, in conjunction with a few other aspects of fraternity life which were galling to him, that he began going to a doughnut shop around the corner. Here he would slump in a booth for hours at a time, sipping coffee and muddling his appetite with various little pastries while he turned through the newspaper or some magazine and brooded over what he was going to do when he graduated and the government stopped paying his expenses. He would have a degree, a Bachelor of Arts degree, which meant that he had been to college for approximately four years and had an elementary knowledge of perhaps half a dozen subjects, with the certain implication that he did not know much about any of them. How many Bachelor of Arts degrees were awarded each year in the United States he had no idea, but there were, no doubt, many thousands, and the more he thought of this the more depressing it became. He considered returning to the Navy, and began to wish he had never requested his release. He had not been doing anything there, and the Navy offered no future; on the other hand, that was the peculiar charm of the Navy. As a seaman he had been under no obligation to bestir himself either physically or mentally, except to meet the minimum requirements of his job.

These hours in the doughnut shop, however agreeable as a respite from the telephone and the harassment he suffered as a pledge, struck him as otherwise unprofitable, so much so that he periodically exhorted himself to do something, but could not then think of much to do. Weeks went by.

One afternoon when he returned to the fraternity house his father was in the lounge.

"I've been waiting two hours!" Jake Isaacs exclaimed. "Where can we talk? You aren't eating enough—you look like a ghost. Come, we'll sit on the front steps of the house, I always wanted to do that. Being in a fraternity, I envy you, such a life." He was already at the door and was beckoning. "I have some news. You must get to know Louis Kahn, who is out of the Army and is in Kansas City intending to marry your sister. None of us could believe it, but it's true!"

Melvin followed him out of the house and obediently sat down on the steps, interested to hear more of Louis Kahn, but at the same time vaguely irritated that his father had appeared, because he had been planning to take a shower and relax in the doughnut shop until supper. There was no way of predicting how long his father would stay; he enjoyed driving to the university, he arrived without warning and might stay no more than fifteen minutes, after which he would go speeding back to the city, or he might remain until it became obvious that he was hoping for an invitation to eat in the fraternity dining hall.

"How soon will you be coming home for a visit?" he insisted, and plucked at Melvin's sleeve. "You must get to know Louis. You can take a bus, it isn't far, I drive here in no time. If you don't like to ride on the bus, don't hesitate to say so. We will drive up to get you. Louis has received a sports car from Italy. Nobody knows how he can afford it. He's a magnificent driver. He'll be happy to come and get you if I am busy."

"I don't understand," Melvin said. "It was just a little while ago that you were threatening to have him arrested the minute he showed up. Now you sound as though you like him."

"Yes, that's true. I was wrong. There's less difference in their ages than I thought. Louis is not even thirty."

Melvin looked at him in astonishment. "Do you mean you're actually going to let him marry Leah?"

"Yes. We are all very happy. He will be good for her. She obeys him, for one thing, I don't know why. She has never paid the least attention to anything I said."

"How can you feel so strongly about a thing and change your mind so quickly?"

"Why not? It's a matter of being informed of certain facts. What's the matter? You don't approve?"

"Well," said Melvin after a while, "if she wants to marry him, and I guess she does, it's a good thing you don't object."

"This Friday we are going to the wrestling matches in the municipal auditorium. Louis was a champion wrestler in the Army. He's enormous. He looks like an oak tree. Next week I am introducing him to my Legion post. We are all extremely anxious to see you. You haven't been home since Christmas. Louis brought presents for all of us from Italy, and has a wrist watch for you. Since Christmas you haven't been home. It isn't far; merely buy a ticket. Here, I'm giving you the money," and he slipped some bills into Melvin's breast pocket.

Melvin got up and walked around uneasily; he did not like the idea of being obliged to accept a wrist watch from someone he had never seen, and whenever his father neatly slipped a little money into his pocket, as frequently happened, he became uncomfortable.

"What's the matter? Are you offended?"

"No, I'm not offended. It's just that I've got a lot of things to do, I mean, studying and so forth."

"Study? You're painting pictures, what is there to study? I have always wished I had talent."

"You don't understand. I don't paint all day, just part of the day, and I've got a course in art history, and the theory of composition and a lot of others, and then there's these non-elective courses like plain English I've got to take to qualify."

"To qualify for what?"

"Well, to get the GI Bill they have these regulations, see, and stipulations."

"You should spend more time studying. Your grades, unfortunately, have never been remarkable."

"Yes, I know."

"After graduation when you apply for a position the employer will request a transcript of your record at the university, you will be obliged to produce it. Grades are important. Nobody will hire you. You should take advantage of your fraternity friendships. I'm going. I would like to remain for supper, but I have business in the city. I will tell your mother you are looking fine, in excellent health, which is not strictly true. You are growing thin, you should eat more. Get a haircut. Good-by. I will tell Louis you are looking forward to meeting him."

As his father drove away, waving and nodding, Melvin slumped on the steps and put his head in his hands.

A few weeks later, considering that already he was twenty-two years old, he took a pencil and paper and spent a while attempting to account for this fact. Spring had come again; from his window he could see through the boughs of a massive, mottled sycamore for a distance of fifteen or twenty miles across the Kaw River valley. The sun was bright and warm, there were no clouds in the sky, and while he sat behind the desk there was a faint, sliding rumble overhead and one last avalanche of snow darkened the window as it cascaded from the eaves and splashed to the ground far below, while the upper limbs of the sycamore swayed from the shock. Then, as if it were truly spring, and they had that instant been released from a cage, two swallows veered by, tilting in noiseless, vertical perfection on some invisible current; he opened the window and leaned out, looking all around, at the wooded hills, the long, winding river, and the great valley, and closed his eyes to gather the full warmth of the sunshine on his face.

Almost a year had passed since the capitulation of the Germans, and it seemed to him quite odd that there had actually been a war, and that he had spent more than three years of his life in military service. Those years had been as real and palpable as his life had ever been, yet now they were gone, and each experience he had known so intimately was gone. He had flown above the Gulf, and, glancing over his shoulder, observed Sam Horne watching him attentively—but now this did not exist. Where, in fact, was Horne? Was he alive? There had been no word from him, not since that postcard in New Orleans, and that was October of last year, no, the year before last. Horne was getting married, was that what he had written? No, he was already married and his wife was pregnant. Yes, and the child was due to be born around Lincoln's birthday, which would mean it would be on its feet by now and speaking a few words, or whatever children did when they were thirteen months old, and yet it seemed like only last year, or the previous year, that they had begun cadet training, running the obstacle course and learning elementary navigation.

Melvin drew his head in the window and looked at a Corsair made of balsa wood and painted Navy blue which hung by a thread from a thumbtack in the ceiling. The Corsair was slowly turning in the breeze. Against the pale green ceiling all perspective was lost and the model became real, turning in the sky; and it seemed to him that he might be somewhere watching Sam Horne return. In a little while the plane would come howling overhead, the flaps descending, the wheels unfolding.

Melvin reached up and with his finger lightly touched the balsa plane, which spun around, rocking back and forth. He wondered again what had become of Horne. Perhaps he had been killed because he had miscalculated a trifle, for just an instant, and the Corsair crashed. Or had he died in the Pacific—shot down, destroyed by a Japanese pilot he never saw? At Saufley Field they talked about this. "All right," Horne said, and Melvin clearly heard him, "you don't know any Japs. Neither do I."

Could such reasoning be justified? At the time it seemed a little strange, but Horne had been so sure, so positive. Now take the dead at Hiroshima—how could the holocaust be justified? On that August morning, he had read, the sky over Hiroshima was perforated by a flash of light that traveled from east to west, from the city toward the hills. A fisherman in a sampan twenty miles out to sea heard the explosion, but there was no noise in the city. There was darkness beneath the cloud, and the people, silent and dazed, with blood pouring from their mouths and nostrils. A hospital collapsed and fell into the river, and there was a man squeezed between two long timbers like a morsel between two chopsticks. Huge drops of water, as large as marbles, fell from the cloud on the burning houses. The animals, too, were burned; the horses, dogs, and cats hung their heads, vomited, and died. There was a woman whose skin slipped from her body in huge, glovelike pieces. A group of children stood in a circle holding hands; their eyes were melted and the fluid ran down their cheeks. In the middle of the city, beneath the center of the explosion, the silhouette of a man was cast on the ground. Later in the day another American airplane flew over Hiroshima, to reconnoiter or gather data on the weather.

The chimes were announcing supper. Melvin washed his hands and went downstairs, still thinking, and his manner attracted the attention of one of the fraternity brothers. Melvin did not hear the brother ask if he was ill, and was annoyed to find someone had caught him by the arm and was ordering him to sing a song. Melvin refused. He was ordered to eat his supper standing up, but this did not suit him either.

The following afternoon he was summoned to the chapter room. There he listened phlegmatically while the vice president, dressed in the mask and billowing gown with the sequin-encrusted crest on the peaked hood, sonorously reread the nine articles of faith and the fourteen perpetual obligations.

Being asked, at the conclusion of this reading, to reaffirm his oath of fraternal loyalty, Melvin balked; then, feeling guilty at this display of ingratitude, for it did seem to him that the members must have privately agreed to lower their standards in order to pledge him in the first place, he slapped one hand down on the waiting book, and raced through the sacred oath. This was not well received; a tense silence ensued, during which he considered whether or not to hear what else they might wish to say, or whether to get up and walk out. He realized that he did not care in the least what they said or did.

Fraternity life, so far as he had learned, engendered song and ceremony, numberless protestations of friendship, promises of a rich future life, and frequent taxes which were known as assessments and which never failed to enrage him. Nor did he know quite why, but the fact that at meals everyone seated themselves in unison at a cryptic signal from the president's table also enraged him. No one outside the fraternity knew about this signal. Being a pledge, he was excluded from knowledge of sanctums Delta, Gamma, and Beta, but the signal to sit down at the table had been revealed to him on the night he made his pledge, for it belonged to Alpha, the lowest order of mystic communication. He understood that when, that is to say, *if*, he was initiated— and as matters were going it had begun to seem doubtful—*if* he was initiated he would be admitted to sanctum Beta, wherein he would be taught the handshake. This had seemed worth waiting for, but now he was not so sure.

However, there were the parties, which he enjoyed and at which he drank a good deal; and the intramural athletic contests, which he enjoyed even more; and on the assumption that perhaps he had been expecting too much and had given very little in return, he decided he might try out for a place on the fraternity track squad. In high school he had been a not incompetent hurdler, for his legs were long, and in mid-air sailing over the barriers he displayed a kind of energetic enthusiasm reminiscent of a wallaby, but because the fraternity boasted two excellent hurdlers he concluded he should become a broad-jumper.

So it was that one fine day in April he got dressed in his old cadet athletic gear which he, together with Sam Horne and a good many other members of the battalion, had wanted to keep and so had reported lost: khaki shorts, white wool socks, black gym shoes, and a reversible T-shirt orange-yellow on one side and Navy blue on the other. In addition, he borrowed a wool sweat-shirt from another pledge, and thus outfitted, with a large towel wrapped professionally about his neck, he went jogging stiffly but cheerfully around the cinder track hoping to be mistaken for a member of the Kansas varsity, or perhaps a visiting Navy athlete. However, nobody else on the track paid much attention and he found himself scrutinizing them as they raced by, wondering which of them were just out for exercise and which were members of the university team. He recognized one—a hawk-faced long-distance runner whose picture was often in the sports section of the newspaper—and jogged after him for a few hundred yards but soon gave up. He lay down on the grass of the football field to rest for a while, fell asleep in the sunshine, did some calisthenics after waking up, and then trotted over to begin broad-jumping; but here he was discouraged by the effort it took to reach the pit, and so, after two or three jumps, feeling slothful and rather embarrassed, he slunk off the field, took a hot shower and got dressed, and spent the remainder of the day in the doughnut shop.

By summertime, when the semester ended, he had established an agreeable routine of painting, studying, and socializing, which had an additionally beneficial effect on his relations with the fraternity—he had become, they thought, more cooperative—and all in all there was no particular reason to take a three-month vacation, so he did not. He registered for the summer session as most of the other veterans were doing, and continued living in the house.

The telephone rang with less frequency during the summer months, since so many students were away, and partly because of this and partly because he had gotten used to books again after seeing so few of them in Texas, he studied more consistently. His grades improved, so much so that in August when the summer session ended he had not only qualified for initiation, but had made better marks than any of the other pledges. Because he had never been first at anything this was a little hard to believe; his father, in fact, hearing the news by telephone, thought it was a bad joke. The pledge class had been small, this was true, and it was equally true that there had been no bright students; all the same Melvin had gotten the highest grades. He was the honor initiate.

Not long after the opening of the fall semester he was blindfolded and led into the chapter room, which, he immediately sensed, was crowded with people, although there was not a sound. Someone whispered in his ear that he should kneel. He did so, after a momentary hesitation, with the indignation he felt whenever he was obliged to get down on his knees. By tilting back his head he was able to peek out from beneath the bottom of the blindfold, and, as he had suspected, there were the fraternity officials in their robes and their peaked hats; he was interested, however, to see that in addition to the officials and the chapter members there were a great many older men, apparently alumni. He had not seen any of them come into the house and he wondered if there could be a secret passage beneath the kitchen; in any event, each man was holding a tall blue candle. They were attempting to look severe, as though this ceremony were of great consequence, which made them all the more preposterous; and, as if this were not enough, at a mysterious signal each man placed his left hand over his heart. The pledges who had followed Melvin into this refuge were also kneeling—he and they together formed a ring. Someone pushed his head down just then so that he could see nothing more, but he had noticed that he was the only one who remained erect on his knees; the others were bent over with their heads and shoulders bowed down almost to the hardwood floor because it was less painful that way. As soon as he had knelt he had begun to feel the pressure, but there had come into his mind the recollection of a photograph, published in the newspaper, of an Australian captive who was about to be executed by the Japanese. The Australian's hands were bound behind his back and he was on his knees with his head bowed waiting for the stroke of the sword.

Melvin lifted his head as soon as the hand was removed; the hand pressed it down again. He did not resist, but a few seconds later when the hand was withdrawn he lifted his head.

Someone whispered in his ear that he must keep his head bowed. He did not say anything, but remained as he was, bolt upright.

After a while he knew he had won. Whoever had been pushing at him left him alone, but by this time the pain in his knees, which he knew, he was inflicting on himself, had become so excruciating that his victory seemed unimportant; he was more concerned with mastering the agony which emanated from the wood and periodically shot up his spine to the base of his skull.

He did not know how long he knelt. His companions moved from time to time and uttered little groans.

They were taught the meaning of various abbreviations, numerals, signs, and eventually the fraternity handshake, which took so long to accomplish and which was so intricate a procedure —the fingers interlaced first one way and, after a pause, another way—that by the conclusion of the act he felt as though he had engaged in some shameful and grossly irregular intercourse.

At last the blindfold was removed. He got up, suspecting his knees might buckle under him, and grimly looked around.

Everyone in the room was staring at him.

What especially struck him at that moment was their sincerity. They stood there and looked at him as though examining some improbable document by the light of their candles.

Later in the evening Kip Silver gave him a present; Melvin accepted it awkwardly, having never known quite what to do or say when accepting a gift. Then, too, he was embarrassed about his recalcitrance during the initiation, for it reflected on Silver, who was his sponsor.

The gift, for that matter, was awkward: it was one of Silver's oil paintings, an enormous abstraction somehow reminiscent of a soiled bed sheet. It was much too large to be hung above the desk and he was afraid that if he hung it above the bed it might draw the nail out of the wall and fall on him in the middle of the night; so, finding no other place to put it, he suspended it from a hook on the door of the closet. There it swung and bumped in a menacing way as though dimly conscious of its own existence.

In addition to this painting he had been given the fraternity pin—diamond-shaped, solid gold, with small rubies enclosing the Greek letters. This was not, properly speaking, a gift; he had paid for the pin and would continue to pay for it he thought, as he weighed it in his hand, for quite some time to come. But it was well made, it was a handsome, distinctive pin, instantly recognizable for what it was, and he took to wearing it on his sweater or on the pocket of his shirt or the lapel of his coat wherever he went, and was gratified by the attention it received. It gave him a status he had never known before, as though he himself were enhanced by merely owning and displaying this pin; before long he depended on it to the extent that he did not like to leave the house without it, and on one occasion when he realized as he was walking to class that he had forgotten it he hurried back to get it. It seemed to him that the pin would somehow solve whatever problems came up and he found it difficult to remember what he had done and how he had gotten along before he joined the fraternity. In a way it was not unlike being in the Navy; there was that same omniscient paternity, the sense of a government or council to which he might appeal but to which he was, and forever would be, subservient, and toward which he would be well advised to maintain an attitude of immaculate and modest obedience. This no longer struck him as distasteful so much as natural, and he considered a little ruefully that if he had only understood this while he was in the Navy he would have made less trouble for himself, would probably have won his commission, and could now be wearing an old aviation jacket with Navy wings and his name stamped in gold on the breast.

Autumn deepened. The leaves, the cool dappled shadows, mild winds—the burning turquoise arch of midsummer had tilted with the axis of the earth. Zinc gray the sky hung, level and constant, low as the sea; and Melvin sprawled on his bed hour after hour and thought of previous autumns. Soon it would be Christmas, and the New Year would follow. The days would grow longer, and the snow, which had not yet begun to fall, would melt into the past; then this year would be gone like the others—and he felt unaccountably dissatisfied.

22

★

A few weeks later he went to Kansas City to attend his sister's wedding. Louis Kahn had invited him to be one of the ushers, and after some hesitation, fearful that he might stumble over the carpet or conduct some privileged guest to the wrong place or otherwise blemish the proceedings, he agreed and made arrangements to rent a tuxedo.

The day before the marriage he was trying on the tuxedo in an upstairs room when he happened to look out the window and saw his sister and Kahn sitting together in the sports car. A few flakes of snow were falling, melting as they touched the fiery red hood of the car. All at once Kahn took hold of her and even from the distance Melvin could see that she had no thought of denying him whatever he wanted. He watched them embrace, saw the snow-flakes falling daintily on her up-turned face, and reflected that the ceremony was going to be a trifle superfluous.

He did not know a great deal about Louis Kahn, except that he had no family and that he was working in a bank, but was aware of a feeling of respect which resulted not only from the tremendous size of him but from a conviction that he could not be easily balked or dissuaded from whatever he meant to do. The curiously thick eyelids had a bluish or purplish shine in certain lights, as though he painted them with cosmetics; and the deadly eyes half-concealed beneath them gave him the hooded, carnal look of some decadent Asian emperor or of a phlegmatic medieval headsman at his leisure, or, for all that, of some mythical and fabulous reptile risen from the water of the Nile, whose stare was fatal. From the day they first met he had sensed, even before accepting the gentle grasp of that primitively shaped hand, that Kahn regarded each man as an individual but looked upon women as belonging to a subspecies, markedly inferior, although equally valuable; and this, in all probability, was the husband Leah required.

Melvin studied the way she reclined in Kahn's embrace; it occurred to him that she might already be pregnant. If not, she would be soon enough. With her depth and breadth and that low, rhythmic, odorous flesh, coupled with an essential stupidity, she must be a continual and irresistible invitation.

He went downstairs and outside. Leah had not moved. She lay supine, breathing shallowly. Her cheeks were flushed, and damp from the snow. Her eyes were bright. She looked at him but he had the feeling that she did not recognize him. Kahn appeared to be half asleep.

Melvin wandered around the automobile, which was furnished with extra mirrors, a spotlight, a horn that would play a little tune, black-leather seats, and a number of other luxuries, and presently asked what they were planning to do on their honeymoon. Kahn said they were going to Las Vegas. Melvin asked what the directors of the bank thought of this idea. Kahn sleepily grinned, raced the engine, and replied that it was none of the bank's business. During the war he had saved a few thousand dollars, he said.

"Excuse me, did I hear correctly?" Jake Isaacs asked, coming out of the house.

"Speedy business in Europe," Kahn conceded, and winked at Melvin.

"If I am not butting in, how much is a few thousand dollars by such standards? Working in a bank, if you were the president, all right. People would say, 'The president has money and an Italian roadster.' Now what will they say? You should be cautious."

Kahn was patiently stroking Leah's bulging hip while he listened. He replied that he would be cautious in Las Vegas.

"He wants to gamble so bad he can taste it," she said indignantly, lying across the seat with her head cradled in one of his arms. She brushed the snow from his sleeve and burrowed against him. "Las Vegas! *Poof!* He won't know I'm alive."

"You will lose money, Louis. Gambling is a mistake. By all means, go to Niagara Falls."

Kahn slapped Leah solidly on the rump and heaved her out of

his lap. She gasped at the insult, but he paid no attention. "I don't lose, Jake," he remarked as he got out of the car, imperturbable as some basilisk with his black crest of marcelled hair, and stood up, tranquilly stroking his bald spot, which, in the wintry afternoon, resembled an egg buried in an oily nest.

The next day, on Leah's seventeenth birthday, they were married. It was near the end of November and snow had been falling since dawn, but there was no wind and the air seemed warm for that time of year. The services took place at eight o'clock in the evening. Leah, with her long hooked nose and musky olive skin, looked tough and expectant, like an Arab in a white burnoose. She was, beyond question, a formidable bride: tall and substantial, with deep, boxlike hips and pendulous, swaying breasts. Kahn, whose crest of hair protruded from under the yamilke, alternately beamed and appeared complacent while the rabbi spoke. After the seven blessings he crushed a small wine glass beneath his heel to symbolize that it would be as impossible to break this marriage as it would be to piece together the shattered glass; and at this Leah, who stood close beside him under the flowered huppah, looked up at him through the veil with shining eyes. When he placed the ring on her finger he said, first in Hebrew and then in English, "Behold, thou art consecrated unto me by means of this ring, according to the law of Moses and Israel," and once more a change came over her face, softening it and revealing her love for him.

Later that evening Melvin observed how she would sometimes rise to her toes to peer over her husband's shoulder, not in order to see what or who was there, but only for the pleasure of measuring herself against him. Melvin was watching her do this, thinking himself unnoticed and thinking, too, that Kahn was not aware of Leah amusing herself, when Kahn slowly turned his massive head and one of the reptilian eyes disappeared in a wink.

Having drunk more than he intended, and feeling neglected, Melvin left the reception and descended to the basement, where he unbuttoned the collar of his tuxedo and squeezed into a nook behind the furnace as he used to do when he was a child and had been scolded or was confused. From within the warm furnace came a ticking noise, and there was a smell of oil. He struck a match and peered around; a roach scuttled up the damp, streaked wall and disappeared into a crevice, and as the flame was dying he caught sight of a tub and an old corrugated washboard. There were some of his father's law books in the tub, spotted with mold, and the pages, as he opened one of the books by the light of another match, were difficult to separate. The tub reminded him of years ago when he and Leah used to give their fox terrier a bath; he remembered how the dog whined and shivered, its skin mottled pink and blue beneath the short, soapy hair. Leah used to sit beside the tub as solid as a doll and hold the terrier by the muzzle to keep him from shaking. It seemed strange to Melvin that what once had been so real could be effaced as thoroughly as algebra on a blackboard.

He was standing silently in the darkness when someone came down the basement steps and switched on the light. It was Leah. She knew where to find him. She began to abuse him for leaving the party, and then she clutched him by the hair and tried to drag him upstairs. His resistance angered her; she slapped him sharply and then, with a shocked expression, she fled with her hands over her ears.

An hour later, having changed from her bridal gown into a wool traveling suit, and extremely drunk, she crept into the basement with a pair of pinking shears and lunged toward him, intending to get at a sparse, furry mustache he had been encouraging; he hopped aside, exasperated and confounded, and caught her wrists and they went struggling through the basement without a sound except the snap of the shears. He managed to push her against a wall and pinioned her there with her arms extended. Her strength amazed him; he was gasping for breath. He ordered her to let go of the shears. She was weeping and choking on her own sobs, cursing him obscenely; all at once she stretched her head toward him like a horse and he felt a painful pull at his lip. He twisted her arms until she cried out; then he let go and stepped away from her. His lip was warm and wet, it was throbbing violently, and when he looked at his fingers they were smeared with blood. Leah had fallen to the basement floor and was sobbing bitterly. He helped her up. There was calcimine on the shoulders of her suit and she exuded a strong odor. He brushed off the calcimine and she went away. After she had gone he took out his handkerchief and pressed it against his lip to stop the bleeding, and noticed on his sleeve a strand of hair so black that it appeared almost blue: he wound it around and around his middle finger, perplexed and obscurely moved.

The next day as he was returning to the university he thought of her again; he could not make any sense of her behavior. But then, he reflected, he could not understand even himself. He knew that he was going to resign from the fraternity; this conviction had steadily grown on him, but he did not know why. There was no reason to leave the fraternity, other than a persistent discontent, and this more than anything embarrassed and puzzled him. He felt certain he would be asked by the members to give some explanation for his decision, and he knew he would not be able to do so. And that was the way it turned out.

He was, however, greatly astonished by the reaction to his announcement. He had expected the fraternity members to be disappointed that he was quitting, but they were not especially disappointed, they were outraged. He was damaging the fraternity prestige. Word would get about that one of the brothers had defected.

He had thought that Kip Silver, at least, would understand; he could scarcely believe it when he heard Silver tell him to get out and never to come near the house again. Melvin instantly put on his jacket, as shocked as he had ever been in his life, and hurried to the doughnut shop, where he sat in a booth until he stopped trembling; then he bought a newspaper and turned to the apartment listings.

Apartments being too expensive, he went through the list in search of a housekeeping room, but there were none available. A few furnished rooms were given, and some sleeping rooms. He started out to look at them, and found most of them rented by the time he got there. A thick, wet, clinging snow had begun to fall. Hungry and miserable, sneezing crookedly and without hope, he trudged up and down hillsides knocking on doors, until, too filled with despair to search any longer, and torn between his aversion for the fraternity and his resentment toward the way he had been treated, he sat down on a bench and tried to decide what to do. It was obvious that the immediate problem concerned a place to sleep for the night; he must either stay in a hotel or return to the fraternity until morning.

It was after midnight when he made up his mind. He would have gone to a hotel but for two facts: he was entitled to sleep in the house because his rent was paid, and secondly—and this was what decided him—he had been told to get out and stay out.

So it was that he entered the house and tramped loudly through the lounge, went up the steps to his room making as much noise as possible, and carefully slammed the door. He waited to see if anyone would try to throw him out, but nobody did. He dried himself off, crept into his bed feeling very wretched, and lay there wide awake all night, shivering and sneezing and anxious for the dawn.

He was up early, with a bad cold, and got out of the house before anyone else was awake. After breakfast at the drugstore he read magazines until eight o'clock, thinking it would be impolite to inquire for rooms earlier, and then began where he had left off the previous night. Shortly before noon he found an enclosed sunporch. It was small, it was warm only in the vicinity of the electric heater, and he would have to walk through the land-lord's living room to make use of the shower and toilet; however it cost only fifteen dollars a month and it was on the opposite side of the campus from the fraternity.

With his head completely stopped up, but otherwise feeling somewhat better, he drank several cups of boiling-hot tea in the drugstore and then returned to the house. The brothers, who were just filing out of the dining room singing one of their favorite songs about good fellowship, ignored him and he was thankful for this. He did not ask any of them for help in moving, and none of them volunteered.

About an hour later he was in his room halfway through pack-ing when he had a visitor, a small, intrepid brunette who told him without a smile that her name was Jo Flanagan, and that she had come to help him move. Melvin gazed at her in stupefaction. She was, if not homely, no better than plain. Her nose was long and sharp; it seemed to proclaim her independence, and her chin had a cleft. She disdained cosmetics, but she had a naturally sweet odor so that he did not back away from her as he was inclined to do at first. She wore glasses, presumably because she needed them, and drew her long hair back into a soft bun. Except for wearing saddle shoes, a plaid skirt, and a baggy lemon-colored sweater with the sleeves pushed up to her elbows, she could have been a frontier schoolteacher.

"You certainly have a lot of junk," she said, with her hands on her hips.

"There's a whole lot more in the closet," Melvin said vaguely, unable to stop looking at her.

"Let's get busy," she said. She picked up a pair of trousers that had been on the floor for a week.

Melvin sat on the desk and fumbled for a cigarette, still watching her. "Aren't you assisting the wrong party?" he asked. "What I mean is, nobody else wanted to help me."

She was going through the closet. "Did you ask for help?"

"No," he said, "I didn't."

She stepped out of the closet to look at him sharply, and exclaimed, "You're exactly the way I thought you'd be!"

Melvin shrugged and began drumming his heels against the desk.

"What's *that?*" she demanded. "Don't tell me you painted that." She had paused before Kip Silver's abstract.

"It was a gift," Melvin said, "except now he may want it back. I don't know what to do—whether to take it or leave it here. It's even heavier than you'd think," he added pertinently.

"It's bunk," she remarked without giving it another glance.

"Well, now, I don't know about that. It stays with you. Those marks—those tracks—whatever they are—if you look at them long enough you can close your eyes and still see them, which proves—well—they have what you could sort of call a disharmonic continuity, I think." This phrase struck him as appropriate, and he continued. "The—ah, associations one discovers in contemporary art are significant. Modern artists have learned to visualize. And the spatial concept, too, is—oh, this is all difficult to explain unless you've studied art, and I don't suppose you have." He paused. "What did you say your name was?"

"Flanagan."

The name meant nothing. He sat on his hands and watched her move about the room.

"How did you know I was leaving the fraternity?"

"I saw you last night. You passed by the boarding house where I live and looked at the sign in the window. I waved to you but

314

you didn't wave back; you only stared at me. Did I frighten you?"

"I don't remember. I think I had a fever last night. Are you sure it was me?"

"It was you," she sighed. "It couldn't have been anyone else. Is your cold getting worse?"

He nodded, sniffling.

At last she said, "There! I think we're ready."

"Good. I want to get away from here."

Outside the fraternity house she asked, "Now which way?"

"I figured you'd know," he said, looking down at her affectionately. "I thought maybe you were my fairy godmother."

"You could certainly use one, brother Isaacs. I never heard of anybody who got into so much trouble."

"What do you mean?"

"For one thing, you exasperate your professors by asking 'Why?' Doctor Peters was getting set to brain you last week."

"He's an imbecile," Melvin said promptly. "I know more about the course than he does. Anyway, he didn't know why half the time." He walked a few steps and said, "How did you know about that?"

"I sit next to you," she replied coldly

"You *do?*"

"It's a good thing you intend to be an artist," she said, "because you're much too tactless to be successful at anything else."

"Flanagan," he muttered. "Oh, sure, that name sounds familiar now." He looked at her again. "You're the one with the books! Every time you come into the room you've got an armload of books. What's your first name?"

"Jo. Josephine. In a way, I'm sorry you're moving because I could see your light burning from my room."

On their second trip across the campus she carried his tennis shoes and racquet, a bag filled with apples and candy bars, and the greasy brown coveralls he had worn at Pensacola.

"Now, honestly!" she remarked as they were nearing the porch.

"What's the trouble?" said Melvin, without looking around.

"Wouldn't you consider discarding this ghastly ensemble?"

He knew she was referring to the coveralls; she had made a face when she found them under the bed.

"I'm not ever going to throw them away," he said. "They mean a lot to me."

"How about letting me wash them?"

"I'll wash them myself one of these days," he answered. "I've been planning to, but there hasn't been time."

"I knew you'd be like this," she said. "I just knew it."

On the third trip he took another box of textbooks while she carried his lamp and an album of phonograph records and marched directly behind him, wearing the lampshade as a hat. He sensed she was keeping step with him, which would make them look all the more ridiculous, but every time he peered over his shoulder she skipped.

"You certainly don't know the first thing about music," she said. "I think I'll drop these records."

"I would imagine you like jazz," he said, and stopped.

She prodded him with the lamp. "What are you going to buy me to eat when we finish moving?"

"Who said I was?"

"I believe I'll have a sirloin steak. I adore steak. And *pâté de foie gras*. We'll have a lovely evening." She began to read the titles on the album: " 'Bury Me Not on the Lone Prairie.' 'Little Joe the Wrangler.' 'The Cowboy's Lament.' 'I'm Sad and I'm Lonely.' "

"I enjoy those," Melvin said.

" 'The Old Chisholm Trail.' 'You Are My Sunshine.' "

"I like them. I'll play them whether anybody else likes them or not."

"Keep moving," she said, and he felt the lamp in his ribs.

"How long have you been sitting next to me?" he asked as they walked up the steps to the sunporch.

"Long enough, brother Isaacs. Long enough."

"It's funny I never saw you. In fact, the more I think about it, the more it gets sort of fantastic."

She sighed, and remarked with an air of boredom, "You only notice blondes. Even a bleached blonde can make your eyes pop. Men are impossible, don't you think?"

She ordered a hamburger instead of a steak, and while they sat across from each other in the booth he saw that she did have

316

a certain slight, winsome charm. Not very much, but a little. She was not totally unattractive. He saw that her shoulders were really quite graceful, and her nose was not as sharp as he thought. She seldom smiled, but when she did he was very much pleased.

"Why do you read detective stories?" she asked.

He had hoped his paperbound thrillers would get by; after all, thousands of intelligent people read them, millions perhaps. He told her he wanted to find out who the killer was. She asked why. He didn't know, but the question struck him as unfair.

"Where did you get that calendar?" she asked.

Melvin winced. The calendar had a picture of a rosy-cheeked blonde lolling on a bearskin rug. "I saw it in a pool hall in Pensacola," he said. "I thought it was attractive, so I bought it."

"But it's several years old!"

"Oh, well," he said. "The days don't change much. Let's discuss something else."

"Who shot the bear? All right! I know! You like the calendar and nobody had better throw it away."

"That's right," he said firmly, and had a drink of water. "Tell me, do you by any chance work for the FBI?"

"Oh, no. Home economics is my field. That seems bourgeois to artists, but it's quite fascinating to me."

"Then you're not here for an education. You're after a husband."

"You're much too direct. Men have so little tact."

Melvin could not think of anything to say to this. As they were leaving the drugstore where he had taken her for dinner he remarked, grinning, that he would have to write home about quitting the fraternity.

She looked up at him, seemed to be considering what he had said, and suddenly asked, "What's funny?"

"Nothing!" he exclaimed, grinning more broadly. "Except that this isn't the first time I've quit something and my father isn't going to like it. He keeps wanting me to get incorporated."

"What a preposterous idea!"

"Who's preposterous?" said Melvin. "Me or my father?"

"Well," she answered thoughtfully, "I've never met him, but I suspect both of you are."

"You know," he said a few minutes later, "you've sure got a

nerve. I don't mean just now—not what you've just said, but everything." He looked down at her curiously. She smiled and avoided his eyes.

Presently she said, "This is where I live."

They stopped walking and looked at each other. Then Melvin said, "Good-by. It's been nice meeting you." He thought she was waiting for him to say something more. "Thanks for helping me move," he added. Still she seemed to be waiting, but after a moment she turned away, a bit sadly, he thought, and went inside.

That evening while writing to his parents he found himself thinking of her. He very much wanted to see her again, but could not imagine why. He decided he was grateful for the assistance, and with that he continued writing.

The letter was delivered sooner than he had anticipated; the next evening his father drove to the university and they argued for several hours. At last, as he put on his hat, Jake Isaacs exclaimed, "Nothing is easier than to get along in the world, to make friends. Is this impossible for you?"

Melvin answered wearily that he supposed it was.

"But if you would try! If you would try, you could be like everyone else! You tell me again and again that something was wrong, something made life in the fraternity undesirable, but you don't know what. All I ask is that you explain what kind of a reason is that!"

Melvin was too exhausted and discouraged to reply. His father plucked at his sleeve and peered into his face with an expression of eagerness.

"Why don't you cooperate? Just once?"

"To tell you the truth," Melvin said after a pause, "I do cooperate."

"Excuse me, you do?"

"I do. It's the others who don't."

Jake Isaacs quickly stepped backward and placed one hand over his heart. "All right! That's the way you feel. I'll go back to the city. Who am I to interfere? Never, not once, have I tried to persuade you, to influence you in any manner. All right, it's settled, I'm going. Do as you wish. Except please make a serious attempt to pass your examinations. Another misfortune, after every-

318

thing that has happened, another one, to be perfectly frank, I couldn't stand."

"I'll do my best."

"Your best! You will do your best, did you say? How good is that?"

"We've gone through all this before. Please, let's not talk about it! How did Kahn make out in Las Vegas?"

"Gambling, he won, how much he doesn't say. Leah, however, is wearing a diamond. It's bad business, gambling. To get back to the subject, however, perhaps this is asking too much; it seems to me you go out of your way to antagonize people, the fraternity for example."

"It's all over," Melvin said. "I'm not going to ask them for another chance, so there's no point in you even suggesting it."

"If that's the way you—"

"It is! It is."

"I'm not saying another word."

"I doubt that," Melvin said. "Anyway, I'll do the best I can on the examinations."

Examinations began the next morning and continued through Friday. What with the argument ringing in his ears and the questions being altogether different from the ones he had expected, he grew increasingly despondent and bewildered. It was as though the examiners had discovered what material he had studied and made certain to avoid it. By Friday afternoon he was convinced he had failed at least two subjects, and perhaps more.

Late that night, too discouraged to sleep, he sat on the edge of his cot for a time, then got dressed and went for a walk. He saw a group of men strolling in the direction of one of the women's dormitories and it occurred to him that they were going to give a serenade, so he followed. Much to his surprise, they approached the rear of the building and one after another furtively entered by means of a basement window. There were no lights in the dormitory, it was long after midnight, and after thinking the matter over a few minutes Melvin also climbed through the window. It was quite dark in the basement. He began feeling his way along, came to a stairway, and went up and found himself in the lounge. Moonlight streamed through the french doors. The lounge struck him as being exceptionally pleasant, and, immersed in moonlight as it was, it gave an air of profound serenity. He picked a magazine from the coffee table and turned through it, looked at some pictures and read half a dozen lines by moonlight, and decided he had fallen asleep and was dreaming this, it seemed so unreal. He dropped the magazine on the coffee table, impressed by the fact that it made a noise, and walked up the central staircase and found himself in the second-floor corridor. It was deserted. He went on up to the third floor. This, too, was deserted. He was puzzled, yet more convinced than ever that he was dreaming, for he could distinctly remember that he had followed a group of men here and if they had been real he would have met them somewhere within the dormitory. He was alone, though, able to perceive everything as vividly as though he were awake. Just then a door opened very close to where he was standing and someone tiptoed out, carrying what appeared to be a woman's undergarment. Melvin tapped him on the shoulder and was amazed to see him spring high in the air with a shriek of fright, and it seemed to him that simultaneously there was shrieking and screaming everywhere. Lights popped on, an insane head half-alive with metallic spools of Medusa hair and pinched narrow-set eyes was unexpectedly glaring at him, someone else raced out of one room into another, out again followed by three women in nightgowns beating him over the head and shoulders, doors slammed, the mad, bristling, night creature took another breath and resumed her infuriating, mindless scream so that he was tempted to strangle her. He felt a stunning blow at the base of his skull, nails raked his cheek, and he flew through the corridor as fast as he could go in search of the fire escape. From nearby came a dismal, blood-curdling whine.

He flung up the window and went stumbling down the ladder blinded by the night, the dormitory lights and the full moon in his eyes; someone clawed him as he went past the second floor, and a moment later he was hanging by one hand from the bottom rung, kicking his feet, unable to see how far he was from the ground. Above him women were screaming and dropping things. It was like an ant hill. He let go, tensed for a long fall, planning to double up and roll at the last moment, and was badly jarred because his feet had been only a few inches off the ground. He keeled over in the snow, mute and stiff with shock. He thought he had splintered his spine. Painfully he dragged himself upright by grasping the fender of a car parked conveniently nearby and discovered it was a police car.

The rest of the night he lay on a bench in the city jail, twisting back and forth, slowly, so as not to throw any sudden pressure on his spine, and got up finally, scratched his name and the date on a wall of the cell, and then sat down with his head in his hands.

At one o'clock the next afternoon he was booked to appear in court. Shortly before that time Jo Flanagan appeared. She was wearing a sweatshirt with a peaked cowl on which there were a few beads of moisture, and UNIVERSITY OF KANSAS stenciled on the front.

He took hold of the bars and said, "I guess it's snowing outside?"

She studied him with no hint of sympathy, her arms crossed.

"I hope they keep you here a week," she said. "They can keep you forever."

"Didn't you bring me anything?" he asked. Obviously she had not.

"I could escape if I wanted to," he suggested, rattling the cell door experimentally. He had never been in jail before and was interested in his own sensations.

"Very well," she said, "you're a *bon vivant*. What now?"

This irritated him; it seemed to him that he was always being criticized. He sat down on the bench and crossed his legs.

"Is there something the matter with your back?" she asked, coming closer to the bars.

"I don't know, but it hurts. It feels like an old cornstalk."

"Did the policemen beat you? Is it true they hit prisoners with rubber hoses?"

"I don't know if they do or not," Melvin said, and carefully straightened up. "Have you got—wait a minute! Wait! Where are you going? Aren't you going to stay and talk to me?"

"About what, may I ask?"

"Well, I don't know," he said. He hobbled toward the door with one hand supporting his back and looked at her intently. "Why did you come here?"

"You don't have the haziest notion, do you?"

He could not think of anything to say. He thought she had come to visit because she liked him, but he did not want to say this.

After the trial he wrote a check to pay his fine, was released, and struggled through the snow to his porch, unshaven and groggy and of the opinion he had not been treated fairly.

He took a long nap, awoke greatly refreshed, and made his way inside the landlord's house by pulling himself from one piece of furniture to the next. He telephoned Jo Flanagan to ask if she would care to have supper with him. She said she would not. He thought he must have misunderstood, so he asked again, and again she said no. He was baffled by this; and not knowing what else to do, he asked again. This time she said no—but not quite so emphatically, so he asked again.

This time she said no, but then she said yes.

That evening, moved by he knew not what, and in periodic discomfort from a stabbing pain in his spine, he began telling Jo Flanagan about his experiences in the Navy—how he had attempted to do what was expected of him and how it ended so disastrously. She did not interrupt. She toyed with her beads and looked at him. He was struck by the expressionless female quality of her hands, the tapering, childish fingers. He noticed how delicately her skin absorbed the light, and he recalled a moment when they had been standing close together and the sweet odor of her body caused him to feel strangely weak. He stopped speaking. He could not remember what he had been saying. The war—the concern he felt for all that happened during those years —what did it matter?

23

★

Melvin saw Jo Flanagan frequently during the next few weeks, and, when they were apart, was surprised to find that so many things caused him to think of her—someone's gesture, the sight of a policeman, a sudden burst of laughter.

One morning while he was loitering on the porch steps wondering if she might like to go to a basketball game that night, he heard the trash collectors trundling barrels from the garage next door; he looked through the hedge and observed in the midst of the rubbish an old, weathered baby buggy. For a moment he stared at the buggy, reminded of something, although he did not know what. Then, with a shrug, he mashed his Navy fatigue hat comfortably on the back of his head, settled himself on the steps, and resumed basking in the pallid midwinter sun. But all at once he sat up with a bemused smile, jumped to his feet, and quickly walked along the driveway to the street and looked for the trash collectors. They were nowhere in sight. He stood there a while, pinching his lip and frowning. The February arts-and-crafts festival was not far off and he had not yet decided what to exhibit. Ribbons were to be awarded in various categories. It would be nice to win a ribbon. Thoughtfully he went to a telephone. After being referred from one bureau to another he got the information he needed: the address of the city dump. And there he went to wait for the baby buggy.

A few shabby men and one old woman with eyes like chinks and her head bound up in a kerchief were picking through the litter. Melvin hesitated, thinking they might have some sort of priority, but as none of them paid the least attention to him he soon came to feel more at ease. With his hands in the pockets of his coveralls he wandered around, whistled through his teeth, and occasionally stamped his feet.

From time to time a truck appeared, dumped its load, and drove off, and he inspected what had been brought.

Eventually a truck arrived with the buggy. He had been afraid an argument might develop over who was to have it, but none of the other scavengers was interested, so, having banged it on the ground a few times for no other reason than that he felt like doing so, he took it home.

The next day after class he borrowed a hammer and a hacksaw from his landlord and sawed off the wheels. He then sawed the bumper in half and twisted the ends upward into a semicircle. After that, he took the hammer and industriously pounded the interior of the buggy outward to fatten it a bit. Having got this far he stopped, somewhat short of breath, and realized the job was finished.

He had planned to construct four legs and a tail from a broomstick and some clothesline, and to paint the object Spanish black, but it had come to him as he stood there panting for breath that the essence of the creature had already been revealed. To add to it would be to pollute the inspiration. It was complete, it was marvelously simple, and it was, above all else, the sort of exhibit to perplex a jury—for he had found himself brooding quite often on the chaos wrought by the Cubists and their innumerable relatives. Ever since 1913 when Duchamp's nude stumbled down the staircase the critics had been notably reluctant to criticize anything that puzzled them, for fear of being thought imperceptive. It might well be, Melvin reflected, that the jurors for this particular festival were, deep in their souls, insecure. And if ever there was an animal to confound them, this surely was it. All it needed was a pedestal.

He spent several days building the pedestal, but when at last it was finished it was a very fine piece of work indeed. The pedestal was made of walnut and cherry wood with an inlaid perimeter of teak. He had sandpapered each segment until his fingers were numb, and had fitted and glued the pieces together with the greatest of care. He had rubbed it and waxed it and by the time it was done he had all but fallen in love with it.

On top of this pedestal he screwed the baby buggy, and he wrote on a little card:

"Yearling Bull"
MELVIN ISAACS
One Thousand Dollars

He did not think anyone would buy the bull for that price, which was the reason he had priced it so. At fifty dollars, say, someone might buy it in order to use the pedestal as a coffee table and he had worked on it so hard that he could not bear the thought of its being sold.

There was a freezing rain on the day of the festival; nevertheless a large crowd attended, and as the exhibition was in the gymnasium the rain did not make too much difference. Paintings hung from burlap screens which stood at varying angles so that an intricate labyrinth had been created, providing niches for sculpture and the different crafts. Burlap corridors, crepe paper twisting overhead from the goals to the stanchions, a sprinkle of sawdust that permeated the gymnasium with a curiously rural odor, a refreshment booth, a string quartet playing with the valiant industry and serious purpose of musicians on a sinking steamer—thus did the festival commence.

Melvin, having delivered his exhibit to the committee a few hours before the deadline, immediately went in search of it. He encountered a vast abstract by Kip Silver—why did Silver's paintings sway and bump when anyone approached?—and hurried along, past the pottery and jewelry, and after losing his way and again being confronted by Kip Silver's painting, he located his bull in a cul-de-sac. He could have hoped for nothing more. Each visitor, turning the corner, was massively blocked by the gleaming pedestal with the buggy on top. Even for one who anticipated the sight, it was a memorable experience. The buggy, originally pale blue with what had perhaps been pink trim, had faded to a uniform beige and was spotted with rust, the crossbar strung with beads which some child, or many children, had played with, and bitten, as they were wheeled along the boulevard. These beads were badly weathered, the paint flaked from the surface, and here and there had split like rotten acorns. The instant Melvin saw them he was appalled, for whoever heard of a bull wearing beads? Nor could he imagine how he had failed to notice them. He thought of dashing to the landlord's house for the hacksaw, but it was too late, the jury was coming, and even if they had not gotten to the bull by the time he returned they would hear the screech of the hacksaw and send someone to investigate. He did not know whether he would be disqualified if he sawed during the judging; in any event the noise would attract attention. It was too late, that was all.

But then he was struck by the thought of the emperor's new clothes and understood that the problem was solved: he had merely to ignore the obvious and pray no child appeared.

So he remained beside the bull, hands locked behind his back, rocking from his heels to his toes with a look of unconcern, keenly attuned, nevertheless, to the remarks of visitors, but most of all to the approach of the jurors. He was puzzled and a little disappointed that the public was neither shocked nor outraged by what he had done; those who came upon it stopped promptly enough, but that might have been simply because they could not go any farther; they looked at the object on display and then at him, suspecting he had something to do with it, and went away. Evidently times had changed since 1913.

At last the jury did come around.

"Gentlemen, there is something Phoenician here," the first juror said. He touched a faded bead. "See the famous Tyrian purple."

"I find myself impressed," said the next—and he cleared his throat—"by the quite extraordinary telekinetic threshold. It is virtually palpable. One may be at variance with the degree of positive realignment, which does not appear to be at less than the irreducible minimum, and on this account I must say I find myself inadequately gratified. Nonetheless, we should be remiss to disparage the intercession of contemporary scansion. At all events, this is a peculiarly inflexible commentary on the current condition. I would say we are dealing with a primitive eclectic."

"You speak of Phoenicia," the third juror said, visibly annoyed. "Perhaps. But I think of the Minotaur. Certainly that is the sculptor's intent. Look around, gentlemen. Are we not ourselves in a labyrinth? And are we not Athenian captives all? Who shall be our Theseus? No one knows, yet surely some Daedalus has been here."

"Nonsense, nonsense!" exclaimed the second with a courteous but admonitory smile. "All being is unity, we know, and approximates the omniscience of truth, from which one concludes, in this particular instance, that a Lascaux-inspired theosophy has become an irrevocable adjunct to the collectarium."

There was a pause.

"The color is quite beautiful," said the first.

"The mythical content is profound," said the next.

"Beyond doubt," the other one said, "we are here confronted by a most stipulatory reaction to the universe, however one may cavil. Shall we proceed, gentlemen?"

The judges walked away, but in half an hour they were back, and one of them pinned a blue silk ribbon to the pedestal. Melvin could feel the blood rushing to his face. He looked at the judges, and at the ribbon, and at the baby carriage, and all at once he was filled with an intolerable sense of helplessness. He turned around with a bewildered expression.

He telephoned his parents to inform them of his success and they were very much pleased. They congratulated him and told him how anxious they were to see this bull. Melvin knew they were under the impression he had created a bull about which there could be no mistake, an animal such as they would find on a farm; consequently he was not eager for them to see what he had made. As he talked to them he repeatedly changed the subject; with equal determination and with an enthusiasm dismally counterweighted by his monosyllabic replies they persisted in asking about the bull.

"Well," Melvin said to his mother, "you know it's sort of in the new modern kind of trend. I don't know whether you've kept up on modern art or not." He was walking back and forth as far as the telephone cord allowed. "It's kind of non-objective, they call it, you know," he added hopefully, and taking a pencil from behind his ear he scratched the top of his head. "It's not what you—ah, might expect." He listened to her answer and understood that she thought he was being modest; she did not grasp what he was trying to explain. He shifted from one foot to another, picked his teeth, and gazed around moodily. He was wearing his khaki pants as low on his hips as they would go without falling off, and now, with four fingers of one hand thrust into the pocket, he gestured with his thumb while he continued to disparage the prize-winning sculpture. The conversation ended with his parents still asking when they would see it, wanting to know if he couldn't bring it on the bus the next trip he made to Kansas City, and himself replying evasively.

During the next few days he was congratulated by a great many people, some of whom he did not even know. Jo Flanagan was the only one who had nothing to say; this began to irritate Melvin. He made certain she had more than enough opportunity —alluding to the ribbon and to a review of the festival which appeared in the campus newspaper. But she only listened, or answered noncommittally if he questioned her.

"How did you like the festival?" he asked.

"I like festivals," she answered.

"Were there some particular works of art you thought had a lot of power and meaning?" he asked.

"I saw some things I liked."

He gazed at her resentfully. In his wallet was a clipping from the newspaper; he wanted to show it to her, since his name was mentioned three times and there was also a lengthy appreciation of the bull.

"What in particular did you like?" he insisted.

She named a few paintings, and described a piece of pottery.

"Did you get around to looking at what I did?" he asked, although she had stopped in the alcove several times while he was there.

She looked at him calmly, frankly, but did not answer.

"It was an old baby carriage nobody would have looked at twice," Melvin said. "I revealed the essential, underlying truth. The essence of it." He thought she would agree to this.

She did not say a word.

"There were some *extremely* complimentary remarks, if you must know," he went on; and when, even then, she obstinately refused to congratulate him, he clenched his fist, choking with rage, and demanded hoarsely, "What more do you want? Look what I did!" He managed to subdue his voice, but his lips quivered and he could not stop trembling. He felt as though he had been seized unaware, bound hand and foot, and he did not know how to get free. The sensation was almost unbearable. Perspiration stood out on his face. He leaned toward her desperately and murmured, "Those animal paintings in the Lascaux caves, in case you're familiar with them, have exerted a considerable influence on my interpretation." He had gone to the library after leaving the festival in order to look up Lascaux, Theseus, Daedalus, and such other critical allusions as he had been able to remember, but even as he said this she turned on him a gaze so deliberate and penetrating that he quickly dropped his eyes.

"The judges saw that I'd gotten to the spirit of it, it was a transfiguration, and the spatial concept had to be altered to coincide with the metamorphosis," he said without looking at her. "I was devoted to the tension and stress of my subject and I reorganized it with rewarding sculptural resource."

"Is that so?"

"Yes, it is!" he exclaimed bitterly. "It said so in the paper. And half the people on campus have come up to me and said something flattering. Everybody except you. I thought you'd be pleased. If you want to know the truth, I'm an important person now. People are talking about me and I'm going to start painting abstract from now on. There's a feature in a magazine I read the other day where it concludes the only possible way for a contemporary artist to get at his full potential, I forgot just how it was phrased, is to be abstract and disclose the innumerable shapes that peer out of the commonest things. That way you appreciate—the public, I mean, will be taught to appreciate how we artists fix moving experiences in images that verify their universality. And that's what I'm going to do. I know how to do it. If you'd heard the jurors you'd know what I'm talking about."

"Glory to you."

"Yes, well, you just watch!" he told her vehemently. "This is only the beginning, and I don't mean maybe. Everybody's going to learn who I am. I've been nobody long enough. All my life I've just been booted around. If it isn't my father it was a Navy officer or a schoolteacher or somebody, and I'm sick and tired of it!"

"I know you are," she said mildly.

"Well, then!"

"Then what?"

"Well, there you are!"

"We know where I am," she remarked, "and don't be so huffy! Have I stung you? You're utterly impossible when you behave like this."

He avoided her for nearly a week, making a point of it by nodding curtly whenever they happened to meet on the campus; yet he found himself listening expectantly when the telephone rang in the landlord's house, hoping she might be calling. And he lingered in the studio after classes were dismissed, because she had often stopped by to see how his paintings were coming along.

Once she had been there, late in the afternoon when the light was altering, and he had looked around, with some brushes in his hand, and found that she was looking not at the painting but at him. For an instant she did not realize his attention had turned to her, so deep was her concentration; then she seemed to awaken, flushing in embarrassment, with shining eyes, and with the gesture he had come to know so well she lowered her head and tucked away a wisp of hair. Often he had recalled this moment; it had revealed more about her than he could ever learn from talking to her.

Having picked up ten copies of the paper in which he and the bull had been so roundly praised, confident that he would need at least that many copies, he grew increasingly baffled and frustrated as he perceived, having tucked one clipping in his wallet and mailed another one home, that he had no idea what to do with the remaining eight. He thought of giving them to his professors, or of mailing them to various influential publications, but could not bring himself to do either. Again and again he studied the laudatory sentences: "Isaacs' subjective statement carries the unmistakable marks of originality, relevance, and a sublime degree of artistic integration. His bull is inexplicably right. The sculptor began with a clear and cogent idea and brought it to eloquent realization by means of the most expressive symbology imaginable. It is this symbolic content, epitomized by the necklace of beads, so inchoate and archetypal, that makes the Isaacs sculpture easy to grasp, yet difficult to interpret."

And so aroused and persuaded was he by these lines that he

decided to grow a beard. He experimented with a stick of charcoal, studying himself in the mirror—since he wanted a beard
which would be flattering and would at the same time identify
him as an artist—but was not pleased with anything he designed.
The Van Dyke he rather liked, except that it made his head
resemble a gourd, and the L-shaped beard of a Parisian existenial-
ist was suitable to the angularity of his features—it gave him a
formidable, ascetic appearance, he thought—but it cried aloud
for a beret and he did not dare walk around in Kansas wearing a
beret. Having considered several other styles and found them even
less satisfactory, he decided, simply, to quit shaving and observe
what developed.

One evening not long after this he was at his desk half asleep,
thinking of the time he had been a cadet, when there came a
familiar, insistent rapping at the door.

"I can only stay a minute," his father said, stepping inside and
immediately looking around for the bull. "Your mother and I are
invited to Lake Quivira tonight, a cocktail party with people we
just met. Unbelievable."

"It's over in the studio," Melvin said. "It's locked up. You can't
see it."

"It must be beautiful. I have always been extremely fond of
animals, sculpture, and music, as you know. If the price is reasonable I will be delighted to make a purchase. We could put it in
the back yard, next to the bird bath. Your mother thinks that
would be nice. How much are you asking?" He began to peel
off his gloves. He was wearing a long, tight camel's-hair overcoat,
a pearl-gray Homburg, and a cream-colored silk muffler with a
fringe.

Melvin, struck by his father's extraordinary resemblance to a
Hollywood gangster, replied that he did not want to sell the bull.

"Ridiculous! Artists hope to—eh! Eh? What's that? Is that a
little beard? You can't be growing a beard, I hope!"

"I'm thinking about it," Melvin said, pulling his chin.

"Excuse me, but you can't do that!" his father exclaimed from
the depths of the Hollywood overcoat. "To be shabby and
bearded isn't wise." Neatly he tucked a few dollars into Melvin's
pocket. "Buy yourself new clothing. The police. This is America.
You could be questioned."

24

★

It had never occurred to Melvin that he might be regarded with suspicion merely on account of his appearance; the more he contemplated the implications of such a philosophy, the more sinister it seemed, and the more outraged he became. He resolved to let his beard flourish, and, rather than buy new clothing, he spent the money on a new phonograph. Having gone this far he felt he had somehow entrenched himself, or fortified himself, and was prepared to defend his position against the Philistines.

Day by day he grew shaggier and more conspicuous, yet no Philistine helmet broke the horizon. A number of strange figures did appear on the horizon, however—people who came to look at what he was painting. He had abandoned realism and was painting nothing but abstractions, which, since they were not impressions of the tangible world, were necessarily statements of a thought or emotion, indisputably personal, and therefore subject to any number of interpretations, and because of this fact they, like the bull, were exempt from criticism—a situation very much to his liking.

At first he had not understood non-objective art, having assumed that an abstract shape or composition was no more than the foundation of a painting, and had commenced, indecisively, one afternoon after the professor and the other students had left the studio. He painted a circle in the center of a fresh canvas, because that seemed a plausible departure, but did not know what to do next. He backed away, trying to avoid thinking of it as a target, and for about fifteen minutes considered the circle, all the while growing more ill at ease. Since he could not then think of a better idea, he added a triangle, stepped away again, with his head cocked, trying to recall how Kip Silver and the other progressives went about the business. Suddenly he dipped a rag in turpentine and washed off what he had done. He walked to the window, where he smoked and stared over the campus. The snow had almost melted from the hill. The wind keening thinly through the trees was not a winter wind. A few birds circled above the stadium. It seemed a long time ago that he was released from military service. He wondered if the bases which had been so congested and purposeful were the same, or if, now that the nation was at peace, they were abandoned. He thought of his cadet friends and wondered if they were alive or dead. How immediate and how significant the war had been not long ago—newspapers full of it, and radio broadcasts. And yet already, so soon, so easily, the war was gliding away, slipping from sight like an iceberg in the mist.

He returned to the easel, on an impulse shut his eyes, and mashed the brush against the canvas. The result, when he looked, was oddly attractive. Furthermore it communicated his feelings, which, in turn, suggested he might have hit on the proper approach to contemporary art. And on this basis he proceeded and had no difficulty. An application of color—if harmonious, fine, it was harmony; if not, why, naturally it was disharmony, that is to say, a spontaneous manifestation of the dissonant elements of which life itself is comprised, a perceptive reflection of the troubled times—a bold stroke there, here a shape, there a form, arabesque and filigree, all topped and crowned, capped and gowned, so to speak, with a daring smear, or, for depth, a symbolic cipher. Very soon he realized he could not possibly do anything wrong; here, at last, was something at which he would not fail.

Prior to the festival nobody had shown the slightest interest in anything he did, but, having won a blue ribbon and been written up in the paper, he was a celebrity of sorts. He could sense people on the campus furtively looking at him and knew they were talking about him. Then, one afternoon in the studio, after he had shown a number of his canvases to some visitors, one of them asked the price of a certain oil painting, Melvin felt a clutch at his heart, a premontion, said fifty dollars, and found he had made a sale. He was so shocked and frightened that perspiration broke out on his face, and when the buyer asked if a check would be acceptable Melvin merely nodded, unwilling to trust his voice.

Then, not two weeks later, he made another sale. And then another. He was completely amazed. There was, furthermore, a good chance of additional sales. He had heard, unofficially, but reliably, that one of his paintings might be purchased for the university library, and if this should come about there was a chance some gallery in Kansas City or Topeka would give him a show. And as if this were not enough, Kip Silver was sick with jealousy, a state of affairs which gave Melvin the utmost satisfaction.

He set to work with great industry, and the more abstracts he manufactured the better he liked them, and he saw that he had been wasting his time attempting to paint comprehensible objects; indeed the modern method had something to offer, and he had never felt so assured, so positive, not only of his talent but of himself. What he chose to put on the canvas, or where, or how, did not matter in the slightest, although it was comforting to putter about with a palette knife—he would paint a while, scrape it off, paint a while longer, and scrape it all off with a groan of anguish for the benefit of whoever cared to observe the artist at work, and this could be pursued indefinitely because nobody knew what he was up to.

Now and then, however, he did become troubled and acutely depressed; he would sit in a corner tugging his beard, or hold his head, and would not respond when someone in the class spoke to him. He was aware that these fits were growing more frequent and more pronounced, and he was worried. Meanwhile he painted his way along, day after day, deeper and deeper, discovering, much to his surprise, that, together with a subtle yet irresistible feeling of guilt, his signature was becoming larger. Soon it came to the point of usurping the beholder's attention—*Melvin Isaacs* seized the eye and would not let go.

His moods, his eccentricities, his flamboyant assaults on canvas, and, to some extent, the ferocity of his black, piratical whiskers, all contributed to the stories growing up about him on the campus, and he was mentioned rather often in the student newspaper, which rolled off the press in the journalism building five afternoons a week:

334

Promising abstractionist Mel Isaacs seen in Navy flyer coveralls descending the fire escape at North Hall . . .

He had accidentally gotten locked into the men's toilet; even so, there was his name once again, and publicity meant sales.

In the campus humor magazine he was startled to find a caricature of himself. He did not think the caricature was very good: the hair was kinky, the nose long and hooked, the feet too big and flat, and the face generally expressed fear and mistrust, and he was further disconcerted to see that it had been drawn by a freshman art student to whom he had paid no attention. He felt both flattered and resentful, and took care to ignore the boy who had drawn this picture of him. He could not make up his mind what attitude to adopt; he felt restricted, and, at times, was seized with such desperation that he thought he was strangling, but he did not know to what or to whom he could turn for advice.

One Sunday evening his father telephoned to read a feature article on the university art department which had appeared in the Kansas City paper. Melvin was mentioned and described as "gifted."

"Such painting, this entire movement," his father said, "escapes me, I admit. Pictures I love, of course. It's an English countryside with cows, a brook, a shepherd and his dog, fine. I have the greatest admiration for art. But to be frank, I'm the first to say I don't have time to keep up with everything, especially art, and if what you are painting is selling—if other people like it, we are all very proud for you. It's fine. Congratulations. Your mother just called from the kitchen. She'll be here in a minute to say hello. Leah and Louis were over earlier today and asked about you. Leah says you should write more often. She plans to send you some cookies. Why don't you come home next week end? A client of mine is back from a duck hunt in Canada and we have three nice birds."

"I'd like to very much," Melvin said, "but I'm going to stay here and paint. I feel that I'm beginning to make some real progress."

"What kind of progress?"

"It's difficult to explain. But my vision is getting more comprehensive now."

There was a long silence.

"I've put up an easel on the porch," Melvin said. "I can't get into the studio on week ends, that's why."

"Fine. Fine. We're glad to know you are serious about something. Come home soon."

"I will," Melvin said. "It's just that finally I'm realizing my potential."

He had tried to bribe the janitor to admit him to the studio on week ends, and failing this—knowing of a second-floor window that was never locked—he once attempted to scale the wall, which was thickly overgrown with ivy, but he became alarmed halfway up when he heard and felt the vines tearing loose and jumped to the ground in his brogan shoes and coveralls with arms outstretched and his beard neatly parted by the breeze.

He much preferred working in the studio, not only for the atmosphere and the north light, but because of the space; the porch was quite limited and he was doing progressively larger canvases. He had taken to broader brushes, since it might require weeks or months to complete a painting with a three-quarter-inch sable; he now got his brushes at the dime store—house painter's brushes they were, glossy, rectangular, and as rigidly thrilling to the touch as a foxtail. There, too, he had discovered that house paint was much cheaper than the finely ground oils for which he had been obliged to pay up to a dollar for a few ounces. The GI Bill gave him an allotment for supplies, but it was insufficient, so he began experimenting with quart cans from Woolworth; he was not displeased, so far, with what he had accomplished, and stimulated by success he had an impulse to try painting with a kitchen spatula instead of a palette knife. He bought several sheets of absorbent gray cardboard, chipboard it was called, placed one on the floor, and got down on his knees with the spatula and the enamel.

Chipboard had a number of virtues, but the thing that most pleased him was the absorbent quality: the paint dried in a few minutes, enabling him to work with great rapidity. So it was that before long he had accumulated a stack of brightly painted cardboards—shimmering yellows, blues, reds, lurid whorls and spirals with such titles as "Ambiguity," "Security," "Anxiety," "Ambition," "War," and "Genius."

336

In addition, he had several dozen cylinders of waxed paper, about two feet in width, on which he had drawn immensely elongated figures with a carpenter's crayon. He drew these egregious figures on the floor, since each was fifteen or twenty feet high, crawling on hands and knees along the immaculate waxen path which unrolled ahead of him with the inscrutable majesty of a carpet in a fairy tale; there was, he reflected, something symbolic about the way the cylinder unrolled, though he could not quite define it. In any event, the attenuated drawings turned out to be mysteriously popular among the campus intellectuals; in particular, he observed, among the Socialists. He could not imagine why, but it was so: the Socialists, who for some reason always managed to look rather hairy, almost bushy, would buy the drawings and roll them up and surreptitiously carry them away while he pocketed the money with a sense of baffled gratitude.

He concentrated on achieving spontaneity above all else, and, having learned from an art digest that something described as "an elusive intimacy" had been revealed by someone in Wisconsin who had hit upon the idea of painting without implements, he eagerly seized on this and commenced dipping up the house paint with his hands. This he found to be exhilarating, and he plunged his hands ever more deeply into the can, squeezing, squeezing rapturously, squeeze, squeeze!—till he felt his very fingers melting and his eyes began to glow with inexpressible affection and concern for everyone, everywhere, squeeze, squeeze, *squeeze!* Soon he could not bear the thought of stopping. He wished all his friends were present so that he could let them know how dear they were to him, how unutterably he was longing for them, ah!—how the paint gushed, spurting, sucking, opulent globules! Was Paradise half so tantalizing?

Divinely at ease after thirty minutes of squeezing the paint, he began to work, choked with sentiment, scooping it by the handful and allowing it to drool down his fingers to spread in widening, gracious pools across the chipboard. Overcome by emotion, alone in the studio, he could not help removing his shoes and socks, and then why should he not squeeze that ineffable paint between his toes? Oh, yes! *Squeeze! Squeeze!* His lips trembled and tears rolled down his cheeks until at last, so stupefied and glutted with sensation that he did not know where he was, or who he was, and could not care less, he felt that he must skate upon this paper, he must perform a glissade before his soul overflowed, and he did, pouring a stream of that indescribable paint ahead of him and singing madly in tune with himself. But then, somehow, he tripped and stumbled and went down, fell, shocked and profoundly mortified even as he caromed off the end of his magic carpet and with the majestic aplomb of a bowling ball went crashing through the easels.

Moodily he spent some time in the washroom with a rag and a bottle of turpentine. The paint in his beard was exceptionally difficult to remove. He walked home and took a steaming shower, but for some days after the accident his beard gave off a curious, unfortunate odor, not unlike a dinosaur egg, perhaps, or a mistake with chemicals.

"Are you doing sculpture?" his father inquired, a bit hesitantly, as though he did not quite know what to call it, the next time they talked on the telephone.

"A little," said Melvin. He had made some bric-a-brac sculpture —soldering, nailing, gluing together fragments of junk from the dump, although everything seemed rather anticlimactic after the bull—a duck constructed from a flatiron and a nozzle and some watchsprings, a camel made of two skillets welded together, and a few other animals.

"Is it selling?" his father inquired.

"Not too well," Melvin replied.

"How many have you sold? Not that I am prying into your personal affairs, but how many have you sold?"

"Not too many," said Melvin.

"How many is that?"

"Well," said Melvin, "none."

"That's too bad, but I'm not surprised."

"I'm doing all right otherwise," Melvin retorted sharply. "Last Tuesday I sold another little oil. I'm doing all right."

"Nobody said you weren't, Melvin. Do you hear from your Navy friend?"

"No, I don't have any idea where he is."

"Do you need anything?"

"No. Not a thing. Good-by."

Late that afternoon he was again in the studio alone, the other

338

students having quit at four o'clock as they always did, when he began to speculate on whether a large abstract on which he was working might not be more emphatic if he could manage to apply the paint to the surface with some sort of actual impact. He backed away and then lunged forward, thrusting the spatula to the canvas. The effect was not radically different from what he had already achieved. But one thing did come to mind—the flexibility of the spatula. It really was extraordinarily flexible. He wiped it clean and tentatively waved it back and forth. He depressed the tip with his thumb, bent the blade, and narrowly observed it whip around when released. He thought about this for a while. Then he proceeded to thicken the paint until it had very nearly reached the consistency of chewing gum; after loading the tip of the spatula he stepped back, crouched, took aim, and let fly. Through the air the globule of pigment streaked in a resolute arc and without compunction dealt the canvas a celestial blow. And as he had leaned slightly forward and risen to his toes as he released his arrow, thus he stood poised, spatula in hand, all gilded and mute as any idol.

Moments later he was busily flinging paint when the spatula slipped in his grasp and with singular radiance akin more to a Roman candle than a comet the paint soared across the studio and out the window. After a horrified pause, anticipating a shriek of rage and anguish, he rushed to the window and leaned out.

There was nobody below.

He shaded his eyes and tried to see where the paint had landed —somewhere in the bushes, he supposed, or, estimating the trajectory, maybe farther down the hillside. At all events it was gone. He was about to draw his head in the window when he became conscious of a bird darting beneath the eaves, apparently building a nest, though he could not see where. He watched it for a while. It was a common sort of bird—a chimney swift, he thought. All his life he had seen them, batlike, hunting insects in the Midwestern summer twilight. He looked again at the sky, to the west where the sun was setting. It was not a winter sunset. He felt on his face a mild, warm breeze. There was an odor of growth, of abundant earth, of life itself, inexorably triumphant.

A few minutes later Melvin walked out of the studio and telephoned Jo Flanagan to suggest they have supper together.

There was a pause.

"What did you say your name was?"

"I know," he replied persuasively. "I haven't called for a while, but I've been busy."

"All right, then," she said at last. "But put on a clean shirt."

After supper they attended a movie, which was not as good as the advertisement claimed; but there was, in addition to the feature, a short subject concerning a talented macaw. This macaw belonged to a commercial artist and one day, with an obvious desire to imitate its master, the bird took a brush in its beak and pressed the brush against a canvas. The artist encouraged the bird, framed some of its works, and submitted them to a gallery specializing in modern art, where they were enthusiastically accepted and placed on display.

After the movie they were walking across the campus when Jo Flanagan said, "Do you know that you're beginning to stammer?" She touched his arm as she said this and they stopped walking. She was looking at him with curiosity. "I've noticed it before," she went on, "but I supposed you were doing it on purpose. You do have a ghastly sense of humor at times."

"I'm not doing it on purpose," Melvin said. "I feel all right. I can't help it, that's all."

And then, to his astonishment, his fists clenched so violently that he could not release them and he exclaimed in a choking voice, "They don't know what it's about! Rubbish! Trash!" he shouted, desperately trying to stop himself, and suddenly flung his arms around the trunk of a tree. He managed to catch his breath, his vision cleared, and he prepared to speak rationally. "They think they're so clever, oh, I don't, I mean-m-m-m—" He could not understand why he was speaking like this. "I've got to start over," he continued, speaking with difficulty, but with fantastic rapidity, with no idea what he would say next. He listened in dismay to the words streaming through his lips. He heard himself tell her again and again with raving insistence that he must make a new beginning, and at first did not know what this meant; then he guessed that he was talking about the painting and sculpture he had done, and then he became conscious of a remarkable sensation: it was as though he could distinguish himself at a great distance, approaching and steadily shouting, while the words continued to pour out of his mouth. He felt strangely grateful; he had no desire to stop off this flow of words, if only it would permit him to meet and merge with the approaching, gesticulating figure.

He discovered that he had stopped speaking, that he and she were standing quite close together and that she was staring up at him with a look of such intensity that he was stunned; gradually he was able to recall what he had just finished saying—he had asked her to marry him. He could feel the warmth of her, she was so near, and he was paralyzed by the blazing black pupil of her eye, which seemed to register assent.

In the morning he went to the barber shop, an establishment he had avoided, and emerged half an hour later reeking of talcum and lotion, rather pleased that without so much hair he could feel the spring sunshine on his face. And, having contracted with himself for the reconstruction of his career as an artist, he armed himself with a hammer, a pair of pliers, and a screwdriver and walked without haste to the studio, where he dismantled and then demolished the already battered baby carriage. The pedestal he kept for a coffee table.

By Monday he had finished cleaning up. The spatula and the quart cans of house painter's paint were in the landlord's basement, in case he wished to paint the house. The astral cardboards, waxed papers, and similar experiments lay in ashes, and such spiritual content as they possessed had been returned to the stratosphere. Some of the canvases, those on which the paint was not too thickly encrusted, he thought he could use, so he scraped them as clean as possible and stacked them in a corner.

He knew that he would now be obliged to find a job. The government was still paying his tuition and enough for minimum expenses, but there was nothing left over, and if he was to be married there should be some money in the bank. He considered making abstracts till the end of the year, not only in hopes of selling a few but because an abstract—the bigger the better— would be just the thing to enter in competition for the annual Ellery Finch Fellowship. The fellowship provided for a year of study at any art academy in the United States or abroad, and Melvin could think of nothing he would enjoy more than a year in Paris, married or not, with all expenses paid. Nor did he need

341

to remind himself of what this would mean when it came time for his first exhibition: whatever he showed, then, would merit serious attention. It would be reviewed. It would attract a crowd. But eventually he dismissed the idea, reasoning that if he succumbed to this temptation he would be apt to give in again, and again.

Without enthusiasm he asked his instructor if he might have the key to the still-life studio. The instructor, a taciturn old Hungarian in a paint-stained smock, regarded him somberly and without a word gave him the key. After unlocking the studio Melvin paused, gazing at the dust that had settled on the colored bottles and plaster casts and on the skeleton which hung by a bolt through the cranium. He knew immediately that when he started to draw from these he would not be ignored. It had been too long since anyone studied fundamentals.

Kip Silver, coming on him seated before the skeleton, was amused.

"Whatever you're about to tell me," Melvin said, "I already know."

Silver took the pipe from his mouth and began tamping it full of tobacco while his eyes winked with malice. "Study your life away, Isaacs," he said. "Do you think you'll ever duplicate the old masters?" He held a match to the bowl and went on, between puffs, "Suppose you could, what? It's been done. You're living in the past," and he strolled away chuckling.

Melvin, as he laboriously copied the skeleton, which, revolving gently in the spring breeze from the window, seemed to mock him, knew that Silver had a right to be amused.

His reputation declined slowly at first because no one could possibly imagine what he was doing. Perhaps it was a new and radical departure. But after a while, when he did nothing spectacular, when, in fact, he did not do anything at all except what he was evidently doing, people lost interest.

At the end of the school year the Ellery Finch Fellowship was awarded to Kip Silver, who was represented in the competition by a single painting, unframed, titled "Variation 6," of such dimensions that it could not be hung and so had been leaned against a wall. It consisted of a grayed rose background in which some gravel and leaves had been embedded, and a trail of purplish marks resembling fingerprints.

A bit sadly Melvin strolled around, looking at the various paintings and sculpture, most of which he had seen before. His own entries—a charcoal study of a Donatello head, and a fretfully painted view of the Kaw River—were not admitted into the final judging.

Seeing Jo Flanagan, he gave her a wan smile and shrugged.

She asked how he was.

"Oh," he said, "fair. I guess I knew it would happen like this. I'm just disappointed, that's all. It makes me feel so familiar. I mean, I'd like to win once in a while. Just occasionally."

"Biting into you is like biting into an old coffee bean," she said. "Will you carry my books and buy me a soda?"

"All right," he answered, "if I have enough money." And he did have enough, though not much more.

25

★

When he returned to the porch he found one of his paintings propped up against the cot as though someone had been looking at it. Anyone could have entered the porch, because he never bothered to lock the door, but he could not imagine who the visitor might have been. He noticed that a book had been moved —taken from the shelf—and was lying on the desk. He picked it up. Under it was a ten-dollar bill. He was about to go into the house to ask the landlord if his father had left any message when the connecting door opened and his father appeared; he had been drinking and was excited.

"I thought you would never come back!" he exclaimed. "Where have you been? Did you find the money? Buy new trousers— people will think you haven't a cent in the world. I've been considering your painting. I'm happy to say it's recognizable; however, to be honest, Melvin, I'm not surprised nobody is buying any more. You had a good business, selling what nobody could criticize, now you've thrown it away! Why? Never mind, we can talk about that later. Stop walking back and forth—you're making me nervous!"

"I'm making *you* nervous? Is that what you said?"

"Yes! You are, yes. Kindly stop pacing the floor. I have something important to tell you, very important. Listen to me, Melvin, it was the other evening at dinner when the doorbell rang and there they stood, both of them—"

"You're talking so fast I can't understand what you're saying."

"Excuse me. Hephzibah and Ilya, your mother's cousins from Europe. We thought they were dead. They will be living with us from now on, in the attic. You remember, we've spoken of them, I'm sure."

"Yes, I remember," Melvin said.

"Hephzibah is at least six feet tall. I opened the door and there they were, Melvin! With satchels and parcels, each with an umbrella, and your mother when she saw them almost fainted. . . ." He was not able to stop talking or to speak distinctly. His eyes were luminous and feverish. He gasped for breath, blinking and shaking his head. Repeatedly he would get up and walk around the porch, sit down again, and cross his legs, gesturing all the while.

Melvin knew that throughout the war his mother had been trying to find out what had become of these women, and that a few days after the invasion of Poland a relative named Leopold who was in the garment industry in New York had sailed to Europe with several thousand dollars in an effort to buy their freedom. Leopold had vanished. Nothing had ever been heard of him. Melvin could not get over a feeling that there existed in Europe at that time an abyss, or a maw, into which human beings were hurled like the horrified figures in a fantastic nineteenth-century illustration of hell.

He saw that his father was preparing to leave.

"Hephzibah and Ilya, I neglected to mention, are sleeping in your bed. They are anxious to make your acquaintance, Hephzibah especially. When will you come home? It has been a long time. How soon can we expect you?"

Melvin answered that he would plan to visit Kansas City over the week end. There was a bus at four o'clock Saturday after-noon.

"Come in the morning, at least. Or Friday, that would be bet-ter. It's been so long. Everybody misses you."

"No, I couldn't make it on Friday, or Saturday morning. I must have forgotten to tell you, but I have a job now. I'm delivering ice."

"Ice? You are delivering ice?"

"Yes. Every morning," said Melvin.

"Frankly, I'm astonished. Since when?"

"I just got the job a little while ago. I'm what they call a helper. Each truck has a driver and usually one of these helpers. We start early and don't finish the route until about noon. I have to meet the driver at the plant at a quarter to five in the morning. Sunday is my only day off."

"I have never understood you. As a small boy you were mysterious."

"I don't know why you should feel that way. It's just an ordi-nary job and I'm glad to have it. My summer session classes are in the afternoon and I ought to be able to earn enough working every morning to save a little."

"Delivering ice. An iceman!"

"If you can find me a better job I'll take it," Melvin said ir-ritably. "I doubt if you can, though. I don't have much to offer for a recommendation. There aren't many jobs available," he went on. "What makes you think jobs are so easy to get? I was lucky to find this! I'm not about to give it up!"

"All right!" his father exclaimed, and stepped backward. "All right! Who's arguing? At least it's an income. Buy new trousers, don't forget. Patches don't look nice. Saturday we'll expect you."

Melvin telephoned Jo and told her he would be gone for the week end, and on Saturday afternoon he took the bus to Kansas City. There he boarded a streetcar, which let him off within a few blocks of his home.

The refugees were together on the sofa. It was evident they had been waiting for him. They were seated like schoolgirls, hands demurely folded in their laps. He had no more than entered the room when Hephzibah, unquestionably Hephzibah, flew at him—a gigantic, ruffled, extinct, moulting bird, phoenix, griffin, roc, purple-and-gold, with a touch of the ostrich in her limbs and the wood pheasant in her barbaric plumage, her slit beak cracked in noiseless, mythical laughter—enfolded and lifted him as though he were a suckling pig. He dug for safety with his toes, arms pinioned against his sides, smothering in the musty shawl. Her harsh, pitted cheek was pressing his, her mouth agape in dreadful mirth. She crushed him to an unyielding muscular bosom and dropped him, washing her hands together, bending forward from the waist to appraise him through eyes suddenly threatening and narrow as tilted coins. Ilya remained on the sofa, regarding him without the slightest expression, only a dim, lusterless apathy.

Ilya whispered in Yiddish; Hephzibah nodded, and shrewdly tapped her teeth.

Melvin straightened his necktie, which dangled askew as though exhausted by the furious embrace.

Hephzibah grinned and took a step forward.

Melvin without hesitation stepped back.

Hephzibah frowned, softly clucking and croaking, and flung up her arms; the tassels of her shawl stood out like hoodoo bells as she whirled to confer with Ilya. They agreed, and nodded wisely.

"Ech! *Love!*" Hephzibah crooned, advancing as he retreated.

"What is this, a gavotte?" said Melvin.

"*Love*, Love, *no*-thing is—how to speak? Should having the *beard*, Love! *Tchk-tchk!*"

"You should have seen me at Easter," he said, and feared he was about to sneeze. She clutched for him; he dodged.

"Tchk-tchk," Hephzibah whispered with unutterable concern and affection.

Later Melvin remarked to his father, "If you think she's going to roost in an attic you'd better think again."

"That's a fact. She's out all day having tea with the neighborhood. She discusses the world situation with delivery boys, plays hop-scotch on the sidewalk with little girls. Now I think I should tell you—I don't know how—a dreadful thing took place. Hephzibah was not here, she was across the street playing dominoes. Little Ilya was sitting quietly on the sofa when, for no reason, she began placing logs in the fireplace. It was a warm evening.

We didn't need a fire. She hobbled to the woodpile on the porch, returned with a log. Your mother and I were puzzled. We didn't say a word. Ilya returned with another log, then another. All at once the meaning became clear. I was horrified. I spoke to Ilya. She didn't hear. Your mother led her to the sofa where she was willing to lie down, docile, as though expecting something, and in a little while she went to sleep." He stopped and took a deep breath. "The two of them were in Auschwitz, that much we know. We can only guess at the rest, at what was done to them there. We don't ask. If they want to speak, they will. But, Melvin, there is one thing I wonder about, although I know the answer. It's this: where have they been since then? Tell me, can you guess?"

Melvin looked uneasily at his father.

"I'll tell you, Melvin. The Russians got them. Since the end of the Second World War they have been Russian slaves." He stood up and beckoned Melvin to follow him. They walked upstairs and along the hall to a trap door in the ceiling. He thrust a hook through a ringbolt and drew the door downward; a ladder came rumbling diagonally from the attic. There was a smell of dried apples and mice and fresh wood shavings.

"Louis tells me we should have a permanent staircase instead of this ladder. I'm investigating the cost. Now, here you see, the air vent is being transformed," he continued as he stepped from the ladder to the floor of the attic. "It's going to become a round casement window. And we're putting in furniture. Your mother is making a rug of colorful scraps. Louis helped the carpenter. He's an expert with tools and comes over every afternoon soon after leaving the bank, wearing a Hawaiian shirt and sandals. Hephzibah tells us Ilya is pleased with what we're doing, and is hopeful there'll be a rocking chair beside the window. She likes to peep through the branches of the trees at the children playing. I'm getting a rocking chair. Hephzibah has been decorating." He pointed to a beaverboard wall covered with decals—pirates, maps of states, ducks, rabbits, steamships, hula dancers, and row after row of pink flamingos. They had not been skillfully transferred; many had slipped and wrinkled, or had been torn and were crookedly pieced together.

"Every morning at the ten-cent store she is waiting when the doors open. Buying gilt-edged stationery, marbles by the sack—

look in the chiffonier, marbles in the top drawer. However, I'm not interfering. Buy everything, I say to her, and give her the money. Fortunately she prefers to shop in the ten-cent store, the drugstore, the supermarket. It could be worse."

Melvin recognized the chiffonier; it used to be in his room. He opened the small drawer where he had kept his handkerchiefs and a collection of arrowheads. The arrowheads were still there, together with hundreds of the marbles Hephzibah had bought. He opened another drawer and saw first of all the green wool garrison cap with the cadet insignia; it was the cap he had been issued at Albuquerque. He tried it on; it seemed a trifle tight, and there was a mustard-colored stain on one side. Also in the drawer were a pair of woolen athletic socks with holes at the heel and toe, a khaki shirt with a frayed collar, a broken hockey stick with electrician's tape wound around the handle, a pair of leather moccasins, some faded pajamas, and a stiff-ribbed tuxedo shirt and a crimson sash he used to wear to dances before the war. He had completely forgotten the sash and tuxedo shirt, and the hockey stick he had not thought of in years. He stared at the moccasins; he knew they had once belonged to him, but he could not remember anything else about them, except that they were so worn he must have liked them and valued them. There were a few other items of greater or lesser consequence, but what interested him most was a spiral notebook: it was his logbook from the airport at Albuquerque. The binding had been crushed and there was a sticky residue inside the front cover, a mashed jellybean or gumdrop.

He placed the logbook on top of the chiffonier and looked at the first page. There was the name of his instructor, Mr. Collins —he remembered this name but nothing else—and the date, the amount of time spent in the air, the velocity and direction of the wind that day—the wind had been important and they had discussed it seriously—and finally, concluding the data, the serial number of the airplane. He read what he had written after coming down from his first flight:

Expected to get airsick, but didn't. Instructed in general plane management under normal flight conditions. Preliminary routine of dives, right and left hand banks, and got to hold the stick a little while on straight and level course. Horizon looked actually curved, and Rio Grande like melted lead with slag on the surface, or aluminum, instead of water. Could see airport move slowly underneath the tire on my side of cabin. Very strange. Mesa covered with snow in every direction. Beautiful winter sunlight on city of Albuquerque. Columns of smoke from chimneys. Saw Flying Fortress (B-17) from Army Kirtland field pass us at terrific speed, *below* us! and could see tail gunner sitting in plexiglass blister. Air smooth during flight, except one big bump near canyon. Mr. Collins says it was caused by updraft, says many updrafts during summer months and can be dangerous. Got foot accidentally caught under rudder pedal during spin demonstration. Didn't hurt, but Mr. Collins very upset. Will be careful in future. Was hungry, maybe because of altitude and plan to bring candy next flight. Like nothing ever experienced.

The next afternoon when he returned to the university he took the logbook with him, and now and then while he was working on the ice truck he would think of Albuquerque. The truck stimulated his imagination, his ability to recall what he had done and even what had passed through his mind years before. He concluded this was because of certain similarities: he was at work on the truck well before dawn, it bounced and swayed along the streets with a motion very like that of the bus to the airport, he was always sleepy, and the huge misty cakes which rumbled and skidded across the bed of the truck and bumped against the sideboards, however unrelated to any sound or movement or substance he had known in the Navy, nevertheless contributed to his mood, with the result that he sometimes discovered himself fast asleep when the truck jolted to a stop. This never failed to embarrass him; he suspected the driver resented his dozing in the cab. Yet it was so satisfying, so restful, that he could not bear to keep his eyes opened, and continued to indulge himself. He would wake with a start, wrench open the door, leap to the ground and rush around to the rear of the truck, unhook the chain, and spring aboard with the tongs in hand just soon enough that he could not be criticized.

One morning while he was bouncing monotonously on and

on, comfortably damp and cool beneath his old cadet coveralls and a brown rubber vest, his head nodding to every bump in the street, he was able to hear, as loudly, as imperatively as though he were still asleep in the depths of the stadium, the blaring notes of the bugle reverberating through that ice-cold concrete-and-iron dungeon an hour before dawn; and it seemed to him that he swiftly rolled from his bunk, put on his clothes in the sudden electric light, and was marching across the gravel parade ground toward the mess hall while Sam Horne sang cadence and snowflakes whirled around the streetlights. Overhead, through rifts in the clouds, the constellations appeared like problems in celestial navigation.

The methodical chip-chip-chip of a pick penetrated his reverie; desperately he flung open the door and leaped out. The iceman did not say a word, but with a melting milk-gray cake on his shoulder he bowed his head and strode away. Then Melvin reflected that he was probably going to be fired unless he could find some way to redeem himself, and remembering that in a few minutes they must deliver a bushel basket of shaved ice to a cocktail lounge he set to work with a basket, a cake, and his trident. Very rapidly he shaved down the end of the cake so that an almost constant stream of shavings for cocktails arched into the basket, and when the driver reappeared Melvin gave the basket a casual tap with his trident to demonstrate his knowledge of the route. The expression on the iceman's face puzzled him; he could not imagine what he had done wrong, and then he remembered that the lounge was closed for alterations.

That evening, after telling Jo Flanagan what had happened, Melvin sighed and added despondently, "He even made me buy it. He took fifty cents out of my wages."

"Well, where is it?" said Jo Flanagan. "I certainly hope you didn't leave it there."

"What could I do with a basket full of ice?" said Melvin.

"What did he say when he fired you?" she asked a moment later.

"Oh, not much," he answered thoughtfully, gazing incuriously and with no great enthusiasm at the way she was dressed. She was wearing lederhosen and a pleated blouse, red canvas tennis shoes and ribbed wool stockings up to her knees, and there was a beret on her head and a bulging alligator-yellow handbag slung across her shoulder.

"Have you just come back from a hike?" he asked. "Or were you playing tennis?"

"There was a folk dance this afternoon. Tell me more about the iceman."

"Oh. Well, where was I? Oh, yes! He wasn't especially sarcastic the way you'd expect. He simply told me frankly he'd have to report me to the plant manager. Actually, I think, it was the company that fired me. I can appreciate the driver's side of the matter. He has all this ice to deliver and it's true I did loaf. I was doing just enough to get by."

"You were doing just enough to get by. Is that what you said?"

"Yes. Why do you look surprised? I was paid by the hour, so it didn't make any difference."

"I know. But for some reason I didn't think you—oh, never mind."

"I was meeting the minimum standard. At least until I fell asleep."

"The minimum standard."

"That's right," said Melvin.

"So you're becoming one of those people."

"Should I do more than I'm paid to do? The company doesn't pay extra for good workmen. The iceman was explaining all this to me one time about a month ago. He wanted me to join the union, and he pointed out that the stronger the organization is, why then the more demands it can make. There are all kinds of advantages to being a union member."

"And you joined."

Melvin remained silent for a while and gazed around uncomfortably. At last he said, "No, no, as a matter of fact, I didn't. I suppose I should have. It would have been to my advantage, there's no question about it. Even after I fell asleep, if I belonged to a union—I don't know exactly how it operates, but I gather they'd make certain I was hired by somebody else, so I guess it would have been smart for me to join."

"But why didn't you?"

Again Melvin fell silent and looked away.

"Once you told me," she said after a little while when he had not answered, and yet had seemed to be struggling to find words, "you told me not long after I came to help you move away from the fraternity that I had no idea what I was letting myself in for. You've probably forgotten, you forget the things most people remember, but once you did say that to me, and I was so puzzled. You were stubborn, I knew—oh, anyone could tell that!—but you were quiet so often, as though you were worried about something, and I couldn't imagine what you meant. But now I think I'm beginning to see why you get into these situations. I only wish I knew of some way to prevent it."

"If you know how it happens you know twice as much as I do," Melvin said gloomily. "That iceman was suspicious of me right from the start. He noticed the paint on my coveralls and asked if I was a painter, so I said yes, but then I realized he meant a house painter, so I had to go and tell him I didn't paint houses, I painted pictures. I should've kept my mouth shut. I don't know why I never learn. It's happened to me about a dozen times. Anyway, when I said that he gave me the queerest look and never mentioned it again."

They had been wandering across the campus as they talked and had come onto a promontory from which the hill dropped away steeply toward the south. They stopped and gazed across the fields, where clouds were mounting and lightning flashed through the twilight. A distant rumble of thunder sounded from the green depths of summer.

"You want to marry me. Is that so?" she asked, and went on without waiting for an answer. "I'm not sorry, for I love you. I've loved you longer than you know. And when the minister asks if I will take you for better or worse I will say I do." She paused. "It's only that better would be so much nicer than worse."

Melvin was embarrassed, and said awkwardly, "I can't help it."

"I know you can't," she replied, and then suddenly cried, "Oh, I can't stand this!" and turned and flung herself into his arms and began kissing him passionately. Just as quickly, then, she quit and pushed him away, but held tightly to his hands.

"I'm afraid there's something I must tell you," she said.

He was struck by her tone and stared at her in alarm. He had no idea what she meant, but then he understood. She was pregnant.

Soon the breeze was upon them, bringing the odor of lilacs and rain and the fecund valley beneath the hill.

26
★

It seemed to Melvin that surely his fortunes had now come to their lowest ebb, not excluding those days on the Texas prairie when he had been reduced to the status of an accomplished gopher. Then, at least, life lacked its present convolutions; it had been, in its way, simple enough, curiously blissful, inasmuch as the prairie had been expansive and he had responded to it. He had not had much to worry about, although at the time he had not been convinced of this, whereas now there was little question but that he and destiny were opposing one another with sinister finality and he was not altogether certain he would emerge victorious. It seemed to him that despite all prudence, temperance, and the most honorable intentions—reasonably honorable at least—in some mysterious fashion life was running away from him. Things were totally out of hand. He had fallen into disgrace as an artist, lost his job, confounded his parents, and impregnated his fiancée. Besides all this he had difficulty breathing and would sometimes remain utterly quiet with a distant expression and with one hand pressed to his heart, which he thought was starting to palpitate.

He resolved to approach his problems systematically and with the same high, serious sense of purpose with which he had approached a number of lesser problems, because, after a great deal of admonitory rumination, he was unable to come up with a better idea. The unsatisfactory state of his career, however threatening, and however contemptuously he was regarded by the other students, was not immediate; to be in disgrace was to be in disgrace, he reasoned, and was essentially nothing more. Secondly, he had lost his job on the truck. This was serious, but there was nothing to be gained by lamenting it; the only thing to do was to hunt for another job. Possibly he could deliver newspapers, or packages if he had a motorcycle—in any event, look for a job.

As for the disappointment and bewilderment his parents must be feeling, well, that was regrettable but he did not know what to do about it.

And so, having mollified his conscience, he was free to brood on the topic that obsessed him.

Having asked Jo Flanagan with a certain desperate levity if she could not be mistaken, and, being told there was no mistake, having argued for some minutes more that there must be a mathematical possibility that she was mistaken—an argument she did not bother to answer—he reluctantly came to a decision.

So it was that, approximately three weeks after learning he would soon be the head of a little family, he caught the bus to Kansas City in order to have a talk with his father, and began this talk by saying that he intended to get married.

"You're too young," his father replied firmly. "I didn't dare to get married when I was your age. Unthinkable."

"Yes, well, if you'll let me expl—"

"In marriage there are children. Have you thought of this? No. You think to yourself: I want to get married. That's all. Fantastic!"

"That's wh—"

"Without a job—impossible! Have you considered? I have money, yes. Naturally I wouldn't see you starve. But you are not being sensible. Not sensible. You should use your head, that's your trouble. Such a situation calls for judicious consideration. Time to consider. You should sit down and ask. Say to yourself with arms folded: Am I in such a rush? I will wait a little while, say to yourself."

"But I don't think you—"

"Who's speaking? You or me? Who is trying to say something? Your trouble is you don't listen. You keep trying to interrupt, I don't know why. In the Navy, did you listen? The officers were trying to assist you, but you were trying to talk, to tell them how to run their business, as if you were the admiral. I never could understand it. The first lesson you should learn is, listen carefully and so discover how to keep out of difficulty. Does that make sense? Am I being unreasonable? What is the name of the young lady?"

"Jo Flanagan."

"A very nice name. You've mentioned it before, but I didn't realize you were serious."

"Look, going back for a minute because you brought it up, I never thought I was an admiral. It was just that once or twice things didn't make much sense, so I—oh, well," he muttered, "it was a long time ago. Let's forget the whole business. The war's over."

"The wise man does not say: It was a long time ago. He doesn't say: Let's forget. The wise man observes: Remember what occurred! I shall profit by my experience. Frankly, do you profit?"

"Well," Melvin answered after thinking it over, "I don't know. As a matter of—"

"Next there was the painting. Abstract. It was a good thing. The money was rolling in. Not enormous sums, granted, yet surprising. I am the first to admit I was amazed. We were all somewhat baffled, but happy that you were a success. So what happened? Where are the customers? Disappeared! I would like to ask a simple question: What happened to the customers? A direct answer, please."

"Well, in a sense, you could say, I supp—"

"Exactly!" his father cried. "Evasion! How does somebody talk to you? I question you regarding sticks; you answer in regard to stones. Why is this? Since you were one day old I have been puzzled by you. A Hindu—I would have more topics in common with a Hindu wearing a turban than with my own son. If, twenty-five years ago, someone had told me this I would have laughed. I'm not laughing now."

"I don't know anybody who is," Melvin said, and then, as his father had momentarily stopped talking, he went on to explain that Jo Flanagan was pregnant. "I was certainly surprised," he said. "You can't imagine. When she told me I could hardly believe it. I thought she was joking, but she wasn't. Well, anyway, I suppose it's sort of in the natural order of things, if you consider the situation objectively. And the statistics about how frequently this occurs are incredible. So that's more or less how things stand at the moment. Actually what it means," he added with an attempt at joviality, "is that you're going to be a grandfather!"

There was a long silence.

"Objectively," said Jake Isaacs at last. "Statistics. What next?"

But Melvin had begun to feel more confident; he felt immensely relieved that he was no longer burdened with a secret. All his affairs now seemed to him less disorganized than he had assumed; with persistence, intelligence, a modicum of decent luck, and adequate cooperation from other people there was no reason he should not be able to restore his foundering vessel to a state of fair equilibrium and sail on, as it were, toward calm seas and that prosperous voyage which surely must be the appanage, the immemorial legacy, of any man.

Thoughtfully he said, "It isn't that this is a cause, it's an effect."

"I don't understand a word," said his father. "Please go on."

"Why, it's very simple," said Melvin. "We're not being married because she's pregnant. I asked her before I knew, quite a while ago. And I have some more news."

"Possibly you should keep it to yourself. I have had enough for one day."

"I've got another job. That is, I think I have. It's a wonderful opportunity with the gas company. I've been interviewed and they liked me and said to come back Monday. It's a very progressive company, the interviewer told me. They believe in encouraging the employees to work their way to the top." Melvin whipped a match across the sole of his shoe and lit a cigarette. "I wasn't sure I'd like working for the gas company," he said, between puffs, "but I've thought it over. I'd like being promoted. I don't think I've had any sort of promotion since I don't know when."

"That *is* good news," his father said. "Delivering ice was not dignified, but this sounds better. There is nothing wrong with delivering ice, except that we were disappointed. To make a comparison, it was the way we felt to learn you were no longer an aviation cadet but a sailor. We couldn't imagine you as a sailor. It was like a dream, even when you came home wearing the uniform. Well—now, this sounds like an improvement, a step forward at last."

"Yes," Melvin said, "I think it is."

"What are you to be doing? Tell me about the position."

"First of all, I don't have to get up so early. I won't be expected at the office until eight o'clock."

"If you enjoy sleeping late, all right, but that's unimportant. I haven't seen the gas company in Lawrence, but they have, I am told, a very nice building, modern, with satisfactory working conditions." Jake Isaacs stood up and rubbed his hands together. "You don't know how encouraging this sounds. Now, at last, you can amount to something. Buy a new suit. It's important. I'll give you the money. Customers don't like to deal with shabby representatives. I can't tell you how happy this makes me. If you work hard and obey your superiors there is no reason why you cannot advance rapidly. I happen to be acquainted with one of the head bookkeepers here. I will speak to him tomorrow, letting him know you will be working with the company in Lawrence. What will you be doing specifically?"

"I don't think anybody would notice what sort of a suit I had on," Melvin answered.

"Don't be silly, of course they notice. I enter an office, the first thing—before anything else—I observe who greets me, how his shoes are polished, the haircut—you should get a haircut—and the quality of the gentleman's suit. If I am greeted by a lady I observe her manners, the coiffure, hands, posture, and so forth. I then know the type of person with whom I am dealing. Nothing is more valuable. Get something appropriate, tailor-made. Pinstripe is always nice and creates a favorable impression, also a hat. Don't forget to wear the hat to the office. The manager will notice and say to himself: I will keep my eye on that young man. Have the tailor send the bill to me. I'll be delighted to pay."

"I don't need a suit."

"Ridiculous. Let's not argue about this. You've never been willing to dress, it's good for you. What will you be doing?"

"Maybe so, but I don't need a suit. In fact I'd look pretty foolish."

"For the last time, what is your position with the company?"

Melvin hesitated. The fact was that if he obtained the job he would be reading meters, and he knew his father had gotten the impression that he was to be a junior executive. Finally, when the silence grew unbearable, he mentioned what he would be doing during a speech having to do with a number of other matters. He was intending to wear his comfortable and, by now, badly worn khakis and brogan shoes on the job. "And suppose it rains," he suggested with persuasive confidence, "what then? I still have my canvas fatigue hat that we were issued in Iowa."

"Gas meters? Is that the opportunity? Reading gas meters?"

"That's right," Melvin said.

"You told me you would be in a nice office."

"No, no, that's what you said, I only said I had to report at the office by eight o'clock, which is right. They give you a book, see, each meter reader gets his route book—it's about so big," he explained, boxing it with his hands, "like a notebook except that it has a metal binding, and there's one page for each house on the route. It shows the location of the meters—you read the electric meter, too. Well, the minute I saw one of those books I thought—I don't quite know what I'm trying to say, but it's sort of a passport, if you know what I mean. For instance, on the ice truck, the passport was my icepick and rubber vest and tongs. What I mean is, nobody asked questions or wondered about me. I was no different from anybody else with a job. I was a member, don't you see? I belonged. Well, so a flashlight and a meterman's book accomplish exactly the same thing."

"I don't understand a word. Not one."

"It's clear enough. All that matters is the—well, there are these stereotypes, let's say. It's assumed if somebody looks like a professor, he *is* a professor. Or, take another example, if you come to attention and salute the flag, you're patriotic. Or vice versa, of course. Now, in this case, I could be Karl Marx, or Machiavelli, but so long as I carry the flashlight and meterman's book nobody will notice me. The point I'm making is that—ah," he stopped, squeezing his lip and frowning, trying to recall the point.

"Marx? Karl Marx, did I hear you say? The Communist?"

Melvin felt suddenly depressed, and thought of how often he

had attempted to explain one thing or another without success. "I should be starting back to the university," he said. "There's a talk and discussion in the auditorium tonight I want to hear. Some librarian lost his job on account of having a Communist mother-in-law, or something like that." He noticed his father looking at him quite strangely.

"You are going to what? A Communist meeting on the campus? A librarian discharged as a security risk is speaking to students? I didn't know that was allowed. You're joking!"

"Security risk?" Melvin asked uneasily. "I never said—"

"A Senate Committee investigating public education and misuse of funds has discovered the new American history texts contain the word 'liberty' no more than twelve times as against a total of nineteen times in the previous edition. No one can explain the reason. The reason, however, is that Communists have infiltrated. Further, if I remember correctly, the word 'Russia' is now to be found a total of seventeen times, as opposed to five times in the previous edition. These are facts I am giving you, not mere opinions. In addition, it has been revealed the name of one of the editors is Lubitov, a native of Russia, born in Moscow."

Melvin was dumbfounded by the expression which had come over his father's face.

"It's time to tell America the facts," Jake Isaacs continued, and got to his feet and began walking back and forth, gesturing as he spoke. "The United States may be forced to defend itself again!" His voice was rising as it did whenever he was irritated or excited. He seemed to be aware of this, and made an effort to speak calmly. "I am reminded of a magazine cartoon showing an American peaceably asleep beneath a tree. Along comes a British soldier with a sword. The American wakes up fighting for his life. The struggle is over and he returns to sleep. Next comes a Spaniard with a sword, the same happens as before. Next a French soldier. Next a German. Each time the same thing occurs. America is now in the process of settling down for another nap, following the defeat of the Axis, unaware of the Russian soldier approaching. It is dreadful we don't learn from experience. Am I correct in hearing you say you are going to listen to a Communist lecture? Possibly I was mistaken. You didn't say any such thing."

"Yes! I did say that!" Melvin exclaimed. He jumped up and thrust his hands into his pockets. "I am! I'm going to that lecture." He ran upstairs to his room for some books and then hurried away to catch the bus. He had not particularly cared about the lecture and had merely given it as a reason for starting back to the university, but now he was determined to attend.

27
★

In the days and weeks that followed he found himself thinking less often of his approaching marriage than of the change which had come over his father at the mention of Communism. It was as though his father had been stimulated by the possibility of another world war. This was so incredible that Melvin could not consider the idea for long without wondering if he himself had become unbalanced. He recalled as much as he could of their conversation. But it was not what had been said that was so frightening; it was the eagerness with which his father had begun to speak, the strength of his gestures, the animation that suffused his voice. And it seemed to Melvin that since the end of the last war his father had been a little discontented, as though some obscure purpose had gone out of his life. The implications of this, too, were frightening, for if it was true that he looked forward to another war, it must follow that he was insane. And yet, because he was not alone in his violent hatred, how could anyone say—and be called sane himself—that thousands, or hundreds of thousands, or millions, perhaps, were mad?

And it occurred to Melvin that if in the act of war, or in the preparation for it, there was indeed the sign of madness—if war was not, as he had once supposed, an instrument of divine providence, but merely a consequence of human intent—some proof of insanity should exist. And he reflected that if this proof did exist he most likely had encountered it already. He might well have met it face to face, day after day, without seeing it for what it was.

He thought of the various bases at which he had been stationed. Somewhere, he was sure, buried in that experience, a clue existed, a glyph or symbol. He remembered the snowy mesa where the Deacon crashed, the tiny red-and-black plane upside down like a celluloid T on a sparkling white tablecloth, and recalled how he had spiraled and circled in the silence that reigned over the wreck, studying and wondering. Then with the wind and inseparable from the wind he went floating over the great river and saw the shining water that descended from the lofty Colorado plains and flowed through Albuquerque on the way to Mexico, through Socorro and Rincon, Las Cruces, El Paso, and Juarez, until, turning to the east, embodied in the verity of that river, he and it together poured onward toward the azure Gulf.

He had been aware of almost nothing except this river flowing through the valley, and had thought of how the rivers joined and mingled in the sea; that one day these waters should again rain down on the mountains—that this should be true, that it had never failed to be true, now seemed to him not only impressive and strangely authoritative, but hinting deeply of some response to the questions which perplexed him.

He thought of the sky above Pensacola, of clouds and darkened earth, and the rain, seeing deep blue lakes in the distance, and densely wooded hills which gradually approached and were not hills but only shadows, of the day he alone flew between two fantastic pillars into a gray and ghostly city where fog swirled and he was lost and burst forth miraculously into the blinding sun while the city drifted on, clouds eternally drifting toward the sea. He remembered that he had seen the shadow of his airplane on a cloud in the very center of a rainbow-colored halo, and it seemed to him this might be an omen. At Pensacola the meaning lay close to the surface.

So it was that the morning after their marriage Melvin and his new wife, carrying a cake box packed with sandwiches and fruit and with a large Thermos bottle of coffee, boarded a train to New Orleans. From there they planned to take a bus to Pensacola. He had obtained a vacation of one week from his job as a meter reader, and, because there were no examinations scheduled for either of them at the university, they had decided they could afford to miss a few classes.

After a day in New Orleans, during which they walked around the city a great deal and paid a brief visit to the air station on Lake Pontchartrain, they got on a bus to Mobile.

In a little while the bus was out of the city and racing along the sandy coast, through Gulfport and Biloxi—one after another the sun-struck southern beach towns flew past the bus windows. Once he had peered down through rifts in the blooming cumulus clouds and distinguished this same highway on which he was now traveling, and had been able to make out automobiles and trucks and buses, and had sometimes seen a train, and here and there an isolated tree casting a shadow in a watery field or across a road. The pine forests had resembled fungus, lichens clinging to an iron-red and umber earth, variegated like damp granite, and he had watched the shadow of his airplane flicker across the highways and fields and forests and ponds with the fantastic rapidity and frenzied energy of a spider suddenly floating, stiffly poised, on the water of some lake, with the shore receding steadily.

He had assumed there would be a number of interesting things to point out to her in Mobile, so they wandered around in Bienville Square, stopped at Walgreen's for a soda, browsed about in the Haunted Bookshop—Pat Cole, who seldom returned from liberty in Mobile without a new book, had one day introduced him to the people who owned the shop—and eventually, fatigued by the relentless heat, they returned to the depot, yawning and fanning themselves. He had not been able to explain successfully that once upon a time Walgreen's drugstore had been of considerable importance in the scheme of things—on two particular fountain stools, still there, which he had pointed out to her, he and his best friend Sam Horne used to wait, and wait for hours, and stare into the mirror at the passersby, at the activities going on behind their backs. They had never quite known what they were waiting for, but they had been prepared for it, whatever it was. They had waited there and scanned the scene in that mirror.

He told her about it as lucidly as he could. "We wasted a lot of time there. Everybody congregated in that drugstore, I don't know why. It was sociable, somehow. Cadoodlers, they used to call us, or did I mention that already? 'Evenin', cadoodlah boy,' some girl might say. 'Wheah y'all from?' Well, then, we'd say we were from Barin Field, though sometimes, if they looked like they came from the bottom of the barrel, Horne would poke me in the ribs and say we were from Corry or Bronson, and he'd introduce us with fictitious names. They were suspicious of us, though, even when we told the truth. I think they figured we had only one thing on our minds."

"They were so right."

"Yes, I suppose so," he nodded, and felt obscurely flattered that nothing else had been on his mind. "We tried to get them drunk and into bed, naturally, and they tried to drink the liquor without getting drunk. We only got one night a week away from the base, that's why."

"I see," said his wife, who did not sound too cordial.

Then they were on another bus speeding through the humid day. In the pine woods were cattle, cream-colored and brindled; he had never noticed them when he was a cadet. Aroused by the bus, they ambled away from the road and trotted with cumbersome udders swaying, deeper into the woods. Vegetation grew in high tropical profusion; telephone poles sunk in marshy ditches alongside the road were half concealed, old vines and fresh tendrils encircled the posts and crept along the crossbars to touch the wires and glass plugs. The tilled fields whose every detail he clearly discerned—tin cans strung up to frighten the crows, each ditch, each furrow methodically turning like the spoke of a wheel as the bus went speeding by—the last time he had seen these fields he had thought of them only in terms of personal security, as places to land in case of emergency. He had looked down on them, estimating their substance, comparing the color of one to another as he flew by, in order to judge how it would support him, meanwhile listening absently to the pulsing roar of the engine, which was like the surf, or the wind on a mountain, and as the cruciform shadow flickered along he glanced ahead more frequently and earnestly to catch sight of the water tower at Barin Field—a stiff-legged, stilt-legged, red-and-white giant standing spraddled with pine trees at his waist and wearing a friendly, preposterous, impossible coolie hat, a red-and-white checkerboard monster all the way around, like some metallic companion of Dorothy, unutterably nonplused but affable just the same, who had gotten lost in the woods on his way to Oz.

Bloody Barin was closed, the gates chained and secured by a rusty padlock. Melvin stood with his hands grasping the fence and stared through the mesh at the distant barracks where he had lived. On the second floor at the central window he used to stand with a billiard cue like a rifle in the crook of his arm while he drank a bottle of Coca-Cola and waited for Sam Horne. From another window on the left side of the barracks—he was not positive which window, although once he had known—he used to stare, idly, feet on the desk and a gunnery manual in his lap, half asleep from boredom, toward the flight line where during interminable winter months the hangars loomed like mausoleums just beneath the sluggish clouds, illuminated and discolored by reflection in the gray-green daylight, while rain dripped from the eaves, and over the field monotonously swept the red beacon, thrusting and darting at the clouds like a fish at the stormy surface. Through the fence to his right was a bunker that separated the landing mat from the road; hundreds of cadets had been standing on it the night the planes collided and crashed and exploding gasoline spouted from the wreckage in flaming diagonal arches. The back steps to the barracks had been crowded, too. The billiard game had stopped. Everyone was silent because Death was visiting once again.

Although he had not seen Death the Horseman that night he thought it must be as they say, riding across a yellow moon with a wooden-handled scythe uplifted. Death that night had come to visit Pensacola, as it often had before, and as he had understood it would again, perhaps for him. So, too, had they all known it might have been for them; they watched the great spurting flames, the incandescent eruption, in such silence—leaving the ivory balls to gleam unattended on the green baize table.

It was at this gate he had stood one drizzling Sunday noon with a cigarette hole burnt in his necktie and his collar smeared with lipstick, his blue uniform soaked with liquor and his shoes half submerged in mucky puddles while he tried persistently to deceive the guard. Now the road was dry as any bone; he moved one foot and scraped a little dust into the air, the dust settled and dimmed the polish of his shoes, as though it, too, had been raised from the void. He looked at the guardhouse. The glass was cracked. A torn spiderweb sagged from the eaves.

With a handkerchief he began wiping the perspiration from his face, and noticed not far from where he stood the tracks of another pilgrim in the dust, and two cigar stubs. He squinted up at the shimmering sun. Barin Field was closed. Weeds were growing inside the fence. There must be nests of mice in the barracks, and roaches swarming in the showers. He watched two squirrels race over the ridge of the barracks roof and stop with tails aloft, like figures on a weathervane.

He nodded to his wife, who had been sitting on the suitcases with a newspaper over her head. She got up, staggering a little, he thought, and took the smaller suitcase; he took the large one and they trudged along the road to the intersection of the highway to wait for another bus.

"Do you love me?" she asked while they were walking.

"Why, of course I do!" he replied without looking around.

"How do I know?" she insisted with a birdlike chirp. "You don't, truly, do you?"

"Certainly!" he said. "Certainly."

She was silent for a little while. "But do you love me as much as you did last Wednesday?"

He stopped; she bumped against him and backed away with a foolish expression.

"I want you to be happy," she said.

"I *am* happy!" said he, rather peeved by such nonsense. "I'm extremely happy." He resumed walking. "However, it's hot today." Their relationship was an established fact; he saw no sense in discussing it or analyzing it, and he did not look around again, although he could feel her reproachful gaze.

Beyond Barin Field the highway led to Saufley. Here, too, they descended from the bus and carried the suitcases to the gate. Carrying them had become tiresome and he was irritated with himself for not having checked them through to Pencacola, but it was too late now.

Saufley Field was in operation. It was smaller than he remembered—so small that it did not quite give the impression of a military base, but rather seemed to belong to a game somehow, or to be part of a summer camp, and the forest grew right up against the barbed-wire fence. Pine branches thrust through the mesh. Not long after this station was abandoned there would be saplings in the clearing and undergrowth approaching the hangars, and in twenty years in this humid climate it would be as lost as the ruins of Chichén Itzá. However it was bustling with activity at the moment: battleship-gray Navy vehicles with big, heavily treaded tires and distinctive markings—a red cross and a thick yellow stripe—were parked in the shadow of the dispensary, obviously ready to go speeding toward the next crash. Course lights revolved from the squadron tower. Row upon row of jet planes were lined up where the old dive bombers used to be, and as he stared at them he realized he did not know anything at all about jet planes—in fact there would be instruments on the panel that he had never heard of. He did not even know what company manufactured these planes. Two SNJ's were parked on the apron, the wings moored to bolts in the concrete; otherwise nothing looked familiar.

He was mystified and disappointed. So many things he expected to find here had vanished.

He was looking at the jets when he heard an unmistakable noise approaching the station. A Dauntless came into view, tilting over the trees, blowing a thin black stream of exhaust, the engine thudding and coughing and the pudgy wheels unfolding, flaps descending mechanically while the plane slowed in the air as though the pilot had stepped on the brakes; it came around like a bucket in the muggy Florida afternoon and floated and floated on currents rising from the runway, over tufts of brownish grass sprouting through the cracks, and finally touched down so lightly that everything he had experienced at this field came back to him with a rush.

"Did you—" he began, grasping her arm. "There! Just then—" but her expression told him that she had only seen an airplane landing, that was all.

"I suppose we ought to get into town for some lunch," he said a moment later, feeling aimless and mildly stunned by the glaring light.

"It's nearly one o'clock," she said. "My isn't it hot today!"

"Yes, it is," he said, and picked up a suitcase. "It always was hot down here, but I don't remember it being anything like this."

He took another look around, the last look: the neat frame barracks on concrete pilings, the huge NO SMOKING signs, and turned once more toward the flight line which had been the focus of his life. Some cadets were playing cards in the shadow of the hangar. They wore coveralls similar to those he and his friends had worn when they lounged in that area, but these cadets did not wear canvas helmets or baseball caps; they had gaudily painted plastic crash helmets. He wondered what they would think if he went over and told them that he had been at this field during the Second World War. Would they be polite and pretend some interest—and ask a question or two, as he himself did whenever his father spoke of the first war?

In Pensacola they had lunch in the coffee shop of the hotel; it was cool and gloomy after the sun-drenched landscape and they rested there, eating spumoni and drinking iced tea, and Melvin turned around several times to study a noisy luncheon party of three ensigns and a Marine lieutenant who he knew had just been commissioned. Their uniforms were crisp and fresh, the gold collar bars sparkled. He thought he detected, too, an aura of liberation about the young officers, an indescribable psychic release which manifested itself on graduation day.

"What's the matter with you?" his wife asked.

"Why," said he, as though nothing could be more obvious, "those are cadets."

She looked again. "I thought the ones with wings and stripes were officers. Isn't that what you told me?"

"Yes, yes," he answered vacantly without hearing what she said.

After lunch they wandered along Palafox Street. He paused in front of a photographer's studio. One evening, on liberty from Ellyson Field, he had not been able to locate Horne and had come wandering down Palafox and discovered him waiting in this studio, evidently about to be photographed, but peeking apprehensively out the window as though he did not want to be seen, his beady blue eyes darting along the street. He had been attempting to comb his hair in preparation for the picture and he was carrying a stuffed alligator. At some invisible summons he whirled and disappeared; and later, in the barracks, he had sensed that Melvin

367

had seen him there, and scowled and fussed about, crumpling papers in his mortification, and finally snarled, "What's so funny? If you got anything to say, let's have it!"

"Why are you grinning?" she insisted, plucking at his shirt. "Answer me. It must have something to do with a woman."

"Sam Horne got his picture taken here."

"Sam Horne," she replied after a pause. "He's the one from Iowa."

"That's right. I guess I've told you about him before. I expect this must be dull for you, but I want to go over to the main station—Mainside, we called it."

"The day is yours. The night will be mine," she said. "I'm ready when you are."

Mainside had not changed, though he had thought it was oriented differently: south now seemed north. But the substantial red brick Colonial administration buildings, the white hospital— these he recognized, though without much sense of recovering the past; not until they walked along the coast toward Fort Barrancas, beyond the officers' club, and he saw the fine white sand drifting over the weeds, and the scrubby pines and twisted brush growing from hollows and hillocks near the Spanish fort. Then, gradually, as though recalling a dream, one incident before another, the interval vanished and when he shut his eyes and listened to the crunch of footsteps on the road he could believe it was not his wife walking beside him, but Horne, or Roska, or Nick McCampbell, and that they were going to meet some WAVEs on the beach, and that someone there would have a portable radio to listen to the news broadcasts: the Marshall Islands had been invaded, a task force was shelling Saipan.

Melvin pointed across the inlet. "That's Santa Rosa Island. We could get a room over there and spend a day or so. It's been a long trip. If you'd like."

"That would be nice."

"I want to visit Ellyson and Whiting. You could stay in town this afternoon and I could meet you. Maybe you'd like to do some shopping."

She immediately shook her head and insisted on going along and he sensed that she was jealous, but of what he had no idea.

As they approached Ellyson Field he stared up in speechless

368

dismay, for the air was swarming with helicopters teetering and flailing in mindless, drunken orbits, oscillating, rocking, dipping and rising straight up and hanging suspended in mid-air, turning around and around after their tails like flea-bitten dogs. He had never liked helicopters; now they had invaded and actually taken over this base, altering the very atmosphere and giving off unfamiliar noises. The dipping, spinning machines struck him as idiotic; he glared at them, mumbled, turned around, and went back to the highway.

After a long wait they got another bus and traveled to Whiting Field, and there, as they were standing outside the gate while Melvin showed his identification cards, she looked up and saw the hawks which lived in the dense pine woods surrounding the base. She pointed them out to him and asked why he had never mentioned them. Melvin shaded his eyes and watched the hawks circling motionless in the currents high above the field and did not answer because he could not remember them. The instrument squadron had been located here and the cockpit had been hooded most of the time he was aloft; even so it was odd that he had not glimpsed the soaring hawks, or noticed them from the ground. He squinted again at the drifting specks in the sky.

And often he thought of them during the next three days as he lay on the beach of Santa Rosa Island, and thinking of them he thought of Louis Kahn, without knowing why, unless it could be that Kahn, like the hawks, had killed as they killed, without remorse, regarding it as necessary to survival.

Uneasily he reached out to touch his wife, and felt her thigh. She was lying beside him in a depression not far from the water, and with that touch he realized he was almost asleep, sinking into the beach, the hour, and the light, with a few grains of sand on his lips and, now, one finger hooked inside the waistband of her bathing suit—as though they slept in Arabia where she might be stolen—while the luminous waves splashed ever closer, and ever and anon on the horizon the burning sun retreated to the high western sea.

He turned his head and wiped the sand from his lips. An offshore breeze was blowing. The beach was cool. He and his wife were alone, but for the midsummer constellations glittering overhead and the small white crabs that scuttled along the water's edge. She was seated cross-legged and was smoking a cigarette with the curious ineptitude of women, as though, having begun, she was not quite certain how it would end. The war for which he had been so meticulously and mysteriously prepared, like a ram for a festivity, was already a subject for historians who could not record the life and death of anonymous men any more than they could record these crabs—these opaque specters dashing to and fro, popping with such alert frenzy out of one hole into another.

He sat up, stiffly. Some hairpins, a mirror, and a comb slipped off his chest. She often used him as a table when he was asleep.

28
★

This impression—that the war which had engulfed most of the nations in the world was already half meaningless, relegated to history no differently than any other war, and that, as veterans died and generations passed, the time would come when this cataclysm would arouse no more than the mild curiosity that he, himself, felt toward the War of the Roses—this impression persisted through the summer and autumn without lessening; it remained with him, indeed, as profoundly as his union with his wife. There were times when it seemed to him that he and she and the implications of that war in which he had not fought were inextricably bound. His life during those days, though he had not clearly distinguished it then, had not been his own to live, and this, he now reflected, was unjust. Having been given life through some power far exceeding that of all mankind, how was he, therefore, obligated to any man, except as he chose to be? His life had proceeded not according to his own need and his desire, but from the omnipotence of an agency whose purpose and nature, he grew positive, were inimical to him; a ceaseless, measureless tide, the consequence of a singular mistrust, and that subsequent multitude of murders sanely eulogized, day by day—this malevolent tide had caught him unaware with all the rest and cast him along the shore and would have drawn him beyond sight and hope of land as though he were not a living man but a derelict raft, or a sea anenome, some sodden ruptured polyp washing senselessly to and fro in the ebb and flow of the littoral foam.

One morning near the end of the year, with his mouth full of tacks and a hammer in his hand, he was repairing the linoleum in a basement apartment that he and Jo had rented. Snow drifted thinly down the steps against the basement door and lay deep in the areaways outside the windows. As he crawled across the floor, pausing here and there to drive a tack into the linoleum, which had warped during the autumn rains, it seemed to him that the tap of the hammer echoing through the gloomy basement was like the tap of a blind man's cane; and he reflected that he himself might as well be blind, since he was being led wherever it pleased the authorities to lead him: two days previous he had received in the mail a letter from the government informing him that he was subject to the draft and that he was to report for a physical examination on the fifteenth of February. He had been so stunned by this news that for a while he thought it must be a joke; but, after reading it through again and again, he opened up a trunk in which he kept various papers and objects he considered valuable and compared it with the order to report for physical examination which he had received at the beginning of the Second World War. The signatures were different; otherwise the two notices were almost identical. It was an official notification by the draft board. There was no doubt of it.

He had placed the letter in a drawer of his desk, beneath some miscellaneous papers, to keep it out of his sight, but it was there, and it was colossal. When he was eighteen years old he had been expecting such a letter, had looked forward to it, and had been anxious to go. He remembered the excitement he felt as he left his parents and sister and hurried down the ramp at the Union Station and plunged eagerly into the crowd.

But here it was again.

He had not told Jo. He did not know what he was going to do. He was not certain how he felt; the letter had been too overwhelming. He did not like to think about it.

All at once a shadow darkened the window. He glanced up, assuming it was Jo who had gone down the hillside to the grocery, but glimpsed a bulky man wearing a green cap and a black overcoat. An instant later there was a furious pounding on the door and the buzzer began, buzzing in Morse code. Then he knew, before the code spelled out the name—Sam Horne—who stood at the door.

"Hello, baby!" Horne growled, blinking and grinning. He looked shorter, older, and he was much heavier, with prominent reddish freckles all over his face. A wattle of flesh dangled beneath his chin and when he turned his head the flesh spilled over his collar and momentarily hid the silver bars. He was a senior-grade lieutenant, two black stripes on the sleeve of his winter green uniform. Below the British-looking embroidered wings on his breast were three rows of campaign ribbons with battle stars and clusters.

"So how long has it been?" he was demanding as he shuffled flat-footed through the apartment. "I shipped out of Diego— hell, when was it? Let's see, I was in operational at Jacksonville before that. Holy cats! It must have been right after designation at Pensy! Sure, that was the last time I saw you."

"You were going to a party at the BOQ," Melvin said, and walked to the stove to put on the coffee pot. He knew quite well when they had last seen each other.

Horne chuckled. His jowls quivered. "Yuh, by God! We had a ball that night, too. And I tried to get you to sneak in and join us, but you wouldn't. I never could figure out why."

"By the way," Melvin said, "you didn't happen to go back to visit Barin not so long ago, did you? I noticed some cigar butts outside the fence and the first thing I thought of was that maybe you'd been there."

"I got a belly full of that hole. That stupid ensign—what was his name?"

"I know who you mean. Frank, or something like that. Brink. Hunt. Lunt. Monk!"

"That's the man! Ensign T. J. Monk. Yes, sir! And one of these days I'll meet up with that plump little turd, and he'll get a reaming to pay him back."

"You're a lieutenant. He's probably a commander by now, if he's still in the Navy."

"I could get to him, don't kid yourself. It's a matter of knowing the right people."

"He never bothered you especially. I was the one he loved to put on the pap sheet."

"I'll tell you something. He's a homo. Once when he summoned me to his room he tried to put the make on me. 'Why not remove our coats, Mr. Horne?' he pipes, and that was only the beginning."

"You didn't mention it. You could have got him cashiered."

"Maybe. But it might be on my record as well as his, and I didn't want anything to spoil my record. I'm going a long way in this outfit and no pansy is going to stop me. Your old buddy is going right up the ladder. I won't make it to the top because I'm not Annapolis, but I can go to captain or maybe rear admiral if I play it right. And I'll play it right, you watch," he added in a low, determined voice. He had been looking at the paintings on the wall with an expression of annoyance. "I thought you'd eventually get squared away, but I should've known better. The international situation the way it is, and you're still in a dream world."

Melvin shrugged. "There's always an international situation."

"Oh, Jesus! If there's one thing that burns me up!" Horne cried and jumped halfway to his feet, but then collapsed heavily in the chair. "Those Commies mean business while you lie around painting pictures! Oh, forget it, forget it, let's not get in an argument. Honest to God, there's something about you that just drives me wild, I don't know what it is. I never have been able to figure out what it is." He loosened his belt and gave a comfortable grunt.

"All the way through that stupid cadet program I kept trying to give you the word, but you didn't pay any attention to me. You had to do things your own way, and I admired you for that, believe it or not. But look what it got you. Living in a moldly basement. What future have you got? You got less future than when you were a cadet. It's the truth." He paused and appeared to be thinking, absently tugging at the flesh under his jaw. Then he remarked in a friendly voice, "You've changed, baby. But I have too. My hair stopped falling out, though. I was afraid I was going to lose it all out there in the Pacific. As soon as I got back to the States I started going to a beauty parlor twice a week. It was the damnedest thing. They sit you down near those dryers, those big aluminum sons of bitches that look like the warhead of a torpedo. Okay, there I was, me, Sam Horne—an hour and a half twice a week for about six months listening to a bunch of ignorant broads quack about percale sheets. Can you feature that? I had to sit there looking at a movie magazine or the *Ladies' Home Journal,* and then some fruit by the name of Donald came around to give me a massage, a massage on the top of the head. I never been so mortified in my whole life. Vinegar and lemon juice and I don't know what. I'm telling you, if it starts to fall out again I'm going to get myself a wig and the hell with it."

There was a pan of breakfast rolls on the stove; he had been studying the rolls as he talked and now got up and helped himself, covered a roll with butter and strawberry jam, and began to eat it with a look of intense satisfaction. After he had finished he wiped the crumbs from his lips and brushed his sleeves. His fingertips were sticky from the jam; he began to lick them, staring around the basement. His eyes, Melvin noticed, were still suspicious and burned frigidly, as blue as a flower or a gem, and they missed nothing. His voice was nearly the same, a little deeper, but as hoarse and abrasive as ever. His face, though, had altered, the features thickened; and his nose had swollen—it was underlaid with crimson veins as though something within him were rising to the surface.

"I thought you'd show up one day," Melvin said. "I've been looking forward to it more than I realized. Lots of times I've asked myself what I'd like to know particularly about everything that's happened since Pensacola, and this is going to sound foolish, but you know how all through the program I was hoping to fly a Corsair?"

"Yuh. And you're lucky you never got to. You don't goof off in one of those, not if you want to be around for supper."

"Maybe so. Anyway, that's one thing I want to know. What it feels like to fly a Corsair. Is it anything like a Dauntless?"

Horne said, "I'd almost forgotten you and that old Dauntless."

374

He hesitated, and the thought of it seemed to puzzle or irritate him. "What were you trying to prove? Why didn't you bail out of that crate?"

Melvin stirred restlessly and took a sip of coffee. Horne and everyone else might forget that crash landing but he had not and knew he never would. At any moment he could see the concrete tilt toward him just beyond the oil-spattered glass, feel the searing heat, the crunch of metal, and the grinding shock, and smell the burning oil.

Horne evidently did not expect an answer. "Speaking of old planes, I saw something last summer that was pretty hard to believe. Me and another fellow had ferried a couple of jets to Phoenix. Well, just outside town there's this junk yard full of World War Two amphibians. It wasn't but a few years ago those planes were picking up survivors, but you know what? A Catalina with 'Adak' stenciled on the fin was actually lying there in the desert on its back—turned clear over! I guess the wind blew it over. It was awful—this great big plane with its hull turned up to the sun. It was like a dead whale, tumbleweed bouncing by, and the dust and the sand. So I stopped and talked to the guy who owned the place and he told me the government auctioned off those PBY's so cheap he bought a dozen, thinking he might convert them into apartments for students, or coffee shops, or some damn thing, but now he's sorry he got them. He says kids throw rocks at them and people climb over the fence at night to steal whatever's loose. Honest to God, I could've cried! The tires are flat, cut to ribbons, and the sides are bashed in. When I think of only a few years ago how glad everybody in service was to see those planes! Nothing ever looked half as sweet as one of those monsters coming over the horizon. And I ought to know," he added grimly, "because I spent practically all night on a raft one time in the Philippine Sea and a PBY picked me up at sunrise just like I was a commuter."

"I didn't know you were shot down," Melvin said, looking at him with interest.

"I wasn't shot down," Horne said. "I ran out of gas." A moment later he said, "It was my own fault, but the strangest thing is, everybody thinks it was heroic. You fall in the ocean, you're a hero. That beats hell out of me! I can tell a civilian exactly what happened and I see from the look on his face he thinks I'm modest. But our squadron exec, now, he knew better. I'd no more than got back aboard and put on dry clothes before he started chewing me out. That man went up one side and down the other. I thought sure I was about to lose my wings." Horne shuddered. "Next time I took off he tapped me on the shoulder and said, 'Lieutenant, aboard this vessel no gasoline coupons are required.' "

"And what did you say?"

"I said, 'Yes, sir, I'll remember that.' And I saluted. What did you think I was going to do—be a comedian and make some bright remark? Not me! Oh—by the way, you may or may not be aware of this, but clear out in the islands they heard about you. Not you precisely, not *personally*, that is. But they talk about a certain cadet, and whoever tells some anecdote claims this cadet was a friend of a friend of his. But it's you who's mainly responsible. I must have heard three or four stories about different things you did—things I know you did, that were supposed to have been done by this sort of mythical Dilbert." Sam Horne plucked another roll from the pan, buttered it and spread jam over it, muttered, "I got to go on a diet," and greedily chewed up the roll, meanwhile staring at Melvin.

"A guy from the Sixth Fleet joined our squadron in the Marianas and one night he started telling about the Corpus Christi cadet who got his foot caught underneath the rudder of an OS2U. So after everybody knocked themselves out laughing I told them it happened at Albuquerque and it wasn't an OS, it was a Taylor-craft. And then I said—do you know what I said? I said, 'That was my roommate!' Yes, sir! That's exactly what I said. All the way out in the Pacific. 'That was my roommate!' I said. Even in the Sixth Fleet they'd heard about you, although, frankly, I can't imagine how."

This seemed to afford him some kind of satisfaction. "One day on the beach at Honolulu," he continued, "I overheard a lieutenant telling about the cadet that tried to shoot down his instructor, only the name of the instructor in this version wasn't Teitlebaum—it had been told so many times it had got shortened to 'Baum' or maybe 'Bowen,' it sounded like. Anyway, you were chasing him the hell and gone around the Gulf trying to line

376

him up in your sights. What do you think of that?" Horne demanded, pinching his belly as he spoke and eying the pan of rolls.

"Have another one," said Melvin.

"All this lard," Horne replied. "I got to cut out eating so much. I don't know what makes me do it. I'm going to work it off one of these days." He got up and walked to the stove, where he studied the rolls, and then without a word selected one, buttered it, and covered it thickly with jam.

"Where's Nick?" Melvin inquired. "Do you hear from him?"

Horne stuffed the roll into his mouth and swallowed it, and poured another cup of coffee. He looked at the pan of rolls again. "These are good," he said. "These really are good."

"My wife made them."

"Is that a fact! Well! Yes, sir, those are all right. Let's see— what'd you just say? You asked something."

"I was wondering if you'd heard from Nick McCampbell."

"No, I—now wait! Let me think. Oh! Isn't that funny I could forget? He's dead. His number came up. I thought you knew. He was killed on an atoll near Saipan. Sure, it's beginning to come back to me now. When I heard about it the first thing I thought was how much you used to like McCampbell, and I figured I'd better write and tell you before somebody else did. Didn't you ever get the letter?"

Melvin shook his head.

"I think I wrote you, but maybe not. I guess not. Well, anyway, he got it just a few weeks after he was assigned to a combat squadron. That's the breaks for you. He hit some flak—he was in a 2C outfit. They were coming back from a strike, I forget where, and McCampbell's engine conked so he bailed out and landed in the surf. They thought at first he was drowned, but after a while the guys overhead saw him get to his feet and come running out of the water headed for some coconut palms. He had a forty-five in his hand. He made it to the palms all right, but there was a squad of Japs at his heels and that was the last anybody ever heard of him."

"He was alive, though, the last they could see?"

"He's dead, don't kid yourself. Those Japs got him—he'd never surrender."

"Wasn't there anything anybody could do?"

"His wing man circled the reef as long as he could, but his gas was running low and the carrier was on its way. McCampbell just had it, that's all. It wasn't anybody's fault. He was a mean little booger," Horne added thoughtfully. "Say! I wonder where the other guys are. There were six of us, huh? You and me. McCampbell's dead, and what's-his-name who spun into the Gulf on that dive-bombing run."

"Elmer Free."

"That's right. And so that narrows it down to Roska and that other guy, the one I couldn't stand. That son of a bitch that acted like he drank from the Holy Grail."

"Cole."

"Yuh. Pat Cole. He's another bird I wouldn't mind running into again, although maybe I'd just as soon not. Wherever he is you can bet he's found a soft touch."

"Do you know anything about Roska?"

"I heard a report he was missing in action, so I guess he's gone, but you never know—he could be running a cat-house in Sioux City for all I know. Or drinking himself to death, which is more likely."

"And you've gone regular."

"Yes. It's not a bad life, not bad at all. The pay is fair, lot of free time, no worries. And besides, the country's going to get suited up again pretty soon, what with the way the situation is developing in Korea, and I like being in ahead of the mob. Right now I'm on route to Washington for a special six-week course given by the Intelligence Department. I set down at Olathe to refuel and figured what the hell, I don't have to log in till the ninth, so I called your old man's office in Kansas City. He told me you were up here going to school and that you'd gotten married."

"Marriage is an understatement. You know when there was a hurricane off the coast in Florida how they used to tie the planes down by ropes from the wings to the concrete?"

"They still do."

"Well, that's the feeling," Melvin said. "I'm nearly a father, too."

"I got two kids," Horne remarked with indifference. "Little boy named Sandy and a girl named Martha. I haven't seen them in

378

about a year. The wife and I separated. And speaking of understatements, that's one. Do you—ah, like it?" he asked, leaning forward.

Melvin glanced around, thinking Jo might have appeared; he could not entirely get over a suspicion that women were able to materialize wherever they pleased. "Well, yes, yes," he said in a discreet voice, "but it's a little incredible. You take, for example, the hairpins. Do you have any conception of how many hairpins women use? Why, it's fantastic! They get everywhere—all over the floor, in the ashtrays, even in bed."

"My wife," said Horne, "used to wake up every morning about four o'clock. She'd rear straight up holding the covers around her neck and sort of gasp. 'Oh!' That's what she'd gasp. 'Oh!' she'd say, and then sink down and go right back to sleep. It was the weirdest thing."

"Well, that *is* strange."

"Yes, and I asked her a couple of times what was the problem— did she hear a noise or something, but I never could get an answer." He frowned.

"We had a good honeymoon," Melvin remarked. "We did a lot of sightseeing and stuff."

"Sightseeing and stuff?"

"You know what I mean."

"Hell yes, I know what you mean. But if it lasts you're luckier than me. The wife and I hadn't been married two months when the squabbles started. Time and again. Over nothing. She always had money, that was one thing. She figured everybody did, or should, and kept wanting me to earn more so we could live higher on the hog. She never could accept the fact I was a farmer before the war. She pretended it wasn't quite true, that it was a joke, like I spent vacations on the farm. Well, she nagged at me to get out of the Navy because that wasn't good enough either, which I did in order to pacify her. I wanted to be an architect once, a long time ago, and thought maybe now was the time. But you don't start out being an architect, so there I was working as a stock boy in a department store and taking a course in drafting. Meanwhile we were living on her income from stocks and bonds. Anyway, the jug turned sour. No matter what I did it was wrong as far as she was concerned. She chipped at me. She kept knocking bits off, day after day, night after night.

"So that's how the situation developed. I meant to write you, but somehow I couldn't bring myself to do it. I was sort of ashamed, screwed up. I got so mad," he said with an interested look, as though he were listening to someone else, "that once I knocked her cold. And do you know, when she hit the floor the first thing I thought was, 'Damn your soul!' and I kept saying to myself while I stood over her and saw her there at my feet, 'You deserved it! You brought it on yourself!' I still think if I had done that to her the first time she tried to run me around—well, maybe not, I don't know. But she kept pushing at me, and pushing at me the way some women do, just begging for it, really, while I kept reminding myself that I was a gentleman, but then all at once it was too late—she pushed one time too often—and what she couldn't understand, I think, was that I stretched her out with no warning. No warning at all. I remember the day. She never knew what hit her. Down she went, stiff as an old halibut. She didn't wake up for about fifteen minutes and I thought I'd killed her. I didn't care. If I'd happened to have a gun in my hand when she started after me I'd have shot her. It's funny—just in a flash something happened and she wasn't my wife, I didn't know who she was, even her name, only that she was driving me mad."

He scratched his head and grunted softly. "I'm paying for it. I'll pay for it the rest of my life. If there's one thing she doesn't need, it's money, but the court ordered me to give her half the property and alimony till she marries somebody else. She wanted all the property. She wept and complained—I couldn't believe it. And at the same time I felt kind of sorry for her, she sounded so pitiful. You know what she does now?" Horne asked, gazing at the floor. "She lives in Santa Monica. She spends every day—all day—from nine in the morning till the sun goes down, lying on the beach. She lies around on one of these great big striped towels in a leopard-skin bathing suit and sits up once in a while to oil herself, and then she lies down again and puts on her polaroid glasses. That's what she does the whole day long. All around her are those ukelele-playing bums in thatched hats and peppermint-stick pants and not one of them would funk a note if Asia sank to the bottom of the sea." He stood up, walked briskly to the stove, and selected another roll. "In court she called me extremely cruel. I'm not cruel. I never been cruel to anything in my life, not even to a fox or a weasel."

"You clobbered me a time or so and frankly I never grew to love you on account of it."

"Those little fights we used to have at Pensacola? Those were in fun."

"You had more fun than I did."

"You never learned," Horne explained while he spread the roll with jam. "You always left yourself wide open. I could never figure that out—every single time! Crazy." He glanced at his wrist watch. "Come on, let's go to Olathe!" he said enthusiastically. "Take a ride. I saw a couple of J's there when I landed."

"I doubt if the Navy would care too much for my presence."

"Balls! They don't know you from Dan McGrew. Come on! I got a station wagon parked outside and we can be at Olathe in half an hour. What do you say, baby? Let's go!" He swallowed the roll and hurried over to wash his hands.

"All right," Melvin said. "Why not? Sure! All right, let's go!"

"Uh, oh," said Horne. "I forgot. What about the wife?"

"I'll leave her a note. She's at the grocery." He tore a scrap of paper from a sack and began to scribble on it.

"Can you do that?"

"Do what?"

"Go when you feel like it?"

"Certainly! Come on, maybe we can get away before she comes back." He put the note on the stove with an apple on top to hold it and ran to the closet for his jacket. "Take some of those rolls along if you want to," he called.

"I was thinking I might," Horne answered. "They really are very good." And he was wrapping four of them in wax paper when Melvin reappeared.

While they were driving toward the naval base Melvin explained what had happened to him after graduation day at Pensacola and what he was now doing. "I plan to use the remainder of the GI Bill," he concluded. "Then, probably, I'll try to locate a teaching position somewhere. Maybe some little college might hire me."

"If they don't know you they might," Sam Horne replied, not with any particular animus, but in a sociable tone, as though it were an established fact.

29

★

Around a bend in the road they came within sight of the base and of the bleak flint hills of Olathe, bare and frozen. Whorls of snow as fine and dry as sugar, or alkali dust, swiftly rose from the fields and gullies and swept through the barbed-wire fences and the ranks of splintered cornstalks like wraiths in the pallid winter sunlight.

Horne brought the station wagon skidding to a stop at the gate. A guard appeared. Melvin, watching the guard's face, saw it assume the customary expression—the man retreating well within the face, leaving it, the voice, and the body, to function as expected.

"Good morning, sir," said the guard, saluting.

"Good morning." Horne returned the salute and drove on.

The sky was clear. A green beacon flashed from the squadron tower. The cups of the anemometer were spinning. A few planes were in the air.

"North wind. Fifteen knots, twenty knots," Horne observed, squinting at the wind sock, "and cold as my Aunt Mona."

He parked near the hangars and pointed to the Corsair he had flown from the West Coast. The bubble canopy was set far back on the fuselage, as close to the rudder as to the engine, and the lowest blade of the four-bladed propeller was almost touching the concrete.

"That must be a new model," Melvin remarked. "It seems different from the ones at Pensacola."

"Yuh, they gave it a few more horses and squared the prop tips."

"I've never seen this greenish color before. The others were always that midnight blue, or else camouflaged."

"It's a new paint they're trying, testing the corrosion, or some damn thing. Come on, it's got only one seat and you ain't about to solo." He whistled into his fists and hopped up and down. The snow came whirling around his feet and he suddenly turned and ran for the hangar. "God above," he muttered when they were inside, "I wish I was in California." He shivered and peeked through a crack in the door. "You wait here, I'll scare up some gear."

He returned a few minutes later dressed in winter flight clothing, with a parachute slung across each shoulder, and had brought a suit for Melvin. "I left those rolls in the car," he said with a worried expression. "I hope nobody eats them before we get down. They certainly are delicious." He scratched his head, frowned, and walked away.

When he came back he had a map, a candy bar, and a number of cigars which he was easing into a pocket of his jacket. In the meantime Melvin had gotten dressed. The musty, brindled helmet was buckled under his chin and his ears tingled. The leather trousers were so heavy and the fleece so thick that he was scarcely able to walk.

"I don't know why it is," Horne said, looking at him, "but you always remind me of a puppet. Come on, let's go," and he started for the door.

The SNJ to which they had been assigned was parked behind some jets halfway down the line. Flurries of snow spun over it and under it, rattling the greenhouse and drifting against the worn tires. It was silver and green with orange squadron markings. They walked around it, examining the surfaces for damage, and climbed on the wing, one after the other, and it occurred to Melvin, seeing himself and Horne so bulky and brown, that from a distance they must look like gorillas clambering into the cockpits. He dropped into the seat, drew the canopy over his head to shut out the wind, and then began to untangle the shoulder harness, realizing presently that he should have arranged it before sitting down. He was still untangling it when there was a leaden thump and the control stick began flopping around between his knees. The pedals sank to the floorboards and the airplane moved a little as the rudder swung against the wind. The stick plunged forward and rocked back, the elevators descended and flipped upward; the tail of the plane did not leave the ground but for an instant it had felt lighter.

Melvin got his arms into the harness and buckled it securely to the safety belt. There was another metallic clunk and Horne's hulking figure dropped almost out of sight; only the top of his helmet was visible in the front cockpit. A moment later he was cranking himself up. The control stick continued banging noisily from side to side. The ailerons loosely lifted and fell in the wind.

Horne started the engine; there was a weary whine, every second more shrill and powerfully protesting, until it seemed ready to burst; then all at once the propeller jerked, flung itself over, stopped, jerked again, and disappeared in a roar of noise. Out of the wavering, colorless hoop the blades emerged, fanning slowly around, first one way and then the other, with a drifting, leisurely motion, while acrid fumes streamed into the cockpit.

Melvin unhooked the microphone from the radio box and said over the intercommunication system, "My feet are cold." He could see Horne's shoulder move as he reached for the front microphone.

"Why don't you open the heater?"

"I forgot where it is."

"On the floor," Horne said, observing him in the mirror, and then added, "I was going to let you handle the take-off. I just now changed my mind."

There was the valve on the floor, right where it had always been; he rotated it with his toe and felt a stream of air, not quite warm and yet not cold, inside the cuff of his trousers. Then he sat with his hands and feet riding on the controls and waited, looking around at the base, at the green beacon, at the distant figures in the control tower.

The brakes depressed, the throttle knob slowly pulled his left hand forward. The direction of the propeller blades appeared to reverse, like the spokes of stagecoach wheels in the movies; the engine was howling. He looked at the instrument panel, for a

384

moment unable to locate the magneto switch, but there it was, and he watched it, knowing it was going to move. It did; immediately he could feel a difference in the quivering fuselage. The tachometer needle was sinking. He tried to remember how much it was supposed to drop when the magnetos were tested.

In a moment the throttle returned to its former position and Horne was signaling to the lineman, who had been standing by with the collar of his peajacket turned up and his back to the wind; the lineman ducked out of sight beneath the wing to kick away the chocks. He reappeared a few seconds later on the other side of the plane with his mittens raised, beckoning, trotting nimbly backward. The SNJ rolled after him like a captive dragon glinting in the January sun, growling but obedient to each command, rocking and waddling in the wind, hunch-backed, bandy-legged, and pigeon-toed, and Sam Horne pushed the throttle forward to blast the tail around.

The lineman waved them on and ran for the hangar with his head buried in his coat.

The wind whistled over the fuselage and the plane seemed to skip now and then as Horne taxied rapidly along the strip toward the far end of the runway. Melvin looked up and saw, not far above the leafless trees, where abandoned bird nests lodged here and there in the forks, a twin-engined transport gleaming in the winter noon, and then, at the same instant, as though they were still flying together at Pensacola, Melvin and Horne turned their heads toward the squadron tower: a red light was shining in their eyes. Horne drew back on the throttle.

Snow spun up from the runway as the transport thundered ponderously by them with its plump wheels reaching stiffly for the ground, and snow was still boiling in its wake across the center of the field when the tower light shone green.

The SNJ trundled forward. The canopy rattled and danced like a teacup. They swerved onto the runway, the metal trim tabs moved as Horne adjusted for the take-off, then the throttle was sliding forward and the plane bumped ahead faster and faster and the tail hesitantly rose from the pavement. Melvin sat with his arms folded, smiling and looking around as he felt with his body for the diminishing bumps and for that subtle, final withdrawal of the earth.

Gently but positively the wheels thumped into their pockets beneath the fuselage; he knew how they would look from below —tightly rolled, clasped there, side by side, like buttons or talons. A wing dipped and the J curved across the station. There was just time to glimpse the high wire fence flickering underneath the wing before a burnt white prehistoric horizon tilted into view —a fragment of decorated pottery from a cave, snow and trees, the solid mottled luster of a frozen pond, all at once a silo and pigs and the pens stark white, and the trampled, muddy, hay-strewn barnyard and one Gauguin horse beside the weathered door, railroad tracks, and the matted weeds beside the bridge. The plane was rising. In the distance was another farm, fenced and angular, all Kansas and honest, and away to the side the suburbs of Olathe itself, an unfinished tract, a cluster of pastel bungalows which belonged in the tropics, not on these bleak plains.

Melvin unhooked the microphone and pressed the button. "Let's go over the university. I have some unfinished business there."

Horne stared at him suspiciously in the mirror, but said, after a moment, "Heading three-one-zero. You got it," and patted the top of his helmet and jerked his thumb backward.

Melvin took the controls and for a while flew straight ahead. Then, cautiously, he began to bank from side to side, then lowered the SNJ into a shallow dive and pulled it into a climb while he followed the heading to Lawrence. The controls felt odd, unlike the pedals and wheel of an automobile. He tried a full-circle turn, pressing the pedals smoothly, but the bubble would not stay in the center of the arch—it slipped ahead of him all the way.

The sheepskin jacket, the leather gloves, the engine fumes, the greasy steel, cold to touch, the knobs and levers, and the dials, the tight discomfort of the helmet, and the clamminess of the fleece, a coarse, hard corner of the parachute pack on which he was seated, and the memory of the odor of canvas after long hours in the summer afternoon—these recalled far more than he had been able to remember when he and his wife were visiting Pensacola. These she could not ever understand.

"What do you remember most about the program?" he asked.

"A couple of sons of bitches I'd love to get even with," said Horne with no hesitation.

386

"I know. But what else?"

"I guess that Christmas dinner at Albuquerque," said Horne after a while. "It was dark that day, that's what I'll never forget. They had to turn on the lights, it was so dark in the chow hall. I've still got the menu, those little printed, folded menus they had set up at every place, I've still got mine somewhere. That was a mighty fine dinner, after all those powdered eggs and cold beans. I just couldn't believe we were going to get a decent meal. All the time I was eating that Christmas dinner I kept expecting the skipper to come running in there and shout, 'What the hell do you people think you're doing? Who gave you permission to eat turkey and cranberry sauce?' Incidentally, if you want to go to Lawrence, you're twenty degrees off course."

Melvin banked the SNJ and Horne's shadow, followed by his own, slid along the wing and disappeared into space. A wisp of smoke floated through the cockpit. He glanced at the mirror and saw that Horne had a cigar in his mouth and was holding a match to it.

"Yes, that was a good dinner," Melvin said. "You know, the other day I got to thinking about that book of nudes. Did you take that with you to Jacksonville?"

Horne removed the cigar and appeared to be thinking. At last he said with a serious expression, "I can't remember. Be damn if I know what ever did happen to that. Somebody must have swiped it. Jesus, by the time we finished Saufley that book was so mangled you'd have thought it went through the wringer. It was a fine book," he added thoughtfully, and resumed smoking.

"Yes, it certainly was," Melvin said. "I never saw anything like it. Six hundred and fifty women."

"Yes, that was all right. That was worth while."

They flew over the wind-rippled snow and Horne remarked, "It's almost like I got cheated out of being an architect. If there hadn't been this war, I'd have gone to the state university—I was saving for it. I'd have worked my tail to the bone, and right today I'd be a junior partner in a firm somewhere. In Omaha, probably —fat, dumb, and happy. Maybe in Chicago. You know, baby, I never told you this but when we were cadets I used to go off by myself sometimes just in order to look at buildings. I'd walk around them, and go inside and look at the corridors and stairs.

And those liberty nights when nobody knew where I was, you know what I was doing usually? In the reading room of the USO, or in the library, or in some park under a streetlamp with a book. Sure, by the time we got through Pensacola I'd practically memorized *Toward a New Architecture*; I knew as much about the Bauhaus as if I'd been there. But we were at war and I felt— *ah!* Forget it.

"Now it seems strange," he continued, "but I used to lie in my sack at Barin and just think with admiration about people like Gropius or Le Corbusier. I used to daydream about the time when everybody would be discussing me and the stuff I was erecting. I was planning to use stone and glass and brick and wood in ways they'd never been used. I was going to design buildings so tremendous that you couldn't help touching them. 'This is by Samuel Thompson Horne' people would say." He fell silent, but then went on in a bemused voice. "I had a funny experience once in the South Pacific. We'd received orders to work over a couple of the islands. I've forgotten why, but anyway there we were—I was leading the section. We came across the volcano and on the beach, right where I'd suspected they'd be, were some troops. At least I figured they must be troops instead of natives, the way they deployed and scrambled for cover when they heard us coming, Anyhow, I was about to open fire when the weirdest thing happened, honest to God! Those people disappeared right in front of my eyes! You think I'm nuts, wait'll you hear this: all I could see was a bird. Can you beat that? There was a web-footed bird flying up at me. It was a big gray albatross. It was a flash of light from somewhere, I think. One of those gooks had a mirror and was trying to blind me, and as soon as I realized that's what it was I was all right. Christ, was I mad! I knew I was in position so I opened fire, even though I'd been completely blinded.

"We went up and down that beach," Horne added a few moments later. "When we got through with that beach nothing moved. Even the water seemed dead. I was a little uneasy. That bird scared the living Christ out of me. Till the day I die I'll believe I saw that bird. But it was a smooth assault, what the hell. We received a Presidential citation." He patted himself on the

388

helmet and took the controls; an instant later the SNJ was rolling and Melvin clutched at the safety belt to make certain it had not come unfastened. He could not feel the rotation, but one wing was rising like a hand and the other was descending and he was able to see directly above his head a red barn and a snow-capped haystack, then a barbed-wire fence and a ragged, scorched cornfield where a few Holstein cattle stood at the edge of a blue-frozen creek veined with submerged branches. He saw the tails of the upside-down animals blowing in the wind. His feet dropped from the floorboards. His hands no longer rested in his lap but wanted to rise. The safety belt was taut. With some difficulty he pulled the microphone to his lips and said, "There's a lot of dust sifting from the bottom of the cockpit—and some straw!" A cockroach struck the canopy. A metal object—it was a coin, a penny—dropped from somewhere and skidded past his head. He tried to pick up the penny but it eluded him and slid wildly out of sight. He became conscious of the steadily thundering engine and the fumes. He began to feel bloated and soggy. His cheeks bulged, his lips felt like flaps, and his eyeballs grew uncomfortably large; he had the impression he must look diseased, swollen, with a snarling or indignant expression. Then the wings began to tilt; soon the pressure on his head was diminishing, it was easier to focus his eyes, and he was able to discern, straight ahead, not far beyond Sam Horne's flaking brown leather helmet, a field which had been plowed after the last snowfall. The furrows were approaching, falling diagonally from above and sinking gradually under the engine. He was not sure what Horne did next, only that they were upside down again, and right side up, and down again. He glimpsed a horseman—it was a boy in a mackinaw on a galloping mule—corkscrewing toward the plane, and just as he was bracing himself for the impact there was a sweeping, sucking roar and he found himself blinking and squinting into the sun, which was pleasantly warm on his forehead.

Horne reached for the microphone. "I can't imagine how straw would get in a J, but it doesn't surprise me. Once I was talking to a fellow who went through primary at Dallas, and he told me he got into a Stearman one day and something ran across his lap and it was a great big rat! And once at Diego I found a woman's glove in an F6F." He replaced the microphone and continued smoking while the airplane climbed across the valley toward Mount Oread and the red tile roofs of the University of Kansas.

In a little while Melvin said, "Do you see that winding road coming up past the smokestack?"

Horne nodded.

"Well, beyond it a little ways, see those tennis courts?"

"I do," said Horne. "So?"

"Well, on the west side of them is the fraternity house, that big place with all the steps in front and the sun deck on the roof. That deck looks strange from this view," he added. "I don't know why, though. Well, anyway, that's it, and what I want to do is make a pass at it. Really give it the business!"

"You want to take over?"

"I'd like to very much, but I'm rusty. I haven't flown in so long, it wouldn't be smart."

"Since when did you do anything smart?" Horne remarked as he banked the J and began looking for other planes.

Melvin was peering eagerly over the side of the cockpit at the fraternity house, which was almost directly below. He had not thought much about the fraternity since the collapse of his relationship with it, other than being conscious of a vague, festering injury, as though he had been bitten; but seeing the defenseless house beneath him, and the people inside so unaware of who was overhead, he became excited. He thumped on the fuselage and pointed. *"Let's go! Come on!"* he shouted, and looked at Horne in the mirror.

Horne did not answer; he continued turning and scanning the sky until he was satisfied there were no other planes in the area. Then he looked down with a studious expression, locating the house and inspecting the angle of the hillside. He circled again, and observed the smoke from the chimney. Finally he pulled around in a swift vertical bank, flipped the airplane on its back, and started down with the sun on the opposite side of the house so that afterward, when people looked up, they would not be able to see anything—the J would be climbing into the sun and the numbers on the wing would be invisible.

Melvin felt himself being drawn down. The greenhouse rattled and hummed as the J spiraled down, and the sunshine struck him full on the head, the warmth of it penetrating his helmet. He glanced at the instrument panel: the altimeter needle was unwinding and he thought of the four French cadets who had been sent to Pensacola for a course in dive bombing and who, apparently enraptured, dove straight into the middle of the target and plopped out of sight like ducks in a shooting gallery: *un, deux, trois, quatre!* He was a bit shocked at how close Horne had come to the earth on the previous dive, and now as he looked ahead he was horrified. His jaw sagged, his eyelids drooped, a chimney shot by the wingtip, the plane slowed and sank toward the fraternity-house lawn as Horne rammed the propeller into low pitch and then, rattling and roaring, they were across the street and somebody's bicycle and the sign in front of the doughnut shop and the rim of the football stadium and going steeply up. Melvin immediately loosened his harness and twisted around in the cockpit. The front door of the house burst open and frenzied little figures were leaping into the snow He shook his fist at them. "That's what I like to see—*fraternity spirit!*" he called. "And let that be a lesson to you! Come on," he said to Horne, "let's do it again!"

"You're out of your head. We're leaving this area right now. Take over. Give us a good five thousand feet. Out of binocular range," Horne added, and tapped the ash from his cigar.

"Did we break some windows, do you think?"

"What do you want to do, go back and ask?"

"No, but I'd just like to find out."

Horne muttered and wagged his head. "We got the job done, why do you have to go back and investigate everything? Leave it alone! Forget it! I don't understand you. Head for Kansas City. The phone company in this neighborhood's going to be busier than sonny boy at the circus, so I'd as soon be identified somewhere else. We can let down on the other side of the city to show our numbers and give us an alibi."

"What if we're the only J up today?"

"If we were," Horne said patiently, "I wouldn't be flat-hatting, bet your life. Three other flights checked out ahead of us, and in the loft I heard a couple of boot ensigns talk about coming over Lawrence this afternoon." He shifted around in the cockpit and squinted in the direction of Olathe. "There!" He jabbed with his cigar. "Just below the horizon, bearing zero-nine-zero. Two pigeons. I bet they're not six months out of Pensacola. Well, good luck, boys! You're either quick or you're dead these days, that's God's truth.

"You know, I used to be like you," he continued, "but I've learned a few things since we saw each other last. When I got overseas I learned something I don't think you'll ever understand because you never fought for this country. Like McCampbell, the more I think about it. Maybe he knew from the start what had to be done, but he never said a word—he just did it."

After a moment Melvin asked, "What did you learn?"

"I don't know exactly," Horne said. "Except I feel different. I feel proud—I really do! Every time I put on this uniform I feel proud. And people on the street look at me. They look at the wings and then they take another look at me. They feel close to me, I can tell. I'm sort of a cop, you might say. It's a good feeling."

They were over the suburbs of Kansas City. Ahead lay the gaping, crenulated skyline and the wide shining bend of the Missouri. They flew down a bright sheaf of railroad tracks to the Union Station. The station resembled a mausoleum, or an old warehouse, with patches of sooty snow on the roof, and a curving line of yellow taxicabs in front. Across the road on the mall, between the two squat, banklike museums, rose the great fluted shaft of the Liberty Memorial.

"By the way," Horne remarked as Melvin guided the plane around the Memorial, "when I talked to your old man on the phone he said to be sure and tell you he was coming to the university for dinner with you soon. He didn't say when."

"He drives up occasionally. Listen, he once told me that on his troopship going to France during the first war the soldiers would sometimes break out cheering. Cheers would just swell from the ranks, according to what he says. That's curious, because all the time I was in the Navy I never once felt like cheering. Did you?"

Horne looked at him in the mirror. "Are you kidding?"

"That was my reaction exactly," Melvin said. "I can remember all kinds of different sensations, such as being bored or scared or infuriated by some stupid officer like Monk, for example. And plenty of times I had a tremendous sense of relief, on account of having gotten down alive, you know. But I just can't understand why anybody in the service would cheer."

"Times change." Horne inspected his cigar and champed on it comfortably. "Used to be the soldats were eager to save the world. No longer. Now all anybody wants is to save his skin. No more illusions, no dreams. Things are rough these days."

"Suppose there was to be another war. Would the attitudes change again?"

"There wouldn't be time for an attitude. You'd be ionized before you even knew war was declared."

"If that's so, why is there so much talk about civil defense? This idea of stationing people on rooftops to watch for enemy planes—why, if you compute the speed of the new jets together with the bomb trajectory, it becomes obvious the spotter would get squashed before he could focus his binoculars. But the government plans to spend millions of dollars manufacturing helmets and arm bands and printing leaflets. Or this idea of bomb shelters. If there wouldn't be time, why bother?"

"Ask me an easy one," Horne said. "But you might as well make preparations, why not? It won't do any harm. It might do a little good, and most of all it keeps the citizens occupied. When you're busy you don't think. If a civilian figures a bomb shelter or a tin helmet is going to save him—fine! Let him think so. Why not? It makes him feel better."

"I suppose a few people really could reach the shelters in time. Don't you think so?"

"Sure! You might save half a million, several million maybe in towns and cities that weren't hit right at first. There'd be fifty times that many dead, of course, no matter if you got shelters for everybody from Rover to Betsy. It's like beef on the farm," he explained. "What you do is, you keep them pacified until it's too late to do anything about the situation. They're in the slaughter-house before they figure it out. That's how you got to handle the citizens. You encourage them to put on a tin hat and dig a hole in the ground and everything's fine. The government's got the right idea—set up the program, get the testimonials, and hope for the best."

"But—"

Horne hit the control stick and the plane jumped. "Why ask *me?* I don't run the firm."

"I was just wondering."

"So are we all. I said it wouldn't do any harm, that's all I said, and it might do some good."

"But is that so? The more I think of it, the more I feel that the longer you cooperate with this sort of reasoning the more you're contributing to the sense of urgency and panic. It actually makes the situation worse."

"I got worries enough without worrying whether I'm contributing to urgency and panic," Horne said. "Frankly, what worries me is how I'm going to get rid of all this lard. I don't even play golf any more. I head for the BOQ as soon as I get off duty and sit around and get so stupid drunk that by chow time I can't tell a pork chop from the skipper's wife." He cranked himself higher in the cockpit and peered at the sky, which was overcast with icy stratus clouds. "Holy jumpin' Jesus—look at that stuff move! Another twenty minutes and we'll get blown halfway to Kentucky. It's time we secured. Where's Kansas City?"

They looked along the river, but the city was nowhere in sight.

"We should have started back sooner," Horne said. "I'll take over." He cleared the engine and put the SNJ into a shallow diving turn that carried them swiftly across the frozen brush and tanglewood along the shore and over the sandbars and hurtling over the rooftops of a town.

"I think I know this place," Melvin said.

Horne shoved the throttle forward, rolled into a vertical turn, and pulled the SNJ around the circle so tightly the wings crinkled.

"I know where we are," Melvin said while the turn drained the blood from his head and sucked the microphone from his lips, "There's the military academy. This is Lexington."

Sam Horne looked over the side of the cockpit. "Yuh, you're right. There's the battlefield on top of the cliff. And there's that spooky house where they were hanging each other. All right, we're in business again. Olathe should bear approximately west by southwest."

Snow was falling when they landed, and as they taxied toward

394

the hangars a red beacon replaced the directional lights on the squadron tower.

"Better stay over and take off for Washington when the weather lifts," Melvin said. "We've got room enough for you at the apartment."

And Horne, after going upstairs to check the aerology reports, said he would.

30
★

Night had fallen when Melvin and Horne reached Lawrence. The town was covered with snow. The wind whistled down the street. The basement apartment was dark.

"Is this a good idea?" Horne asked. "Women don't like their husbands bringing home strangers. Besides, it looks like she's already gone to bed."

"My wife won't mind," Melvin said confidently. "She's heard me talk about you so often she'll be delighted. I wonder why there aren't any lights on." He turned up the collar of his jacket, jumped out of the station wagon, and hurried down the steps with Horne right behind him.

"It smells like something's burning," Horne said.

"I know," Melvin said. "I wonder what it is."

"You better open the door and find out," Horne said, stamping his feet and blowing through his fists.

"I think I just dropped the key in the snow," Melvin said. "I can't see anything, it's so dark down here. Have you got a match?"

Inside the apartment there was a crash; a dog barked, a door slammed.

"If I were you, I'd look for the key in the morning," Horne said. "I think something's on fire." He raised his fist to pound on the door but at that moment the door opened, Hephzibah looked out, gave a shriek, and vanished.

Melvin rushed in, but stopped in amazement. In the center of the apartment stood what appeared to be a new aluminium garbage can, a green sales tag dangling from one of the handles. Dozens of little packages were scattered on the floor. The room was dimly lighted by candles. An English sheep dog with a nose as black as a prune and a long pink tongue dangling stupidly from its mouth like a comedian's necktie was crouching on the sofa. The dog reared up with its nose pointed at Melvin, soared like a rug over the back of the sofa, and went bounding into the bathroom, where it gave an immature but tremendous bark. The kitchen was full of smoke.

"You're home!" cried Jake Isaacs. "Ah, lieutenant!"

"*Ech! Tch!*" Hephzibah muttered, striding back and forth wringing her hands. "Such a night, such a night! *Ech! Ech!*"

"Where's Jo?" said Melvin.

"I'd better be going," said Horne.

"Take off your things, lieutenant!" exclaimed Jake. "You can't leave now, you just got here!"

"Where's Jo?" said Melvin.

"Really, I think I ought to get back to the base," said Horne. "This weather may clear up and I've got to get to Washington."

"Washington, lieutenant? You're just passing through? I've been looking forward to a little visit. You can't be in such a rush."

"Listen, what's going on here?" Melvin said. "Where's my wife? What's happened to her? Will somebody please tell me what's going on here?"

"She's not feeling very well, I'm sorry to say. She's in the bedroom. Nothing serious. The fact is, she won't come out. Take off your hat, lieutenant."

The sheep dog came soaring from the bathroom and collapsed on Melvin's feet.

"What's this? Where did this dog come from?" he demanded, becoming excited, and ran to the door of the bedroom. The door was locked. He rattled the handle and tapped on the panel. "Jo?" he asked. "Are you there?"

She did not answer.

"Are you all right, Jo?" he called.

396

Still she did not answer.

"Did you know there's a big dog in the living room? Down! Get down!" he said sharply to the dog, which was standing up like an old friend or a drunken cadet with a paw across his shoulder and was gazing into his face with a look of devoted admiration.

"*Ach! Schön!*" Hephzibah murmured, "*Liebling!*" picking up the dog in her arms as though it were a child. She walked away, nodding and crooning, and the dog did not struggle.

"Whose is it?" Melvin said. "I never saw it in the neighborhood."

"It's a puppy by the name of Bundy. A birthday present from Louis to Leah," said his father.

"That's a puppy?" Melvin said. "How big does it get?"

"Nobody knows. Louis neglected to inquire. It eats a pound of horsemeat like *that!*" He snapped his fingers. "Very affectionate."

Melvin rapped on the bedroom door and said, "Jo? Why don't you answer? Is anything wrong?"

"The cake fell. That's when she began to cry. Just then the lights blew out. It's been snowing heavily for an hour, a power line must be down."

"Horne and I wondered what that burnt odor was. We thought something was on fire."

"Yes, but it wasn't the cake. You were smelling the steak."

"I can't figure out why she would be cooking steak," Melvin said after a moment. "This is ordinarily the night we have casserole or chipped beef."

"It's your anniversary. That's the reason."

"It is *not* my anniversary," Melvin said. "We just got married last summer."

"You've been married six months. These things are important to women. Nobody knows why."

"She doesn't usually get upset. Something else must have happened." He turned and stared at the garbage can and the packages on the floor. "What's that? What's in there—in those little brown paper packages?"

"Ah! I've been waiting for a chance to explain. In fact, it was then the difficulty began. She ran into the kitchen while I was explaining."

"Jo?" Melvin said, rapping on the door. "Are you all right? Why don't you come out? I want you to meet a friend of mine."

"I really ought to be leaving," said Horne. "You've probably got some things to talk over and I—"

"Nonsense, lieutenant!" said Jake. "You're staying for dinner. We'll be delighted to have you."

"What are we going to eat?" Melvin said. "It sounds like everything's burned up." He walked into the kitchen and his father followed him. The beginning of a salad lay on the drainboard. There was a bottle of wine with two glasses; evidently she had not been expecting guests. Melvin looked into the broiler at the steak, which was as black as leather. He tapped it with a fork. There was a saucepan on the stove. He lifted the lid and fanned away a cloud of steam.

"What was this? It looks like boiled pine cones."

"Artichokes, I believe. I love artichokes," his father said, peeping over his shoulder. "Possibly they're still good."

"Get away," said Melvin to the dog. "I haven't got any horse-meat."

"He'll eat the steak."

"I may eat it myself," Melvin said. "I don't know why there's always so much confusion everywhere I go. I'm really getting sick and tired of everything. I'm just about to do a flip, and I don't mean maybe!" As he listened to himself talk he began to grow excited. "I come home from Olathe looking forward to a nice dinner and a quiet evening and it looks like a hurricane struck the place! The dinner's all burnt, my wife won't come out of the bedroom—she won't even speak to me!—and there's a big dog I never saw before that acts like it lives here. I'd just like to know what's going on, that's all! Is that asking so much?" The lights flickered, came on, and he paused.

The lights went off again.

"It doesn't matter what I do!" he said bitterly. "Nothing ever turns out right." He looked at his father, who shrugged.

"There should be a delicatessen in the neighborhood. I'll run out and get a little something we can eat."

"I lost my appetite," Melvin said.

"Consider your guest. What about his appetite?"

"I'm tired of considering guests! I'm sick and tired of everybody and everything! And besides, if you think that sheep dog's got an appetite, just wait'll you see Horne at the table. Anyway, he isn't a guest. I've known him too long." Melvin felt himself beginning to tremble; he walked quickly away from his father and stood looking out the window into the basement area-way, which was nearly filled with snow. It occurred to him that he and Horne could have remained at the naval base overnight; he was sorry they had not done this. He thrust his hands into his hip pockets and pretended to stare out the window, although there was nothing to see but a wall of snow outside the glass. "I'll be all right in a minute if everybody will leave me alone," he said. "It's just that it seems like no matter which direction I turn there's some kind of disaster. Either something's happened, or is about to."

"Yes, that's true," his father said. "I know the feeling. There's no solution. All we can do is to make preparations as wisely as possible. As the saying goes, a stitch in time saves nine. Not always, perhaps, but in general it's the truth. That's the reason for the packages you were asking about."

Melvin continued to look out the window. "Did you bring that stuff?"

"Yes. It's everything you will need. It's a gift from me. You know what happened in nineteen forty-one—the Japanese attack succeeded because the United States did not like to consider the possibility of war. If the country had been alert, prepared for a treacherous assault, it wouldn't have happened. We're in the same situation today in regard to Russia. It's incredible so many Americans are blind to the obvious fact! A world-wide conspiracy to overthrow our government is being directed by the Kremlin. This has been definitely proved, I don't know how many times. It's beyond my understanding why so many Americans ignore this. How long are we expected to wait—until vehicles with the red star come rolling through our streets?"

"What do you recommend? It seems to me—"

"What do I recommend?" exclaimed Jake Isaacs. "What a question! Who'd listen to my recommendations? I could fly to Washington with a tape recording of the Russian plan of attack, but could I get by the receptionist? I'm a private citizen without a voice. I vote, I'm proud to vote, although my vote doesn't change the situation. If anybody listened I would say, first of all, national security is of paramount importance. That would be my first recommendation. The employment of questionable individuals is certainly not in the best interests of national security. The standard for refusal of employment, or removal from employment, should be reasonable doubt as to the loyalty of the persons involved. Substantial defects of character as well as persistent and ill-advised associations should be taken into account. Any doubts whatsoever must be resolved in favor of security. Ah, lieutenant," he exclaimed.

Horne stood in the doorway with an interested expression.

"Lieutenant, please give us your opinion," Jake said, laughing gaily, with his eyes fixed on the campaign ribbons pinned to Horne's blouse. "The question, in the simplest terms, is whether we shall continue to live in freedom or as slaves of the international Communist conspiracy."

Horne was aware that his campaign ribbons were impressive; he unbuttoned his blouse, thrust his hands into his pockets, and slouched against the doorway. He remained silent for a while, frowning into space, but then said, "That's very coincidental, sir. Yes, that's a strange coincidence, because just about a month ago an old buddy of mine who has access to the USTEP files was telling me some extremely sobering facts."

"I'm tempted to inquire," Jake said, laughing. "Nothing confidential, naturally. Simply the nature of this material of which you speak. Pertaining to what?" he asked, looking eagerly from Horne's face to the ribbons. "The extent of Communist infiltration, perhaps?"

"You appreciate that I can't give out direct information, sir," Horne began, and was ready to say something else, but did not have time.

"Of course!" Jake said, and stepped forward to touch him on the arm. "Excuse me. I'm afraid I've embarrassed you, lieutenant."

"Not at all," said Horne.

"You're right, lieutenant—we can't be too cautious. I've learned a lesson, thanks to you. I won't ask another question! I've been of the opinion for some time that there should be an inquiry into the subject matter available in public libraries, to say nothing of university professors, guest speakers, and so on. In the libraries someone to supervise unobtrusively—proctors to record who is reading what. This would be invaluable when the emergency arises. It will simplify relocation of potential subversives as well as facilitating immediate imprisonment of traitors. It's a privilege to have you here, lieutenant. You don't know how much this means to me."

Horne took a deep breath and for the first time the uniform hung slack around his waist. He screwed up his eyes and nodded. "I don't know quite what ought to be done with subversives. It's a problem, for sure. On the one hand, we're supposed to allow free speech in this country. But on—"

"Free speech! Excuse me, lieutenant. I didn't mean to interrupt. But aren't you confusing the term free speech with treason? Naturally I don't like to overstate the case, and frankly no one is more concerned than myself with the rights and privileges of the individual in a democracy. However, it goes without saying you cannot allow traitors to go around doing what they please. In that event they will soon have destroyed the very freedom we cherish and defend. Free speech, lieutenant—it's a privilege to be earned. Or am I wrong?"

"No, of course not, sir," Horne said, flushed with embarrassment. "I certainly didn't mean—"

"I shouldn't have interrupted. Excuse me, lieutenant. I know we agree. It was a slight case of misunderstanding, nothing more. I'm concerned about what's happening to America, that's the reason. We must have peace and security. Peace without security is the peace of a lamb in the wilderness. Pacifism never fails to be attractive to sensitive persons and nobody admires such people more than I. However, war is imposed by moral obligation as well as by military necessity. For peace we are indebted, not to pacifists, but to those who are willing, when inevitable, to risk the dreadful danger of war rather than to witness the destruction of those institutes and ideals which make peace possible. Excuse me for making a speech. If pacifists were given their way it is appalling to imagine the condition of mankind, enslaved by despots, divided by rival tyrants. In military service there is distinction and high honor, a fact our children are forgetting. It should be taught in school. There is no greater honor than to die in defense of one's country."

The sheep dog came shaggily trotting into the kitchen, peered through the hair covering its face, and in a berserk, good-natured manner started to bark.

"Be still," Jake said to the dog. "Frankly, Melvin, I'm puzzled by your attitude. Communists have infiltrated our public schools and universities, propaganda floods the libraries, and it has been established definitely there are spies in the State Department. But you don't care. Would you mind explaining *why* you don't care? Is that asking too much?" With both hands pressed to his chest he followed directly behind Melvin who walked to the door of the bedroom, listened, and then knocked.

"Jo!" Melvin called. "You come out of there!"

"Possibly she's asleep," his father whispered. "Maybe you should knock again."

"She's not asleep," Melvin said. "She heard me."

"How do you know?"

"I can tell. She's wide awake, lying there on the bed. She's mad. She was crying a few minutes ago, but she's mad now."

"What makes you so sure? There hasn't been a sound."

"I don't know," Melvin said, "but I can tell."

"Have it your own way. I was attempting to make a point when something interrupted. It's this: I have no love for the Germans. However, we must admit they will be invaluable allies in the forthcoming struggle." He stopped, as though astonished by the expression on Melvin's face.

"By the what?" Melvin asked. "What did you say? What was that again?"

"The forthcoming war between America and the godless despots of the Soviet Union. The German soldiers are excellent, everyone admits, in contrast to the poorly equipped, unimaginative Russians. Don't you remember the remarkable advance of the German army in nineteen forty-two under extremely adverse conditions? They reached Stalingrad! Now, with American supervision, not even the Russian winter will stop them. This will give us control of the Volga and access to lumber and fisheries, which are vital to supply." He coughed into his fist and continued to speak while walking rapidly around the apartment. "I shouldn't say this, perhaps, but the lieutenant will be interested. A very close friend, whose name I won't mention, whose sister-in-law is employed in the Pentagon, has seen with her own eyes a secret copy of a list, smuggled from the Kremlin, of ten American cities destined to be destroyed by the first wave of Russian bombers. Kansas City is on the list, in fourth place. Because of the stockyards. I can tell you something else: each Russian cadet is personally assigned one city in the United States. It's an examination. He draws up the master plan for attack. It's the final examination for a Russian military cadet. Copies of this plan are now in the secret files of the FBI."

"I'm beginning to feel crowded," Melvin said, turning around so quickly that his father stepped back in astonishment.

"Let's ask the lieutenant for an opinion."

"I don't have to ask anybody for an opinion!" Melvin shouted.

The dog sprang to its feet and resumed barking with an expression of enjoyment, looking first one way and then another to see who was impressed. Hephzibah strode back and forth with her hands clasped over her head. Horne had been listening uneasily, without attempting to speak, and gave the impression of straining, as though he had grown somewhat deaf.

"Open that door, Jo?" Melvin asked, rising on tiptoe. "I'm going to count, Jo. One. Two! Do you hear me? One. Two! *Three!*" and he pounded furiously on the panel. Then he stopped, breathing hoarsely. There was a crash on the other side of the door.

"She's not asleep. She threw something at you," said his father.

"I told you she wasn't asleep."

"She's been in there a long time. Tell her to come out. I'm sure your guest would like something to eat."

"I'm not really very hungry," said Horne. "In fact, I was just about to leave."

"Lieutenant, you can't go! There's something I want to ask your opinion about."

"Why should she be mad at me?" Melvin asked. "I haven't done anything." He turned to the door. "Listen, Jo, I don't see that there's anything to be gained by acting like this. I don't know what the trouble is, but let's look at it logically." There was a swishy noise, as though a garment had struck the door. The dog trotted up and sniffed around and looked at Melvin with the benign, preposterous expression of a simple-minded caveman, the tongue hanging out one side of its mouth. Melvin knelt and buried his hands in the huge puppy's coat. "What do you think about?" he asked, and gently shook the dog. "Do we have similar problems? Suppose you were in my place, what would you do—everything considered? Tell me, what would you do? On the eve of Armageddon is it better to adopt the motto of the Boy Scouts, or gather up your courage and say no? That's the question. You look so wise. You should know. What must I do?"

The dog studied him with deep affection.

"Well, then," Melvin said, "tell me what they're doing." He pointed toward his father and Sam Horne.

The dog got up as though intending to have a look, but then sat down and wildly scratched its ear.

Melvin walked to the card table, where his father and Horne had just finished unfolding a large map of the world. The map had been printed and distributed by a veterans' organization. From Russia a number of red arrows arched over the North Pole to major American cities. Smaller arrows spread across the North Sea to England and France. At the bottom, in red type, was the text:

> One-two punch leads off with massive flight of Tupolev and Ilushin long-range turboprop bombers unloading A-bombs on U.S. plants and industrial complexes. Synchronized hail of torpedos on East and West Coast shipping from 300-strong submarine fleet. Communist underground erupts—sabotage with small atomic weapons, newer types of poison gases, midget nuclear explosives. Red bombers strike overseas bases, viz., Iceland, Greenland, Turkey and North Africa, with simultaneous assault on potential allies.

Horne grunted and scowled. He worked the stub of a cigar across his mouth and squinted at the map. On the breast of his green blouse the slim golden wings glinted in the candlelight. One of his hands was on the map, holding it flat—a blunt, used, positive hand, creased and stained by nicotine, with a thumb like a hammer and fingernails as flat and broad and limited as an array of chisels. His features, when he leaned over, slowly gorged with blood. Melvin no longer recognized him, but had the impression he had seen this man somewhere—in a newsreel, or on the cover of a magazine just after he had circled the earth in the latest bomber or testified before the Senate.

"They got a base in that area," he muttered, pointing, "sure as God made apples."

"We need more information, lieutenant. Latest reports indicate troops being massed along the border."

Melvin looked at his father and was struck by the radiance in his eyes. There was no doubt that the possibility of another war fascinated him. Melvin turned away and wandered around the apartment, thinking deeply. Presently he found that he had stopped at the garbage can and was staring at the packages on the floor. The packages were neatly sealed and labeled. He picked up one and saw that it was a pint of chlorine. He picked up another and saw that it was a rubber sheet.

Just then the lights came on.

"Ah!" his father said, straightening up from the map. Seeing Melvin with the packages, he hurried over. "Now I have a chance to explain. I'm glad you're interested. The government recommends one of these containers packed with emergency supplies for each family. Here, for example, you have a pound of raisins. And here you have sausage. Right here is evaporated milk. This is canned bread. Next, some tea bags. Pressed pork loaf. Vegetable juices. Various dried fruits. Here in this group are the utensils—bottle opener, paper plates, a refuse bag of sturdy material, a little measuring cup, and so forth. Over here I arranged the soap. DDT, and so on. Here are the household tools—a wrench, screwdriver, a very practical miniature flashlight, and this shovel, which is collapsible." He demonstrated how to unfold the shovel, then put it down and held up some pamphlets. "These are published by the government. Be sure to read them. Next, I have here the official filing cards. They should be filled out in ink. Print, don't write. Simply give the first name, middle name, and last name, the same as always. You're familiar with this sort of card. Occupation, business address, and here's the space for service preference. You write 'Navy.' The space for criminal record you leave blank." He turned the card over. "Here we have the air-raid signals. A steady siren blast of from three to five minutes: Alert, attack probable. A wailing noise: Attack imminent. Take cover promptly. Crouch behind the bed facing away from the windows.

It is very possible to survive. According to information in one these little booklets, in Nagasaki more than sixty per cent of the people a mile from the bomb are still alive. Some, of course, have died of radiation since the publication of these statistics, however think of the percentage: sixty! How many people know about that? We are apt to suppose everybody was killed. That is not true. Today thousands of people live in new houses where the old houses used to be, a fact I didn't realize until reading this booklet." He began to turn the pages, evidently looking for something, but was unable to find it and laid the pamphlet aside and began looking through another.

"Here, listen close. This will surprise you. Anywhere within one-half mile of the center of the explosion, the chance of survival is one out of ten. Naturally such odds are not favorable, however listen to this—I am going to quote the exact words of the official in Washington. 'From one-half to one mile away, you have a fifty-fifty chance.' Did you know that? It changes the picture entirely. Now consider: exactly how much chance is there that the bomb is going to be dropped within one-half mile of this apartment? Very little, practically none at all. You have, therefore, a fifty-fifty chance, at least, if you obey instructions. Your chances could be much better." He licked his thumb, turned a page, turned another, and another, frowning in concentration.

"I want you to listen closely. I am going to quote again—yes, this is the information here. 'A modern atomic bomb can do heavy damage to houses and buildings roughly two miles away.' We are aware of the fact. However, listen. 'But doubling its power will extend the range to only about two-and-one-half miles. In the same way, if there were a bomb one hundred times as powerful, it would reach out only a little more than four-and-one-half, not one hundred times as far.' How many people are aware of that? They say the new, improved bombs will kill everybody. That's not true. The United States Government says it is not true. Look at this pamphlet! It is called 'Survival Under Atomic Attack' and is being distributed by the Office of Civil Defense. A wonderful piece of work, very well thought out. Nicely printed.

"To prevent blindness the government instructions are to bury your face in your arms for a period of ten to twelve seconds after the explosion. This also helps to keep flying glass out of your

406

eyes. If you work in the open you should always be sure to wear full-length, loose-fitting, light-colored clothing and do not go around with the sleeves rolled up. Always wear a hat; the brim of the hat may prevent serious facial burns. Here is another fact I will read: 'Naturally, the radioactivity that passes through the walls of your house won't be stopped by tin or glass. It can go right through canned and bottled foods. However, this will not make them dangerous, and it will not cause them to spoil.' This booklet has a great deal of useful knowledge. 'Go ahead and use them,' it says, 'provided the containers are not broken open.' That speaks for itself. As soon as you hear the siren, if there is no time to reach the basement—we are already in the basement, that's true, excellent—simply close all windows and draw the blinds. Such precautions lessen the danger of fire sparks and radioactive dust. Keep at least one flashlight handy. There beside the pressed pork is the flashlight. Be certain not to strike a match after the attack because if the mains have been shattered—a very good chance this will be the case—you will have gas and oil fumes. A bad explosion could result. Also, an ordinary newspaper will protect you from radioactive dust or raindrops if you are out of doors. After getting up, however, do not forget to discard the newspaper, which will be contaminated. You should bury it. You have the shovel. Dig a little hole, bury the newspaper, and leave a notice to the effect. Inside the house, I don't need to remind you, broken windows should be covered with blankets or pieces of cardboard because the bombers will probably come again, especially if the destruction has not been total." He had been standing motionless while the words poured from his mouth. He wiped his lips with his handkerchief and continued.

"Now for the evacuation plan. I have marked in blue pencil on a little map of Lawrence the route you will take. Either of two streets you can follow down the hill to the highway, turning right to be in accord with the flow of evacuees from the metropolitan area. After the bomb falls there will be thousands from the city fleeing in this direction. Highways will be jammed, an accident will make escape impossible, so drive cautiously but do not waste time and be positive you do not attempt to drive against the crowd. Go the same direction as everyone else, otherwise you will be lost." He closed the flue of the fireplace and hurried to the radio. "I am marking the Conelrad frequencies," he said as he took a pen from his vest pocket. He drew two stars on the radio dial.

Melvin walked quickly around the room, sat down and crossed his legs, but a moment later jumped up and stood with his fists clenched behind his back. His father ran up to him, stopped, and spoke in an urgent voice. Melvin was no longer listening; he was thinking of the notification to report for military service. Ever since receiving the order he had been wondering what to do. He had no idea what would happen if he defied the government. He was under the impression that if he belonged to some religious organization he might be exempted from duty, and had considered whether or not he might join such a group. It would not be difficult to pretend belief in the articles of faith, to lock himself to the organization, so to speak, as he might have locked the controls of the Dauntless heading out to sea. No one would be the wiser. But to oppose the government by himself would be disastrous. If he alone, on the basis of his own conviction, refused to comply with this order, some punitive action must follow. What this would be, he did not know; he supposed it would consist of a fine and imprisonment. Possibly there was a choice; but to pay the fine would negate the principle, since payment implied acquiescence. It became reasonably certain, therefore, that if he did not wish to declare himself devout, and did not choose to enter military service, he would soon enough be entering a federal prison. This thought did not particularly disturb him; he knew he could endure it, having been well tempered by the Navy. What concerned him was the mortification and the shame his imprisonment would bring down on his parents and his sister, and, of course, what it would mean to his wife, and, later, to his child.

He reflected that more than anything else he had always wanted to be free, and since he would be sacrificing that freedom if he should accede to this demand, he concluded he had never had a choice. There was no decision to be made. He knew what he would do. Just then he heard his father's voice and looked around.

"Concerning emergency sanitation during nuclear attack, this official booklet is extremely helpful. Among other things, it is necessary, for instance, to maintain an adequate supply of safe drinking water. Instructions are contained in this booklet, such as how long to boil the water, how it should be labeled, and how long it will keep, together with vivid explanatory pictures. The flat taste caused by boiling water is easily removed. Simply add a pinch of salt. Or, if you prefer, the government suggests pouring the boiled water like a magician from one container to another until—"

At this instant Melvin's hand reached forth, as it had done once before to save him from annihilation, and took the pamphlet. He tore it in half, looked around, and, catching sight of the garbage can, lifted the lid above his head and brought it down with a crash. Up went the sheep dog, high in the air with a phenomenal bark; over went the card table, end over end, the world and all, while Hephzibah shrieked and fled.

"Get it out of here," Melvin said.

"What? What?" his father exclaimed, stepping backward in dismay.

"Now I know what happened to my wife. She won't accept this equipment and I won't either."

"This is what our government recommends! I was explaining it when all at once, for no reason, she became hysterical. I was going to draw a little plan for a bomb shelter—a major general has testified before Congress that private shelters can be ninety-four per cent effective—but she ran away! I don't know why."

"You don't, but I do," Melvin said. "She and I feel the same. You take this garbage can with you when you go."

"You don't care to live?"

"I care," Melvin replied.

"Exactly!" said his father, and gestured toward the supplies. "All of us want to live. There's the answer."

"Do you think so?"

"Certainly!"

Melvin looked at his father, and saw him for the first time.

"What's the matter? Aren't you listening? I'm pointing out how we can survive." And he went on speaking, but Melvin did not hear a word.

Would it be the way to live, truly? To live underground, feeding from a garbage can, subdued, eternally fearful, helpless, wondering, caught like the most lowly creature. Would this be liberty—or would it be death? To emerge when the danger was past, anxiously studying the sky, only to scurry underground again, and again, and again, each time a shadow sailed overhead. It seemed to Melvin that this, more truly, was death. To exist like a rodent and perhaps be trapped while frantically seeking escape, or to stand up and behold the unity of the world, certain of the ultimate worth of mankind—perhaps thus to die, yet, if that came to pass, to die in freedom—these were the paths before him and he knew he must choose his way forever.

"When you go," he repeated, quietly, to his father, "take with you what you've brought. I'll live my life as I wish, and my wife also. We don't intend to hide, not now or ever. We're not digging any more holes. I'm in deep enough as it is," he added, and walked to the desk where he rummaged about until he found the notice from the draft board. Having cleared his throat he said, "Greetings from the President," and read the letter aloud.

"Amazing!" his father exclaimed when he had finished. "We live from day to day."

"I doubt if they'll actually send you to Korea," said Horne.

"That's irrelevant," Melvin said. "I'm not going into military service again ever, that's all. My mind is made up. I'm not going. I won't go. I will not go. I refuse."

"Impossible!" his father cried. "What will you do?"

"I don't know," he said. "But I know what I won't do." And here he paused. There was nothing more to say.

Printed in the United States
by Baker & Taylor Publisher Services